"You've had patients more reluctant than me?"

"Oh, yes," she said with a definite nod. "There are more people who don't like to admit they need help."

"It's hard," he admitted. "I didn't want to admit in front of you that I wasn't as strong as I used to be. That I was weak."

"I've always thought that it takes great strength of character for anyone to recognize honestly what they can and can't do." She gave him an encouraging smile. "Some take longer than others, but you did come to that point, and I think that's honorable and manly."

"I think what I struggled with most was I felt I wasn't the man I used to be."

"None of us are what we used to be," she said. "We've both come through our lives with wounds mental as well as physical."

"What wounds do you carry?"

Her heart suddenly felt like it was pushing heavily against her chest, filling it with its racing beat. She took a slow breath. Should she tell him now?

A HERO'S REDEMPTION

CAROLYNE AARSEN
AND
BELLE CALHOUNE

2 Uplifting Stories

A Family for the Soldier and *Heart of a Soldier*

LOVE INSPIRED
INSPIRATIONAL ROMANCE

LOVE INSPIRED®

INSPIRATIONAL ROMANCE

Recycling programs for this product may not exist in your area.

ISBN-13: 978-1-335-43060-1

A Hero's Redemption

Copyright © 2022 by Harlequin Enterprises ULC

A Family for the Soldier
First published in 2015. This edition published in 2022.
Copyright © 2015 by Harlequin Enterprises ULC

Heart of a Soldier
First published in 2014. This edition published in 2022.
Copyright © 2014 by Sandra Calhoune

Special thanks and acknowledgment are given to Carolyne Aarsen for her contribution to the Lone Star Cowboy League miniseries.

For questions and comments about the quality of this book, please contact us at CustomerService@Harlequin.com.

Love Inspired
22 Adelaide St. West, 41st Floor
Toronto, Ontario M5H 4E3, Canada
www.LoveInspired.com

Printed in U.S.A.

CONTENTS

Carolyne Aarsen and her husband, Richard, live on a small ranch in northern Alberta, where they have raised four children and numerous foster children and are still raising cattle. Carolyne crafts her stories in an office with a large west-facing window, through which she can watch the changing seasons while struggling to make her words obey.

Books by Carolyne Aarsen

Love Inspired

Visit the Author Profile page at LoveInspired.com for more titles.

A FAMILY FOR THE SOLDIER

Carolyne Aarsen

But those who hope in the Lord
will renew their strength. They will soar on wings
like eagles; they will run and not grow weary,
they will walk and not be faint.
—*Isaiah* 40:31

To my dear husband,
who knows everything and still loves me.

Chapter One

The hospital room felt suddenly too small.

Chloe clutched the chart of her patient, Ben Still-water, as his twin brother, Grady, limped through the doorway of Ben's room. In spite of the single crutch supporting him, Grady's presence filled the space.

He stood taller than she remembered. Broader across the shoulders. His eyes had taken on a flat look, though, all emotion leeched out of them; lines of weariness bracketed his mouth. It was as if his time serving in special ops in Afghanistan had shown him sights he wanted to forget.

"Hello, Chloe," he said. His chocolate-brown eyes, shaded by dark eyebrows, drew her in as his eyes shifted to her left hand. Chloe unconsciously flexed her fingers. Though her divorce from Jeremy had been finalized a mere four months ago, Chloe had removed her ring eight months before when she'd discovered Jeremy had been cheating on her.

"A lot of things have happened since you went away from Little Horn," she said, setting Ben's chart aside, then covering his legs with a sheet. He looked so pale compared to his twin brother, who now joined her at the foot of the bed.

She had come into Ben Stillwater's hospital room hoping to do some physical therapy with him. But for the moment, all thoughts of her patient fled as the man who had once held her heart came to stand by her side.

"I know. My cousin Eva getting married, among many other things," he said.

All of Little Horn had buzzed with the news of the injured vet's return from Afghanistan two days ago, the day after the New Year had been rung in, the day of his cousin's wedding.

Eva Stillwater and Tyler Grainger had been engaged since Thanksgiving, but they had surprised everyone by announcing that they'd decided to get married as soon as her cousin Grady could come home.

"I heard it was a lovely ceremony," Chloe said. "I'm happy for them."

"Me, too. I think they wanted to start adoption procedures as soon as possible. That's why she stepped up the date." He held her gaze. "It's good to see you again."

Chloe gave him a tight smile, disturbed at how easily old emotions had intruded. She'd known she would run into him eventually. She just wished she could have had some advance notice.

So you could have put on some makeup? Do your hair?

You're a divorced woman and he's a war vet with an unexpected child, she reminded herself. *And you have other complications. Too tangled.*

Besides, she had promised herself when she discovered Jeremy's cheating that no man would hold her heart again. No man would make her feel vulnerable.

"I'm sorry. I'll leave you alone to spend time with your brother," she said, moving past Grady only to come face-to-face with her stepsister.

"Hello again, sister of mine," Vanessa Vane said, tossing her red hair, her bright smile showing off thousands of dollars' worth of dental work and a puzzling nervousness. Vanessa had never been one to show anything but overweening self-confidence.

Last month she had waltzed into Little Horn, crashing the Lone Star Cowboy League's annual Christmas party and laying claim to Cody, the baby who had been dropped off at the Stillwater ranch four months earlier. Vanessa had cried crocodile tears, telling anyone who would listen how badly she felt about abandoning Cody at that time. She should have owned up that Grady was the father and stayed around.

But she was back now and wasn't that great?

For Chloe, not so much. Vanessa's redheaded vivaciousness was a bright contrast to Chloe's wavy brown hair and calm demeanor. And whenever Vanessa saw Chloe she liked to remind her of those differences, as well as the deficiencies of Chloe's now-deceased father, Vanessa's stepfather.

"Hello, Vanessa. How's Cody doing?" Chloe asked.

Though Chloe had heard Grady and Vanessa were an item a year ago, seeing Cody, the physical evidence of their relationship, created a surprising and unwelcome heartache.

"He's great. Such a sweetie." Vanessa smiled up at Grady, batting her eyelashes.

Grady's own eyes narrowed and he didn't return her smile, which surprised Chloe. Vanessa's expression grew taut as she looked from Grady to Chloe again, and her auburn hair glistened in the lights of the hospital room. "Isn't my baby adorable?"

"He is," Chloe agreed, wishing she could be less inane. More sparkly and interesting.

Like her sister.

Every time Vanessa came into a room, eyes were drawn to her; men took a second look at her long red hair, slim figure and vivacious personality.

"Can you give me any information about my brother, Chloe?" Grady's resonant voice broke in over Vanessa's prattling. His eyes, deep set and dark, held hers in a steady gaze, resurrecting old feelings she couldn't allow. "Do you know when he'll come out of it? Do you know if there will be any long-term damage?"

"Don't be silly, Grady," Vanessa put in, walking past him to stand beside Ben's bed. "Chloe can't tell you anything about your brother. She's only the physical therapist."

Chloe ignored Vanessa, unconsciously tucking back a strand of hair that had freed itself from her ponytail. "The only thing I can tell you is that he will experience some measure of muscle atrophy, given how long he's been in a coma." Chloe put on her professional voice, trying not to let Vanessa's patronizing attitude get to her. "The range-of-motion exercises we perform on him will help maintain as much of his muscle tone as possible and at the same time prevent sensory deprivation."

"Ooh. Long words," Vanessa said, the joking tone in her voice negated by her flinty look. "Still trying to impress Grady? I wouldn't bother."

"Do you know anything about the coma?" Grady continued, obviously ignoring Vanessa. "At all?"

Chloe heard the hurt and fear behind his questions.

She guessed the bond identical twins often shared made him more anxious.

"I only know what you know," she said. "The fall from the horse was the root cause, but there have been no other internal injuries that we can ascertain, no brain injury. No hematomas." She stopped herself there. As Vanessa had said, she wasn't a doctor. "You'll have to speak with his doctor to find out more."

"Thanks for that information at least," Grady said, his smile holding a warmth that could still make her toes curl.

"You're welcome," she said, trying to convey a more brisk and professional tone. "We hope and pray he will come out of it. That's all we can do."

"I'll take care of the hoping and leave the praying to those more capable." The bitterness in Grady's voice made Chloe wonder again about his war experiences overseas and what they had done to his once rock-solid faith.

"How long are you back for?" Chloe asked, holding up her head, determined not to let the effect he had on her show.

"For good. I got an honorable discharge from the army. I'm home."

She forced herself not to look at the crutch he leaned on to support himself.

"We can all be so thankful Grady made it back from Afghanistan. And a hero to boot," Vanessa said, the edges of her lips growing tighter, as if she had to work to maintain her vivacity.

Each word she spoke felt like a tiny lash. Her stepsister had known Chloe had a crush on Grady when they were in high school. In fact, once Vanessa had discov-

ered this, she'd made an all-out attempt to charm and
captivate Grady just to spite her. Chloe, a tomboy at
heart, had known she couldn't compete with her glam-
orous stepsister, so she'd given up on that dream.

Given that Vanessa claimed to be the mother of
Grady's supposed baby, Chloe could only reason Vanessa still held some attraction for him.

"I still can't get over how much Grady and Ben look
alike." Vanessa gave Chloe an arched look as she fiddled with the sheets draped over Ben's body.

"They do look similar," Chloe murmured, trying to
find an opportunity to make her escape while her stepsister chattered away.

"Similar? They are like two peas in a pod," Vanessa
said, her narrowed gaze flicking from Ben to Grady. "If
it weren't for Ben being flat on his back, you'd never
know the difference. And did you know that twins have
identical DNA?" she asked, turning to the cards on the
windowsill.

And why did Vanessa think she needed to impart
that particular piece of information?

"I'll leave you to visit with your brother," Chloe said,
taking another step toward the door.

To her surprise and shock, Grady touched her arm,
as if trying to make a connection. "It's good to see you,"
Grady said, lowering his voice. His eyes held hers.

Unable to look away, Chloe felt her heart quicken.
Then a faint queasiness gripped her. Vanessa called
out again and she dismissed the emotion as quickly
as it came.

Vanessa claimed that Grady was the father of her
child.

And Chloe had enough problems of her own.

* * *

Chloe's reaction to his wound still stung.

Grady fitted his crutch under his arm and made his way over the snow-covered sidewalk to the ranch house. The chill January wind biting into his face promised bitter weather to come and seemed to sum up how he felt. Vanessa had driven him in her car to the hospital. Grandma Mamie's car and Ben's truck filled the garage, which meant they had to park it outside.

All the way home he replayed that moment when he'd stepped into his brother's hospital room. He would have had to be blind not to have seen Chloe recoil from him.

Not that he blamed her. A crippled soldier and, according to Vanessa, the father of a child born out of wedlock. A child from her own stepsister.

Grady knew Cody wasn't his, and though part of him wanted to tell Chloe, he knew it was neither the time nor place; he wasn't even sure if it mattered to her. He was still frustrated at how glibly the lies had tripped off Vanessa's tongue when she had confronted him at the ranch, Cody in her arms. He had come directly here once he was discharged and the first person he'd met at the ranch house had been Vanessa.

She had unleashed a stream of innuendo and falsehoods about how she and Grady had been intimate at a party that he and Ben had attended. Initially she had said he was too drunk to remember, but Grady wasn't a drinker. Nor was he the kind of guy who slept around. At all. But the DNA test had shown Cody was a Stillwater, so Grady guessed, given his brother's wild living, Ben had fathered the child at that party.

When he'd confronted Vanessa with that information she had conceded that maybe she'd had a bit too much to drink herself and quickly claimed it must have been Ben. The trouble was, though he had made it very clear to Vanessa that he wasn't Cody's father nor was he interested in her, she still flirted with him. It annoyed him and even though he didn't encourage it, he could only guess how the situation looked to Chloe. Not exactly the hero he had hoped he would return from the war as.

Injured, with the whiff of scandal surrounding him and his family.

Precisely the thing he had left Little Horn to escape after his father's debilitating injury had sent his mother away, unable to live with a crippled man. The shame of his mother's defection and subsequent divorce had caused Grady to join the army, looking for discipline and meaning to his life. It had sent Ben on a path of hedonism and self-indulgence. Their mother's death while traveling abroad hadn't helped matters, either.

It seemed both their lives had come full circle. Now he suffered from a life-changing injury that had cut short his army career and Ben lay in the hospital after being thrown from a horse. Both living echoes of their now-deceased father.

"Slow down, soldier," Vanessa called out as she got out of her car behind him. "Let me help you."

He tried not to cringe as he kept going, tucking his chin into his jacket against the cold, trying to banish the picture of Vanessa standing beside Chloe, their differences so obvious.

Chloe with her sweet, gentle smile. Vanessa with her overly loud voice and tactless attitude. He knew he shouldn't compare, but he couldn't help himself.

Vanessa hurried ahead of him as he struggled up the stairs to the covered veranda that wrapped around the Colonial-style house. "You know, I can never figure out which of these doors to use," she muttered as she grabbed the handle of one of the double doors. She pulled it open just as Grady came close, and the door connected with his leg.

He bit down on a cry as he stumbled, his crutch slipping out and away.

"Sorry. I didn't mean to hit you." Vanessa clutched his arm as he regained his balance, pain shooting up his leg and clouding his vision.

He rode it out, then shook off her hand, frustrated at his helplessness. "I'm okay. Please."

"I'm just trying to help you," she complained as he fitted his crutch back under his arm. "You don't need to get all huffy."

"Sorry," he said, unable to say more than that as he stumped into the entrance of the house. As Vanessa closed the door behind them, heat washed over him blended with the scent of supper baking and his frustration eased away.

He was home.

Beyond the foyer a fire crackled in the stone fireplace that was flanked by large leather couches. He wanted nothing more than to sink into their welcoming depths, close his eyes and forget everything that had happened to him the past few years. The war. The secret mission he and his team had been sent on and the hard consequences.

He just wanted to find the simple in life again.

But the sound of a baby crying upstairs broke the peace of the moment and reminded him of his obligations and how complicated his newly civilian life would be.

"Grady? Vanessa? Are you home?" his grandmother called out from somewhere in the house.

Vanessa sauntered past him to the living room, ignoring his grandmother's question.

Just as Grady shucked off his heavy winter coat, his grandmother came down the stairs toward him, carrying Cody, who was fussing and waving his chubby arms.

In spite of knowing Cody wasn't his, it wasn't hard to see the resemblance. The little boy's brown eyes and sandy hair were exact replicas of his and Ben's, and he looked identical to Grady and Ben when they were babies.

He could see how people might believe he was the father. That Chloe might believe he was bothered him more than he cared to admit.

"Is he okay?" Grady asked, hobbling over to his grandmother, the injury in his leg making itself known as he faltered.

"He's just fussy. Missing his mom, I think." Mamie Stillwater shot a meaningful glance over her shoulder at Vanessa, who was now lounging on the couch leafing through a magazine she had bought on their way back from the hospital.

Vanessa must have caught the tone in Mamie's voice, however, because she shot to her feet, her hands out for Cody. "Hey, sweetie," she cooed, taking him from Mamie's arms and walking back to the living room. "Did you miss your momma?"

"Can I get you something to drink? Some coffee? Hot chocolate?" his grandmother asked him, her eyes still on Vanessa who sat on the couch again.

"Coffee would be great," he said.

"I'm fine," Vanessa said to her, then turned to Grady with a coy smile and patted the couch beside her. "Come and sit down, soldier," she said.

Grady hesitated, then walked over, wavering between politeness and his own struggles with Vanessa. Though he knew Cody wasn't his child, he was clearly Ben's and therefore his nephew. However, Vanessa didn't seem very motherly.

His thoughts whirled as he struggled to find the peace that had been eluding him for the past few years. Ever since that hay bale had fallen on his father and injured his back, Grady's home life had spun out of control. His father's chronic pain had created tension, which had led to fights, which finally had sent his mother away.

Living with his father had been difficult before; it had become almost impossible after the accident. Reuben Stillwater had turned into a bitter, angry and critical man.

Grady, who had often wanted to leave the ranch and Little Horn, saw his chance when he met with a recruitment officer from the army at high school. As soon as he'd graduated, he'd joined the army looking for discipline and order. He desired adventure and an escape from Little Horn. He had joined special ops, wearing his green beret with pride.

But escape had resolved the issue only temporarily. Running special ops in Afghanistan had drained him. Had created an increasing yearning for home. When he'd been injured that horrible day, he'd known his career was over.

However, coming back to the ranch to discover a woman he neither admired nor desired was telling everyone he had fathered her child wasn't the vision he'd held in his head during the lonely nights in Kandahar, Afghanistan. He had longed for the open spaces of the ranch, the simplicity of working with cattle and horses.

As he leaned back and glanced at Cody gurgling his pleasure in Vanessa's arms, a picture of Chloe flashed in his head. She looked as pretty as ever. Prettier if that was even possible, with a simple charm he remembered from their youth.

As if someone like her would look at someone like you, he reminded himself.

"He sure knows his mommy," Vanessa said, tickling the little boy under his chin. "Don't you, darling?"

His grandmother returned with two steaming mugs of coffee. She set down one within arm's reach of Grady and settled herself on the large leather couch across from them both, her eyes on Vanessa and the baby.

"Busy happenings in the county today," Mamie said, her gaze flicking from Vanessa, still absorbed with Cody, to Grady sipping his coffee. "Yesterday Tom Horton discovered a couple of his brand-new ATVs were stolen."

"They figure the same people who've been rustling the cattle and stealing equipment are to blame?" Grady asked.

"Lucy Benson is quite sure it is. This must be so difficult for her." Grandma Mamie tut-tutted. "Byron McKay is calling for her to quit as sheriff and she's not getting any closer to the culprits."

"Byron McKay likes to throw his weight around," Grady said.

"He's a big-time rancher, isn't he?" Vanessa put in, tucking Cody against her while she opened the magazine with her free hand. "I heard he's got one of the biggest spreads in the county."

"He's wealthy enough," Mamie said. "And he likes to let the members of the cowboy league know it."

"He's not president yet, is he?" Grady asked.

"Oh, no," Grandma protested angrily, as if the idea horrified her. "Carson Thorn still holds that position and the other members will make sure Byron doesn't ever get in charge."

"This league… That's the one that threw the fancy party I was at two weeks ago. What do they do exactly?" Vanessa asked.

"The league formed over a century ago as a service organization," Grandma Mamie said. "They provide help and resources to the ranchers in the area. There are chapters all over Texas."

"What kind of help? Like with the branding and stuff?" Vanessa seemed quite interested in the dealings of the league, which puzzled Grady.

"It started to fight cattle rustling and give support when times got hard for fellow ranchers." Mamie gave Grady a warm smile. "Grady and Ben's great-grandfather, Bo Stillwater, was one of the founding members."

"They aren't helping much for all the cattle rustling going on," Vanessa said, still turning the pages of her magazine one-handed, seemingly oblivious to her little boy, now, thankfully, sleeping in her arms. "I heard that Byron McKay got some fancy machinery stolen and another cattleman lost some animals. And that town sign thingy is still gone. Not too on the ball, are they?"

"I'm sure they're doing what they can," Grady said, cradling the cup of coffee, feeling a sudden chill. Coming home to stories of a rash of thefts of cattle and machinery and equipment was disheartening. The community of Little Horn, with the help of the Lone Star Cowboy League, had always pulled together. Though he had been back only a few days, he already sensed mistrust growing between the local ranchers.

"Funny how nothing's disappeared from this place, though," Vanessa said with a sly look. "Maybe the thieves are those kids you've got working on that, what is it, ranchers something or other?"

"Future Ranchers program," Grady said, shooting her a warning look. "And you might want to watch what you say about the girls we've got helping here. The Markham sisters' ranch has been hit, as well."

"But that Maddy Coles. I mean, she's a foster kid. She probably has all kind of weird friends."

"That's enough," Grady snapped, angry at her allegations, then frustrated at his shortness with her.

Too many things were happening at once, he thought. His brother, Ben, in the hospital, Vanessa and her ever-changing insinuations, all the upheaval the thefts had caused in the community.

Seeing Chloe hadn't helped his equilibrium, either. He'd thought hearing about her marriage would ease away the feelings he still harbored, but now she had come back to Little Horn. Single and as attractive as ever.

He felt a clutch of pain in his leg and all thoughts of Chloe vanished with it. He wasn't the man he used to be and he had nothing to offer any woman. He shot a glance at Vanessa. Especially not with someone like her entangled in his life.

"What puzzles me is all the things other people are receiving," Grandma said. "The new saddles at Ruby's, the cattle at the Derrings' and the clothes for their foster children. It's all very nice and generous, but it's puzzling."

"Well, I wouldn't mind getting some of the stuff being handed out." Vanessa tossed the magazine aside then stood in front of Grady and held out the little boy, who had woken up again and was stirring in her arms. "Can you take him? I'm tired. Didn't sleep a wink last night."

Grady hadn't slept much, either, but he said nothing. Instead, he set his coffee on a nearby table and took him from Vanessa. Cody stared up at him with bright eyes and gurgled his pleasure, and Grady felt a tug on his heart. He was such a cute little guy.

"I think you should see about getting that Eva chick back, that nanny you hired," Vanessa said. "I don't think I can take care of this little boy by myself."

Then she sauntered off before Grady could say anything more.

When she was out of earshot his grandmother got up and sat down beside Grady, letting Cody grab her finger with his. "I wish we could hire Eva again, but she's married now and I want to give her time to concentrate on her husband and married life. I wish I knew what to do."

"We will take care of him," Grady said firmly. "He's a Stillwater. Our flesh and blood. Our responsibility."

But even as he spoke the brave words, he felt a tremor of apprehension. Ben lay in a coma. He had his own injuries to contend with. His grandmother was getting on in years.

If Vanessa wasn't stepping up, what would Cody's future look like? Grady knew getting married wasn't in the picture for him, so he couldn't count on creating any kind of family for Cody.

His thoughts, unexpectedly, drifted to Chloe. Her warm smile, as generous as always. Her easy nature.

He pushed them aside as irrelevant. He would never be marriage material.

His mother hadn't been able to live with an injured man; how could he expect Chloe to?

Chapter Two

"Got a new patient for you. Is Salma here?"

Chloe looked up from the makeshift desk she had been given in one corner of the physical therapy department at the doctor standing in front of her. With his droopy moustache and thick eyebrows, Dr. Schuster looked as though he should be riding the range rather than diagnosing and treating patients. Dr. Schuster had taken advantage of this impression and adopted an aw-shucks attitude that put many of his patients at ease.

However, right now he looked anything but as he tapped the file he held against his other hand, the frown on his face giving her cause for concern.

"She's gone for lunch. Can I help you?"

"I thought she would be around."

"You look worried. Is it a difficult case?"

"I've got other things on my mind," he said. "But this patient does bother me. He said he doesn't need therapy."

"Do you want me to talk to him?" Chloe asked, not sure she could make a difference, but sometimes another voice helped.

"You mean turn on that Miner charm?" Dr. Schuster joked. Then he shook his head. "No. I can't ask that of you."

"It's my stepsister who has all the charm," Chloe returned. Ever since yesterday when Vanessa had shown up with her arm hooked in Grady's, grinning that smug Cheshire smile, Chloe had struggled with envy and frustration. So often in the years after Vanessa's mother had married Chloe's widowed and grieving father, Chloe had wished she and Vanessa could be close. As an only child she had looked forward to having a sister.

Instead, Vanessa had been difficult and contrary, trying at every opportunity to either discredit Chloe or treat her with contempt.

"Vanessa definitely has a certain appeal." Dr. Schuster's smile deepened. "She's been the talk of the town since she descended on the party last month claiming to be Cody's mother. But I doubt she has as much staying power as you."

"Words to make a girl's heart go pitty-pat," Chloe said in a dry tone and held her hand out for the file. "Who is the reluctant patient?"

"Another Stillwater. Grady."

And now Chloe's heart did, in fact, go pitty-pat. And then some. She took the folder from Dr. Schuster and opened it, scanning the contents, trying to maintain her distance.

"This patient will need quite a bit of time spent with him." Chloe flipped through the file, shifting into professional mode. "He'll need to get started sooner, rather than later, if he wants to regain full mobility."

"He only arrived Friday, last week," Dr. Schuster

said. "He came to see me yesterday on the recommendation of his surgeon in the army."

"Okay. I'll contact Mr. Stillwater. See what I can do."

"Good. Great. Make sure you let Salma know, as well. I suspect once you get Grady cooperating, as senior therapist she'll be doing most of the work."

Chloe understood this, but worried that Dr. Schuster thought she wasn't as competent as Salma. He looked as if he wanted to say more, then left, his lab coat flaring out behind him as he hurried off.

Clearly in a rush, Chloe thought, setting the file aside.

She had hoped to talk to him. Tell him about her personal situation. Guess it would have to be another time.

There were no other visitors in Ben's room when she got there, and the only sound was the faint hissing of his oxygen, the steady beeps of the monitors. "I suppose you've heard about all the happenings in and around the county," she said to him while she got him ready for his exercises. Talking to patients while she worked was part of the therapy. "Thefts and unexpected gifts and all sorts of stuff. Kind of crazy. So far, though, nothing from your place, so that's good, I guess. And now your brother is back." Chloe's smile faded as she did a series of hip flexions and abductions, thinking of Grady.

"You know everyone says you look the same. I can see some minor differences," she continued. "Grady's eyelashes are thicker. Hope that doesn't bother you, though I can't imagine either of you could care about that. And his one eyebrow slants off to one side. I think he's a bit taller. Maybe because of his army training. Makes him stand up straighter."

A cough behind her caught her attention and she

flushed, suddenly self-conscious about her chatter as Mamie Stillwater entered the room holding a sleeping Cody, a large quilted diaper bag hooked over her narrow shoulder.

"I'm sorry," Mamie said. "I didn't mean to interrupt."

"I'm just doing Ben's exercises," Chloe murmured, thankful she hadn't said anything more.

"Do you mind if Cody and I watch?"

"Not at all." Chloe felt a stirring in her soul at the sight of the little boy, so innocent, his rosy cheeks begging to be touched. Vanessa and Grady's son. The thought hurt her more than it should.

At least this child has two parents. As opposed to mine.

She tried to fight the thought down. *I'll do the best I can*, she reminded herself, thinking of the child she carried. At four and a half months, she thankfully wasn't showing yet, so she hadn't told anyone. Not even her close friend Lucy. She was too ashamed. Sooner or later, however, she would have to tell the hospital administration, and then everyone else.

Mamie dropped the diaper bag on an empty chair by the window, shifted the sleeping baby in her arms and stood on the opposite side of Ben, her free hand resting on his head while Chloe did some hamstring stretches.

"You've been doing this awhile?" Mamie asked, fingering Ben's hair away from his face.

"About two years. It took me six to get my degree."

"And you came back here…"

"I was offered this job." Part-time and only temporary, she'd been told, but she'd wanted to come back to Little Horn badly enough that she took the chance it might turn into full-time work.

"I was sorry to hear about your father," Mamie said.

"So was I." Chloe had made a visit seven months ago for her father's funeral, then returned to Fort Worth and Jeremy.

How much had changed since then, she thought.

Her father's ranch had been sold, barely paying off the debts incurred against it from his accident, and Jeremy had started divorce proceedings once he'd found out she was pregnant.

She had felt rootless and lost. Taking this job had become her way of finding her footing.

Chloe moved to work on Ben's arm when the rhythmic thump of a crutch on the floor gave her another start. Grady had arrived.

She pressed her lips together, sent up a prayer for strength and continued working.

"Good morning, Chloe," he said, his deep voice creating an unwelcome shiver of awareness. She gave him a nod, her cheeks warming as he made his way around the bed. He wavered, catching the rail of the bed to steady himself. He wasn't wearing his brace today, she noticed.

"Are you okay?" his grandmother asked.

"I'm fine." His curt voice and the clench of his jaw told Chloe he wasn't fine at all. She guessed his hip was causing him trouble, as was his knee. From what she'd read in his file, he'd been shot in the thigh, damaging many muscle groups and compromising the ligaments of his knee. "Do you want me to hold Cody?" Grady asked.

"He's okay. And Chloe said we could stay while she does therapy with Ben," Mamie said in a falsely bright voice. "It's interesting to watch her work. She's very capable."

"I understand from Dr. Schuster that you'll be coming to visit me in the physical therapy department," Chloe said, piggybacking on what Mamie was saying.

"I doubt it," Grady muttered, the tightness around his mouth another indication of the pain he dealt with. "I don't have time with everything at the ranch falling on my shoulders now. And this little guy." He glanced down at Cody, touched his chubby cheek with one finger, and Chloe's heart hitched at the warmth of his smile. This man would make a good father.

Was a good father, she corrected herself.

"Plus I've got Ben and the Future Ranchers program he started at the ranch to keep me busy," he continued. I don't have time to run around for appointments that won't make a difference."

"But if you don't take care of the low mobility in your knee and hip, you could be facing chronic pain later on," Chloe suggested.

Grady shot her a frown, as if he didn't appreciate what she had to say.

"As a physical therapist, I feel I must warn you the pain you are dealing with now will only worsen with lack of treatment." Chloe manipulated Ben's fingers, half her attention on helping the one brother while she tried to convince the other to accept what she could do for him.

"The pain isn't that bad." He dismissed her comment with a wave of his hand. "I know my dad managed through his. Your dad, as well. Just have to cowboy up."

Chloe kept her comment about that to herself. She didn't know everything about his father and care. However, she still maintained that, in the case of her own father, if he had received proper care and treatment, he would have been better able to do his work. "Being tough only gets you so far," she carried on. "Your injuries will, however, only cause you more problems with lack of immediate care."

She stopped then, sensing she was selling herself too hard. Grady looked as though he didn't believe her. Didn't or wouldn't—she wasn't sure which was uppermost.

"Are you working here full-time?" Mamie asked, stroking a strand of hair back from Ben's forehead, shifting to another topic.

"I am here as a part-time, temporary worker." Speaking the words aloud made her even more aware of her tenuous situation.

"Where will you go after this?"

Chloe shrugged, working with Ben's fingers, stretching and manipulating, not sure she wanted to talk about her hopes and dreams to start up a dedicated physical therapy clinic in town. Finding out how little was left after settling her father's estate had put that dream out of reach.

"There are other opportunities in Denton or Fort Worth, I'm sure." Opportunities she had passed up when she'd taken this job. She wasn't a city person. Coming back to Little Horn had filled an emptiness that had grown with each day she was away.

"I see." Mamie held her eyes, nodding slowly, as if her mind was elsewhere.

"I need to work on Ben's other leg and arm," Chloe said, setting Ben's hand down beside his still body. "So I'll have to ask you to come over to this side of the bed."

Just as Chloe came around the end of the bed, Cody whimpered, opened his eyes and started to cry.

"I should get something for him to eat," Mamie said, jiggling him as she dug through the large diaper bag she had been carrying. She looked over at Chloe as Cody's cries increased. "I'm sorry to ask, but can you hold him a moment?"

"Of course."

"I can take him." Grady shifted himself so he had his hands free.

But Mamie had already set Cody in Chloe's arms.

She held the wiggling bundle of sorrow. His cries eased into hiccups. His dark brown eyes, still shining with tears, honed in on Chloe's.

A peculiar motherly feeling washed over her. This little boy, so sweet, so precious. She cuddled him close and he quieted as he lay his head against her shoulder.

"You have a way with him," Mamie said, pulling a jar of baby food out of the diaper bag. "Just like his previous nanny, my niece, Eva, did."

"He is a sweetie," Chloe murmured, rocking him to keep him quiet.

"I can take him back now," Mamie said, taking the boy from her. "I should find a place I can heat this up."

"There's a microwave at the nurses' station I'm sure you can use," Chloe said, walking to the sink in Ben's room to wash her hands again.

Mamie walked out, leaving Grady and Chloe alone. She moved to the other side of Ben's bed and started with his leg exercises.

"Does that do anything?" Grady asked. "I mean, he's not participating."

"No, but it's important we keep his abductors flexed, his hamstrings from pulling." Chloe glanced over at Grady, disconcerted to see him staring at her. She dragged her attention back to her patient. "It's a type of stimulation, as well. And if we don't do these exercises, his muscles will seize up and when he gets out of the coma, he will have a much longer recovery ahead of him."

"You said when."

Chloe glanced up from Ben, thinking of the theories of coma patients being able, on a subliminal level, to hear what was said around their bed.

"I said when and I mean when," she said, her voice firm. "He will come out of this. We just have to do what we can for him while we wait."

Grady sat down in the chair, setting his crutch aside. "I like the sound of when. I have things I need to settle with my brother. Ben and I... Well, we had words before I left."

"A fight?"

"A disagreement about his lifestyle," Grady said. "I want to make it right."

Out of the corner of her eye, Chloe saw Grady drag his hand over his face. He looked exhausted. She was sure some of it was the burdens he carried, in addition to the pain.

"Then, this is a chance for you to talk to him," Chloe said, picking up Ben's arm and stretching it gently above his head. "A chance for you to tell him what you feel. Tell him how you care for him."

"So you think he can hear me?"

"I'd like to think he can." Chloe gave him a gentle smile. "Sometimes talking aloud can be as much for yourself as for him."

Grady nodded, then looked up at her, his expression growing serious. "You think it will help?"

"Confession is good for the soul," she said.

"In that case, I'll wait until you're gone. I don't want you hearing all my deep, dark secrets."

"You have those?" And how did that semiflirty note get in her voice?

"Don't you?"

She held his gaze a split-second longer than she should have, thinking of the last time she and Jeremy had been together and the repercussions of that. The child she now carried.

She had no right to talk this way to him. No right at all.

"If you're referring to Cody's parentage, I feel I need to tell you, he's not my son. At all." His gaze locked on hers, suddenly intense.

"He's not?"

"No."

Chloe seemed surprised and yet, at the same time, pleased that he wanted her to know.

"So why is Vanessa—" she stopped herself. She almost asked him why Vanessa was acting as if she had some claim on Grady, but it was none of her business.

Yet he seemed to think she needed to know. A tiny finger of awareness trickled down her neck. Was he trying to tell her something else?

She pushed it away as she returned to working on Ben. He was simply concerned about his reputation, that was all. Besides, it seemed that Vanessa, in spite of Grady not being Cody's father, seemed to have laid her claim on Grady.

There was no way Chloe could compete with her very attractive stepsister.

A few minutes later she had finished. Before she left,

she couldn't help a glance Grady's way. But his entire attention was on his brother. So she made a notation on Ben's chart then left.

Dr. Schuster stood by the nurses' station, but he looked up when she came near.

"Chloe. Just the person I need to talk to." His grim expression made her apprehensive.

She swallowed down her nervousness. "What do you need?"

Dr. Schuster tugged at his moustache, then steered her toward a small room just off the nurses' station. "I had hoped to do this in my office, but I don't have time." Another tug on his moustache. "I'm sorry to tell you this, Chloe. But I just got the word that I have to cut back on the budget. I know I promised you a job for longer than this, but I'm afraid I have to let you go. I don't have much choice."

"Excuse me?" Chloe wasn't sure she heard him correctly. "I've lost my job?"

"The position was only temporary," he reminded her.

"For a year." She fought down her rising panic, trying to maintain a professional attitude, trying not to sound as though she was pleading. "I need this job, Dr. Schuster."

Her life had been turned upside down the past four months. She had counted on this year to catch her breath, make other plans.

"I'm sorry, Chloe. You're a hard worker and I'd love to keep you. We could certainly use a fully staffed physical therapy department. But it's not going to happen. Sorry."

"When do I leave?"

"I'll pay out your two weeks' salary, but Friday will

be your last day." He patted her awkwardly on the shoulder and left.

Chloe leaned back against the wall, fighting down an unwelcome urge to cry. Silly hormones, she thought, closing her eyes and breathing slowly.

Help me, Lord, she prayed. *Help me get through this.*

The prayer had been her constant refrain the past year. Each time she felt that she had caught her balance, life spun her around again.

She covered her face with her hands, pulled in a wavering breath, then slowly released it.

"Are you okay?"

Mamie Stillwater's concerned voice behind her made her straighten and force a smile to her face before turning around. "I'm fine," she assured the elderly woman, still holding Cody, who slept again. "I'm just fine. Just tired. How's Cody?"

"He's tired, too." Mamie gave her a careful look. "I better get back to see how Ben is. You take care of yourself, okay?" She patted her on the shoulder with one thin hand, then trudged away, her own shoulders stooped, as if carrying Cody was more than she could bear, either.

Chloe gave herself a few more moments to compose herself. But as she walked past Ben's room, she glanced sideways only to catch Grady looking directly at her. She gave him a wan smile, then carried on. She had one more patient and then she was done for the day.

And where was she supposed to go after that? How was she going to take care of her child on her own? Jeremy had disappeared after he found out she was pregnant, disavowed any interest in her or her child, and she hadn't been able to find him. Nor did she have the energy right now.

Help me, Lord, was all she managed as she made her way to the next patient's room.

"Boy, does it smell bad in here."

Grady cringed as Vanessa's shrill voice echoed down the hallway of the barn.

"You in here, Grady? I need to talk to you. I'm not coming in."

"Will you excuse me a moment?" Grady said to the three young girls standing by the doorway of one of the horse stalls. "I need to speak with Vanessa."

Maddy Coles, Lynne James and Christie Markham were part of the Future Ranchers program his brother, Ben, had initiated to help high school students get extra credit. They came to the ranch whenever they could to work with the horses and to assist with their training and care.

"Do you want me to clean out the stalls?" Maddy asked, grabbing a fork from the wall.

"That would be good. Start with Apollo. Lynne and Christy, you can go outside and get Bishop, Shiloh and Chief in. Saul said he wanted to check their hooves when he comes here. I'll be right back."

The girls nodded and Maddy, eager as ever to work, stepped into the first stall.

Grady hurried down the alleyway, the thump of his crutch on the wooden floor echoing through the cavernous horse barn. A chill wind whistled toward him as he neared the open door where Vanessa stood, her winter coat wrapped around her, her mouth turned down in a grimace of disgust.

"I don't know what's nastier, the weather out here or the stink in there." She waved her hand delicately in front of her face as if to dispel the scent.

"What can I do for you?" Grady asked.

"First off, Mamie wants you to come to the house. She's not feeling that great and Cody has been crying the past half hour."

"And you can't take care of him?"

"I told you. Hire that nanny back. I'm headed to Austin. I've got a fitting for a dress I ordered. I'll be back tomorrow."

Grady could only stare at her, the suspicions that had been hovering in the back of his mind growing stronger each moment he spent with her. "So you're leaving your son with his great-grandmother?"

Vanessa shrugged. "I don't have time for this. I have to go." She turned and hurried off, her high-heeled boots slipping in the snow that had fallen overnight.

Grady watched her go, heaving out a sigh. He shouldn't have pushed her. He blamed his lapse on the steady pain in his leg and the headaches he'd been fighting the past two days. He took a deep breath and worked his way back to Maddy and the other girls. After giving them instructions for work that would keep them busy for the next hour, he hobbled back to the house to help his grandmother.

Cody's heart-rending wails were the first thing he heard when he stepped in the house.

He shucked off his coat, banged the packed snow off the bottom of his crutch, then, moving as fast as he could, followed the little boy's cries. He had trouble negotiating the stairs, Cody's distress adding to his own growing panic. He burst into the nursery, hurried to the crib, his ears hurting from the noise the little boy emitted.

Where was his grandmother?

He set aside his crutch and grabbed the tiny, upset bundle of baby. Cody arched his back, his fists batting the air, screeching with eyes scrunched shut as Grady tried to lift him out of the crib.

Grady wobbled on his feet, trying to hold the squirming child. Cody turned away again, screaming even louder, and Grady lost his footing.

He was going down.

He twisted, shifting his center of balance so that Cody would land on top of him.

Excruciating pain drilled through Grady's thigh, up his back and into his head as he landed hard on his bad leg. Cody let out another squawk.

Grady rode out the waves of agony, breathing slowly, then he lifted his head to see Cody staring at him, finally quiet. Thankfully he was unhurt.

"Grady. What happened?" Grandma Mamie burst into the room and hurried to Grady's side, taking Cody from him. "How did you fall? Are you okay?"

Grady sucked in another breath, the pain slowly subsiding. "I'm fine," he said, though he felt anything but. His leg felt as though it was on fire and his head as if someone had pounded a nail through it.

Mamie cradled Cody on her hip and hooked her arm through Grady's as if to help him up.

"Please, don't," he protested, gently pulling away. "I need to get up on my own." Besides, he didn't want to pull Mamie down with him in case he lost his balance again.

He rolled to one side, got his good knee under him

and, using the bars of the crib, pulled himself upright. A red-hot poker jabbed him again and he faltered.

"You're not okay. You're hurt."

"I'm fine," he ground out as the pain subsided, leaving in its wake the residue of humiliation and embarrassment. Couldn't even pick up a baby out of his bed. How was he supposed to keep up the workload created by the ranch? Not everything could be given to the hired hands. He carefully got his balance and reached for his crutch.

"You look pale," Mamie murmured, still hovering, her hand raised as if to help him again.

"How's Cody?" He turned the attention to the little boy.

Mamie shifted her gaze to the little boy, now lying still in her arms. "He seems okay."

"Should we bring him to see Dr. Tyler?" The pediatrician would have a better idea if Cody was sick or not, Grady figured.

"You're the one I'm worried about."

Grady grabbed his crutch, wishing he didn't feel so helpless. "You don't need to worry about me. Vanessa should have been here to take care of the baby."

"I think we need to confront her," his grandmother said, a note of steel in her voice that Grady remembered all too well as a child. Mamie Stillwater might come across as easygoing but when push came to shove, she could be as immovable as half of Texas.

"When she comes back we'll deal with this once and for all," Grady said, massaging the back of his neck with one hand, trying to ease away the tension that seemed to be his constant companion.

Mamie looked down at the baby reaching for her

glasses. "We know for sure he is a Stillwater. I think we need to know for sure if he is a Vane. I think we need to do a DNA test on her."

"That would either corroborate her story or rule her out," he said.

But if Vanessa was the mother, they needed to have a sit-down with her about her responsibilities. She needed to take on more and not count on Mamie.

But if the test proved she wasn't Cody's mother, that left them with the troubling question of who was.

Grady rubbed his head, the pain there battling the pain in his leg.

You should let Chloe help you. Maybe she can do something for you?

Grady held that thought a moment, trying to imagine himself showing exactly how vulnerable he was in front of a woman he hadn't been able to stop thinking about.

He couldn't. He just couldn't.

Chapter Three

"So what are you going to do now for employment?" Lucy Benson took a sip of her coffee, her green gaze flicking around the patrons of Maggie's Coffee Shop.

The place was busy. Abigail Bardera zipped around carrying plates of steaming food, her long black hair pulled back in a glossy ponytail. Maggie poured coffee, helping take orders.

"Blunt much?" Amelia said with a note of reprimand, shaking her head at their friend, her blond curly hair bouncing on her shoulders.

"May as well lay it out on the table," Lucy said.

As soon as Lucy had heard about Chloe's situation, she'd called Amelia and insisted that they take Chloe out for coffee and pie at Maggie's.

"I don't know." Chloe poked her fork at the flaky apple pie Amelia had insisted she order. "I already talked to Maggie about working here, but that's a no-go." She fought down the too-familiar sense of panic at the thought of being unemployed.

She was supposed to have worked today but yesterday Dr. Schuster had told her to consider Thursday her last day. He had hoped it would give her some more time to find a job.

"Would you move back to Fort Worth?" Amelia asked, her tone concerned.

"Too many bad memories there, though if there's work there I might. To coin a phrase that has been the mantra of my life lately, beggars can't be choosers." Her stomach roiled again at the thought of having to leave. Start over. Find her balance again on her own.

Just her and her baby.

"I know things are bad when you're resorting to clichés." Lucy tucked her short blonde hair behind her ear, her eyes holding Chloe's as if trying to encourage her.

"My life is a cliché," Chloe grumped, then waved the complaint off. "Sorry. I shouldn't whine. It's just getting hard to find the silver lining."

"Well, every silver lining has a cloud," Lucy quipped. "And it's not your fault Jeremy cheated on you. I always knew he was a jerk."

If she only knew how much of a jerk.

Chloe cut off that thought. She didn't want to give Jeremy any space in her mind. Bad enough he didn't want to have anything to do with the baby she carried. And that he had disappeared after emptying out the bank account.

"At least you're not going to tell me I told you so," Chloe said. "You did warn me not to marry in haste."

"Are you not listening to Lucy?" Amelia said with a warning wag of her finger. "You're spouting clichés again."

A sudden burst of laughter at one end of the café caught Chloe's attention. Carson Thorn stood by a table of people, laughing at something one of them had said.

"Carson looks more relaxed lately," Chloe said.

"Getting reunited with his childhood sweetheart probably helped mitigate the stress of all these thefts that he and the other members of the league have been dealing with," Lucy said with a wry tone. "Nice that there can be happy endings in this town." She shot a glance over at Amelia. "And speaking of happy endings, how are you and Finn getting on?"

To Chloe's surprise, her friend blushed. She hadn't thought spunky and vivacious Amelia knew how to blush.

"Quite well. Making plans."

Lucy sighed. "Like I said, I'm happy for happy endings."

Chloe gave her apple pie another stab, wishing she could hope for a happy ending in her particular story. She doubted any man would want to take her on now.

"You're looking pensive," Lucy said. "I thought that was my job?"

Chloe knew Lucy had been on edge the past few months, the pressure of all the thefts in the area making her extratense and vigilant. "That's why I'm trying not to complain. I know you're under a lot of stress lately."

As well, Chloe wasn't ready to divulge her secret to Lucy and Amelia. Not while she was still adjusting to the idea, trying to figure out what shape her life would take.

"This string of thefts has been a frustrating nightmare." Lucy looked as if she wanted to say more when someone stopped by their table.

"Good afternoon, ladies." Mamie Stillwater's smile encompassed the three of them, the light from the windows beside them glinting off her glasses and polishing her gray hair. "I'm sorry to interrupt, but is it possible to talk to you alone, Chloe?"

"I have to head out right away," Lucy said, giving Chloe a look she interpreted as "tell me everything later."

"And I have to meet Finn to go over some wedding plans," Amelia said, getting up as well and dropping a few bills on the table. "This should cover everything."

Chloe was about to protest but Amelia just shook her head and gave her a bright smile. "And now we'll leave the two of you alone."

"Thanks so much."

"We'll talk more later." Amelia walked toward the entrance, but Lucy stopped by the table where Carson stood. Chloe guessed she would be asking him if he had heard about more thefts or people receiving anonymous gifts.

"You know we have little Cody at our house," Mamie said as she sat down in the chair Lucy had vacated. "My niece Eva used to be his nanny, but she's married now. I have a cook but Martha Rose went to go help her mother who broke her leg, which means I can't spend as much time with Cody as I'd like. And Grady was supposed to be doing physical therapy with you and he isn't."

She stopped there and Chloe waited, not sure where Mamie was going with all of this.

Mamie gave her a tight smile. "I'm sorry, but I overheard Dr. Schuster talking to you about your job, or lack of one…"

"How did you know about that?"

Mamie paused, her hands folded, fingers tapping against each other as she gave Chloe an apologetic look.

"I didn't mean to listen in. I was in the room behind you when I heard him say that."

Chloe's cheeks warmed. A witness to her firing. But Mamie seemed genuinely sorry and Chloe guessed it wasn't her fault. Dr. Schuster should have been more discreet.

"Again, I'm sorry," Mamie continued. "But what I was wondering, given that we have Cody to take care of and Grady who won't go to therapy, would you be willing to work for me? I thought if you were actually at the house, Grady would be more amenable to participate in his recovery. And, truthfully, I need someone to help us with the little boy."

"I thought Vanessa was staying with you?" Chloe asked.

Mamie shot a look around the café, as if checking to see if anyone was listening, then leaned closer, concern etched on her features. "I know she's your stepsister, but truthfully, she doesn't seem to want to spend the time with Cody that he needs. It would help us out a lot if you would be willing to work for me."

Chloe wasn't sure she wanted to stay in the same house as Vanessa. It was too easy to recall the stinging comments her stepsister had steadily lobbed her way when they'd lived together and how Vanessa had often put her down in front of her friends.

But the cold facts of her life made her shelve her pride. Truth was she needed a job.

"So how long would you need me for?"

"Not sure." Mamie sighed. "As long as Ben is in a coma and Grady is handicapped by his injury…" Her voice trailed off and as she pressed her lips together Chloe felt a flash of sympathy for the poor woman. It must have been so difficult to see her grandsons both dealing with difficulties as well as deal with the extra strain of taking care of an unexpected great-grandbaby.

And then there was Vanessa.

"All right. I'll do it. When do you want me to start?"

"Whenever you're done at the hospital."

"Yesterday was my last day."

"Can you come now?"

The weariness in her voice, plus the light touch of Mamie's hand on Chloe's, made her stifle her objections and give in. "I'll come today."

"Excellent. Thank you so much." Mamie sank back in her chair, the relief on her face palpable. "I'll go directly to the ranch and get your room ready."

"My room?"

Mamie looked taken aback. "Yes. I thought you knew. I'm sorry if I didn't make that clear. I was hoping you would be staying at the ranch overnight. To help with Cody."

Chloe sucked in a breath at the thought of having to face Grady, Vanessa and Cody all together day and night. It was a small comfort to know that Grady was not Cody's father, but that still left Vanessa and her flirtatious ways.

But a job was a job, she reminded herself. Something she needed until she could figure out her next move.

"Okay. I'll pack my things and meet you at the ranch."

"Why don't I go with you and we can drive back with each other? You remember where the ranch is, right?"

Too clearly, Chloe thought, remembering a trip she had made with Vanessa to the Stillwater ranch. The day she'd first seen her stepsister kissing the boy she had cared for so deeply.

* * *

"Hush now, Cody. Please go to sleep." Grady stood by the crib rubbing one large hand over the baby's back in a vain effort to get him to settle down. Vanessa was still gone and his grandmother had left on some mysterious trip to town.

Cody had been crying for an hour now. Grady felt more out of his league than he had that time he and his fellow soldiers had been pinned down by crossfire. At least then he had training to fall back on.

He had no training to deal with a kid who wouldn't settle down.

He should call Eva. Or her husband. They would know. He was just about to do that when he heard voices. And with relief he grabbed his crutch and stumped over to the door to listen. Was Vanessa back?

He heard footsteps coming up the stairs, and a figure rounded the corner. She was slim with long wavy brown hair spilling over one shoulder of a plaid shirt tucked into snug blue jeans. Beautiful and sweet looking.

Grady blinked. Chloe? What was she doing here?

His grandmother materialized behind her, a grin taking over her face. "Isn't this wonderful?" Mamie said. "Chloe has agreed to come help us out."

"And from the sounds of things, I better get to work," she said, giving him a vague smile. "Is he hungry?"

"No. He just had a bottle."

Chloe gave him a tight nod and hurried past him into Cody's room.

Grady looked from her to his grandmother, who stood in front of him looking mighty pleased with herself.

"What is going on?" he whispered, moving her away from the door so Chloe wouldn't overhear them.

The cries from the nursery stilled and he heard Chloe's gentle murmur as she settled the baby.

"We said we needed to do something about Cody. Chloe lost her job at the hospital. And you need therapy and you won't go. Martha Rose is gone. So I thought this was a perfect solution for all of us. Chloe can help us with Cody and she can work with you, leaving me free to help with the cooking and where I'm needed. Win, win."

Grady could only stare at his grandmother, trying to absorb what she had just told him.

"Chloe? Do physical therapy with me? Here?"

"One question at a time," his grandmother said, wagging her finger at him, a definitely mischievous smile on her face. "Chloe. Yes. And yes, I do want her to do physical therapy here. You know that is what you need to do. I can see by the grimace on your face and by the way you walk. It's only getting worse and, I fear, will continue to get worse. You have to take care of yourself."

Grady clenched his jaw, knowing his grandmother was right but not sure he wanted Chloe seeing his helplessness.

"You are the only man I have around," his grandmother said, playing a last, devastating card. "I need you to help me as much as possible."

Surely there had to be another way?

"I agree that we need help with Cody," he conceded. "As for the rest, well, we'll see."

And that was all he was giving her.

"That's fine," his grandmother said with a bright smile. "One step at a time."

He watched her leave, eyes narrowed, feeling as though he had just agreed to something he would regret.

He returned to the nursery to check on Cody.

Chloe stood in profile to him, rocking the baby, such a maternal smile on her face that Grady's knees grew weak. This was what a mother looked like, he thought, taking in the sight of this beautiful woman holding this baby so tenderly.

"I think he's asleep," Chloe whispered, her attention still focused on Cody. As she gently laid him down, Cody started, his hands shooting into the air, then as Chloe stroked his face he settled again, his breathing growing deep and even. It was amazing, he thought, envious of her ability to soothe the child, yet so grateful she could.

She gave his face another stroke of her hand and stepped away.

"We can go now," she said, keeping her voice down.

She left ahead of Grady and he gently closed the door behind him. Together they walked down the hallway.

"Thanks so much for your help," Grady said, following her to the top of the stairs. "I didn't know what to do anymore. You seem to be a natural mother."

She stopped there, her hand gripping the railing, her knuckles white, a look of fear on her face.

Had he said something wrong? Hurt her in some way?

She turned, folded her arms over her stomach. "Before we see your grandmother, I need to know how comfortable you are with working with me. I don't think my coming to help you was your idea."

Grady held her steady gaze, appreciating her straightforward honesty, such a refreshing change from her manipulative stepsister.

And that's not the only thing you appreciate about her, a perfidious voice teased.

He shook it off, his injury a grim reminder of why she was here and what he had to offer someone like her.

"It wasn't my idea. For now, let's just leave it at you taking care of Cody."

"But I saw your file. You need to keep working on your mobility."

"I will. I just don't have time yet. I've got the ranch and the program Ben set up to oversee. If Ben hadn't been so foolhardy…" He stopped himself there. Chloe may be employed here, but she didn't need to know all the ins and outs of their lives. "Anyhow, let's go have some coffee with my grandma, because I'm sure she's getting some ready."

"I have your assessment. Dr. Schuster gave that to me so we could start from there."

"You don't give up, do you?"

"One of the characteristics of being a physical therapist. A quiet stubbornness."

He laughed at that, glancing sidelong at her. But he didn't look away and neither did Chloe. Their eyes held and a peculiar feeling of awareness rose up. An echo of older emotions she had once created.

She swallowed and he saw her take a quick breath.

Did she feel it, too?

Then he took a step closer and his foot caught on the carpet of the hallway. He faltered, thankfully just for a moment, as reality shot down any foolish thoughts he might have entertained.

She turned away, went down the stairs, quickly outpacing him.

And as he made his slow, painful way behind her he was reminded once again the foolishness of allowing himself to feel anything for any woman.

The only trouble was Chloe wasn't just any woman. At one time he had cared for her. But she'd given him no indication that she returned his feelings. And then Vanessa had come along. After that, the war.

Now his life was a tangle of obligations and unmet expectations. He knew he had to be realistic. He couldn't offer her anything. Not anymore.

"So you took the job?" Lucy was asking.

Holding her cell phone close to her ear, Chloe sat back on the bed of the room Mamie Stillwater had shown her to. It was off the nursery and a full floor away from the room Grady stayed in, which was a good thing.

Her room was lovely, though. Painted a soft aqua, trimmed with white casings, the room was large, cozy and welcoming. A chair and small reading table were tucked into a corner beside an expansive bay window that overlooked the ranch. The bed filled another corner, and a small walk-in closet and en suite gave her all the privacy she needed. It was lavish and luxurious compared to the cramped furnished apartment she had been renting.

"I didn't have much choice," Chloe said.

"Won't hurt to see Grady every day," Lucy teased.

"It's strictly professional," Chloe said, trying not to let the image of Vanessa fawning over Grady get to her. "Besides, I don't know how much one-on-one time

I'll be spending with him. He seems intent on avoiding therapy."

"If he's as stubborn as his brother, you've got your work cut out for you."

Lucy sighed lightly and Chloe sensed her friend's extra stress. "You sound tired. Have there been more thefts?"

"Another one at the Cutler ranch last night," Lucy said. "Some ATVs and a horse. I'm getting worried that this is more organized than people think."

Chloe twisted a thread from the cuff of her worn blue jeans around her finger. "Do you have any leads?"

"None. Though something has been puzzling me greatly. The Stillwater ranch is the only large ranch that doesn't seem to have had any thefts at all. A few of the smaller ones have been avoided as well, but I'm still trying to see if there's a connection. A pattern that I can't find. I was hoping you could help me out."

"How?"

"Just keep your eyes and ears open. Maybe get closer to Mamie. I don't know."

"And report anything I might hear back to you."

"Please."

"Okay. I'll see what I can find out." She stifled the feeling of guilt that accompanied her statement. She was thankful for the job and she didn't want to take advantage of that.

Yet Lucy was her friend. And she would be helping her and the community out.

"I should go. Mamie said that dinner was in a few minutes."

"Hey, thanks for doing this for me," Lucy said. "I appreciate any help I can get."

Chloe said goodbye, then made quick work of changing her flannel shirt and pants for a clean pair of blue jeans and an aqua silk shirt. She brushed her hair and, giving in to an impulse, applied some blush and mascara.

For Grady?

Chloe lifted her chin and looked at her reflection in the mirror. For herself, she thought, clipping part of her hair back with a couple of bobby pins. She couldn't allow herself to think of Grady. Not while she carried another man's baby.

Before she could give in to doing any more primping, she left. She paused at the door of the nursery, but all was silent.

She hurried down the stairs. However, no one was in the kitchen by the table, so she followed the conversation to the formal dining room.

Grady sat at one end of the table and as she came in, Vanessa got up from her end and sat by him. As if trying to show Chloe where things stood. Grady didn't seem interested, however, which gave her a small encouragement. He looked up, struggling to stand.

Vanessa frowned at Grady. "Just relax. It's only Chloe." Then Vanessa's icy glance ticked over her. "That's an interesting look."

Chloe's heart turned over as she mentally compared Vanessa's silky dress and perfect makeup with her own clothes. She had thought she looked okay, but now she felt drab and dull. She didn't think she needed to dress for dinner.

Vanessa gave her a wry look. "Well, I guess it's too late to change."

Chloe wished she could ignore her stepsister's dismissive attitude.

"I think you look great," Grady said.

His words shouldn't have made her feel as good as they did.

Mamie, who wore plain dress pants and a shirt partially covered by her apron, entered and set a platter of ham beside bowls of steaming potatoes and salads and vegetables. At least she looked more casual.

"Do you need any help?" Chloe asked her.

Mamie waved off her offer as she removed her apron and laid it on a side table. "No, dear. This is the last plate. Please sit down." Mamie pulled a chair away from the table, leaving the only empty spot available opposite Vanessa but beside Grady. Chloe sat down and plucked her napkin out of the ring, ignoring Vanessa's calculating look.

"Is Cody sleeping?" Vanessa asked, leaning close to Grady, as if staking her claim on him. Again.

"He is."

"Poor baby. I think I wore him out playing with him," Vanessa said with a smug smile.

"Well, here we are all together," Mamie said, but Chloe caught a strained note in her voice.

"One big happy family," Vanessa chimed in, and reached for the salad bowl. "Grady, can I serve you some salad?"

"I thought we would pray first," Mamie said.

"Oh. Right." Vanessa fluttered her hands in an "I'm silly" gesture, then gave Grady another arched look. "I always forget."

Just before Chloe lowered her head, however, she

couldn't help a glance Grady's way and was disconcerted to see him looking directly at her.

Then she felt a tinge of nausea, a remnant of what she had been struggling with the first four months of her pregnancy, a reminder, and she quickly drew her gaze away.

Mamie prayed a blessing on the food, asking as well for some solution to the thefts, thanks for family and another request for Ben's recovery.

Chloe kept her head bowed a moment, adding her own prayer to stay focused on her work here and not be distracted by inappropriate feelings better left buried.

"I heard there was another theft at the McKay spread," Vanessa said, her voice bright, her expression holding a forced gaiety when Mamie was done.

"I'm sure Byron was upset about that," Mamie replied.

"And you guys haven't had anything stolen?" Vanessa asked, taking a tiny bite of her salad.

"Not yet, thankfully." Grady handed the platter of ham in front of him to Chloe. "Would you like some?"

Chloe felt a start of surprise, her mind as much on the job Lucy had asked her to do here on the Stillwater ranch as trying not to be so aware of Grady sitting only a few feet from her. "Sure. Thank you." As she took the plate, however, she caught Vanessa's narrowed gaze.

"That's interesting," Vanessa said, dragging out the word, larding it with innuendo. "Makes one wonder if it's not that foster girl you've got working here who could be behind the thefts. Maddy something or other. She doesn't come from the best family. Sort of like Chloe here. Having an alcoholic father can't be easy."

"I think that's enough," Grady said, a harsh note of reprimand in his voice.

"Well, it's true." Vanessa stabbed at her salad. "About Maddy anyway."

The supper conversation limped along after that. Vanessa picked at her food, shooting glances over at Grady, who steadfastly ignored her. All the while Chloe was far too aware of Grady's eyes on her and of Vanessa's occasional glower. The tension was noticeable and Chloe was thankful when the meal was finally over.

Chloe declined dessert as she got up from the table, saying she should check on Cody.

As she hurried up the stairs, second thoughts nipped at her heels. She shouldn't have taken this job. How long could she put up with Vanessa and her judgmental attitude and snide comments?

But even as those questions plagued her, she knew Grady's presence created the tighter tension.

She slipped into the nursery and stood by the crib, her arms wrapped tightly around her midsection. She could feel a bump that she knew would start to show soon. For now, however, she could still wear her regular clothes.

And what will you do when you can't?

She doubted Mamie would let her go. After all, they had taken in Vanessa, who was an unwed mother. She doubted Mamie would judge her.

But even as that thought formulated, she thought of how Grady avoided Vanessa in spite of her flirting. She wondered if his attitude toward her had something to do with Vanessa's situation—being an unwed mother.

Cody lay on his side, arms curled up, looking utterly adorable.

A confusing brew of emotions stirred within her as she pressed her hand to her abdomen in a protective gesture.

"He's sleeping?"

Grady's voice from the doorway made her jump. She spun around just as he joined her by the crib.

"He looks so peaceful," Grady said, leaning on the rail as if to get a closer look. Then Grady looked over at her and gave her a cautious smile. "I'm sorry about what Vanessa said over dinner."

"You don't have to apologize," Chloe said. "I heard a lot worse growing up."

"I keep forgetting you two are sisters."

"Stepsisters," Chloe reminded him. "And Vanessa only lived at the ranch for a while."

"If I may ask, what made her mother leave?"

Chloe's conscience fought with a desire to tell him the bare truth. There hadn't been enough money for Etta Vane. The ranch hadn't been as prosperous as she had thought.

"I don't think ranch life suited Etta. Or Vanessa. The reality was a shock for them."

"Somehow she seems to like our place just fine," Grady said.

Because there's money here.

But she dismissed the thought. The little boy sleeping in the crib in front of her was her stepsister's reason for returning. As was the man standing beside her.

"I… I should go," she said.

To her dismay, she felt Grady's hand on her shoulder as she straightened. The warmth of his fingers through her shirt sent a tingle of awareness down her spine; the glint of his eyes in the soft glow of the night-light created an unexpected and unwelcome attraction. "Don't take to heart what Vanessa said to you."

"I'm used to it," Chloe said, struggling to keep the breathless tone out of her voice.

"Was it hard? Living with her?"

Chloe shrugged, then gave him a faint smile. "I just wished we could have been closer. But maybe there's time now that she's here."

He held her gaze, his expression earnest. "I feel as if I need to tell you because you're working here now, with Cody, that while I know I'm not his father, neither do I believe she's Cody's mother."

"What?" Vanessa's screech from the doorway broke into the moment. "How dare you say things like that? I'm his mother, Grady Stillwater." She rounded on Chloe. "You were feeding him some lies, weren't you? You always were jealous of me. You're so plain and dumpy. You could never compete with me. You and your useless father. I can't believe my mother even married him. He was a lousy rancher and a crippled drunk."

Chloe fought her inborn urge to defend her father. It wasn't his fault his grandfather hadn't left as much money as Etta had hoped. It wasn't his fault he'd been injured when he had his ATV accident.

"Vanessa, that's enough," Grady snapped.

"Enough of what?" Vanessa said, rounding on him. "You don't need to stand up for her. You need to face the truth."

"If we're talking about truth, it should be an easy matter to get a DNA test done on you," Cody said, his voice surprisingly calm. "That should give us the truth about who Cody's biological mother is."

Vanessa paled at that, glancing from Chloe to Grady,

her eyes wide. "I can't believe you doubt me. I can't believe you think I'm not his mother…" Her voice drifted off and with another accusing glare at Chloe, Vanessa spun around and strode away.

Grady blew out a sigh as he shoved his hands through his hair. "Again. Sorry about that," he said. "I shouldn't have confronted her. Made her say those things about you and your father."

Chloe looked down at Cody, who lay fast asleep and blissfully unaware of the drama unfolding in his nursery. "I'm just glad he didn't wake up" was all she could manage.

Grady touched her again and she turned to him.

"You always were a pure, sweet person," he said.

Once again her former attraction to him bubbled to the surface.

Then Chloe felt another flicker of nausea.

She pulled back, turned away from him, the feeling a stark reminder of the main reason she couldn't encourage him. Couldn't be with him.

The child she carried. The child conceived with her ex-husband.

Chapter Four

"Have you seen Vanessa this morning?" Mamie asked, beating some eggs in a bowl.

Grady looked up from the laptop he had propped on the eating bar of the kitchen. Ben had all the livestock records, all the bookkeeping, all the information on the Future Ranchers in files on the computer, and Grady had been poring over them in an attempt to get up to speed.

"No. I thought she was sleeping in."

"I had to get something from the closet in her room and knocked on the door but when I opened it, there was no one in the room. Her bed was empty." Mamie beat the eggs, the frown on her face clearly expressing her concern. "I'm glad we hired Chloe to help us."

"I am, too." Grady's thoughts skipped back to that moment last night in the nursery. Seeing Chloe standing by the crib, smiling down at Cody, had created a mixture of emotions he had a hard time processing. He knew he was attracted to her. And he sensed something building between them.

But all it took was one shift of his weight on his leg,

one look at the crutch to remind him of the foolishness of letting these feelings take over. He wasn't the man he once was.

No. She deserved better than this.

Just as he made this resolution, she came into the kitchen, Cody cuddled up against her. The baby still wore his sleeper. He was rubbing his eyes, his rosy cheeks holding the imprint of one of his chubby hands, his blanket tucked under one arm.

Grady felt a warmth kindle in him at the sight.

Trouble was he knew it wasn't the sight of Cody that caused it, but the woman holding him.

"Good morning, Chloe," he said, giving her a wary smile.

She just nodded at him, suddenly impersonal. Clearly he had stepped over some line she had drawn last night.

"Hey, sweetie." Mamie reached for the boy, beaming at the sight of Cody holding out his arms to her in answer. "Did you have a good sleep?"

"He woke up once early this morning," Chloe said. "I went to see what was wrong and Vanessa was in the nursery. I thought she was picking him up, but she just stood by his crib and then left. I found this on his night table when I got Cody this morning." She tugged an envelope out of the back pocket of her blue jeans and handed it to him.

Grady frowned as he slit it open and pulled a single piece of paper out.

"Dear Stillwaters," he read aloud. "I decided to leave. You were right. Cody's not my kid. But I'm guessing he is Grady's, because that's what you Stillwaters are like. Love 'em and leave 'em. Have a good life. Vanessa."

"So why did she write that now?" Mamie asked, her fingers pressed against her lips.

Grady folded up the letter and put it in the envelope. "I told her that a simple DNA test could easily prove if she was the mother or not. I'm guessing she knew we would find out the truth." He thought of the cruel things Vanessa had thrown at Chloe as she'd left, yet was thankful Chloe wouldn't have lingering doubts about his relationship with Vanessa.

But Chloe was filling up a bottle with formula for Cody and not paying attention to him. Clearly that moment he thought they had shared was over.

Not that he blamed her.

"When Cody is down for his morning nap, I thought we could start doing some therapy," Chloe said to Grady, her entire focus on getting the milk into the bottle. Obviously the job required intense concentration.

"I need to talk to the kids this morning. Maddy Coles is coming to do some work with our horse trainer."

Chloe gave him a sharp look. "Is Maddy the girl who Vanessa referred to?"

"Yes." Grady ground out the single word, still angry at Vanessa's insinuations.

"Vanessa can be thoughtless," Chloe said, screwing the lid on the baby bottle. "I don't think she always realizes what she is saying."

"I can't believe you can defend her," Grady said. "Especially after what she said about your father. Her comments were uncalled for and unkind."

Chloe's gaze shot to his, the surprise in her eyes shifting to gratitude as she took Cody from his grandmother. "Thanks for that. Dad was… He had his difficulties."

One of them being Vanessa's mother, Grady was sure. "Your father was a good man who had some bad things happen to him. And I should know. My father had his own issues after his injuries."

"Thanks for understanding." Chloe's smile wormed its way past his defenses.

"Did you want some breakfast, Chloe?" Mamie asked, dipping bread into the egg mixture. "I'm making French toast."

"That sounds wonderful," Chloe said. "I'll feed Cody and then I can help you."

"You just sit down and take care of that little boy," Mamie said, patting Cody on his cheek and giving Chloe a warm smile. "I'll take care of breakfast."

Wasn't too hard to see that his grandmother liked Chloe, Grady thought. Most likely one of the reasons she'd hired her.

Against his will his mind returned to last night. To that brief connection he and Chloe had shared. And then to her sudden turn away from him. It was a vivid reminder of his situation.

He finished his breakfast and got up.

"I'm going out to the barn," he said, balancing his plate and mug in one hand as he maneuvered past the table to the kitchen counter.

"Will you be coming back to the house later on?" Chloe asked.

"For lunch, maybe." Grady knew she referred to the therapy she wanted to do. But he didn't want to spend more time with her than he had to. Didn't want to be reminded even more clearly of his shortcomings.

"Do you mind if I go out to the barns?" Chloe stood in the doorway of a small room just off the master bedroom where Mamie slept. The older woman was bent over a sewing machine sitting to one side of the room. She was making quilt squares from what Chloe could tell.

The older woman looked up and pushed her glasses back down on her nose. "No. That's not a problem."

"Cody is down for his afternoon nap. He'll be good for at least two and a half hours."

"Are you going to try to talk to Grady?"

"*Try* being the operative word," Chloe said with a wry smile.

Mamie sat back in her chair and folded her arms over her chest. "I think you'll be able to charm him," she said with a twinkle in her eye.

"I was hoping to set up downstairs in the recreation room, if that was okay? I noticed some exercise equipment in there that I might be able to use."

"That's fine. Do you need any other equipment for him?"

"Some mats and foam rollers once I do my own assessment. I've already spoken with Salma, the physical therapist at the hospital. She said she would be willing to rent some of what I need, if that's okay with you."

"Whatever you need," Mamie said with a wave of her hand. "You just let me know."

"Thanks." Chloe was about to leave when Mamie spoke up again.

"He's a good man," Mamie said, her voice almost pleading. "I know the war has changed him. I know he feels less of a man than he was. He's pulled into himself, but deep down I know he's still the same honorable and loving man he was when he left. And you know that he and your stepsister were never…"

"I know and I understand," Chloe said, holding up one hand to stop the dear woman's defense of her grandson. It was hard to listen to because she spoke Chloe's own thoughts aloud.

Last night, after she and Grady had shared that moment in the nursery, she had lain awake for too long, one hand resting on her stomach where her baby grew, the other on her chest to ease the sorrow in her heart.

"I want to ask another question," Mamie said. "And you can say no if you're uncomfortable, but we'll be attending church tomorrow—"

"I'd love to come," Chloe said.

"Wonderful." Mamie gave her a bright smile, then turned back to her sewing.

Chloe grabbed a jacket and headed out the door. As she left the shelter of the porch, a chill wind snatched her breath away and tossed her hair around her face. She shivered and hurried down the path toward what she guessed was the horse barn.

Muted voices echoed down the long alleyway, her footfalls softened by the wooden floor. Chloe inhaled the scent of the barn, so familiar it created an ache. While her father had never been able to afford a facility such as this, the old barn they'd used for the horses had held the same smells—oil, leather, old wood and horses.

A horse nickered at her as she passed, poking its head over the top of a stall.

Chloe smiled at the mare, took a moment to pet her, then reluctantly left, following the voices to the end of the barn. She turned a corner to a large area that was roofed in but open to the weather.

Grady held the halter of a palomino, stroking its neck while a heavyset man with a shock of white hair was bent over one of the hooves he had tucked between his legs. Chloe recognized Saul Bateman, the local farrier and one-time friend of her father. The sight of him hurt. Though Saul and her father had been friends, Saul hadn't attended her father's funeral and she hadn't seen him until now.

A young girl—Maddy Coles, Chloe guessed—stood beside Saul, her head tilted to watch him work. She was small, slender with a darker complexion and black hair. A pair of earbuds dangled from a cord hanging out of the chest pocket of her worn denim jacket.

"You might want to put that fancy new iPod away before you drop it on the ground," Grady was saying.

"Sorry, Mr. Stillwater," she said with a shrug and a grin. "I don't want to lose it."

"I still find it interesting that iPod and all that other stuff just showed up at your place," Grady said. "Did you ever find out who brought it?"

Chloe stopped where she was, remembering the buzz about how Maddy's foster parents, Judd and Ann Derring, had received some cattle, farm equipment and some clothes for the children, as well as the iPod Maddy now tucked back into her pocket. Maybe Maddy would say something Chloe could pass on to Lucy.

"Not a clue," Maddy said. "Though it was exciting. Timmy hasn't had his nose out of those books since he got them."

"I think it's weird," Saul commented as he dug into the hoof of the horse. "Weird and wrong to steal from people. Then to give other people gifts. Can't figure out why Lucy hasn't found whoever is doing it."

"It can't be easy. It seems to be so random," Grady added. He turned back to Saul. "So why don't you tell

Maddy what you're doing, Saul?" Clearly Grady was done talking about the thefts and wanted to move on.

"Of course." Saul shifted his weight to accommodate the sudden movement of the horse. "You need to make sure you get all the dirt and snow out of the hoof before we trim the hooves and then shoe them," he said to Maddy. "We use this hoof pick for cleaning."

The horse Grady held looked up and whickered at Chloe. Grady glanced back, frowning when he saw her. "Hey, you," he said with a nod. "Cody sleeping?"

"Which is why I'm here," she said, wishing his frown and dismissive attitude didn't bother her as much as they did. "I thought we'd get started on your exercises today."

"I'm kind of busy right now," he muttered, turning back to the horse.

Saul looked up and gave Chloe a half smile. "Hey, girl. How you doing?"

"I'm good."

"I heard Vanessa is gone."

"Yes."

"I'm sorry about the funeral."

Chloe only nodded her acknowledgment of Saul's comment. It had hurt that her father's old friend hadn't attended, but she suspected it had much to do with the falling out the two of them had had over his marrying Etta and the consequences thereof.

Saul had warned her father not to get involved with Etta Vane. But her father, lonely and grieving, had jumped too quickly into another relationship and cut Saul out of his life. "And I'm sorry," he said, holding her gaze, his expression full of regret. "Sorry about your father. He didn't deserve what happened to him. That Etta woman was pure poison."

"Well, Vanessa is gone and I doubt she'll be back," Chloe said. "But for now I have work to do. Grady, are you able to come?" She didn't want to talk about her father and the circumstances of his life. He hadn't been all that happy in this life; she knew he was much happier now.

"I can hold Charger and watch Mr. Bateman work so you can go," Maddy offered, her voice eager.

"It's okay. I'm fine," Grady said. "Just keep going."

Chloe tried hard not to sigh, but his reluctance to let her help him was annoying.

"I'm not going anywhere," Chloe said.

"Great. You hold Charger still while I get the next horse."

"Okay." She took the halter rope and almost laughed at the surprise on his face. She wasn't leaving him alone until he agreed to start therapy.

"Fine. Then I'll get the next horse."

"Sure. You do that."

He frowned at her as if wondering if she was poking fun of him, which she was. He grabbed his crutch and headed out into the paddock.

"You taking care of Cody now?" Maddy asked, carefully digging at the hoof with the pick under Saul's tutelage. "I thought you worked at the hospital."

"The job was only temporary and so Mrs. Stillwater offered me a job here."

Maddy bent over and the earbuds of her iPod fell out of her pocket again. "Whoops," she said, tucking them back in.

Chloe thought of Lucy's request to keep an eye on things at the ranch. "Have you received any other anonymous gifts?" she asked, hoping she sounded more casual than she felt.

"No. Just this stuff." Maddy shrugged and buttoned the pocket this time. "Makes me feel kind of special and creeped out at the same time."

"Have any of your friends at school gotten anything?"

"No." Maddy grunted and dug at the hoof with her pick.

Saul shot her a puzzled look and Chloe decided to stop her questioning. No need to draw attention to herself.

The horse she held nickered and she glanced back to see Grady trying to lead the other horse with one hand and handle his crutch with the other. The horse he was leading balked, his crutch clattered to the floor and he stumbled, grabbing the horse by the mane to right himself.

Chloe took a step toward him to help, then heard Saul clear his throat as if warning her.

She caught his look then turned away, pretending she hadn't seen what had happened, though it bothered her deeply to see this proud man so helpless.

Maddy, intent on getting every last bit of dirt out of the horse's hoof, thankfully didn't know what was going on.

A few moments later Grady joined them, his crutch under his arm again, leading the horse. "I'll tie him up here," he said, breathing heavily.

Chloe fought down a beat of frustration. Why couldn't this man see he needed her help?

But until he agreed, she could do nothing.

"I think we're done with Charger here," Saul said to

Maddy. "I need to trim the hooves, but I'll have to do that on my own."

Just then a noise behind them drew Chloe's attention. Mamie walked toward them holding Cody.

"I'm sorry," Chloe said, feeling suddenly guilty for spending time out here. She held up Charger's halter rope. "Can someone take him? I need to get Cody."

"I'll hold the rope. You can go," Maddy said.

"I just came out to tell you that I got a call from the hospital," Mamie said as Chloe took Cody from her. "Ben's temperature is up. I know we talked about going tomorrow after church, but I'd like to go today."

"I'll take you," Grady said.

"I have a few things to get ready yet," Mamie said, her hands worrying each other. "If that's okay?"

"No problem."

Mamie hurried back, leaving Chloe and Grady behind.

Cody gurgled at Chloe as if he recognized her, and suddenly lurched away from her, his chubby hands flailing.

Chloe almost lost her balance, laughing as she realized Cody wanted to touch the horse. "Ah-dah. Ah-dah," he squealed in excitement.

Charger nickered, then leaned toward Cody. Chloe brought him closer and he reached out, his plump fingers batting at the horse's nose. Charger didn't so much as blink.

"I think he likes the horse," Maddy said.

"Son of his father," Saul said.

Chloe caught Grady's frown, wondering if he was thinking of Ben, Cody's father.

Grady touched the little boy's cheek with a large

forefinger, the simple gesture warming Chloe's heart. Then he pulled away. "We better get going."

He walked back down the wooden alleyway. Chloe easily caught up to him and slowed her pace to match his.

Chloe glanced at the empty horse stalls. "Why don't you keep the horses in here?"

"We only use the stalls for the mares that are in foal. Sometimes we'll put a couple of the stallions in here. They cause nothing but trouble when they're out," Grady said, stopping at the stall that held the horse that had watched Chloe's progress earlier. "Hey, Sweetpea. You going to give us a nice little baby in a while?"

"She's in foal?"

"Due in a few months, as are Babe and Shiloh. Ben had them all bred to a cutting horse. He had plans to…" His voice faltered and Chloe gave into the impulse and put her hand on his shoulder in comfort. The news from the hospital must have been weighing on his mind.

To her surprise, he covered it with his own hand. Large. Warm. Welcoming.

He looked over at her and once again Chloe felt the emotions that had risen up between them that night in Cody's nursery.

Cody's squeal inserted itself into the moment, returning Chloe to reality.

"He sure seems to like horses," Chloe said, disliking how breathless she sounded.

"Like Saul said, son of his father." He looked over at her again. "I'm glad you're here to help take care of him. I know it's a job to you, but with what is going on with Ben and all, it just makes that part of our lives easier."

He gave her a careful smile and her breath quickened.

Another wave of nausea washed over her, her own reality making itself known.

"Are you okay?" Grady asked. "You look a little pale."

"I'm fine. Just tired, I think." When she'd seen the doctor before leaving Fort Worth, he hadn't seemed too concerned about the nausea. She knew she would have to make another appointment to see him soon. She could mention it then.

She walked ahead of him, her lips pressed together, holding Cody close as if to protect him.

She wondered if she was wise to encourage him to work with her and how she could maintain her distance while she did.

He was far too appealing and growing more so every day.

Chapter Five

He had forgotten about the stairs in the church.

It was Sunday morning and Grady and his grandmother had been making their way across the foyer to the sanctuary, chatting with fellow members, catching up.

And now he had to navigate these carpeted stairs.

"We can take the elevator if you want," his grandmother said with a bright note in her voice.

He knew Grandma Mamie was only being helpful. But he didn't know which would be worse—riding the elevator with dear, eighty-year-old Iva Donovan and her walker or running the risk of stumbling on the stairs.

"I can manage at home. I'm sure I can manage here."

Though as he took the first stair, he wished once again he hadn't given in to his grandmother's pleas this morning to come to church with her and Chloe. He was far too aware of the crutch he needed for support and the sympathetic glances he got from people who stopped to say hello. And he was fairly sure church would be a waste of time. He'd seen too much of the darkness of life to believe that God even cared what happened on earth.

"Are you okay?" Mamie asked, resting her hand on his arm.

He just nodded and was about to take the next step when he felt a hand on his shoulder. "Hey there," a deep voice said.

Turning, he faced Tyler Grainger, an old school friend now married to his cousin Eva.

"So glad to see you here, buddy," Tyler continued, giving him a rough, one-armed hug.

Tyler pulled back, looking into his friend's eyes as if trying to see what Grady had witnessed during his time overseas.

You'd never understand, Grady wanted to say.

"So how are you finding married life?" Mamie asked Tyler, rescuing Grady from replying to Tyler's unspoken question. Grady was thankful. He didn't want to discuss his lack of spiritual fervor in the foyer of the church. Especially not with a man who at one time had wielded strong influence in Grady's faith life.

"It's wonderful," Tyler said. "But Eva does miss working with Cody. Though I heard you have a new nanny."

Tyler gave him a knowing look at the same time Chloe joined them. If his injury made him self-conscious, Chloe's presence only increased that emotion.

As did Tyler's discreet poke of his elbow.

"Don't you need to find Eva?" Grady asked.

"Right. I should go," Tyler said. But he gave Grady a wink and jogged up the stairs ahead of him, a vivid reminder of the physical differences between them. It was hard not to feel frustrated or less of a man.

Grady took a breath and worked his way up the stairs, Chloe right beside him, looking everywhere but at him. It seemed every moment they spent together alone only increased either his awareness of her or her retreat from him. Yesterday, when they'd stood by Ben's horse, he'd thought they had shared a small connection. Then she'd pulled back. She'd stayed home when he and his grandmother had gone to the hospital, claiming Cody was fussy. This flimsy excuse had netted him some direct questions from his grandma as to what he had done to her.

As far as he knew, he had done nothing more than cover her hand with his. Clearly a mistake, because she hadn't so much as made eye contact since then.

"Do you think Cody will be okay in the nursery?" Mamie was asking Chloe as they reached the top of the stairs and the entrance to the sanctuary.

She nodded, her gaze meeting his, then skittering away. If she was this jumpy around him after spending a few days together, why should she be surprised that he wasn't about to start physical therapy with her?

"He's settled in nicely. Of course, it's familiar to him," Chloe said, brushing at the skirt of her dress and fussing with the belt she had put on. She looked uncomfortable, as if she wished she were wearing something else.

"Well, well, look at my friend. Looking all pretty and pert in her cute dress."

Lucy Benson joined them, her bright eyes flicking from Chloe to Grady, as if he might be the reason Chloe had made this transformation.

"I told you I owned a couple of dresses," Chloe said, sounding a bit short.

Lucy patted her on the shoulder. "And now you've

proved it." She glanced over at Grady. "How are things back at the ranch?"

Grady heard the subtext in her question. "No thefts yet."

Lucy just nodded. "That is intriguing. Do you have any idea why?"

"Maybe whoever is stealing feels sorry for my brother."

"Maybe. But I doubt it." Lucy gave him a cheeky look, then turned back to Chloe and frowned. "You feeling okay? You look a little green."

"And with just two comments you've effectively negated anything positive you just said," Chloe returned.

"Give with one hand, take away with the other. That's what the long arm of the law does," Lucy said with a grin. "Anyhow, I gotta go. Promised my mom I'd help her out with coffee this morning." With a flip of her blond hair and a wave of her hand, Lucy was gone.

"She's certainly a ball of fire, isn't she?" Mamie said, her tone admiring. "Always on the job."

"A bit too vigilant," Grady mumbled, not certain he liked Lucy's insinuations. He didn't know why the Stillwater ranch hadn't been robbed yet, but he guessed it was simply a matter of time until they were hit. He doubted they would be on the receiving end of any largesse on the part of the Little Horn Robin Hood.

"Can we go sit down now?" Mamie asked. "I want to make sure there's enough room for the three of us," she added, beaming as she looked from Chloe to Grady.

Grady wasn't sure he liked the satisfied look on his grandmother's face. As if seeing Chloe and Grady together made her happy. He was fairly sure she had hired Chloe for more than nannying and therapy, but he wasn't about to confront her on that.

They found their place at the end of the pew, situated in the center of the sanctuary. Grandma and Grampa Stillwater had laid claim to this spot when they'd married, and through the ebb and flow of the Stillwater family, it had become "theirs."

Grady stood aside while Grandma and then Chloe entered. Which meant he would be sitting beside Chloe.

He sat down slowly, easing his way into the seat, trying to find a place for his crutch. It fell; he bent over to pick it up and tried to lean it against the pew in front of him. Wordlessly Chloe took it and laid it on the floor at their feet.

"Thanks," he said, giving her a smile.

She returned the smile and there it was again. The awareness that sparked between them like a live thing.

This time she didn't look away as quickly.

The pianist began playing and a group of young kids came to the front. With a clang of chords from a guitarist and the piano, they started singing. Grady didn't recognize the song, but it seemed Chloe did. She sang along, her voice bright and clear and melodious.

Grady clung to the sound, the purity of her voice easing away the memories that plagued him from time to time. Reminding him of a happier time when he and his fellow soldiers had been on leave in Kandahar and had stopped to listen to a street group singing. A young girl, her voice as clear and true as Chloe's, had been singing, laughing and dancing. It had been a bright spot in that particular tour.

A day later everything had changed.

He stifled the dark thoughts, massaging his leg,

clinging once again to the music to which Chloe sang along.

"'My hope is only in You, Lord, my solid cornerstone, my strength when I am weak, my help when I'm alone,'" she sang.

Grady closed his eyes as the words soaked into his soul. When the song was over he glanced at Chloe. She returned his look, a sidelong grazing of her eyes over his. But her smile lingered in his heart.

And he wondered if he dared let what he sensed was happening between them grow.

He held that thought and then Pastor Mathers came to the front of the church. He looked around, smiling as he welcomed the gathering, his blue eyes shining with friendliness. He made a few jokes, then asked everyone to bow their heads to pray.

His prayer was the usual invocation asking God to bless their worship time. To watch over them as they opened God's word. He also prayed that the past events of the community would not turn people against each other and that, instead, everyone would come together to help and support one another.

As the pastor prayed, Grady felt again the uneasiness that gripped him as he thought of the thefts that had been going on. It was making people testy.

Pastor Mathers finished his prayer and invited the congregation to turn to their Bibles. Grady followed along as the pastor read from *Isaiah* 40. He tried to listen but he was distracted by the beautiful woman beside him, her eyes on her Bible, a faint smile teasing her lips as if the words she read pleased her. He pulled his attention back to the pastor in time to hear him read, "'Even youths grow tired and weary, and young men stumble and fall, but those who hope in the Lord will renew their strength. They will soar on wings like eagles, they will run and not grow weary, they will walk and not be faint.'"

Pastor Mathers closed his Bible and looked over the congregation, pausing as if to let the words settle into their collective mind. "In our culture and society these verses can be tough to swallow. We want to be strong. Independent. These are qualities we admire in ourselves and other people. But as Christians this is not how we are called to live."

Grady looked down, struggling with the pastor's words. It was as if the sermon were tailor-made for him.

You're a soldier, he told himself, mentally arguing with what the pastor said. *You have to be tough and strong. Weakness is death.*

But you're not a soldier anymore.

The other voice, the practical one he had spent the past few weeks ignoring, sifted back into his thoughts.

Didn't matter. He had to be strong. His brother was in the hospital. His grandmother needed him. Cody needed him.

He looked over at Chloe, who was looking at the pastor, her face holding a peculiarly skeptical expression.

As if she, too, struggled with the sermon.

Again he sensed she was keeping something to herself and again he wondered what.

In spite of his curiosity, he shook off the thought. He had enough going on in his own life. He didn't need to take on anything Chloe was dealing with.

"I miss you, buddy," Eva said to Cody, holding him close. The murmur of the people visiting after church rose up around the table they sat at in the hall attached to the church. Chloe felt a pang as she looked around the room. She recognized many of the people here, and as she and Eva chatted, a few members of the congregation stopped by to give her their greetings.

It was home and, for now, she was thankful for a job that kept her there.

"I think he misses you, too," Chloe said, reaching over to wipe some drool off his chin.

"Poor little motherless guy," Eva said. She looked over his head at Chloe, her expression curious. "I hear that Vanessa is gone. What do you think that means?"

That I don't have to put up with her condescending attitude.

Chloe simply shrugged. "I think she didn't like the fact that Grady was on to her lies."

Eva shook her head in dismay. "I sure hope we find out who he belongs to. Every baby needs a mother and father."

Chloe's heart skipped in her chest as she took Cody back from Eva. And what of her baby? She swallowed down a knot of panic, reminding herself of the song she had just sung. God was her refuge and fortress. He would guide her through the precarious place in her life.

"And Grady is most definitely not the father," Chloe said, settling Cody on her hip. He tried to grab for her necklace but she caught his hand, kissing his chubby fist.

"I'm sure that's a relief," Eva said with a coy smile.

Chloe pretended she didn't understand, unwilling to analyze her changing feelings for Grady. Sitting beside him in church had been more difficult than she had expected. She saw how earnestly he had listened to the pastor. How he had seemed to be pondering the message.

The same message that struck a chord with her. After she'd discovered that Jeremy hadn't returned to give their marriage another try as she'd believed, but had simply come to toy with her emotions, she'd promised herself she wouldn't let any man have any control over her again. She wouldn't let any man make her feel weak.

Yet now she was in a position of weakness, and though she didn't like it, she also knew it made her more dependent on God's guidance and provision.

All through the sermon she had kept wondering how Grady heard the message. Then she became frustrated that all her thoughts circled back to him.

"So, barring any other Stillwater coming out of the woodwork, I would guess that leaves Ben as Cody's father," Eva continued.

Chloe pulled her attention back to Eva and nodded. "It would seem that way."

"I just want to tell you how glad I am that you're helping at the ranch," Eva said, moving in closer as if she had some deep secret to impart. "Grady seems happier than when I saw him last."

Chloe frowned. "What do you mean?"

Eva gave her a mischievous smile. "I think you know what I mean. Though Grady has devoted himself to the army, he always said that one day he wanted to settle down at the ranch. Find himself the perfect girl and raise the perfect family."

The perfect girl.

That certainly wasn't her anymore.

Then across the room she saw Grady talking to Olivia Barlow, widowed mother of three children. Olivia brushed back her dark brown hair as she caught the hand of one of her triplet sons, frowning down at him as if warning him. She looked tired, and Chloe didn't blame her. The thought of raising her child on her own frightened her. She couldn't imagine doing it with triplets. Grady patted Olivia on the shoulder, as if in sympathy, then said something to the young boy. When Olivia left, Grady looked up, unerringly finding Chloe across the room. Their gazes locked. Chloe's breath slowed and her heart raced. She pulled her eyes way only to find Eva watching her with a bemused expression.

"Someone just like you," Eva said with a self-satisfied smile. "I think you're exactly what my cousin needs."

Chloe's heart twisted at Eva's words. She knew she was starting to like Grady too much. She wished she knew what to do about it.

Chapter Six

"Smells wonderful in here." Mamie Stillwater stepped into the kitchen carrying a pile of dish towels that she had just washed and folded.

Chloe set the pan of freshly baked muffins on the counter, smiling at the results. "I thought I would bring some of these out to the hands. I'm sure they miss Martha Rose's cooking."

"I'm sure they do, though the boys can certainly manage without her until she gets back." Mamie set the towels in a cupboard beside the pantry and walked to the high chair Chloe had set close to the counter so she could watch Cody while she baked. "He looks tired."

Cody was rubbing his eyes, a piece of banana stuck to the back of his hand.

Chloe wet a cloth and quickly wiped him down. "He is. I just wanted to finish up here before I put him in bed. Sorry I didn't do it sooner."

Mamie waved off Chloe's excuses. "Honey, I wasn't trying to criticize you."

Chloe gave her a tight nod, realizing that her protest was automatic, hearkening back to her life with Jeremy. His constant criticism and harping had made her become overly aware of her shortcomings. It made her angry that he still had some influence on her behavior. She had promised herself she wouldn't be defined by his treatment of her.

Mostly she had kept that promise, but from time to time remnants of her old self returned.

"I can lay him down if you want," Mamie offered.

"No. I need these muffins to cool anyway." Chloe shucked her oven mitts and set them neatly aside, then pulled Cody out of his high chair.

A sudden and strong wave of nausea washed over her and she grabbed the edge of the counter to support herself. This was the worst she'd endured yet.

"Are you okay, child?" Mamie asked, suddenly concerned.

Chloe swallowed and swallowed, praying fiercely this would pass.

"Just feeling a little light-headed," she said as the vertigo receded. "I think I forgot to eat breakfast. And yes, I know breakfast is the most important meal of the day. My mom used to tell me that."

Mamie put the last towel in the cupboard and leaned back, her arms folded. "Do you remember much of your mother?"

"Bits and pieces. I was only ten when she died."

"That must have been hard for you and your father."

Chloe shifted Cody in her arms, tucking his warm head into the crook of her neck as her mind sifted back. "It was. My father was adrift without my mother. I think he barely remembered he had a daughter at times." She shook her head as if dislodging the memories, disliking the self-pity creeping into her voice.

"And then he remarried," Mamie said.

Chloe held Cody even closer as she recalled that moment when she'd realized Vanessa's mother did not see her as an asset, but rather as a rival for her father's affections. "That wasn't a good situation." She gave Mamie a wry smile. "Very Cinderella but with only one stepsister. And my dad didn't die. Etta left before that."

"Can I ask why she left?"

"A number of reasons," Chloe said, her voice growing hard. "She thought my grandfather would leave my father a boatload of cash, and when he died that was a disappointment. And then my father had his accident. He couldn't give her what she needed. Couldn't provide for her, and he had his injury, and what woman can live like that?" She gave Mamie an arch look, underlining the irony of her comment.

Mamie smiled sadly, clearly understanding what Chloe was saying and her slightly sarcastic inference.

"That can be hard," she said.

"I'll put this munchkin down and then I'll head out."

"I'm going to lie down," Mamie said. "I haven't been feeling well."

"I'm sorry to hear that," Chloe said, giving her a concerned look. "I can stay in the house if you want."

Mamie shook her head. "No. Cody will sleep. You go bring those boys some muffins. I'm sure they miss all the fussing they usually get from Martha Rose. I'll be fine."

Chloe nodded, then left with the little boy, but as she walked up the stairs she felt another wave of nausea and wondered how long she could keep her condition a secret.

And if it was fair to the Stillwaters to do so.

I just need this for a few more months, she promised herself. *Just until I can figure out what to do and where to go.*

The thought clung to her with icy fingers because at the moment she had no idea.

"That was a short break," Saul said, looking up from the horse he had just tied to a rail.

"Changed my mind," Grady said brusquely.

"Thought you said you needed a rest."

He had. His leg bothered him and while he resented resting it, part of him had been hoping to see Chloe. Until he'd overheard what she said.

...couldn't provide for her, and he had his injury, and what woman can live like that?

Though he didn't know the context of the words, it wasn't hard to infer what she meant, and it underlined his view of himself. Sure, he could take care of someone financially, manage the ranch from a desk like his father had, but that hadn't turned out well for his father, either.

A nasty wind with a bite to it swept through the alleyway, making Grady shiver. The forecast was for unseasonably cold weather. They would have to increase the cows' feed to compensate.

Josh Carpenter, one of the hired hands, led the horse Saul had just worked on back to the pasture. When he saw Grady, he stopped.

"Hey, boss, just wondering if I can take a day off this week?" he asked. "My dad needs my help setting up some surveillance cameras on his place."

"Has he been hit, too?" Josh's father wasn't even a rancher. He lived on acreage on the edge of town.

"No. He's just getting paranoid that he might. Must

have bought seven of those cameras. I tried to tell him that no one would want his old stuff, but to him it's precious."

"Should be okay." Emilio and Lucas would be around, so he could certainly spare Josh.

Josh gave him a goofy grin, which puzzled Grady until he realized the hired hand was looking at someone past him. He caught the same whiff of baking he had in the house and from the way his neck prickled he figured Chloe had just arrived.

"Hey, Chloe, good to see you," Josh said, threading his fingers through the reins of the horse he was still leading in a nervous gesture. He looked somewhat smitten and Grady couldn't blame him. Chloe seemed to have the same effect on him, except he tried a little harder than Josh to hide it.

"Good to see you, too," Chloe returned, stopping right beside Grady. In one hand she held a plastic bag, in the other a plate of muffins covered in wrap, their warmth creating a cloud of vapor on the covering. "I though you all might enjoy a snack."

"Just let me bring this cayuse away and I'll be right back," Josh said with a bright grin.

Though it had been only a couple of hours since breakfast, the smell of the baking made Grady's stomach growl. However, the thought of sitting all cozy and cute sharing some muffins with Chloe after what he had overheard was too difficult.

His mind scrambled to come up with a reason to leave, but then he made the mistake of looking at Chloe, who was smiling at him, her eyes bright and inviting, and he couldn't think of much at all.

"I could use a break," Saul said, lowering the horse's

hoof and straightening. He patted the horse on the rump and walked over to join them. "I think we could set down right here." He hauled a couple of square bales together, making an impromptu sitting area. "You just set yourself down here, Chloe. Grady, you can drop down here." He grunted as he pulled over another bale. "And me and Josh can park ourselves right here."

Grady was now boxed in. Chloe to his right, the piled-up bales to his left and no escape.

He was fairly sure Saul had arranged that on purpose, so with a resigned sigh he sat down.

"So what kind of muffins are they?" Saul asked as he did the same.

"These are carrot pineapple," Chloe said, handing the muffins to Grady. "Can you unwrap them while I get some plates out for everyone?"

His stomach growled as he carefully took off the plastic, memories assaulting him as he inhaled the scent. His mother in an apron while he and Ben ostensibly helped by cracking eggs, grating carrots but mostly making a nuisance of themselves, he was sure. The warmth of the kitchen, the giggles he and his brother had shared.

His heart hitched as he thought of the fight they'd had before Grady shipped out, his brother's anger at Grady's condemnation of his lifestyle.

"You okay?" Chloe asked, handing out the plates to Saul and Josh, who had quickly rejoined them.

He shook off the sorrowful memory, adding yet another prayer for his brother to come out of his coma. To give them another chance to be together.

"Yeah. I'm okay." He took a muffin and returned the plate for her to pass around. "These are my favorites."

"I got the idea from your grandmother," Chloe said as sat down beside him, the plate of muffins balanced on her lap. "She said you would appreciate them."

Grady took a bite and sighed. "These are as good as the ones my mom made." He took another bite, closing his eyes in bliss.

"You look happy," Chloe said.

He gave her a sidelong glance. "You sound as if that's important to you."

"It is, because I'm softening you up."

"Whoa, here comes the favors," Saul chortled, slapping his knee.

"What do you want?" Grady asked, feeling wary.

"To start physical therapy with you. Tonight. We already did the assessment, but you've been avoiding following through."

He stopped chewing, the muffin in his mouth suddenly tasting like sawdust.

"Besides, that's why your grandmother hired me," she continued, her hands folded primly on her lap, her head tilted to one side as if studying and analyzing him.

Her hair glistened in the light and the smile edging her soft lips resurrected a memory of her when they had been in school together. When he'd thought maybe there might be a chance for him.

He pushed that back, along with other dreams he'd had to discard along the way in his life.

"I don't need physical therapy," he said after swallowing the rest of the muffin. The last thing he wanted was Chloe seeing him more vulnerable than she already had.

"I know you do, and I know it will make a difference for you."

Grady quickly got to his feet. He didn't want to have this discussion, and he especially didn't want to have it in front of his hired hand and his farrier.

"I can take care of myself," he muttered, grabbing the crutch from the bale beside him.

Don't hurry, don't hurry, he told himself as he made his way down the alley of the horse barn.

The last thing he wanted, after that, was to fall down in front of Chloe.

And as he left her words seemed to taunt him. *He had his injury, and what woman can live like that?*

Chloe could only stare as Grady slid the heavy barn door closed behind him, effectively shutting her out.

Suddenly her little bribe seemed rather pathetic and ill thought-out. Had she really thought that waltzing in here with his favorite muffins would make this proud and stubborn man change his mind?

Josh jumped to his feet muttering something about the horses, leaving Chloe behind with a plate of still warm muffins and Saul's quiet company.

"Sorry about that," Saul said, reaching across the distance between them and covering her hand with his. "Grady hasn't been the same since he came back from Afghanistan. He would never admit it to me, let alone you, but I've known that guy since he was a kid. Always proud and self-sufficient. Always trying to be better than he was. I think he was always trying to make up for Ben's antics. Sometimes I think he took on too much. Joining the army was, I think, his way of bringing honor to the Stillwater name. It became a large part of who he is, and now he can't do that anymore." Saul leaned forward, stroking his handlebar moustache as he pursed his lips. "I think he sees himself as weak. For someone who has always tried so hard to be strong, this is a difficult thing. Especially with someone like you."

"What do you mean? Someone like me?"

Saul gave her a wry grin. "You haven't noticed how he acts around you?"

She didn't want to blush, thinking of that moment they had shared in the nursery.

"Doesn't matter," she said with a decisive note. "He needs to do the exercises or his muscles will pull his bones crooked, and we're looking at potential dysplasia and a host of other complications." She caught herself, realizing that Saul didn't need to know all that.

"I'm glad you're passionate about this," Saul said, patting her on the knee. "'Cause I think you will need every ounce of that persistence to get that man to agree. But just remember, he has a lot of pride. If you can find a way to work around that, you'll find a way to get him to agree. And if that doesn't work, just turn on your charm. I know that will be the ticket."

Chloe gave him a wan smile as she thought of the moments when their glances met and she'd felt an arc of awareness. But with that came a glimmer of sorrow. She wasn't the same innocent girl he had once cared for.

Chapter Seven

"I'm going to town today to see Ben," Grady announced after breakfast the next day. "Would you like to come along, Grandma?"

He thought if he kept himself busy today, he could stay out of Chloe's line of sight. Yesterday, when she corralled him in front of Saul and Josh, he had felt taken off guard. And that wasn't happening again.

Right now she was upstairs, busy with Cody. Even in the kitchen he could hear her singing as she bathed him, her voice as clear and true as it had been in church.

And as appealing.

His grandmother looked up from her breakfast and reluctantly shook her head. "I don't think I will. I didn't sleep well last night."

"Oh, no. I'm sorry to hear that," Grady said, rethinking his plans. He had counted on his grandmother driving him. He might have to get one of the guys to do it, though he hated to keep them from their work while he visited with Ben.

"Sorry I can't help you, but Chloe can come with you and take Cody along."

Grady frowned at that. "Why?"

"It would be good for Ben to spend time with his son," Mamie said, her voice firm, clearly misunderstanding his reluctance.

"You're right," he conceded. This would solve his transportation problem, but not the proximity problem. It was growing harder and harder to ignore Chloe. Harder and harder not to give in to the attraction he felt around her.

Well, it looked as if they would be spending the next few hours together. He slowly stood, stacking his bowl on his plate when his grandmother stopped him, as she always did.

"Here, let me take that."

"Grady can manage," Chloe spoke as she came into the room, Cody on one hip, her arms holding him close to her.

"But he has his crutch," Mamie protested.

"He can manage," Chloe said, her voice firm as she set Cody in the high chair and buckled him in.

Grady shot her a frown, wondering what she was up to.

"He doesn't seem to think he needs physical therapy, so I don't think he needs any help, either," Chloe said. "Clearly, he can take care of himself."

He grinned as she tossed his words of yesterday back at him. "I guess I can," he said. He held the plate, balancing it precariously as he limped over to the counter. He had to focus to make sure he didn't drop anything. No way was he making a fool of himself in front of Chloe.

"I'm leaving in a couple of minutes to visit Ben, but I'll need a ride," Grady said, turning to Chloe. "Would you be able to do that for me? And I was thinking we should take Cody, as well."

"If you can give me five minutes, I'll be at the front door."

He nodded, then worked his way down the hallway to his room, thankful it was out of sight of the dining nook. At the door to his room he took a moment to massage his leg. The past couple days the pain had been getting worse. He knew part of it had to do with all the walking around the ranch he'd been doing, checking on the cows, supervising the maintenance of the equipment that happened over the winter months, working with the girls in the Future Ranchers program.

Just do the therapy already.

Grady let the thought linger a moment, still not convinced it would make a difference.

But it won't hurt. And maybe you could go riding again.

Which was a consideration if his brother never came out of the coma.

He couldn't think that. Couldn't allow that to enter his thoughts.

But as he got ready to leave, it nagged at him.

"Has anyone told you about your brother's progress?" Dr. Searle, the neurologist, stood at the end of Ben's bed. He flipped through Ben's chart before glancing over at Grady and Chloe.

"No. We just got here," Grady said, looking from the doctor to his brother, who lay just as still as he had the first time Grady had visited. If there had been progress, he couldn't see it.

"We are seeing signs of Ben coming out of the

coma," Dr. Searle said making a note on the chart and putting it back. "Last night he opened his eyes for a few seconds, then again this morning. That may not sound like much, but given how unresponsive he's been, it's significant."

"So do you know if he'll be…normal?" Grady hated to ask, but he needed to know.

"We have no idea of his mental or physical capacity as of this moment, but we are much more hopeful after the past twenty-four hours."

"So will he wake up if I talk to him?"

Dr. Searle simply shrugged. "We have no idea, but I think you should talk to him as if he were conscious. Just act normal."

Grady looked down at Ben, feeling awkward. Talking to someone who didn't talk back still struck him as odd. "I feel kind of foolish doing that," he muttered.

"Just remember, it's not about you. It's about him," Dr. Searle said. Then he glanced at Chloe. "And how are you managing?"

"I'm working for the Stillwaters now," Chloe said, brushing a strand of Cody's hair away from his face.

"I was sorry to hear the hospital let you go. I hope you can eventually find something in your field."

Chloe just nodded, then looked back at Grady. "I'm thirsty. I'll go grab a coffee so you can talk to him alone."

Grady shot her a grateful look, thankful for her consideration. She gave him an encouraging smile and left with Dr. Searle. Grady dragged his attention back to his brother.

Ben looked pallid. The weeks spent in the hospital seemed to have shrunken him down. The tubes snaking in and out of him created a panic like an icy fist. What if his brother never fully regained consciousness? What if the angry words Grady had thrown at Ben just before he left were the last memory Grady would have of him?

"I'm sorry." He touched Ben's shoulder, then grasped it more tightly. "I'm sorry I said what I did. I know I sounded judgmental, but I said what I did because I cared...no, care about you," he corrected. "You're my brother, and I didn't want to see you throwing your life away. You've always been the only one who gets me, understands me, and I hope you get that I just wanted the best for you." He stopped there, feeling his throat thicken as he looked down at his brother, once so vital and alive, now seemingly inanimate.

He wondered if he should pray. Though he had enjoyed being in church, he still wasn't sure what to make of God's seemingly erratic answers to prayer. Had God truly been listening, He would have kept his fellow soldiers from being injured.

Would have kept him from being injured.

Yet as he stood by his brother's bed he felt two words rise up.

"Please, Lord" was all he whispered, and as he did, he gazed more intently at his brother, as if waiting for an answer.

But there was no change. No movement, just the steady beep of his heart monitor, the whirring of the IV machine. He could hear the muted chatter of the nurses beyond the ICU. The coming and goings of a hospital.

He should have known.

He stood a moment, looking intently at his brother's eyelids, willing Ben to open his eyes, but when the silence grew more difficult than talking, he started telling Ben about the ranch, the program he'd begun and how well it was going. He brought him up-to-date on the goings on—the thefts and the gifts, puzzling aloud why the Stillwater ranch hadn't been hit.

"Maybe it's because they feel sorry for you," he said with a light laugh. He chatted a bit more, slowly feeling less and less foolish.

Fifteen minutes later Chloe joined him, Cody still smiling and reaching out to him. "Ah, da, da, da," he burbled.

"Does he think I'm his dad?" Grady asked, suddenly alarmed.

"No. It's just a sound he makes. Apparently, that and *ah* are one of the first ones they make, so don't panic," Chloe said with a grin.

"Okay. Just to be clear. There's been enough confusion as to who this baby's father is," Grady said, relieved.

"I'm sure you're wondering who the mother is."

Grady looked back at Ben. In spite of his apology, Cody's presence only underlined the erratic and irresponsible life his brother had been living. "I wouldn't even have the vaguest idea," Grady said. "Ben had so many girlfriends and because I was gone so much I couldn't begin to keep up."

"In spite of being twins, you're very different," Chloe said.

"We weren't when we were younger. Dad always called us the Terrible Twos, and I think Mom's hair got grayer after we were born. But things shifted when we hit high school. I got more serious and Ben got wilder."

"I remember that," Chloe said, shifting Cody on her

hip. "It got easier and easier to tell you two apart because Ben was the one always teasing me."

Grady just shook his head, not sure he wanted to know what Ben would be teasing Chloe about. "I just hope he knew when to quit."

"He quit when he got a rise out of me, so I learned to fake some anger or hurt or something so he could laugh and walk away."

"Was he mean?"

"No. Never mean." Chloe gave him a shy smile.

Grady held her gaze and his thoughts ticked back to that time. Ben used to tease him as well, telling him that sweet Chloe Miner had a huge crush on him. But she'd never indicated that she did. Then Vanessa had come on to him and they started dating. Which had only lasted a couple months—until graduation. Chloe had moved away after that and he never found out if it was true or not.

"I know he liked to exaggerate," Grady said. "He seemed to have this idea that you had some kind of crush on me." He added a laugh, as if to show her that he didn't believe his brother.

To his surprise Chloe blushed.

Was it true?

"What can I say? I was young and impressionable and had a thing for cowboys." Chloe laughed it off, but Grady felt his own heart quicken at the thought.

He held her gaze, unable to look away, and before any second thoughts could assail him he said, "I wanted to believe my brother, but you never gave me any idea." His voice was quiet, sincere.

Chloe just stared at him, her blush deepening. But she didn't look away. "I was shy. And Vanessa told me

that she liked you and that I better back off. I didn't
think I stood any chance against her."

"You stood more than a chance," he said. He took a
step toward her as if to close the distance between them.
However, he didn't shift himself enough to raise his foot
properly off the floor and he stumbled. She moved so
quickly and caught him so easily, it was as if it hadn't
even happened.

Except Grady knew it had and he couldn't stop the
flush heating his cheeks.

He knew part of it had to do with the humiliation of
almost falling in front of her, but he also knew it had
as much to do with Chloe's proximity. The warmth of
her arm around his back. The scent of apples that he
guessed came from her shampoo. The warmth of her
breath on his cheek. He shifted and their eyes met again
and it seemed his resolve weakened again. He couldn't
allow himself to be distracted by Chloe and her gorgeous green eyes. Her sweet and gentle nature.

He pulled away and moved closer to his brother,
resting his hand on his arm, creating a connection between them.

"It must be hard for you," she said, moving Cody to
her other arm. "Seeing your brother like this."

"Do you think he'll come out of it?"

"I wish I could tell you one way or the other. I'm
not a doctor."

He just nodded, releasing a harsh laugh. "I was just
talking to him like you suggested. Apologizing for what
I said to him before I left for my last tour." He tightened his grip on Ben's arm as if hoping by force of will
to wake him.

"What did you need to apologize for?"

Grady wasn't sure he wanted her to see him for who he really was, an irate and judgmental man who thought himself better than his brother, but he felt a need to tell someone. And who better than this gentle, caring woman?

"I got angry with him. I told him he was living a life unworthy of the Stillwater name. Told him that he didn't deserve to be a Stillwater. That he had to clean up his life." As he spoke, Grady heard again the harshness and condemnation he had thrown at his twin.

"What did he say to that?"

Grady caught his brother's limp hand, despairing over how lifeless it felt. How cool to the touch. As if Ben already had one foot in the grave and all it would take was one tiny push—

"He told me I didn't have any right to judge him. Told me that I was turning into a self-righteous jerk who thought he was better than anyone else." Grady stopped there, the pain of his brother's anger still so fresh.

"Was that the end of the argument?"

Grady nodded. "I walked away from him, got in my truck and left for my base. I shipped out the next day. We haven't talked since then."

Chloe was silent a moment. "That must be so difficult for you."

"I just wish I knew how to fix it." He gave her a sorrowful look. "When we were little we both had bad tempers. Whenever we fought, our parents would walk us through the reconciliation process. Now they're gone and I can't put this on my grandmother."

"I think you are taking too much on," she said. "The fact that Cody is here and clearly a Stillwater says something about the life your brother was living."

Grady felt an instant moment of defensiveness for his brother at her comment, but he relaxed. "I know. He hadn't embraced faith the way I had. My father's accident and my mother's leaving made him turn away from God. Which makes me feel even worse about our fight. The fact that it's unresolved. The fact that I should have been a better example of faith at work."

"You told him right? That you feel bad?"

Grady released a harsh laugh. "I did. For what it's worth."

"It's worth a lot. He knows now. And even if his brain can't sort it all out, I am pretty sure he can feel your love. As for his faith, that's in God's hands." She set Cody down beside Ben on the bed, close enough so he could touch Ben, but not so close that Cody could grab at the many tubes connected to him. "I'm hoping that by bringing Cody to see him, he builds an unconscious attachment to his son."

Grady looked from the baby to Ben and felt an unreasonable burst of jealousy. His brother, so irresponsible, had a son. A child.

Something he wanted for himself.

"This might sound a little strange to you, but how do you feel about praying with your brother?" Chloe said, shooting him a glance over her shoulder. "I know when you first came here you made a comment about leaving the praying to those who are more capable."

"It was a reactionary comment," he said, remembering that moment. "I still struggle with my faith, though. I've seen things that made me wonder about God."

Chloe reached over and touched his shoulder. A brief contact, but it was as if a current hummed between them. He knew he couldn't deny his attraction to her, though he still felt he couldn't act on it.

Her casual words from the other day still hung fresh in his mind.

"I'm sure we'll never understand what you've had to deal with, and this may sound like a cliché, but I know that God understands. I think we forget that He also carries the burdens of the world."

Grady shot her a wry glance. "You're smart for a young whippersnapper."

"I'm only two years younger than you."

"That's all?"

"It seemed like a lot in high school. At this point, it's minuscule." She shrugged. "And I've had my own difficulties." She said those last words quietly, as if to herself.

"Are you talking about your father?"

She blinked, as if she hadn't understood what he'd said, then she nodded quickly. "Yes. Of course. Yes, I was talking about my father."

But as she looked away from him he caught a flare of anger in her eyes, a set to her jaw that was so completely out of character it jarred him.

He sensed she spoke of something else when she said that she'd had her own difficulties.

He wanted to ask her more, but she picked up Cody, walked around the other side of the bed and took Ben's other hand in hers.

"Did you want to pray with your brother?" she asked, avoiding his gaze.

Maybe God listened to her, he reasoned.

"I guess it can't hurt," he said, taking Ben's other hand, the unconscious man between them their only bond.

But just before he lowered his head he looked at her again and this time caught a look of utter sorrow in her eyes.

Chloe, it seemed, had her own secret sorrows.

And he wanted to know what they were.

Chapter Eight

"So have you discovered anything I can use?" Lucy rested her elbows on the table at Maggie's and released a heavy sigh, rubbing her forehead with her fingertips.

Though she had been in town yesterday, Chloe had asked for this morning off. Her father's lawyer wanted to meet with her to sign off the last of the papers for the estate. Lucy wanted to meet with her and Chloe had agreed, feeling as if she needed a break from Grady. He was growing far too appealing and his actions toward her were so confusing.

"Maddy Coles, the girl who got some gifts from the anonymous donors?" she said. "She works at the ranch through a program that Ben started."

"Really? Since when?"

"Since before I started there."

"Do you think it was before the thefts started?"

"I can find out."

Lucy stroked her chin as if thinking. "Maybe Maddy is the reason the Stillwater ranch hasn't had any thefts."

"Maddy was carrying around her iPod, but she didn't

know who it was from. I didn't have a chance to talk to her any more than that."

"It's a start." Lucy sighed and pulled her hands over her face. "I just wish I could get one solid lead."

From the little bit of buzz Chloe had heard, people were growing increasingly weary of the thefts and the lack of action on the part of both Lucy's office and the Lone Star Cowboy League, which also was supposedly looking into the burglaries.

"But enough about me," Lucy said, an edge of determination in her voice. "How is your work at the ranch going?"

"I'm good. Cody is a sweetie and easy to work with."

"A far cry from Grady, I'd imagine," Lucy said with a wink. "Have you talked him into doing his exercises?"

"A work in progress," Chloe said taking a sip from her mug of tea. "I live in hope."

"You always did where Grady was concerned," Lucy goaded, picking up her coffee. "And now you're blushing even harder. Don't tell me you're falling for him again?"

Chloe knew that if she gave Lucy even the vaguest hint of what she felt for Grady, Lucy would drag every emotion, every nuance of every conversation between her and Grady out of Chloe. But she also knew Lucy wouldn't quit pushing until Chloe threw her even the tiniest crumb.

"It's…complicated," she said.

"What's complicated? You like him. You work there. You let him know. You're a beautiful girl, and you've got a lot to offer someone like him. Don't sell yourself short, my dear," Lucy said.

"Ever the matchmaker, aren't you?" Chloe said.

Lucy shrugged. "May as well try to get other people together. Guys usually don't go for the tomboy type like me."

"Now you're the one selling yourself short. You're a beautiful woman." *And you don't come with as many complications as I do*, Chloe thought as she tried to pull in her stomach. It was getting harder to hide her pregnancy. She knew sooner or later it would have to come out.

Lucy waved off her compliment. "I know who I am, and right now I've got more than enough to keep me busy. No time for romance."

"At least you have a job," Chloe said in a moment of self-pity.

"You've got a job now," Lucy said.

Chloe nodded. "I do and, don't get me wrong, I'm thankful for it, but I want to focus on physical therapy work. That's what I'm trained for."

"So what would be your dream job?" Lucy asked.

"What I'd like to do is open my own physical therapy clinic. With proper equipment and consistent care. The hospital does okay, but the program is not a priority there. I often think that if my dad had gotten better care and follow up he might not have ended up where he was."

"Can you use the money from your dad's estate to start it up?"

"I just met with dad's lawyer to finalize the estate, and it's official. There's nothing left. I won't be starting a clinic here or anywhere anytime soon." She blew out a sigh as she glanced around the bustling café and coffee shop, recognizing many of the people. When she had first moved back to Little Horn, she had nurtured some hope that somehow she would be able to stay here. This was home to her, and with a baby on the way, she wanted to be in a place where people knew her and she knew they would support her.

Fort Worth had been a cold, lonely place for her, but the way things were going, she knew she would have to move back there or some other large urban center where she could get steady work in her field.

Lucy touched her hand in sympathy. "That's too bad. I know you were hoping that could happen when you first moved here."

"It was a dream and I guess it will stay that." Chloe gave her a smile, then glanced at her watch. "I should get going. I promised Mamie I wouldn't stay long."

"I should, too." Lucy drank the last of her coffee and pulled her jacket off the back of the chair. "So you'll let me know the second you find anything out about Maddy or hear even the tiniest bit of gossip you think I might be interested in?"

"I will."

Lucy shrugged on her coat, adjusted it, her eyes still on Chloe, who was winding her own scarf around her neck. "And I still think you should give Grady a chance. I think you two would have ended up together if that snake of a stepsister of yours hadn't gotten in the way."

"If he really wanted to be with me—"

"I'm positive he would have, if you had let him know. Just like I'm sure something could happen between the two of you now if you just give him an idea of what you're feeling."

Chloe knew better, but her friend's encouraging smile ignited a spark of hope. She thought of that electric moment in the hospital yesterday when she had helped Grady after his stumble. When they had stood virtually face-to-face.

Could something truly happen?

She tried to dismiss the thoughts as she got up from her chair and pushed it back.

Lucy smiled at her and looked as if she was about to say something more when Byron McKay shoved past Chloe, almost knocking her over. He was a tall man, imposing, with a stomach protruding over the large, ornate silver buckle of his belt. His steely blue eyes seemed to impale her, as if it was her fault she had stumbled.

His teenage sons trailed behind him, hands in their pockets, their hoodies unzipped, shoulders hunched forward as if trying to make themselves invisible.

"Well, I'm sorry, missy," Byron said, his voice, as usual, carrying over the buzz of the café. He caught her arm to steady her. "Didn't see you there. You okay?"

Before Chloe could reply, Byron thankfully let her go and turned his attention back to Lucy. "So, Miss Sheriff, I don't imagine you've found out anything?"

"I would have reported it to the league if I did," Lucy retorted, her shoulders straightening, her chin up. "But now that I've got you here, I was wondering if you've heard anything from your cousin's daughter, Betsy McKay?"

"Why do you want to know about that crazy girl?" Byron said, his hands dropping on his hips in a defensive gesture, his voice growing belligerent. "Haven't heard a peep from her since cousin Mac died."

Chloe knew exactly why he was so prickly. Everyone in Little Horn knew Byron hadn't done anything for his cousin, Mac McKay, a struggling rancher who had ended up losing his ranch and, as a result, fighting a losing battle with alcohol. Mac had died about six months ago, and according to town gossip, Byron hadn't been bothered even to attend his funeral.

Mac's daughter, Betsy, had fled Little Horn in shame before she'd graduated high school. Hers was a sad story, but Chloe was curious why Lucy wanted to know about her.

"I was simply wondering how that poor girl is doing."

Byron snorted. "If she's anything like her loser father, she's probably getting into trouble." He laughed at his comment, looking over at his boys as if asking them to join in.

"That's a lousy thing to say, Dad," Gareth snapped, shoving his strawberry blonde hair back from his narrow face with an angry jab.

"You shouldn't talk that way about her father or her," Winston joined in, his hands now balled into fists at his sides. "She's our cousin."

"Can't think why you'd want to have anything to do with that washout family," Byron snorted.

Winston just shook his head, and both boys looked visibly upset with their father.

Gareth turned to Lucy. "We haven't heard from Betsy since she left Little Horn, but we're guessing she might be in Fort Worth."

"Probably living on the streets," Byron put in.

Winston's eyes narrowed and Chloe could not understand how the man could be so obtuse.

"Do you boys know Maddy Coles?" Chloe asked, thinking they might have heard some gossip through their other friends in high school as to why she ended up with the gifts she had. "She works at the Stillwater ranch."

"Other than that she was friends with Betsy, not much," Gareth suggested with a shrug. Winston simply shook his head.

"Stop this." Byron spun around, stabbing one long, thick forefinger at her, and Chloe felt a shiver of fear. "Why do you think my boys would hang around with some foster kid?" He glared at her and for a breath Chloe understood how this man could intimidate so many people.

But as he stared her down her back stiffened. Jeremy all over again.

And she wasn't allowing anyone to push her around again.

"Don't yell at me," she snapped, pushing his finger down and away from her.

Byron's eyes widened and Chloe felt suddenly sorry for the members of the cowboy league who had to put up with this man as their vice president, and for Carson Thorn who, as president, probably had to rein him in from time to time.

But to her surprise Byron didn't do anything more.

"Enough of this useless talk," Byron said, shooting one last glare at Chloe. "Boys, we're out of here."

He marched out of Maggie's, indignation trailing behind him like a cloud, and a sudden silence falling over the café.

Chloe pulled in a wavering breath, her knees suddenly weak after that confrontation.

"Wow, girl. I didn't think you had it in you," Lucy said, admiration tingeing her voice.

I didn't, either, Chloe thought, pulling in another breath. "I don't like pompous men yelling at me" was all she said.

"I'm officially impressed," Lucy said, zipping up her coat. "And glad you thought to ask about Maddy. I can't help think there's some connection between Maddy's gifts and the fact that the Stillwater ranch still hasn't been burglarized. Maybe Grady has some idea?"

They stepped out of the café just as an icy gust of wind caught them. Lucy shivered, pushed her hands deep into her pockets and nudged Chloe with her elbow. "Hey, maybe you can get closer to Grady," she said with a mischievous grin. "You could be my honey trap. Use your charm and feminine wiles to get what you can out of him."

"He's been back only a couple of weeks," Chloe protested. "He doesn't know anything."

Lucy sighed. "I was just trying to convince you to flirt with the guy a little."

"He's my boss. There will be no flirting," Chloe said.

"I think you need to live a little. Who knows where it might get you this time?"

Chloe let that thought register for a moment, but then, right then, she felt a movement low down in her abdomen.

She stopped, eyes wide, her hand flying to her stomach as if to verify.

"What's the matter?" Lucy asked, stopping to see what was wrong.

Chloe's heart began racing. This was the first time she had felt the baby move. She felt it again, stronger this time. And in that moment the pregnancy that had felt so vague was now very real with all its consequences.

"Are you okay?"

Chloe just nodded and gave Lucy what she hoped was a reassuring smile. "I'm fine."

But as she walked out the door of the café and down the street to her car, she knew it would be a while before she would truly feel fine again.

Was that rain?

Grady rolled over in his bed, shedding the sleep clinging to him as what sounded like icy fingers tapped on the panes of glass. Frowning, he stumbled out of bed and looked out the window. Through the lines of frozen moisture on the glass he saw the blurry glow of the yard light.

Snow and sleet poured down, creating a sheen on the snow that had fallen overnight, and Grady groaned.

The forecast had been for a few scattered showers, which would have created its own difficulties. But this?

Freezing rain mixed with snow was a disaster in the making. He would have to wait until the sun was fully up before he knew just how bad things were.

He flicked on the light beside his bed. At least the power was still going, but if this sleet and snow continued, it could coat the lines enough that they would possibly snap.

He got dressed, more slowly even than yesterday morning, his leg even more uncooperative.

He rubbed the cramp in his thigh and breathed through the pain as he worked his pants up over his feet. Despair clung to him as another muscle spasm seized him and he wondered if this would ever ease off, but finally he was dressed. He grabbed the crutch, leaning on it even more heavily than before.

The thought of a cup of coffee lured him to the

kitchen, as did a few moments of quiet before Chloe woke up.

It was growing increasingly hard both to avoid Chloe and to stop thinking about her. Thankfully she'd been gone yesterday morning so he could rest in the house for a while without worrying that she would give him that sassy little smile of hers that showed him she wasn't quitting.

The smile that made him far too aware of her appeal.

He knew he'd have to get past his changing feelings for Chloe. He kept hoping that time would ease them back into the past where they belonged, but every time he saw her they seemed to get worse. Trouble was he didn't know how long she would have to stay at the ranch taking care of Cody.

As for his own therapy, he knew he would have to give in sometime, but he also knew he couldn't work with Chloe. Maybe he could see someone in Fort Worth.

A long drive, which meant more time away from the ranch that he could ill afford.

He popped a pod into the single-serve coffeemaker, feeling the weight of his responsibilities. Then he heard a muted squall from upstairs. Cody was awake, which meant Chloe would be coming down soon, her green eyes probing as if waiting for him to give in.

He went to take out another mug for Chloe, but as he reached up into the cupboard another shard of pain shot through his leg and up into his back. He clenched his teeth, riding it out.

"Are you okay?"

Grady jumped, almost dropping the mug. He drew in a long, slow breath, leaning on the counter with one hand, and thankfully the pain subsided as it usually did.

"Yeah, I'm fine," he said, flashing her what he hoped was an assuring grin.

She wore an old plaid shirt hanging loose over a pair of jeans so faded they looked gray. One knee was ripped and the hems were ragged. Her feet were bare, her hair still tousled, though she had made an attempt to tame it by pulling it back. A faint line of mascara still smudged her eyes.

Yet she still managed to make his heart beat faster.

She stared at him with what he thought of as her professional look. As though he was some specimen she was examining. But to his surprise she said nothing about therapy or exercises, even though he was obviously leaning on the counter to take weight off his injured leg.

"I thought I heard Cody," he said, setting one mug on the coffeemaker and pressing the button.

"He's fussing a bit, but not fully awake. Kind of like me," Chloe joked, walking past him to pull the creamer out of the refrigerator. She set it on the counter, then took a couple of spoons out of one drawer and put them by the coffeemaker. "Sounds as if it's blowing hard out there," she said, stifling a yawn.

"It looks quite nasty. Snow mixed with sleet. I'm wondering what the roads will be like."

The lights flickered and both of them looked up at the ceiling as if waiting for them to extinguish.

Chloe pushed away from the counter, walked to the bay window and shoved aside the heavy curtains. "Doesn't look good," she said. "I don't think anyone will be going anywhere in this."

"I guess I'll have to make some calls," Grady said,

getting another cup ready. "No sense having our hands risking an accident just to get to work today."

"Can you manage without the hands around?"

Grady shrugged, the gnawing pain in his leg a reminder of the extra work he had done yesterday with Emilio and Josh as they'd fed the cows that were close to the ranch. "Cows will be good for a couple of days. I'll have to get Emilio to feed the cattle at the other place. He's got a tractor there at his disposal, so they should be okay."

They would have to get a few of the horses in, however. Two more besides Sweetpea were in foal, and he didn't want to risk them falling on the ice and losing their babies. He would have to figure out how to do that; the thought of navigating the ice with a crutch gave him the willies.

"You should call Maddy and the other girls and let them know, as well."

"I doubt their parents would let them come anyway," Grady said, stirring in some sugar and cream into the coffee and setting her cup on the eating bar by the counter. "Your coffee is ready."

She came back to the kitchen and was about to pick up the creamer when he stopped her.

"I already did that."

She pulled her head back in surprise. "Really?"

"Yeah. One sugar and about a quarter cup of cream."

"Not that much," she protested.

"Pretty close," he teased.

She settled on a stool across from him, cupping her hands around her mug, and gave him another smile. "Thanks so much. I'm surprised you remembered."

"All part of my training to observe."

She took a sip of her coffee and released a sigh of pleasure. "That's just perfect." She rested her elbows on the eating bar, her coffee cup cradled between her hands as she watched him. "You've been in the army since graduating high school, haven't you?"

Grady nodded, stirring some cream into his own coffee. Most of his life he drank it black but that was more convenience than anything. Cream was a luxury he never indulged in except when he was stateside. "I've been in special ops for the past three years."

"Green Beret, I understand," Chloe said, her voice full of admiration.

Grady felt a dull ache in his chest. "Not anymore."

Chloe nodded as if acknowledging his loss.

"Though it's just as well right now with Ben in the hospital," he said before she could jump in with some platitudes about how if he did the work he could be back at his old job in no time. The same facts his army doctor had thrown at him. The facts immediately negated by the physical therapist he had worked with in the hospital. "I've got enough happening in my life anyhow."

"When Ben comes out of his coma, would you go back? To the army?"

Grady thought of the training position his superior had offered him as he took a sip of his own coffee, one hip leaning against the counter for support. It didn't hold any appeal. "I can't go back to doing something less than before." Then he gave her a melancholy look. "But I like you how said *when*, not *if* when you talked about my brother. As though it's a foregone conclusion that Ben will come back to us."

"I'm not the kind of person to throw out things just to make people feel good. The last time we visited Ben the doctor said Ben was showing signs of wakefulness. I feel fairly positive."

"You always were a positive person," he said.

"Not always so positive. There were times…" She let the sentence slip away unfinished.

"What times?" he prompted, curious as to which part of her life she referred to, wondering if it was connected to the sorrow he saw in her eyes that afternoon in the hospital.

She pulled in a deep breath, her face holding a puzzling hurt, then she shrugged as if shucking off whatever memories clung to her. "Doesn't matter."

But suddenly it did. To him.

Cody started wailing in earnest, Chloe took a gulp of her coffee and without another look his way slipped off the stool and hurried upstairs. Grady watched her, yearning to find out what she was talking about.

Then the phone rang.

Grady answered. Josh was on the other end telling him that he couldn't come to the ranch. He was stuck in his yard.

After Grady hung up he walked over to the window. Though the day was dawning, it was still dark and gray outside, but there was enough light to show him ice and snow clinging with a treacherous grip to fences, buildings and roads.

No one would be coming and no one would be leaving.

Until the storm let up and the weather got substantially warmer, Mamie, Cody, Chloe and Grady were stranded.

Chapter Nine

"**W**here are you going?" Chloe asked as she came down the stairs.

Grady wore his heavy winter coat and was limping toward the porch.

"Is Cody asleep?" he asked, not answering her question.

"Down for his morning nap."

"How's my grandmother?"

"She's reading in her bed."

This morning after she had fed Cody his breakfast, Chloe had gone to check in on Mamie Stillwater, who hadn't gotten up at her usual hour. The dear woman had said she was too tired to get up, so Chloe had brought her some tea and toast, both of which had been gone when Chloe got back.

"Do you think we'll need to take her to the doctor?"

"No. I think it's just a cold," Chloe said, carrying what was left of the bottle she had given Cody to the sink. "She doesn't have a fever and thankfully she's not coughing." She emptied the bottle's contents and rinsed it out, then put it in the dishwasher.

Chloe suspected his grandmother was simply tired and run down. The past few months had been stressful for poor Mamie. It was no surprise she might be coming down with something.

"I better get going," Grady said.

"Where?" Chloe had checked the weather on the computer in the office and it talked of school and road closures and travel advisories. Though it was still storming, she could tell the yard was also impassable.

"I have to bring the horses into the barns."

"Surely you're not doing that now? By yourself?"

"I have to. Two of them besides Sweetpea are in foal and need to come inside."

Chloe couldn't stop her glance down at his leg and the crutch he was picking up. She wanted to protest but then thought of what Saul had told her about Grady feeling less like a man as a result of his injury.

"I can help you," she said. "Cody and your grandmother are both in bed and won't need me for at least an hour."

"I'll be okay," Grady said.

"Of course you will, but it wouldn't hurt to have an extra set of hands around horses in a storm."

Grady gave her an oblique look, as if he wasn't sure of her motives but then, to her surprise, he gave her a tight nod. "Okay. Just make sure you don't fall on the ice."

Chloe clamped down an automatic response. "I'll let your grandmother know what's happening and I'll get my cell phone in case she needs to get hold of us."

But by the time she came back down, Grady was already outside.

"Stubborn man," Chloe muttered, yanking on her

coat, tugging a stocking cap down over her ears and pulling her gloves out of her pockets. She got her winter boots on quick enough and stepped out the door. Her feet slid out as soon as she set foot on the sidewalk. Flailing her arms, she regained a precarious balance on the slick ice and snow, and moved more slowly across the yard as the sleet beat at her with icy needles. If she squinted she could just make out Grady's dark shape ahead of her, his crutch far out to the side, giving him support.

She caught up to him just as he got to the barn and before he could protest, which she knew he would, she reached past him and pulled hard on the handle. The door, probably frozen on its rails, didn't budge. She tried again, bracing herself. This time Grady helped her and together they manhandled the door open.

Inside, the barn was a haven of darkness and quiet. The storm, muted by the heavy wooden walls, sounded less menacing in here.

Chloe brushed some snow off her hair and turned to Grady, who was closing the barn door. He flicked a switch and golden light bathed the cool interior.

"So where are the horses?" Chloe asked, shivering as a piece of snow melted down her neck. Sweetpea nickered at them, as if telling them they needed to get the other ones inside.

"Out in the pasture off the training pens," Grady said. "We'll need to get most of them into the corrals first before we can sort out which ones we want in the barn."

Though Chloe had worked with the horses on her father's ranch, she also knew that she would have to be cautious working with someone else's animals. She didn't know their pecking order or their behaviors. She would have to be careful and, at the same time, watch Grady. She took a quick breath, sent up a prayer and then followed Grady to the tack room.

"We'll hang these just inside the door. I don't want the horses seeing them until we've got most of them penned up."

"Good idea," she agreed.

She walked alongside him, trying not to ignore his hurried but awkward movements. The last thing she wanted was another accident, she thought, her palms growing damp inside her gloves.

"Ready?" Grady asked as they arrived at the far door of the horse barn leading to the horse corrals. He gave her a conspiratorial grin and she felt herself relax. Grady had faced far worse than this, she reminded herself. He had been born and raised around horses and knew them.

Chloe tugged her hat down on her head, then nodded. As soon as they stepped outside, the wind sucked her breath away and ice stabbed her face. She kept her focus on Grady ahead of her. In the distance she heard the whinnying of horses as Grady opened the fence to the pasture. The sun was coming up, turning the pitch black into a dark gray. As she squinted through the blinding snow, a vague outline of dark shapes ran toward them, growing clearer with each step.

"Here they come already," Grady shouted. "Open the gate to the corrals. Ten feet ahead of you to your right."

Slipping and sliding over the icy snow and clinging to the fence for support, Chloe made her way to the gate. With chilled hands she fumbled with the latch of the chain holding the gate closed. Finally she got it undone, the howling wind unable to mask the growing thunder of the horse's hooves. She pushed on the metal gate with its frozen hinges, stifling her own panic.

She heard Grady shout, the momentum of the horses slow and as she got the gate open, they swept past her, throwing up snow and ice, panting as they ran into the corral.

"The ones I want are in that bunch," Grady called out. "Close the gate. Close the gate."

The horses, now milling in the corral, seemed to sense they were hemmed in and were already turning to come back out when Chloe pushed the gate shut, her feet skidding on the slick ice. The gate clanged shut and the lead horses stopped, slipping and sliding, but, surprisingly, keeping their footing.

"You're better on ice than I am," Chloe grumbled, her hands frozen as she wrapped the chain around the fence post and the corral gate. Her gloves were stiff and her fingers unresponsive, but she finally clipped the chain closed.

She leaned against the gate, shivering as she breathed out a heavy sigh of relief.

Grady came up beside her and clapped a hand on her shoulder. "Great job. Thanks. I couldn't have gotten them in myself."

She nodded, realizing that only part of their work was done. The pen was icy and the horses, most likely riled up by the storm, tossed their heads around, snorting and restless. She didn't look forward to going in there.

"Which ones do you want?" she asked, hunching her shoulders against the biting cold.

"Babe and Shiloh. The roan mare with the blaze and

the appy." Grady blew out his breath, as if also antici-
pating the difficulties they would face.

"I'll get the halters."

When she got back, Grady was already in the pen,
oblivious to the ice pelting him, his hand out, calming
down the horses. She was surprised at how much they
had settled already, but she knew catching the pregnant mares and getting them separated from the herd
would still be dicey.

She climbed the fence, slowly and deliberately just
as her father had taught her, her pants sticking to her
legs, her thighs and hands numb with cold.

Keeping the halter behind her back, she walked toward Grady, who stood in front of the group of horses,
holding his hand out to calm them down.

"Do you dare go to Shiloh, the appy, and get her?"
Grady said, raising his voice just loud enough for her
to hear. "I'll get Babe."

Chloe bit her lip in apprehension, but she nodded
as she handed Grady the halter. She moved toward the
horse, wishing she could have come up beside her rather
than head-on, a gesture horses often interpreted as a
threat. As Chloe approached, Shiloh tossed her head,
as if establishing her independence but, to Chloe's surprise, didn't move. Chloe wrapped her arm around the
horse's neck, grabbing the halter rope and slipping
it around. Then she got the halter on, fumbling with
the buckle with unresponsive fingers. One down, she
thought, tugging on the halter rope when the horse
didn't want to move.

Chloe brought Shiloh to the fence and tied her up,
then went to see if she could help Grady.

He had managed to get the rope around Babe's neck,

but she tossed her head, resisting. Grady clung to the rope with one hand, to his crutch with the other as he wavered on his feet. Babe pulled back, Grady's crutch slipped on the ice and he spun around.

With a pained cry he barely kept his balance, but the rope fell out of his hand, the halter fell to the ground and Babe, with another toss of her head, ran around Grady, the other horses following.

For a panicky moment all Chloe saw was milling horses and through their legs, Grady, trying to find his crutch.

Chloe waved the horses away, yelling at them. Thankfully they trotted to the other side of the corral, and Chloe hurried to Grady's side.

"Are you okay?" she asked, grabbing him by the shoulders, her panicked gaze flicking over him.

"I'm okay," he grunted, fitting his crutch, now coated with snow and dirt, under his arm, staggering. "I'm fine."

But she could see by the way he pressed his lips together and his narrowed eyes that he wasn't. She helped steady him, grabbing on to his coat with her frozen hands.

They stood, their eyes locked, their breaths mingling. Chloe felt her heart quicken as Grady reached up and touched her face with one gloved hand.

"Chloe," he said, that one word encapsulating everything building between them.

Then another gust of wind pelted her with snow, bringing back reality with an icy slap.

"Stay here. I'll get Babe," she said.

Grady protested but she ignored him. She grabbed the halter rope from the ground, hunched her shoulders against the bone-chilling cold and with cautious steps walked toward Babe. Chloe knew enough about horses that the mare would be harder to catch the second time around, but Chloe was cold and miserable herself, her emotions riding a mixture of anger and fear at Grady's near miss and in no mood to be trifled with.

"Come here, you nutty creature," she said, her low-pitched, singsong voice masking her anger. "Time to find out who is boss."

Babe watched her approach as if debating what to do. Chloe took advantage of the horse's hesitation, moved directly toward her and with quick, sure movements got the rope around the horse's neck. She gripped it tightly with one hand while she flexed the frozen fingers of her other hand and slipped the halter on. Her gloves made handling the buckle awkward so she tugged them off with her teeth. The cold buckle stuck to her fingers, but she disregarded the pain as she forced the unyielding strap through.

Done. She grabbed her gloves and brought the horse back, hoping she would be able to untie Shiloh with her numb hands.

"I'll take her," Grady said, but Chloe ignored him, pulled on the bowline knot she had tied on Shiloh's halter rope. Thankfully the icy rope pulled free and without a backward glance at Grady, she brought both horses to the gate. She unlatched it and got the horses through. A quick look showed that Grady was close behind her, latching the gate.

The barn door slid open on its rollers and she quickly led the horses inside, shivering with reaction at the cold penetrating every square inch of her.

The barn was warm in comparison to the storm raging outside. Sweetpea put her head over the gate, whinnying as if welcoming the newcomers. Chloe put Shiloh in the first open stall she found, shut the door with one hip and then put Babe in the one next to her. By the time Grady was back in the barn, she had the halters off and was shutting the door on Babe's pen again.

She stood, halters hanging on the ground, her hands like two blocks of ice, glaring at Grady as he turned to her.

"You scared the living daylights out of me," she said, her voice controlled, masking a fury that gripped her in an icy fist.

"Sorry. It was an accident." He yanked off his hat, slapping it on his thigh to dislodge the snow.

"Caused by your stupid pride and your disability."

Grady's head whipped up at that and his eyes narrowed. "What are you saying?"

"I'm saying that this is enough," she said, shaking the halters at him. "You have held out long enough. Yeah, I get that you're tough and independent and too manly to accept help, but you could have been killed out there. If you were by yourself, you might have."

"I've faced death before," he returned, his voice growing harsh, cold. "I'm not afraid to die."

"Very brave and very noble. But you've got people depending on you, so you don't have that choice anymore. Ben needs you, Cody needs you and your grandmother needs you. Those kids that your brother has started that program for need you." She stopped before she could add "I need you." It was there, hovering, like a live thing but she knew she could never voice that thought. She had no right to need him.

She pulled in a breath, calming her anger, her hands

now resting on her hips in a gesture of defiance and challenge. "Tomorrow you and I are starting your physical therapy. You have no place to go and neither do I until the roads are cleared, so get ready 'cause it's happening."

Then, to her surprise, he sank down on a bale by the door and shook his head. "You're right. I need to do this."

She was momentarily taken aback. She had already been marshaling her arguments, ready to beat down any protests he might make, but clearly they weren't necessary.

"Okay. Tomorrow morning in the exercise room downstairs. Right after Cody's breakfast." She'd had the room ready since she had come. Now she could finally use it.

"Sure. I know I've been fighting it, but...whatever." He shoved his hand through his hair in a gesture of defeat.

"I'll need you to work hard. *Whatever* isn't enough get you through this."

He looked up at her, then gave her a crooked smile that didn't help her own equilibrium. "I'm sure you'll put me through my paces. I saw you with Babe. I don't think I'd want to cross you."

"Darn tooting," she said.

"You were amazing out there," he said, his smile softening. "I'm suitably impressed. You have a way with horses."

"I grew up on a ranch, too," she said, feeling a bit too breathless as an unwelcome perplexity gripped her. She felt as if the world turned in quiet, increasingly smaller circles, with them at the center. Nothing else existed in this moment. She cleared her throat, trying to chase away her confusion. "I was always more of a tomboy than my stepsister."

"Vanessa has nothing on you, Chloe Miner. And don't let yourself fall into that way of thinking. You're twenty times the woman she is and many others besides."

Chloe swallowed, his praise creating a flush that chased away the chill that had stung her cheeks only moments ago.

"Let's get these horses some feed and then we can go," she muttered, feeling as if the breath had been sucked out of her chest.

Stay focused, she reminded herself. *You'll be spending a lot of time with him. Keep yourself aloof.*

But as they dumped hay in the stalls, she ignored the sensible voice and chanced a sidelong glance only to see him looking at her. And for a moment, neither looked away.

"This silly exercise can't be doing anything," Grady grumbled as he pushed his thigh over what Chloe called a foam roller. "This isn't even my injured leg and it hurts."

Chloe had set up some mats downstairs by the exercise equipment Ben had set up at one time. "To make myself buff for the ladies," he had told Grady when he had asked him about it.

Now it sat there, unusable by both Ben and Grady.

"Pain is just weakness leaving the body," Chloe joked, kneeling beside him, supervising. "But as for not doing anything, this silly exercise helps loosen the muscles of your outer thigh. Because you tend to favor your injured leg, your other muscles overcompensate and slowly go out of whack."

Grady stifled a groan as needles of pain stabbed his thigh. "Whack. Is that a technical term?" he ground out.

"It's Greek for messed up."

Grady couldn't help a responding laugh, which was stifled by another jolt of pain. He had done some physical therapy when he was flown back to the States, but he had cut the program short when he'd found out about his brother. So he had left, promising to follow up.

He certainly hadn't thought the follow-up would involve working with Chloe.

Outside the storm still blew, creating havoc for anyone wanting to drive. Thankfully the mares were safely in the barn. The rest could fend for themselves.

Cody was sleeping and his grandmother, who had been quite tired the past couple of days, said she would take care of him.

At this moment it was just him and Chloe. If it wasn't for the fact that she had her professional face on, he wondered if something else wouldn't be happening.

"Do you think my grandmother is okay? Should we phone someone?" he asked, grunting as he did a few more passes over the roller, trying to distract himself from Chloe's presence. "Do you think we should call a doctor?"

"I think she's just tired," Chloe said. "I'm no doctor, but from what I can see she's healthy, eating well. Just feeling a bit peaked. It's just as well we're stranded for a few days. It will give her some chance to catch her breath and get some rest."

"You're a woman of many talents, you know," he said, flashing her a smile.

To his surprise she blushed. He knew he hadn't imagined the uptick in his own heart rate at the sight. Precisely the thing he had been concerned about when he'd discovered Chloe would be working with him, was happening. His feelings for her were growing with every moment they spent together.

He returned his attention to his exercises, promising himself he would stay focused, and for the next few minutes as Chloe shifted the angle he was working, it was all he could do to work through the pain.

Finally he was done, and as he eased himself off the roller, he lay on his back looking up at the ceiling of the basement rec room, surprised at the sweat beading on his forehead. Though the exercises Chloe had set up for him seemed basic and unchallenging he found himself breathing hard now, heart pounding.

"Congratulations," Chloe said, handing him a towel and holding out a bottle of water as he sat up. "You've just completed your first round of physical therapy with me."

"First of how many?" Grady asked, taking a long drink of water.

"That will depend on your progress and how long your grandmother wants me around."

Grady set the bottle aside and wiped his face, trying not to think about the upcoming sessions. He'd had a hard time being objective around Chloe when every time she had to show him how to position himself he'd been far too aware of her touch. Of the fresh scent of her hair.

She held out her hand to help him up, but he ignored it, struggling to his feet and walking over to the weight bench. Hard not to feel less of a man when you could barely stand on your own.

At one time he'd been the guy other men looked up to. He'd been the guy other guys wanted to be like. A Green Beret.

Now he was reduced to rolling his thigh on a foam roller, the most basic of exercises reducing his muscles to a quivering mass. At one time in his life he could run fifteen miles with a fully loaded backpack. Now a few leg lifts and stretches took everything out of him. He couldn't imagine trying to get on the back of a horse.

The thought gutted him and he pushed it aside. Another time. Another place. Right now he had other priorities.

"It gets better, you know," Chloe said as he regained his balance and sat down on his brother's weight bench. He needed to rest his tired muscles a moment. "And if it's any consolation, you aren't in as bad a shape as I thought."

"A minor consolation." He took another drink and slung the towel around his neck, watching Chloe gather up the equipment. "I know it's late, but thanks again for helping me with the horses yesterday. I couldn't have brought them in without you."

"I was glad to help," she said, her smile creating a current of awareness that he had a harder time ignoring each moment they spent together.

"I was glad to have your help, though it kills me to admit it."

"Why?"

He released a short laugh. "No man likes to admit he needs help."

"Especially not a Green Beret?" she teased as she

set the roller aside. "Don't tell me that you did all your missions on your own. Solo. By yourself."

"No. Of course not."

"You were part of a team and each member had their own strengths. You depended on each other."

"Yeah. We were a team."

"I think that's what life is all about," she said, folding the towel he had just used and laying it in the laundry basket. "Helping each other. Leaning on each other."

He said nothing at that, trying to put what she said into his own life.

"I can tell you don't believe me," she continued.

He sighed, then turned to her, feeling that since she had seen many of his weaknesses the past few days, what did he have to lose by showing a few more?

"It's not that I don't believe you. It's just that it's hard for me to see myself as less than who I used to be."

"Why less?"

"I'm not the same man. I used to be able to do so much more. I feel as if I lost part of myself. Part of who I was proud of."

"Well, you know the old saying, 'Pride goeth before a fall.' And I'm sure you've had enough of those, as well."

In spite of himself, he laughed at her gentle teasing. "And will probably have more, so I guess I better get used to swallowing. My pride, that is."

Chloe laughed at that, as well.

"I have to ask, do you think I'll be able to ride a horse again?"

"Of course you will," she said. "Once you get your muscles working the way they're supposed to and you've got some more strength in your leg. No reason at all. In fact, riding will be good therapy for you. Your muscles are always working."

"So you rode a lot?"

"I loved riding."

"How many horses did your father have?" he asked.

"Only four. Mostly for pleasure riding. Dad used an ATV to round up the cows. Not much of a cowboy purist."

"Plus his land is flatter, which made it easier to get around with one of those," he said. "So what is happening to your father's ranch?"

"It's sold now. Clark and Jane Cutter bought it."

"That's too bad. He didn't want to will it to you?"

"There was nothing left to will. Dad owed too many people too much money. Left a few hanging."

The short tone in her voice made him realize a few more things were going on that she seemed reluctant to share.

"I'm sorry. I didn't know." He watched her, suddenly remembering the exchange between her and the farrier.

"Saul knew your father, didn't he?"

Chloe nodded, folding up the last of the towels she had used. "He was an old friend of the family."

"What did he mean when he said that he was sorry? About the funeral?"

Chloe's hands slowed, her brow furrowed, and Grady guessed he had strayed into territory she didn't want to follow.

"I'm sorry," he said, tossing the empty bottle of water into a bin. "I shouldn't be so nosy."

"No. It's fine," she said, her voice quiet. "Saul and my father had a huge fight just before my father died.

Knowing Saul, I'm fairly sure it was about my father's drinking."

Grady heard the shame in her voice and wanted to console her somehow. "That must have been hard for you. Not to have him come to the funeral."

"I don't blame Saul on the one hand. They had drifted apart long before that. Saul had warned my father not to marry Etta, but he did anyway. That was the beginning of the end of their friendship."

"Etta being Vanessa's mother."

Chloe turned away from him, nodding.

"That marriage must have been hard for you, too?"

"My father was so lonely after my mother died, and when he met Etta I think he figured she would fix that." Chloe picked up the empty water bottle he had set aside and put that in the basket as well, not looking at him, her expression pensive.

"So what happened between them that made her leave?"

"A few years after they got married, my grandfather passed away. And we got to find out how badly Gramps had managed the finances. My father didn't inherit as much as Etta seemed to think he would. Then my father had his accident with his ATV. She couldn't live poor and with a disabled man, so she left."

"So how long were Etta and Vanessa at the ranch?"

"About three years. Most of high school. I was excited when Vanessa first moved in," she continued. "I was looking forward to finally having a sister, but…"

She stopped herself there and Grady guessed what her next comment would be. "She wasn't the easiest person."

"I had so hoped to be close to her," Chloe said, grabbing a spray bottle and cleaning cloth. "But that never happened. I liked riding and being outside and she preferred makeup and magazines and boys. We were so completely different." She sprayed the mat he had just used and glanced up at him. "I guess you can't identify. You and your brother always seemed so close. I guess it was because you are twins."

"We used to be close," Grady said, rubbing his hand over his still-sore thigh. "Used to do everything together. But after high school, after Dad had his accident and my mother left, we drifted apart." He released a harsh laugh. "You'd think we would have become closer after that, but we didn't. I signed up for the army after my mother left. My way of coping…of making sense of life. Ben chose his own path."

"I'm sure losing your mother was a difficult time for you both."

"And you know what that's like, don't you?"

"You feel adrift."

Chloe sounded wistful and he felt sympathy flood his soul as their gazes met in an instant of shared grief. "But you found your way, didn't you? You became a physical therapist. You got married."

"I did," she said, turning away, wiping the mat and pushing herself to her feet.

"So how did you and your ex-husband meet?"

"Not my best moment. We met in a bar. He seemed nice." She grew quiet and he sensed an underlying disconnect.

"Seemed nice?"

She released a short laugh. "I was impressionable."

Which only made him more curious. He knew he

had to stop. He was moving into places in her life he had no right to go.

So why did her terse replies only raise more questions he wanted the answers to?

He watched her, letting his feelings for her rise up, wondering if he dared act on them.

Then she looked over her shoulder at him and it was as if an electric current hummed between them.

He felt as though it wasn't a matter of *if* he would give in to the appeal she created, but *when*.

Chapter Ten

"You did good today," Chloe said to Grady as she poured a cup of coffee for him. "Your second day of therapy and I can see some progress. Couple more weeks of this and I'm sure you'll notice the difference."

Grady just groaned his response, his eyes closed, head resting on the back of the leather couch he had dropped into after supper. He had just come in from feeding the horses for the night.

The storm, now in its second day, still raged outside, still cut them off from everyone else. Chloe and Grady had gone out this morning to check on the horses and then, when they'd come back, Chloe had put him to work.

She had managed to get in another session this afternoon, but now they were done for the day.

A fire crackled in the fireplace of the living room, sending out blessed warmth. The lights had been turned low, creating a cozy, intimate setting. Mamie sat on the couch across from Grady, reading a book, a blanket wrapped around her legs. For someone who was supposed to be ill she looked quite perky, Chloe thought.

"The second day of therapy is always the hardest," she said. "Mamie, did you want more coffee?"

Mamie looked up from the book she was reading and pulled off her glasses. She released a heavy sigh. "No. I'm still not feeling well. I think I might turn in."

"I still think we should call a doctor," Grady said, lifting his head to frown at his grandmother.

"I'm not that ill. I just need rest." She gave Chloe a wan smile. "I'll check on Cody before I go to bed. You two just stay here." She set her book down on the small table beside the couch, glasses neatly on top, set her blanket aside and made a show of getting to her feet.

Chloe watched her little performance, and her feeling that Mamie wasn't being entirely truthful was borne out when she got a faint wink from Mamie as she walked past.

Was she deliberately leaving the two of them alone?

The thought made her flush again. She wasn't sure what to do about her changing feelings for Grady, and she knew being alone with him would make it harder to keep herself aloof from him. In fact, the past few days her determination to stay focused on her job had been more difficult the more she got distracted by attraction she sensed growing between them.

She placed her hand on her stomach, as if to remind herself of the single reason she had to keep her heart whole. The secret she knew she couldn't keep quiet much longer. Sooner or later she had to tell Mamie at least. But it was her innate sense of self-protection that made her keep her secret. Thankfully she could wear looser clothing today while she worked with Grady so she could demonstrate some of the exercises she wanted him to do. But her clothes were getting tighter. She was getting close to five months now. She knew she would start showing soon.

"I should get to bed, too, but I'm too lazy," Grady said, easing out a sigh as he reached for his coffee. "I figure I've done enough work today that I should be able to sit around."

Because Grady had no other obligations, Chloe had extended the afternoon session as long as she dared, working different muscle groups each time. He had willingly gone along, even though she knew it had to be hard for him. "Like I said, you did good today."

"It will be a long while before I can climb into a saddle."

"You won't be roping any time soon, but riding is certainly not out of the question in time," Chloe said, hoping to encourage him. She guessed it was difficult enough for him to feel disabled. To not be able to ride must feel horrible. Of all the things she'd missed while living in the city, the ability to go out for a ride was one of the biggest.

"If I can get on."

"You're only limited by yourself," she said, taking a sip of her coffee. As soon as the words left her mouth she realized how trite they sounded. "I'm sorry. I shouldn't be mouthing platitudes at you. Occupational hazard."

"Do you enjoy your job?"

"When I'm working, yes. I do."

"How did you get into that line of work?"

"I think part of it was a reaction to what happened to my father."

"He was injured riding his ATV, wasn't he?"

"Which is ironic. He got the thing because he had

been thrown from a horse once and didn't want that to happen again." Chloe cradled her warm mug, her thoughts melancholy. "He never got over the injury. I think after losing my mother, and his accident and divorce from Etta, he lost all will to do anything. He just stayed at home, started drinking and things just went downhill from there. Including the ranch. I always wished I could have helped him more, but unfortunately I had—" She stopped herself there. Grady didn't need to know all the sordid details of her past.

"You had what?" Grady prompted.

"Doesn't matter."

"Does your 'doesn't matter' have anything to do with your ex-husband?"

He was far too astute, Chloe thought.

"Why do you want to know?" she asked, looking down at her cup of coffee, avoiding his direct gaze. Part of her wanted to tell him, to let him know precisely what Jeremy meant to her. Precious little. Even though they had been married for three years, she had felt alone in their relationship for most of that time.

It was that loneliness that made her vulnerable to Grady's attention.

That and the fact Grady was one of the first men in her life to hold her heart. Though she had tried to dismiss her initial attraction to him as a silly schoolgirl crush, images and memories of him had stayed with her the entire time she'd been gone from Little Horn. When she'd found out he had signed up for the army, she'd guessed that she would never see him again. So she had put him out of her life.

Then she had met Jeremy.

"I'm guessing the fact that you, of all people, are

now divorced makes it pretty clear that things weren't right between you and your ex-husband. Plus, I'm curious." Grady put his coffee cup down, got to his feet and hobbled over to the fireplace. He knelt and threw on a couple of logs on the fire. Sparks flew up the chimney. He stayed there a moment, looking at her, the fire casting a glow over his handsome face, creating interesting highlights in his sandy brown hair.

For a few precious moments the only sounds were the crackling of the fire in the fireplace and the sighing of the steady wind outside.

"I also want to know what I'm up against," Grady continued.

Chloe's breath caught in her chest like a knot. "What do you mean?" The question was superfluous. She knew exactly what he meant, but she felt she had to try to keep a distance.

Then, to her shock and pleasure, Grady moved to sit beside her on the couch.

"I mean that I want to fill in the gaps between then and now in our lives." He brushed a strand of hair back from her face. His hand lingered on her cheek and she swallowed the attraction she felt building.

"I'm not that interesting and my life with Jeremy—" She stopped there.

"Was what?" he asked. "What was your life with Jeremy like?"

Chloe looked down, her eyelashes shielding her eyes, her lips pressed together.

"Tell me," he whispered, his fingers lightly caressing her cheek.

Shame suffused her at the memory of her marriage, but she also felt a need to unload. To let someone know.

Her years with Jeremy had been so lonely. She'd had no mother or father to confide in, and all her friends had been either gone or busy with their own lives.

"He was nice at first. Very charming. But I found out afterward that he was very charming to more women than just me." As she had throughout her marriage, she struggled to separate Jeremy's actions from her life. "I tried to make it work, but it was a failed effort from the start. Jeremy never had any intention of staying faithful. I'm still not sure why he married me."

"Because you're a sweet, caring person," Grady said.

Her heart tilted and she put her hand to her chest as if to hold its errant beat still. Grady was growing harder to resist.

"And that's kind of you to say, but I think he simply saw me as a challenge. I told him the first time we met that I didn't think he was the marrying kind, and he seemed determined to prove me wrong, and I eventually fell for his shtick." It still embarrassed her to admit she was so gullible.

So weak.

"Sorry, I have to go." She swallowed down a sob as shame suffused her.

But Grady's hand was still curled around her neck and he didn't release her.

"What's wrong, Chloe?" His hand was warm, his voice soft and encouraging. "Tell me what's wrong."

Don't look at him, she thought. *Don't give in again.*

"Please?"

It was that single word that broke down her defenses. That word spoken so softly she might have imagined it but for the way his arms tightened around her as if letting her know she was safe.

A word she'd never, ever heard from her ex-husband. So she gave in.

"Like I told you, we met in a bar," she said. "He was charming. I had just gotten a new job working at a physical therapy clinic, and I had just found out that two of my good friends had gotten engaged. Two others were already married. I guess I wasn't in the best frame of mind to have an attractive man flirting with me. He asked me out and I accepted and soon we were seeing each other regularly.

"Like I said, I made the mistake of telling him I didn't think he was the marrying kind. That's when he turned on the charm. We were married six months after we started dating. Of course it was too quick, but what did I know? I was flattered and I thought he cared about me." She stopped, memories she had suppressed for the past few months returning with a vengeance. Confrontations about his cheating. His lackadaisical attitude. His assurance that if he hadn't married her, no one would have. "It was a mistake that I've regretted ever since."

"Why?"

"It's embarrassing."

Again he said nothing, as if waiting for her to fill the silence. So she did.

"Jeremy cheated on me most of our relationship. I found out afterward that this was going on even before we got married. Information that would have been helpful before I said 'I do' and made promises that I had every intention of keeping and he didn't." She knew it wasn't her fault, but the shame that had filled her when she'd found out how she had been duped returned too easily.

Thankfully Grady said nothing, just held her as if giving her statement weight.

"So you divorced him?"

"I should have. But when I confronted him about his unfaithfulness, he told me he was filing for divorce. He was good friends with a judge and hustled our divorce through the courts. I think he couldn't stand the idea that I might actually divorce him first."

She stopped, thinking of the reason Jeremy had divorced her. He had never wanted children. And she had gotten pregnant.

"The divorce was finalized only two months ago," she continued. "It wasn't what I wanted, but I realized, afterward, it needed to happen."

She stopped there and, as if in response to her declaration the baby she carried moved and Chloe closed her eyes, all the joy in the moment receding. She was carrying another man's baby.

Grady tipped her face up to his. "You don't have to feel ashamed of what happened to you. If anything it has shown me that you are a faithful, caring person." He stroked her face with his fingers, his very touch seeming to ease away her fears. "I think we've both got our stuff to deal with, but I like to believe that we can get through whatever happened. I've discovered one thing since I've come back here. I'm not alone in what I'm dealing with and neither are you. We've got a community and family and support. And we have an amazing life here. I've seen some difficult things to make me realize what we have been blessed with."

She leaned back, her hand still on his chest, keeping the connection between them. "Do you talk about it much? What you saw overseas?"

"Haven't much. I came back to quite a storm of events. Between Vanessa claiming I was Cody's father and Ben's coma and the ranch stuff, I felt as if I had to simply dive in and do what came next."

"Was it hard to come back?"

Grady looked away from her, his eyes taking on a faraway look as if he was returning to Afghanistan. "I saw a lot over there that made me angry, sad, guilty and at the same time so incredibly thankful for the life we have here. It was hard seeing what I saw and experiencing what I did. But I made a decision early on in my career that I wasn't letting my experiences define me. I lost my way from that declaration for a while…" His voice faded.

"You said it once before that you didn't believe God hears prayer," Chloe prompted.

"I think He hears it but I'm not sure what He does about it."

His words bothered her, but she could see that in spite of their harshness he didn't seem entirely convinced of their truth.

"I know it's hard to see God through the storms, but I know He has helped me through many," Chloe said quietly. "I know you had a strong, sincere faith at one time."

Grady sighed. "I did. It's still there, but I'm not so sure God wants me with all the questions I have now. I have to confess I'm struggling right now. Trying to find my footing. In more ways than one," he said with a short laugh.

"'Even strong men stumble,'" Chloe quoted. "I don't think God minds our questions. I think He prefers that to indifference."

Grady seemed to weigh that, his expression serious. "I know that I miss that closeness."

"God is still there, Grady. Maybe you'll just have to move a bit closer yourself and take your questions along."

"I think you might be right," he said.

"I know I've always had to learn that this world is God's. He's ultimately in control. And He's a just God, so sometimes some of the questions will have to wait." She felt as if she was speaking as much to herself as to him. "I know in my heart that while I may wonder where my life is headed, I believe that if I hope in the Lord, like the pastor preached on Sunday, that my strength will be renewed. I think you can believe that, too."

Grady looked down at her, smiling. "You really are amazing."

She tried not to read too much into his comment, into the way his dark brown eyes drew her into their depths, seeming to promise a peace she hadn't felt since her mother died.

Part of her called out a warning. Jeremy, too, had promised much.

But even as the voice reminded her of her past mistakes, she also knew that Grady was nothing like Jeremy.

She knew she could trust him.

"I know I've had to believe that God would lead me through the valleys I've dealt with, as well," she said. Then she gave into an impulse and touched his face, tracing a faint scar on his cheek. The promise that someday she might know the story behind it gave her a gentle thrill.

She wanted to be a part of his life.

Yet her life was such a jumble. She dragged the weight of what had happened to her and she didn't know what to do with it.

She turned to him and as their eyes met she felt as if everything wrong in her life faded away. It was just her and Grady.

To her chagrin, an errant tear slipped down her cheek. She reached up to scrub it away but Grady caught it with his thumb, easing it away.

"Why so sad?"

"Old memories," she said.

He gave her a crooked smile. She felt her resistance ebb like sand before a wave, and before she could say anything more, he bent closer to her, blotting out the light. Then his warm lips were on hers and everything wrong in her life dwindled and died.

Grady leaned his forehead against Chloe's, his eyes closed, his hands resting on her shoulders. He eased out a sigh, then pulled her against him.

She fit against him as though she belonged, her breath warm on his cheek, her hand resting on his shoulder.

He leaned back against the couch, taking her with him. She nestled in his arms and he pressed a kiss to her forehead, releasing a sigh weighted with many of the losses of the past year.

"I feel as if this has been a long time coming," he said.

"What do you mean?" Her voice was soft, as if hardly daring to disturb the moment.

"I think you know what I'm talking about," he said

with a soft chuckle, sensing her question for what it was—a woman's foray into the examination of relationships.

"I do, but I like to talk about it," she said, lifting her head and stroking his hair back from his face, her gesture creating a gentle warmth that he hadn't felt in a long time. As he looked down on her smiling face illuminated by the firelight's glow, he felt, for the first time since he had returned, that he was home. That he was in a place he belonged. He brushed a gentle kiss over her forehead and smiled.

"I've always known who you were," he said, laying his cheek on her head, holding her a bit more tightly as if she might disappear again. "Always been attracted to you, but you never seemed to know I even existed. I remember you talking to my brother and it seemed that you were kind of flirting with him, so I thought he was the one you were interested in."

"I was flirting with Ben?" she said with mock horror. "I thought I was flirting with you all that time."

Grady gave her a gentle shake. "Please tell me you're kidding."

"Of course I am. I could always tell you two apart." Chloe nestled closer, her hand resting on his chest, her finger tracing the line of the buttons on his shirt. "When Ben teased me and I played along, I always hoped you would come and join us and then I could talk to you. You always seemed so aloof, and when Vanessa came I got the feeling you were interested in her."

"That was only because she flirted outrageously with me and you didn't give me any indication that you liked me."

"Classic communication breakdown," she said with a chuckle. "Blame it on me being a bit shy."

"I wonder how things would have turned out if we had actually talked to each other instead of just assuming things?"

"Guess we'll never know," Chloe said.

"Guess it doesn't matter," Grady returned, fingering her hair away from her face. He brushed another kiss over her forehead and eased out a sigh of satisfaction. "You're here now and so am I, and all the twists and turns of our life led us here."

"I like here," Chloe whispered.

He couldn't stop himself from kissing her again. Then he pulled his head back, his hand cupping her cheek. "So where do we go from here?"

"Seeing as how the roads are glare ice and there's a travel advisory out, nowhere, I guess," she said with a tight smile, deliberately misunderstanding him.

He gave her another gentle shake. "You know what I'm talking about. I don't get the idea that you're a casual person when it comes to relationships."

"I don't know. I did marry Jeremy."

"And you honored your promises even though you knew he wasn't doing the same."

Chloe lowered her gaze, her expression suddenly serious.

"That means more than you can know," Grady said. "You are an honorable person. That's rare."

"Don't give me too much credit," she murmured.

Grady felt a niggle of unease at her words, then realized she was being self-deprecating, which made her even more charming.

"I think I've always admired you," he said, stroking

her cheek with his thumb. "While I didn't know exactly what your life with Vanessa was like, I do know that you never spoke ill of her. Never said anything against her while she, on the other hand, seemed to have a more negative attitude."

"That's a kind way to say she didn't like me," Chloe said, smiling again.

"You can joke about that?"

"Now I can," Chloe admitted, laying her hand on his chest. "Listening to her and her mother constantly put down my father was harder, though. I loved my father in spite of his failings."

"You truly are a faithful person," Grady said. "I am so thankful that you came back into my life. You mean more to me than ever before."

"And I'm thankful I'm here," she said.

Then, to his surprise and dismay, another tear slid down her cheek.

"Hey. Babe. What's the matter?" The endearment slipped out even as he touched the track of moisture.

"I don't know," she said, hurriedly swiping away the next tear. "I'm just happy, I guess."

He felt his own heart lift in response. "Me, too," he said, pressing a kiss to her lips. "Me, too."

But as he held her close he realized she hadn't told him the real reason she was crying.

Chapter Eleven

The wind howled around Grady as he made his way across the yard the next morning. His footing was precarious and he slid more times than he cared to count, but thankfully he didn't fall. He pulled his hat down over his ears and tugged up the collar of his jacket, keeping his eyes on the yard light above the door to the barn. Sleet beat at his face and got into his eyes, but finally he made it.

The heavy door slid open and he stepped inside.

He shook the snow off his coat and heard a questioning whinny from the far end of the barn where the horses were kept.

"I'm coming," he called out in answer, shivering as he made his way down the semidark alleyway. He pulled open the door of one of the empty stalls where Josh had stacked some hay. It took him a while to bust open a new bale, but he had time, he told himself.

Though part of him was eager to return to the house. And Chloe.

He broke loose the bale with his crutch then, grabbed a pitchfork and dumped a few forkfuls into the alleyway, pivoting on his crutch with every movement. When he had enough to feed the horses, he did the same, moving the hay a little more each time. It was tedious and frustrating and he had to fight his annoyance with his limitations.

But he also noticed his hip wasn't as tight as it had been a couple days ago. Though his leg still ached and each movement created a surge of pain, for the first time since his injury he felt a sense of optimism.

Mostly that came from Chloe, who firmly believed that with time and hard work he could regain the majority of his mobility.

He managed to fork the hay into the pens, and when he was done, he was sweating from the exertion.

He dropped onto a bench close to the pens and stretched his leg out in front of him, massaging it to ease the cramp that had come up.

Sweetpea whinnied at him, her head hanging over the stall as if asking him what he was still doing there.

"I know, Sweetpea. I want to go back to the house, but I need to take a moment," he said, thinking aloud. "Need to figure out where I'm going."

This netted him a faint snort.

"Don't mock me," he said. "I can't just jump into this. Chloe is a wonderful person and she deserves the best. I just don't know if that's me."

Sweetpea just stared at him.

"Plus I've got this ranch and Ben and Mamie…" He felt the weight of each of these obligations, yet even as he listed them he kept thinking about Chloe.

He pulled in a long, slow breath, letting his mind settle, thinking about what she had told him last night. How God welcomed him and his questions.

"I don't know what to do, Lord," he prayed. "I have lots of things I want to ask You about. Things I saw and experienced that I don't know the answers to."

He stopped, feeling a bit foolish, but at the same time feeling a gentle peace surround him.

"I used to be able to talk to You more easily. But I felt as if You didn't listen or didn't care." As he spoke the words aloud, it was as if he heard them for what they were. A lie.

"I guess I know You care. I just wish I could get some direction. Especially now. With Chloe. I feel as if I'm not strong enough to do this."

My hope is only in You, Lord, my solid cornerstone, my strength when I am weak, my help when I'm alone. The words of the song they'd sung last Sunday sifted into his mind.

Maybe he was trying to do too much on his own. Maybe he had to put more of his hope in the Lord.

"Help me to put my life in Your hands, Lord," he prayed. "Help me to put my growing relationship with Chloe there, as well."

He sat a few seconds longer as if to let the prayer soak into his being and returned to the house.

"One final set of stretches and we're done," Chloe said as Grady slowly got off the exercise bike. His range of motion was still restricted, but Chloe could tell that, given time, he would regain more mobility. Maybe not as much as before, but enough to resume most of his former tasks.

"I think I need some encouragement," Grady said, rolling his neck.

"Like what?" she asked, with a teasing smile.

When Grady had come down to the exercise room this morning, he had greeted her with a kiss as natural as breathing. As if they had been dating for months instead of just getting to know each other now.

"I think I could use another kiss," he teased, catching her hand and pulling her close.

Chloe felt her cheeks warm, but she laughed and brushed a kiss over his mouth.

"Oh, c'mon, we're not in junior high." He draped his other hand around her neck and drew her closer yet. His kiss was warm and it gave her exactly the right little thrill.

She pulled back, unable to stop smiling. This morning at breakfast she and Grady had sat side by side, their hands twined together under the table. Mamie had sat across from them looking quite self-satisfied and healthy. Once again Chloe doubted her story about how ill she felt, but she wasn't about to challenge her. She had guessed Mamie had ulterior motives for hiring her in the first place, but right about now, she didn't care.

"Does that help?"

"Immensely," he said. "Now what am I supposed to do?"

"Lie down, arms beside you, and I'll tell you." She walked him through the series, correcting his movements as he worked. "Just make sure you don't push too hard," Chloe warned as he completed the last set. "You don't want to strain your muscles and put yourself back."

"Guess I just want to get better quick." Grady finished, then dropped onto his back on the exercise mat, one arm flung over his eyes. "I'm an impatient man."

"That could be a detriment," Chloe said, kneeling

beside him. "Patience is the main ingredient in any therapy program."

"You always have an answer," he groaned as she twisted his leg just enough to stretch the calf muscles.

"We get an app when we graduate that we put on our smartphones as well as a book that matches comment to complaint," she said, settling back on her haunches while Grady rolled over and got to his feet. He wavered as he reached for his crutch, but she didn't help him, knowing how independent he was. As long as it didn't look as though he would fall she knew enough to leave him alone. "I've used it many times with some of my more reluctant clients."

"You've had clients more reluctant than me?"

"Oh, yes," she said with a definite nod. "There are more people who don't like to acknowledge they need help."

"It's hard," he said. "I think I was dealing with false pride." He gave her a sheepish smile. "I didn't want to admit in front of you that I wasn't as strong as I used to be. That I was weak."

"I've always thought that it takes great strength of character for anyone to recognize honestly what they can and can't do." She gave him an encouraging smile. "Some take longer than others, but you did come to that point, and I think that's honorable and manly."

"I think what I struggled with most was I felt I wasn't the man I used to be."

"None of us are what we used to be," she said, cleaning up the equipment she had used today with a spray bottle. "We've both come through our lives with wounds, mental as well as physical."

"What wounds do you carry?"

Her heart suddenly felt as though it was pushing heavily against her chest, filling it with its racing beat. She took a slow breath. She had put this off too long. It was time to tell him the truth. She clutched the bottle, her back to him, steadying her breath, readying herself. But the sound of the baby crying broke into the moment.

Chloe spun around just as Mamie came into the room holding a red-faced, screaming Cody, whose cries filled the room. "I'm sorry, Chloe. I don't know what's wrong with him. He just woke up. I know he's supposed to be sleeping a bit longer."

"No need to be sorry," Chloe said, hurrying to take the squalling infant from her. "I'm sorry I wasn't there to help."

"Working with Grady is as much your job as taking care of this little one," Mamie said, handing Cody over. "So you have nothing to apologize for."

Chloe settled Cody against her, rocking him, shushing him, stroking his warm, damp head. Immediately his cries eased into hiccups and he lay his head against her shoulder.

"You certainly have a way with him," Mamie said with admiration. "A natural mother."

It was a simple, innocent comment, but it was a reminder of what she had yet to tell Grady.

Not yet, she thought. *Not yet*. She didn't want anything to upset what was happening between them. Part of her felt dishonest, but she simply wanted the ordinary time of being with Grady without all the complications that would come with her news. She knew things were growing, moving to a serious, solid place. She just wanted them both to have their footing before she created more instability.

Isn't that a bit self-serving?

Chloe stifled that unrelenting voice. It wasn't selfish, she reasoned. It was practical.

"I'll go take care of Cody," Chloe said, turning to Grady. "You're okay for now?"

He gave her a discreet wink. "More than okay."

Chloe blushed again. Tucking Cody against her, she turned and followed Mamie up the stairs. She sensed that the older woman wanted to say something, but Chloe wasn't ready to bring out into the cold light of day what was growing between her and Grady. It was so new, so tender. Something she had yearned for, for so many years, and she was afraid too much dissemination could destroy its fragile fabric.

So she just kept going up, bringing Cody to the nursery. She lay the little boy on the changing table, smiling at him as he gave her a drooling grin, his cupid's-bow lips glistening.

"You are a little stinker, aren't you?" she cooed as she took off his pants and changed his diaper. He had a rash, which, Chloe suspected, had woken him in the first place.

Outside, the storm, which hadn't abated since it had begun, roared on, pelting the window with snow mixed with rain. Chloe felt safe in this place. Centered. As though this was where she was meant to be.

She got Cody cleaned up, then sat in the rocking chair in one corner of the nursery cuddling him and trying to ease him into sleep. His warm body melted against hers and she felt a flush of maternal joy. What would it be like to hold her own baby?

Her heart clenched at the thought. Where would she be when that happened? Here? With Grady?

Somewhere else?

Help me, Lord, she prayed, fear wrapping an icy fist around her heart. *Help me to do the right thing. To find the right time to tell him. Please help Grady to understand.*

The thought that he might not was too difficult to contemplate. For the first time in her life she felt as if the boundaries of her life were falling into pleasant places. She was back in Little Horn, and the man she had spun so many dreams around had kissed her. Had told her how much she meant to him.

Did she dare disrupt that?

You'll have to sooner than later. You can't hide that pregnancy forever.

"Please help him understand," she prayed aloud, holding Cody even closer, feeling sorry for this poor child who didn't know his mother and whose father was still unconscious. "And be with Ben," she continued. "Please return him to this family."

She eased out a gentle sigh, rocking the little baby, singing to him and her own child at the same time.

From below she heard Grady and Mamie's murmured conversation, then the sound of the shower running. The ordinary sounds of a household. A home.

Cody finally fell asleep and Chloe laid him gently in his crib, stroking the little one's downy head. "Sleep tight, little one. May God watch over you," she whispered.

And me, as well, she added.

She left the room, gently closing the door behind her. When she arrived downstairs she saw Mamie pulling out her bread pans.

"Here, let me do that," Chloe said, hurrying over to

her side. "You rest. You're still recuperating, I'm sure. Did you want some tea?"

"Yes of course. Tea would be lovely," Mamie said hurriedly, dropping onto a nearby stool and sighing as if she had to remind herself how ill she was supposed to be. Chloe stifled a smile.

Chloe plugged in the electric kettle and looked out the window over the yard. She could barely see the barn through the storm and once again was thankful she didn't have to go outside. Thankful for this place of shelter and refuge.

She looked over the bread recipe, humming as she gathered the ingredients.

"You seem happy," Mamie said as the water began to boil.

"I guess I am," Chloe said, her cheeks flushing as she guessed that Mamie knew exactly what the reason for her lighthearted attitude was.

"So does Grady. Not only that, he seems content. Something I haven't seen in him for a while."

Chloe felt the weight of that statement, as if Mamie was hinting that she might be the reason for that.

"I'm glad. He's making decent progress. Of course, we've only just started, but he's determined to do well, and that means he probably will. It took a while to convince him, but I think he's motivated now."

"Of course he is," Mamie said with a smug tone. "He has the best reason in the world to improve himself now."

Chloe wasn't sure what to say to that leading statement.

"I know my grandson may not always be the most cooperative," Mamie said. "But he's a good man."

Chloe looked over at her, realizing that Mamie knew exactly what had been going on.

"He is," Chloe agreed. "The best."

This was exactly the right answer, judging from Mamie's smug look.

When the water boiled Chloe made tea, poured a cup for Mamie and herself and returned to mixing up the ingredients. The yeast had soaked long enough and she could add the rest. Thankfully Mamie found a magazine and paged through it as she drank her tea, not saying anything more and leaving Chloe to work in quiet. As she cracked eggs and added oil to the bread dough, Chloe felt a curious peace slip over her. It had been years since she had done any baking. Jeremy had been seldom at home to eat it and when she had attended school, she hadn't had time.

She turned on the mixer to knead the dough just as Grady came into the kitchen.

Chloe felt her heart skip a beat when she saw him cleaned up, his hair still damp from his shower, cheeks shining from his shave. And when his dark eyes found hers, locking on to her gaze, she felt a sense of homecoming.

This is right, she thought. *This fits. This is where I belong. Everything else will come together.*

It had to.

Chapter Twelve

The next morning, Grady got up, stretched and then groaned as he felt muscles he had forgotten were part of his anatomy. He was even more stiff and sore than yesterday. But it was a good sore. The kind he used to feel after a hard workout.

He rolled his neck and beyond the door of his bedroom he could hear Cody banging his spoon on the high chair and Chloe talking to him in lilting tones. He felt a surge of happiness he hadn't felt in years.

He was home, and the woman he cared about more with each passing minute was under the same roof. These past few days had given them a time out of time. An opportunity to simply be together without all the complications of the outside world.

Then he heard it.

Silence. He walked to the window and pushed aside the curtain, lifted the blinds. Gray clouds still blanketed the sky, but the storm had passed. No wind blew; no snow slanted sideways over the yard. All was calm.

Which meant that soon life would return to normal.

He felt a touch of concern at the thought. What would happen to him and Chloe then?

Then he laughed that foolish idea off. As if their changing feelings could only thrive in this little bit of space and time they had been granted. He'd cared for her before, and he knew she had cared for him, as well. He felt in his heart that what he and Chloe had would only grow.

To where?

The question hovered, creating both concern and anticipation. He knew he wanted more than simply to date Chloe. Though what was happening between them had come up quickly, he also knew she wasn't a casual dater, either.

He looked out over the yard at the ranch he and his brother had inherited. A legacy going back many generations. Though he had given so much of his life to the military, he'd never realized how important this place was to him until now.

And to the life he could give any future family.

He got dressed quickly, finding his crutch, praying that someday he wouldn't need it anymore, then made his way to the kitchen and Chloe.

Warmth braided with delicious smells greeted him as he stepped into the kitchen.

His grandmother sat on the other side of the table drinking a mug of tea, paging through a magazine. A batch of cinnamon buns, the reason for the home smells, lay cooling on the counter. Chloe was trying to coax breakfast into Cody's cereal-encrusted mouth. The little guy was banging a spoon on the tray of the high chair, babbling his pleasure. His hair stuck up, and when Chloe held a spoon of food in front of him he batted it away, netting a smile from Chloe instead of a reprimand.

She was so incredibly patient, he thought, watching as she wiped the cereal from the high chair and from her arm with a cloth.

"Are you done, munchkin?" she asked, wiping his mouth, as well. "I hope so because I'm ready to eat, too."

"I'm hoping those cinnamon buns are for breakfast," he said, popping a new pod in the coffeemaker.

Chloe spun around, and when she saw him her bright smile warmed his heart.

"Good morning," she said.

"Chloe made them," his grandmother piped up.

"You must have been up before dawn," Grady said, grabbing a mug out of the cupboard and flashing her a warm smile.

"They're overnight cinnamon buns," she said. "I haven't made them for years. But I'm sure they're fine."

"I'm sure they are, too," Grady said. The coffeemaker burbled, pouring a stream of brown liquid into his mug. "Looks as if the storm has cleared. Things should be getting back to normal soon."

"That's good, I suppose," his grandmother said. "I imagine you'll be back to work once the roads clear."

"I'll have to. After breakfast I'd like to check on the horses again." Then, just to see what his grandmother would do, he stopped by Chloe and pressed a kiss to her soft, warm neck. "Good morning," he whispered.

She ducked her head, but he caught the edge of her smile then looked over at his grandmother, who grinned like the Cheshire cat.

Breakfast was a quiet affair. Cody sat on Chloe's

lap as she ate, watching Grady as if trying to figure out what he should think of him. Mamie made small talk. Chloe gave Grady a shy look from time to time.

When breakfast was over, Chloe sat Cody in his chair and started clearing the table. But Mamie stopped her. "You just go and change Cody. I'll clean up and then watch him. You should go help Grady in the barn."

"He's been managing the past few days without me—"

"I wouldn't mind the extra help," Grady interrupted before Chloe could formulate a reason not to come. He guessed she was trying to be all noble and responsible, but if Grandma wanted to give them a few moments alone, he was taking them. Once the roads were cleared, the ranch hands would be back, then Maddy Coles and the other girls would return and there would be precious few quiet moments for them. "I'd like to check on the other horses outside as well, and I'd like your help for that."

"In that case, I'll take care of Cody and be ready in fifteen minutes."

It was actually five, which made Grady smile. It seemed Chloe was as eager as he was to spend time together.

The air still held a hint of moisture as they walked across the icy yard. Grady took his time, his steps deliberate. There was no way he was falling down in front of Chloe. When he went out on his own to feed the horses, he didn't care as much about finesse. He had slipped and slid, but that hadn't mattered. He hadn't had an audience then.

Now, he knew he was being proud, and Chloe had

seen him at his weakest, but he still felt the need to show her that he was capable.

The barn was silent when they stepped inside, then Sweetpea whinnied at them followed by Babe and Shiloh.

"They're probably hungry," Grady said, his halting steps echoing in the cavernous barn.

"Do you want me to help feed them?"

"Nah. I'll be okay." He had things down to a system and though it took time, he wasn't as ungainly as he had been the first time he'd done it.

Sweetpea, Babe and Shiloh hung their heads over the gates of their pens, watching patiently as he approached them. "Hey, girls," he said. "How are you doing?"

They whinnied back, their replies echoing through the barn.

"You care to translate?" Chloe teased.

Grady pushed open the door of the stall holding the hay with his crutch and shot her a grin over his shoulder. "Sweetpea is asking me why I had to bring that gorgeous girl in here, and Babe is asking me where her breakfast is. Very selfish, that one. Shiloh is just curious."

Chloe laughed at his lame comments, making him feel as if he might actually own a sense of humor.

She walked over to Babe, stroked the horse's head. "Your meal will come in good time," she said.

Grady tried not to rush. His pride made him want to look competent in front of Chloe, but his more practical nature reminded him to take his time. If he fell down again, he'd look even more foolish.

Then, without saying anything, Chloe walked into the pen where the hay was, grabbed another fork and stabbed it into the bale. She brought it over to Babe and dumped it into the stall. Then went back for another. Grady bit back his protest, knowing on one level he should be happy for the help. The less time he spent awkwardly making his way back and forth with the hay, the less chance he had of falling or embarrassing himself. And Chloe knew what she was doing.

A few minutes later they were done, the horses munching loudly.

"Amazing how they can make that dry old hay seem so tasty," Chloe said, hanging over Babe's stall, watching her eat.

Grady set aside the fork and while she was looking at Babe, stretched out a kink in his leg, grimacing at the sudden and unexpected stab of pain. He tried not to feel disheartened, knowing it would take months before the pain would ease off. Chloe hadn't promised him any sudden recuperation, and he knew better than to expect that, but it was still frustrating to be so hampered in what he could do when he wanted to show how capable he was.

"When are they supposed to foal?" Chloe asked, joining him on the bench by the stalls.

"Sweetpea is due in April, Babe and Shiloh in May."

"I remember we had one mare who had a foal. I named and raised her. Saul helped me train her. He also tried to talk me out of calling her Shayalama. Said it would take me too long to train her because it would take me too long to say her name every time I wanted her to do something."

Grady smiled, though he heard the hint of sorrow in her voice. "What happened to this Shayalama?"

"She was sold when things went bad for my father."

She rested her elbows on her knees, her chin in her hands, her eyes seeming to be looking to another place.

Grady stroked her shoulder in commiseration. "That must have been a hard time for you."

"I was gone for the worst of the decline. Which brings its own load of guilt. The last few years, when things got really bad, I was..." Her voice drifted off and she pressed her lips together.

"You were married to Jeremy."

She nodded, giving him a rueful smile. "I should have paid more attention to what was happening. I should have helped my father more. His life was so scattered."

"I know how you feel," Grady said. "I had the same difficulty with Ben. Being away, yet knowing what kind of life he was living. I guess I shouldn't have been as angry as I was with him."

"It's hard to watch someone make bad choices."

"I didn't need to be as hard on him as I was."

"You did it because he matters to you," Chloe said, turning back to him, taking his hand in hers. "In our studies we talked about the special bond that twins share. I think you become more invested in each other's lives. And as a result, you probably care more. You told him what you did because you love him, not because you wanted to be some kind of policeman."

Grady squeezed her hand in response, chuckling in spite of his regrets. "You are so perceptive. That's exactly what Ben had accused me of doing. In fact, he informed me that I was a solider, not a cop."

"I guess we're on the same wavelength, too," she joked.

He curled his hand around her neck, pulling her in for another kiss. "I'd like to think so."

She lay against him with a gentle sigh, her hand resting on his chest, her other around his waist. "I like this place."

"This barn?" he said, deliberately misunderstanding her.

"Being in your arms in this barn," she said with a chuckle. "I like being here on the ranch."

"Do you miss your work?"

"It was what I trained for. I hope that someday I will be able to do it full-time again."

Her comment reminded him that her stay here was temporary. Did he dare assume she would want to make it permanent?

The thought jolted him. Was he ready to make that commitment?

Was she?

The stillness of the barn, broken only by the munching of the horses, made Chloe feel a gentle push-pull of emotions. Grady's appeal; the reality of the baby she carried. The honesty they had just shared; the secret she held close.

She had to tell him before she moved so far down this path she couldn't find her way back.

Her heart stepped up its tempo as she scrambled for the right words to convey the information, the right time.

Now, her mind told her.

Later, said her heart.

"I guess we should get back to the house," Grady

said, breaking the soft silence with his comment. "Don't want Grandma to worry about us."

"I doubt she's worried," Chloe said, feeling the relief of the momentary reprieve.

"You're probably right. In fact, I think that Mamie's illness was either contrived or exaggerated."

"And why would she do that?" Chloe asked.

Grady gave her a conspiratorial smile. "So that we could do this." He gave her another kiss.

Was this really her? Chloe thought as she drew back from him, her hand on his shoulder, her eyes locked with his. Was this really Chloe Miner kissing Grady Stillwater for real instead of those endless fantasies she had spun up in her room, hugging her pillow, pretending it was him?

"I like doing this," she said. Then she kissed him back. For real.

"I do, too, but I should get hold of Josh, Emilio or Lucas and see which of them can come in. The cows will need to be fed either today or tomorrow."

So soon, Chloe thought. So soon the outside world would descend into their lives with obligations and ordinariness.

But who know what would come with it?

Grady grabbed his crutch and stood, his movements awkward. Chloe suspected most of his stiffness resulted from the workouts she had done with him. Had she pushed him too hard?

"I should go visit Ben as soon as possible," Grady said as he set his crutch under his arm. "I hope he doesn't feel as if we've abandoned him."

"Just tell him what happened. He'll understand."

"I love how you talk about Ben as though he knows exactly what is going on."

"Like I said, it's subliminal. He might not remember, but I believe it enters his subconscious and takes root there."

"I guess sooner or later we'll have to tell him about Cody," Grady said as they made their way to the door.

"I wish I could tell you when the right time to do that is."

"I know. I don't want him to feel as shocked as I did when I heard that Vanessa was parading Cody around town telling everyone I was the father." He pulled open the large sliding door, the outside light a sharp brightness compared to the gloom of the barn. "I tell you, much as I love that little guy, I am thankful he's Ben's child." He gave her a warm smile, touching her cheek. "Starting a relationship with the responsibility of a child is a heavy, difficult thing to deal with."

Chloe blinked in the bright sunlight, cold blooming in her chest, spreading to her hands, her head, her feet.

Her first response was flight. Run. Get away from the words that chilled her soul.

The responsibility of a child. Heavy, difficult thing to deal with.

His words wound around her heart like an icy fist.

Good thing you didn't tell him about the baby.

She hurried ahead on the ice, her feet slipping in her rush, but thankfully she didn't fall.

"Chloe? What's wrong?" Grady called out behind her.

But she kept going, the house ahead of her. Sanctuary.

"Chloe," Grady called again.

Then she heard a clatter as his crutch fell, a muffled thump and Grady's cry of pain.

She spun around in time to see Grady sprawled out on the ground, his one leg at an awkward angle.

"No, oh, no," she cried, hurrying to his side, hoping, praying that he hadn't done more damage to his injured leg.

She dropped to her knees beside him as Grady scrambled, trying to regain his footing.

"Here. Let me help," she said, fitting her shoulder under his armpit as she had been taught.

Grady groaned and Chloe felt another flicker of regret. But even as she helped him to his feet, she knew that as soon as she could, she would retreat to her room. For now, however, she was Grady's physical therapist and she had to help him get back up.

"You okay to stand?" she asked as they managed to get up.

He simply nodded and she got his crutch and handed it to him. He didn't look at her as he stumbled toward the house. He was probably in pain, but she also knew Grady well enough that he would never admit it. Especially not to her.

However, she was in pain as well, and every moment walking alongside him created her own agony.

With each hesitant step his words reverberated through her mind. *Heavy thing. Heavy thing.*

Too heavy for him, it seemed.

They got to the house, and as soon as they were inside Chloe made her escape, mumbling some excuse to find Cody, even though Mamie told them he was sleeping.

Chloe said no to coffee, the thought of sitting down

with Grady and Mamie and acting as if all was well unbearable. She hurried upstairs, her feet unable to move fast enough.

Difficult thing to deal with...responsibility of a child...heavy...difficult. At least she had kept her secret to herself.

She dropped into the rocking chair in the nursery and lay her head back, ignoring the moisture trickling down her cheeks. Now what was she supposed to do? If Grady had a hard enough time thinking about taking on Cody, whom, for a moment, everyone thought was his, how could she expect him to take on another man's child?

A man who was less than honorable. A man who had easily renounced any claim to his own biological child, then disappeared.

She closed her eyes, rocking, praying in snatches, sending out ragged petitions consisting of only two words. *Help. Me.*

Cody stirred in the crib and she got up to check on him, but he dropped back into the deep, innocent sleep of a baby, his lashes resting on his chubby cheeks, one dimpled hand beside his head.

Chloe stood over his crib a moment, her hand splayed over her own stomach as if protecting the child who grew within.

"Guess it's just you and me," she whispered, her sorrow threatening to choke her as she returned to the chair and her rocking.

And now what? How could she continue to work with Grady knowing how he felt? Knowing that if he found out about her baby he would surely reject her to her face?

She couldn't bear that.

But how could she leave Cody? The poor child had already been through so much. Another change would be detrimental.

And where would she go if she left? She had no job, no home. She pressed her hands to her stomach, her mind churning as she tried to think of where in this cold, unfriendly world she was supposed to find sanctuary for herself and her baby.

She closed her eyes and as she rocked, her prayers were sent up.

Help me to trust, Lord, that You will bring me where I should be. Help me to love this child and to love You. To put my life in Your hands.

And help me not to cry the next time I see Grady.

Chapter Thirteen

"Are you feeling okay?" Mamie asked Grady as he straggled into the kitchen the next morning. "I saved some breakfast for you." She glanced at the clock, an old habit of hers when the boys had had an especially late night. Her quiet reprimand.

Grady knew exactly what time it was. It had surprised him as well when he'd looked at the clock this morning. Nine. Meant he had lost half the morning already.

"I'm fine. I'm tired," he said.

Exhausted would be a better word. He hadn't fallen asleep until about four this morning, his mind going over and over what happened yesterday.

After he had fallen on the ice, Chloe had found all kinds of reasons to avoid him the rest of the day, telling Mamie, not him, that she wasn't feeling well.

He knew she was fine. Or had been fine as they talked in the barn, edging toward vague plans, hesitantly delineating the parameters of their relationship.

He'd thought they had been getting somewhere.

And then he'd fallen.

She'd seen him helpless before. It was this helplessness he wanted to hide from her, hence his reluctance to do physical therapy with her. But he had given in and she'd helped him, seen him at his weakest.

But then, with startling clarity, he realized she had never seen him fall before. Had never seen him sprawled on the ground like some landed fish flopping around. He tried to dismiss the picture, but he couldn't lose the idea that Chloe had backed away from him because of it.

His mother hadn't been able to deal with his father's disability. Had seeing him on the ground reminded Chloe exactly how weak he truly was?

Part of him didn't want to believe that of her, but it was the only explanation for her sudden retreat.

"Did Chloe say what she was doing today?"

Mamie shot him a sharp look, as if he should know this himself.

"She said she was taking Cody out for a walk with his little sleigh down the south ridge now that the weather has cleared. Are the boys coming back today?"

"Last night I called Lucas and Emilio and sent a text to Josh, and so far they're all able to come. I think the girls should wait a day or two yet." He rubbed his forehead, thinking of all the work that needed to be done now that things were getting back to normal. "Is Martha Rose coming back?"

"I hope so. If the boys are back, they'll need meals made, and I don't have the energy or time." She sighed lightly and Grady shot her a look of concern. His grandmother had always seemed indestructible, but he'd noticed she wasn't as spry as she once was. One more concern on his mind.

As he put on his coat to leave for the barn, he heard

footsteps coming down the stairs and his heart jumped as he heard Chloe talking to Mamie. "Just thought I would let you know I'm taking Cody out now."

His grandmother's reply was an indistinct murmur. Grady quickly buttoned up his coat, then realized to his dismay that he had left his crutch leaning against the counter in the kitchen. He knew he couldn't navigate the still slippery yard without it, but he didn't want to go back to get it and face Chloe.

He was about to leave anyway when he heard footsteps again. And there was Chloe, holding his crutch out to him, a stark reminder if ever there was one. "You forgot this," she said not meeting his eyes, her voice cool.

He took it, questions burning in his chest, pride keeping them unvoiced.

"And I won't be able to do therapy with you this afternoon," she said, her hands folded primly in front of her, a protective gesture.

"That works out good," he replied. "I'll be busy all day." Yesterday he had been looking forward to another therapy session with her. To pushing himself again, to showing her what he was willing to try.

But not now. Not with her expression so cool and reserved.

With a murmured thanks he made his way past her, resisting the urge to look back. He didn't want to know if she was watching him, but he acted as if she was, taking his time, taking cautious steps. As he walked, his mind ticked back to a comment she had made that he had overheard. ...*couldn't give him what she needed and what woman can live like that?*

And as an icy claw gripped his chest, he paused, unable to walk for a moment.

So that was what this was all about. Her retreat. Her silence. She realized she couldn't live like *that*. Just like his mother couldn't. Like Etta Vane couldn't.

He finally got to the barn, thankfully without falling or even slipping, and once inside he leaned against the door, his emotions a swirl of confusion, anger and sorrow at the injury that had incapacitated him. The disability that had made him less of a man. Just like his father.

"Boss? Is that you?"

Josh poked his head out of Sweetpea's stall.

"Yeah. I'm here. You're here early."

"Just wanted to make sure everything was okay. What with you laid up and all."

"I'm hardly laid up," Grady snapped, feeling overly testy, and then immediately feeling bad when he saw the surprise on his hired hand's face. "Sorry, Josh. Didn't sleep well last night, so I'm a bit short this morning."

"At six foot some, no one could call you short," Josh said with a laugh, in one comment acknowledging and dismissing Grady's apology. "So I figured we need to get those cows fed and see how the horses are," Josh said. "I should also check those cameras."

"I doubt the thieves were out and about during the storm," Grady said.

"Yeah, but it wouldn't hurt to make sure they're all still working."

"Have you heard about any more thefts?"

Josh shook his head. "Nope. But then, like you said, with the storm and all maybe the thieves decided not to risk anything the past few days. What else is on the list for today?"

"The Massey tractor needs some work on the bale

forks before you feed, and the John Deere needs an oil change. I was hoping to get it done this week, but didn't feel like tackling it on my own."

"Are we getting muffins again this morning?" Josh asked with a hopeful gleam in his eye.

"Unless Martha Rose makes it back here, I doubt it."

"Chloe's busy?"

"Yeah." And that was all he was saying about that.

Chloe trudged over the snow, pulling Cody behind her on the sled. His happy squeals were the perfect antidote for the knot that tightened with each minute she was apart from Grady.

The sun was shining, promising hope, but Chloe couldn't find it to latch on to it. Hope seemed as far away as summer did right now. She shivered and looked back at Cody all bundled up, his stocking cap sitting crooked over his face, obscuring one eye. But he was waving his arms, laughing at everything he saw.

"You are so adorable," she said, feeling a motherly burst of affection for him. He laughed at her as if he agreed, then suddenly leaned over in the sled, looking past her.

Chloe couldn't stop the lift of her heart at the thought that it might be Grady, but when she turned it was only Emilio walking toward her, carrying a large envelope. Even though the air was still cold enough to turn his breath into vapor, he wore his coat open, and only a shabby straw cowboy hat on his head.

"Hey, Chloe. Grady told me I might find you out here," he said as he came near.

Chloe's heart jumped just a bit thinking Grady had

been watching her, then she realized that Mamie must have told him.

"I was just taking Cody out on his sleigh. It's so nice."

"So glad the weather turned decent. I was getting worried about you guys stuck out here, and Grady and all, but I'm sure you managed just fine." He gave her a gap-toothed grin, as if sharing some inside joke, then knelt to tickle Cody under the chin with one large, grease-streaked finger. "Hey, little guy. You having fun with Chloe here? You making sure she and Grady behave themselves?"

His innocent words, assuming a relationship between her and Grady, hit her like hammer blows.

It won't happen, she thought, despair tugging at her.

She couldn't give in, however. She had to think of her baby and what was best for him or her.

"I got something for you," Emilio said, straightening and handing her the large envelope. "Grady asked me to pick up the mail while I was coming through town and this came for you. Whoever it was knows you're staying here, I guess."

Chloe frowned as she took the large, heavy envelope with her name scrawled across the front. The only attempt at an address was "Chlo at Stillwater Ranch," and there was no return address anywhere on the envelope. Her name was misspelled, so whoever had sent it didn't know her well.

"Looks mysterious," Emilio said with a wink.

"It certainly does," Chloe agreed. "Thanks for getting it for me."

"No problem. You coming to see Grady? He and Josh are working on the tractor. I'm sure he won't mind if you stop by." His assumption of a relationship was like another hook in her heart.

"I should bring Cody back to the house and find out what's in here," she said with a forced smile, holding the envelope aloft.

"Are you bringing muffins later?"

"No. I'm...busy. I promised Mamie I would help...help her...with her knitting." Chloe floundered around, scrambling for any kind of excuse.

"Well, I'll tell Grady you said hey."

"That's not necessary," Chloe said with a dismissive wave of her hand.

Emilio looked puzzled, then shrugged. "Sure. Well, see you around." He waggled his fingers at Cody, then sauntered off, hands jammed in the pocket of his jacket, whistling as he walked.

She had to leave, Chloe thought as she turned and trudged back to the house. It was as if every encounter was a stark reminder of what she could never have.

...starting a relationship with the responsibility of a child...heavy thing.

All night Grady's words had resonated through her mind, circling like ravens, pecking at her insecurities.

She was a divorced woman, carrying another man's child.

She was fairly sure a man of honor, a soldier such as Grady, would struggle with that idea, especially when she had told him the exact state of her marriage to Jeremy.

The house was quiet when she stepped inside. Mamie must be sleeping, and it didn't sound as if Martha Rose was here yet. So she took Cody upstairs, changed him and played with him until he started rubbing his ears and fussing. Then she laid him down, sang him to sleep and retreated to her room.

Once there she took out her Bible, needing comfort and spiritual nourishment. Needing the reminder of God's faithfulness.

Her hands turned to Lamentations, easily finding the passage in chapter three that she had drawn from so often.

"The steadfast love of the Lord never ceases; His mercies never come to an end; they are new every morning; great is Your faithfulness."

She had clung to these very promises of God's faithfulness through all the years she had been married to Jeremy, struggling to stay true to her vows when she knew her husband wasn't. The promise of God's faithfulness had helped her then, and she prayed it would help now. God's love was all encompassing and faithful and unending.

She closed her eyes, pressing the palms of her hands against her cheeks, trying not to let fear and despair take over, trying not to think of what she had lost with Grady. Instead, she tried to remind herself that God's love was sufficient for her.

"Please help me to hold on to that," she whispered, continuing her prayer, praying for her baby, for Ben, for the people of the community and finally for continued healing for Grady.

She knew he needed to continue his physical therapy sessions, but she also knew she couldn't work with him.

Not anymore.

She finished her prayers just as her phone rang. It was Lucy.

"Hey there," Chloe said, leaning back against the head of her bed, tucking her legs under her. "What's up?"

"Thankfully not much, what with the storm and all. No thefts and no gifts."

Which made Chloe suddenly remember the letter she had received. She had left it in Cody's room. "I got something this morning that seemed a little odd," she said, getting up and slipping into Cody's room, glad for the distraction from Grady and the sorrow clinging to her.

"What is it?"

"Just a minute," Chloe whispered, picking up the envelope and checking on the little boy. He lay with his head to one side, his chubby cheeks pink from the cold, his tiny hand curled up beside his head. Her heart wavered at the sight, then she quickly left, hurrying back to her own room.

"Are you still there?"

"Yeah. I just got the letter from Cody's room."

"Letter? Who from?"

"No return address and it was sent to me via the Stillwater ranch. Whoever sent it spelled my name wrong, so that could be a clue." Chloe sat cross-legged on her bed, phone tucked under her ear as she slit open the envelope. Another envelope, thick and heavy, fell out as she pulled a single piece of paper out.

"What's inside?"

"A letter…" Chloe scanned over the contents. "From Robin Hood, apparently. He's giving me a little something to help me with my dream of staring up a physical therapy clinic." Chloe frowned, read the letter again.

"Is it handwritten?"

"No. Typed. Not signed, obviously. Probably printed

on a computer…and now I've put my fingerprints all over it."

"Relax. This isn't *CSI: Little Horn*," Lucy said with a light chuckle. "I doubt I would be able to figure out whose prints they are if they're not in any criminal database. But I need to see it. What's in the envelope?" she asked, just as Chloe picked it up and carefully peeled it open.

A huge stack of one-hundred-dollar bills fell out. Chloe's mouth fell open as she stared at the cash now spilled on her bed.

"Money. Hundreds of dollars." She did a quick calculation, flicking through the bills. "Nearest I can tell it's close to about ten thousand dollars."

Adrenaline mixed with fear shot through her veins. How had this person known about her dream? How had he tracked her down here?

"This creeps me out," Chloe said, pushing the money away from her as if it might contaminate her.

"No kidding. But you know you can't keep the money."

"I don't even want it," Chloe said, staring at the pile of bills, her arms wrapped around her legs. "Who could have known about this?"

"Grady?"

"I doubt he would resort to this," Chloe said.

"I think you're right. But like I said, you have to give the money up. Carson has called an unexpected meeting of the cowboy league this Saturday. Grady will have to sit in as Ben's replacement. You could give the money to him to give to me then."

"Sure. I can do that." She could give it to Mamie, she

figured. Mamie could hand it over. She didn't want to face Grady. Not if she could avoid it.

"By the way, how is that handsome soldier?"

Lucy's innocent question created an ache in Chloe's heart.

"He's…he's…good."

"Good? Be still my heart. That's all you can say about the guy you've loved since grade school?"

Chloe drew in a slow breath, trying to stay on top of her scattered emotions. She didn't want this taking over her life. "I don't want to talk about him."

A beat of silence greeted that statement. "Since when? I know you're attracted to him. You two just spent three days all secluded from the outside world with only an older woman and a baby. Don't tell me that something didn't happen?"

"Something did." The comment burst out of her, the need to share what she was dealing with overcoming her natural reticence. So she told Lucy, "He kissed me. I kissed him."

"What? That's amazing. I'm so happy for you."

Her enthusiasm was like salt on the wound.

"So things are moving forward?" Lucy continued. "I know you've always liked him."

"I have. I do." She released a short laugh. "I've never cared for anyone the way I care for Grady. And I thought things were getting somewhere."

"Thought? What happened?"

Chloe cradled her stomach with her arm, as if assuring her baby of her love. "He made a comment about kids. How glad he was that Cody wasn't his. That he couldn't think about starting a relationship with the responsibility of a child."

"So why is that a problem?"

Chloe looked down at her stomach, and in spite of everything that had happened the past while, she felt a smile curve her lips. Life was growing inside her. A baby was developing. Flesh of her flesh.

She knew she could keep the secret no longer.

"I'm pregnant. That's the problem."

Another time Lucy's gasp would have created a surge of shame, but Chloe couldn't allow that to happen. She was this child's mother. Its first line of defense.

You and me against the world, she thought.

"Jeremy is the father," she continued.

"Oh, Chloe…"

"And once we got divorced, he ducked out. Haven't heard anything from him, and I don't know where he is. Part of me doesn't want him in my child's life, but the fact that he would abandon us like that makes me so furious."

"Oh, sweetie," Lucy murmured. "I wish you would have told me sooner."

"I was ashamed at first, and I wasn't sure exactly how to tell you."

"I wish I could come over."

"No. It's fine. You're busy enough with everything that's been going on."

Lucy's tired sigh underlined Chloe's assumption. "I am. It's taking over my life, and people are starting to ask for my badge. I just wish I could crack this thing."

"You will. You just need one good break."

"Is that a pun?"

Chloe chuckled. "Not intentional."

"Good to hear you laughing. As for Grady—"

"Like I said, I don't want to talk about him. He also

has a lot going on in his life. He doesn't need the complication of a pregnant woman."

"I know he cares for you," Lucy said. "You should tell him about the baby."

"I can't. I heard what he said, and I can't face any kind of rejection from him." The thought of his turning away from her thickened her throat.

"Are you leaving the ranch?"

"I can't yet. Cody has had too many disruptions in his little life."

"But if you and Grady—"

"I'll be fine," Chloe interrupted. "I just have to focus on my baby and do my job."

But even as she spoke those brave words, Chloe knew it would be much, much harder than that.

Chapter Fourteen

"Sorry I didn't come sooner." Grady settled himself in the chair beside his brother's bed, wincing as pain seized him, almost making him spill the cup of coffee he had bought for himself before coming up. Once again he felt sympathy for his father. How had he dealt with his pain day in and day out?

And, even harder, how had he faced their mother's rejection of him?

"It took me longer than usual to get here," Grady said. "Stubborn. Wanted to prove I could do this on my own, so I drove myself."

His leg still throbbed from being in one position so long. Thankfully his brother's truck had an automatic transmission. No clutch.

He had hoped to duck out without telling his grandmother he was going on his own, but she'd caught him before he left and handed him a thick, heavy envelope full of cash. Told him Chloe had received it and he had to give it over to the league. Thankfully she had said nothing about him driving to town.

But the envelope had bothered him. Chloe couldn't even be bothered to give it to him in person.

"We got stuck up at the ranch the past few days," he continued. "Freak snowstorm. Shut everything down."

He watched his brother closely, hoping, praying for even the slightest acknowledgment. The nurses had told him that Ben's eyes had opened again this morning, but now his brother lay perfectly still.

"Started doing some therapy, though I've skipped the past few days."

He had wondered how much good it would do. He could feel that he was stiffer today. But Chloe had been studiously avoiding him and hadn't said anything about therapy, and he wasn't about to ask, even though it was one of the reasons his grandmother had hired her.

"But the weather's turned, so that's good," he said to Ben as he shifted his position on the chair, trying to get comfortable. "Sun's shining and the snow is melting. It's a bluebird sky out there."

It was ironic that while storms blew around his house, he had felt more serene and at peace than he had at most any other time in his life.

Because of Chloe.

Now that the sun was shining in a tranquil blue sky, his heart felt tossed and beaten and battered.

Because of Chloe. Who couldn't even be bothered to give him that lousy envelope in person.

"There's supposed to be another storm front blowing in. At least according to the forecaster. I sure hope not. The yard is still a sheet of ice, and I'm worried about the horses." He paused to take a sip of coffee, surprised at how much easier it was to talk to his brother now. Especially sitting here alone with no one waiting or hovering. Just him and Ben.

And because he was alone, he felt he had the space to tell his brother the things weighing like a rock on his mind since their last meeting. "I don't want to just talk about the weather," he said, looking down at his coffee cup, pulling together his apology. "I want to say again how sorry I am over how I left things between us before I left for this last tour. I'm sorry I was angry with you. You had a lot to deal with after I left. I had no right to be so self-righteous. I left you behind to deal with Dad and the ranch. I thought I was being all brave and heroic and honorable, but you were the brave and honorable one. You were the one who kept things going. I left you to do it alone and then judged how you did it. You're still my brother and I love you."

He stopped there, as if to let his confession settle somewhere in Ben's mind.

A cart pushed by a lab tech clattered past. Nurses at the station laughed at something.

Life flowed on regardless of the macro and micro tragedies of the world.

"I know that you're the easygoing one and I'm the worrier, so I should tell you that, as usual, I'm worried again. My leg doesn't seem to be getting any better and it hurts. A lot. Made me think of Dad and how hard it was to live with him."

Grady set his coffee aside, leaned forward in his chair. On a whim he took Ben's hand in his, surprised at how warm it felt. Still a horseman's hands with scars and rope burns and calluses.

"Remember how angry he got that time we took his truck out on the hayfield with some friends, burning doughnuts and acting like idiots? Fourteen years old and we had the world by the tail. Good thing Mom intervened or we would have been in worse trouble." He laughed lightly at the memory.

"I miss her, though I still get ticked at her for leaving Dad. I know he wasn't the easiest to live with, but I'm finally getting how hard it was for him. It's hard not to feel like less of a man when you can't do what you used to."

He stopped there, his own emotions suddenly in flux as he thought of Chloe. He felt his heart shift, shook his head and carried on.

"A couple of days ago I fell. It was bad enough to be sprawled out on the ice looking like some spavined mule, but it had to happen in front of Chloe. Yeah, the same Chloe who came here the last time. She's at the ranch now taking care of Cody and supposedly doing therapy with me, though she hasn't the past few days."

He stopped again, frustrated at how close his emotions were to the surface.

"I think she's given up because she saw what a hopeless case I am. Like Mom, after spending enough time with me she must realize I'm not getting better. That I'm this crippled man who has little to offer someone as wonderful as her." To his dismay, his voice broke.

"Listen to me," he said, adding a short laugh. "I've seen so much pain and sorrow overseas and here I am feeling sorry for myself over the loss of a woman. Trouble is this isn't just any woman. This is Chloe. Now, I know I've never been as good with girls as you have, so it might sound kind of pathetic to you, but I don't know what to do. I don't want to end up like Dad. I don't want her to be disappointed in me. I feel as if I've had something special, and now I don't know what happened to it."

He stopped there, feeling as if he had said too much. Opened himself too wide. Made himself too vulnerable.

Then he caught himself. What did it matter?

He bent his head, feeling as though he had hit the bottom.

And he knew what he had to do.

He held Ben's hand between his, bent his head and closed his eyes.

"I know I'm proud, Lord. I know that too often I want to do things on my own. But I'm facing big things that I can't fix. I can't push through with my will or my strength. You'd think I would have learned that overseas. I care for Chloe and I want what's best for her, but I can't make her love me. Take care of her. Watch over her. Be with my brother, as well."

He said amen, and stayed with his head bent a moment.

Then Ben's hand twitched in his. A slight movement, but a movement nonetheless.

He squeezed Ben's hand back and his heart dropped when Ben's hand moved again. Grady's eyes flew to Ben's face and to his amazement he saw Ben's eyelids drift upward. It was agonizing to watch. His lids fell shut again, but then once more, they slowly lifted. Ben blinked, then again and his head turned toward Grady. His hand twitched in Grady's again, then his fingers tightened for the briefest of moments.

Was that a smile?

Grady felt his heart quicken.

"Ben. Can you hear me? Squeeze my hand if you can hear me."

Ben's hand tightened briefly, then fell limp in his and his eyes closed again, and once again he lay still and unmoving.

Grady stood, watching, waiting for a few more minutes, but there was no more movement on Ben's part.

His heart filled with a mixture of expectation and disappointment.

What did he expect, that Ben would sit up and start talking?

Grady knew better than that, but even so it was a start. A tiny ray of blessing on a week that had been darkness and loneliness.

Fifteen minutes later he was on his way to a hastily called meeting of the Lone Star Cowboy League, his heart feeling just a bit lighter. As Ben's brother and a Stillwater, Grady had been elected to take his brother's place.

A number of vehicles were parked in front of the league building when he arrived. It looked as if most everyone was inside. With a grimace, Grady got out of the truck, pulled the hated crutch from behind the seat, locked his truck and hobbled up the snow-covered path to the door. Inside, he was greeted by the sound of angry voices, one of them Byron's.

Grady wasn't looking forward to this meeting. Though he had been back for a while now, he hadn't had much to do with the community as a whole, other than attending church on Sunday. The questions surrounding Cody's parenthood still seemed to cling to him, even though almost everyone should have known by now that the allegations were false. Vanessa was long gone and her accusations with her.

Nonetheless he took a deep breath, sent up a prayer for patience and walked into the building.

"Well, hello, Grady." Ingrid Edwards, the secretary of the league, sat at the desk by the entrance to the boardroom, her red hair hanging loose around her face. She pushed her glasses up her nose and got up, her hand out as if to help him. "I'm glad you're taking Ben's place."

"I hope I'm up to it," he said, taking a step away from her.

"So sad what happened to him." Ingrid gave him a shy smile. "And I was sorry to hear about your injury, too. That must have been so hard for you! Do you need a hand? I can hold your crutch while you take your coat off."

"I'm fine," Grady said, a little more gruffly than he should have. Ingrid meant well; she just wasn't the most tactful person.

It was just that her view of him seemed to underline how he felt about himself. And how he was sure Chloe saw him.

Carson was standing in one corner of the room chatting with Lucy, who wore blue jeans and a faded denim shirt today, giving her a more approachable look than her uniform did. But this was negated by the frown beneath her blond fringe of hair.

Byron sat at the table, bent over some papers, glowering at whatever it was he was reading.

Carson looked up as Grady came in.

Was he imagining the look of pity on his face?

Grady knew he was being oversensitive.

"Well, the war hero is here," Byron said, getting

up. "Mighty proud of you, son. You are a credit to our community."

Grady grew uncomfortable with the man's obvious bluster, and his discomfort only increased when Byron pulled a chair out for him.

"Here. Let me help you."

Why did everyone seem to think he was so helpless?

Maybe because he was, he thought, remembering his ungainly fall the other day.

"I can manage," Grady said, shaking off Byron's hand on his arm.

Then Lucy saw him and waved him over. "Grady. I need to talk to you."

"Excuse me," Grady said to Byron, who was frowning at him, obviously displeased that Grady had refused his help. But Grady wasn't about to try to soothe the man's ruffled feathers.

He made his way around the chairs to where Lucy stood, suspecting she wanted to discuss the thick envelope Chloe had left on the counter for him to pass on to Lucy. She was still avoiding him, and his grandmother was still trying to find out what had happened, but Grady didn't want to talk about it.

"Grady, good to see you here," Carson said, holding out his hand in greeting. "Though the reason you are here is less than ideal. How is Ben?"

Grady shook Carson's hand then shrugged. "Actually, there is some small improvement. Very small, but the doctor assured me he is moving in the right direction."

"We'll continue to pray for him," Carson said, giving Grady a tight smile. Then he turned back to Lucy.

"I need to talk to Ingrid before we get started. Will you excuse me, please?"

Lucy nodded, waiting until Carson was out of earshot. She moved to the far corner of the room, turning so that her back was to the room. "Do you have the envelope?"

"Locked in my truck."

"Good. I'll have to present this to the meeting. Are you okay with that?"

"Yes. Why wouldn't I be?"

"It's just that the money came to Chloe while she was on your ranch. And Maddy, who also works at the Stillwater ranch, got some gifts, as well. Add that to the fact that you still haven't noticed anything missing…" She let the sentence hang as if expecting Grady to finish it.

He pushed down his anger at her unspoken suspicions, knowing she was simply doing her job. "I have no idea why we haven't been hit and people on our ranch have been getting things," he said. "Unless you suspect someone on the ranch."

Lucy blew out her breath, shooting another glance backward as if checking to see who might be listening in, but Byron had left the room as well, leaving the two of them alone.

"I don't suspect any of your employees, but you have to admit, it does seem odd that you haven't had anything stolen. I feel as if there's a connection, but I can't figure it out yet." She was silent, but Grady didn't add anything to her suspicions. He knew Josh, Emilio and Lucas couldn't possibly have anything to do with what had been going on. He trusted those men implicitly. As for the girls, he knew beyond a doubt they weren't involved.

"And how was your visit with Ben?" she asked.

"Like I said, very positive. I'm tempted to tell him a couple of lies, hoping he will try to wake up to set me straight."

Lucy gave him a sympathetic look. "But it's a good sign."

Grady nodded. "A very good sign."

"Chloe seems optimistic about your recovery, as well," Lucy said.

Even hearing her name hurt.

"We're not talking about...that."

Lucy bit her lip, looking back over her shoulder again at the empty room. She took a few steps closer and lowered her voice.

"So what happened with you and Chloe? I thought you two were getting somewhere?"

Grady pulled back, frowning at Lucy.

"Oh, don't get all 'mind your own business' on me," Lucy chided. "I talk to Chloe all the time. One minute she's all sappy and moony, the next she's weepy and miserable. What did you do to her?"

Grady could only stare. What was she talking about? Chloe miserable?

"What did *I* do to her?" He released a bitter snort. "She was the one who pulled away. Who cancelled my therapy sessions because she couldn't stand to be near me. Because she couldn't face the idea of maybe ending up with a man who wouldn't be able to do all the things he used to. Just like my mother couldn't." He didn't mean for that last comment to come out. He blamed it on his minitherapy session with his brother.

Lucy narrowed her eyes, watching him as if she

couldn't understand what he was saying. "How do you figure that?"

Grady ground his teeth together, determined not to let Lucy and what she was talking about get to him.

"What makes you say that?" Lucy pressed. "She didn't say anything about your leg or disability. Just that she didn't think you would want to be with her because of her—" Lucy stopped there, holding up her hand, waving it as if to erase what she had just said.

"Because of her what?"

"Never mind. Talking too much. Blame it on being in civvies," she said, easing out a sigh.

"If this has something to do with what is happening between me and Chloe, you need to tell me."

"It's not my secret to tell," Lucy said, folding her arms over her chest, her feet planted slightly apart. Holding her ground.

"Secret?"

"You need to ask Chloe. Not me," Lucy said.

"But she's not talking to me." Grady clenched his fist, struggling to maintain his composure.

"Find a way. You're not the only one with pride, you know."

Grady couldn't help it. Hope fluttered deep in his soul, a fragile thing he hardly dared acknowledge but didn't want to ignore.

"Talk to her," Lucy said, adding a meaningful look. "Don't let her get away from you."

Grady held her gaze a moment, sensing that there had been more to the situation than his interpretation, and the flutter of hope grew. Just a bit.

"So why are we having this meeting, or are you two just going to sit in the corner sharing secrets?" Byron

McKay called out, his loud voice breaking the silence that followed Lucy's comment. "Maybe you'd like to bring the rest of us into the loop. Tell us if you've solved any of the crimes. Maybe get that stolen Welcome to Little Horn sign back."

Lucy spun around, straightening her shoulders as if readying herself to face down Byron. "No secrets to share, Byron," she said as Carson, Tom Horn, Ingrid Edwards and other members of the Lone Star Cowboy League filed into the room. "As for the Welcome to Little Horn sign, I am looking into getting a new one made."

"Let's get going," Byron called out, looking around as people settled into their seats. "Guess we'll have to find out just how incompetent our sheriff has been over the past week."

"That's out of order," Grady said.

Bryon rounded on him and Grady stared him down. Then Byron gave him what, for Byron, seemed to pass for an apologetic smile. "Right. Sorry."

Grady felt a small victory, but as he settled into the chair he had a hard time concentrating on the meeting. Over and over he thought of what Lucy had told him. Her truncated sentence about Chloe that raised more questions.

Because of her *what*?

He knew one thing: as soon as he got back to the ranch he was going to find out.

"What are your plans for this afternoon?" Mamie asked Chloe as she packaged up some cookies. "I was hoping to take these to Iva Donovan. See how she's doing."

"I thought I would take Cody out for a walk." Chloe finished giving him the last of his lunch and wiped the baby's mouth with a cloth. Cody tried to push away her hand, and in spite of the heaviness weighing on her heart she had to smile. "He's been cooped up quite a bit, and now that the sun is shining I'd like to get out, as well."

This way she would be out of the house when Grady came back from his meeting with the league. She knew she couldn't avoid him forever and would have to resume his physical therapy sessions soon, but she needed a few days to settle herself in this hard place.

Chloe wiped Cody's hands and got up to bring his bowl to the sink. She returned to the high chair and unbuckled his harness, then picked him up. After she settled him on her hip, she cuddled him close, pressing a kiss to his head. Tears pricked her eyelids. The past few days it was as if her pregnancy was making her feel even more maternal and fragile.

"Honey, is everything okay?"

Mamie's quiet voice and gentle hand on her shoulder didn't help Chloe's precarious emotions.

She swallowed the knot in her throat and struggled to regain her composure.

"Yes, everything is fine."

But her assertion didn't come out as strongly as she had hoped, and her voice trembled on the last word.

"I don't think it is at all," Mamie said, slipping her arm around Chloe's waist and steering her gently toward the living room. "In fact, I think we need to talk."

Her words created an ominous feeling inside. Did Mamie know about her pregnancy? Was she about to get fired for misleading her? Where would she go now? What would she do?

Just wait. Don't borrow trouble.

Chloe pulled in a long, slow breath and sat down, holding Cody a little tighter than necessary. He wiggled as though he wanted to leave, so she set him on the floor.

"He just keeps getting bigger and bigger," Mamie said as she sat down on the couch beside Chloe. They watched him crawl away, then sit up, smiling proudly at his achievement.

Then Mamie turned to Chloe, took her hand.

Chloe swallowed, and swallowed again, trying to stifle the fear clawing up her throat.

"I promised myself I would never be a meddling grandma," Mamie said, giving Chloe's hand a gentle squeeze. "But I'm going to now. I noticed that you and Grady seemed to enjoy each other's company. I thought you were attracted to him and vice versa. In fact, I was kind of thinking the way things were going that you and him were building a relationship. But now..." She shrugged, waited as if hoping Chloe would fill in the blanks, but Chloe, not trusting herself to speak, said nothing.

"I know that working here isn't the same as working in the hospital," Mamie said with a sense of finality. "And I think you know that I asked you to come for a bunch of reasons and not just because I needed help with Cody. I could have asked any number of people to help me. And yes, I was hoping you would be able to convince Grady that he needed to do therapy, but I'm sure I could have done that myself."

Mamie gave her a rueful smile. "I may as well tell

the truth. I was hoping that you and Grady would get together. I know you used to like him in high school, and I'm positive he had a thing for you until that Vanessa girl got her claws in him." This was followed by another long-suffering sigh. "And then, for a while, it seemed that you two found each other. That you were, well, falling in love. But now you two can't even spend time together in the same room. So I'm coming right out and asking…what happened?"

Chloe looked down at their joined hands, so close to the growing swell of her stomach. Talking about Grady still hurt too much. She didn't trust herself to be objective. Not to cry.

If she told Mamie about the baby, which would be hard enough, she might be distracted enough not to ask her any more painful questions about Grady.

Sending up a prayer for strength, she took a breath and held Mamie's questioning gaze.

"I'm pregnant."

"I know."

Chloe could only stare. Mamie's blunt response was not what she had expected at all.

"How did you know?" she asked when the shock wore off.

Mamie shrugged. "I didn't know for sure. I just guessed, but I guess I know for sure now." She gave Chloe's hand a comforting squeeze. "Don't worry. I haven't told anyone. And it doesn't matter. I'm thinking that your ex-husband is the father?"

"Jeremy. Yes. I got pregnant and he didn't want a baby. Didn't take him long to get rid of me thanks to his close friendship with a judge."

"It's okay, sweetie. You don't have to explain."

"But I feel as if I do. I took this job under false pretenses."

"I'm thinking Grady doesn't know?"

Chloe shook her head, the last words that he'd spoken to her still ringing in her mind.

"Why haven't you told him? I know you care for him."

Chloe heard the faint reprimand in Mamie's voice and tried not to feel defensive. "I was afraid. Everything happened so quickly and it was so wonderful." She looked up at Grady's grandmother, praying she would understand. "You are right when you say I've cared for Grady a long time. We were on our way to building a relationship and everything was working out so well. I was so happy."

"What happened?"

Chloe bit her lip, casting through her mind for the right words.

"We were talking about Cody and he said that he was thankful that Cody wasn't his because he didn't…didn't want to start a relationship with the responsibility of a child. He said that was heavy stuff. And at that moment I knew I couldn't tell him about my baby."

Mamie's silence underlined Chloe's insecurities.

"He kept telling me how much he appreciated my honesty and innocence," she continued. "And here I am, not only divorced, but pregnant by the man I just divorced. It just makes me feel…unworthy."

"Oh, child, never think that," Mamie hastily said, giving Chloe a hug. Then she framed Chloe's face with her hands, shaking her head as if in disbelief. "You are indeed a pure and innocent person. You were trying to stay true to your vows, and that is already beyond admirable. That you got pregnant doing so was not your fault."

"Thank you for that," Chloe said, catching Mamie by the wrists, smiling at her. "But it doesn't negate the fact that Grady doesn't think he can take on a child."

"You don't know that for sure. You don't know exactly what he was referring to. What he meant. I still think you should tell him."

"For what purpose? I doubt he will change how he feels about taking on the responsibility."

Mamie said nothing to that, which only underlined what Chloe knew she had to do.

"I know you hired me to work with Grady, but I don't know if I can do that anymore." Chloe bit her lip, looking over at Cody, who was gumming on a small teddy bear, looking up at them, his eyes sparkling. Her heart lurched in her chest. "I don't want to do this to Cody, and if you want, I will stay to take care of him—"

"Honey, don't make any decisions right away," Mamie said. "You have a home here as long as you need it."

"I also have a furnished apartment in town," Chloe said with a forced laugh.

"That's not a home."

Chloe agreed, but she couldn't see that she had any choice.

"You know you can stay here as long as you need to," Mamie said.

"Thank you," Chloe said.

"And I think you should talk to Grady. You need to tell him about your baby and let him decide how he feels about it."

"But he said—"

"I know what he said, but that was about Cody. For all you know, he might have felt guilty because he thought he couldn't take care of him given his injury." Mamie was quiet a moment. "I don't know if you know the full history of Grady and his parents."

"All I know is that his parents got divorced when Grady was in junior high."

"Did you know why?"

"I was young then. I can't remember." Plus she'd had had her own drama going on in her home. That had been about the time Etta and Vanessa had come into Chloe's life.

Mamie pulled in a slow breath. "I think what happened with my son and his wife has had an impact on both boys, and not for the better. My son, Reuben, had an accident a couple of years before the divorce. He was feeding cows and a bale fell on him and injured his back. After that he was in constant pain and couldn't do as much as he used to. He wasn't the easiest man to live with before, and he became much more difficult after that. Shirley couldn't handle living with him. Two years after the accident, she left him.

"Grady was angry and humiliated, and as soon as he could, he joined the army. I always thought he figured it was a way of redeeming the family name. Grady and his father were always close, and after he left, Reuben became even more bitter. While Grady could always get along with him, Ben couldn't. Which caused problems in Ben's life." Mamie was silent a moment. Then she gave Chloe a gentle smile. "I may be wrong, but when Grady got injured I wonder if, on some level, he didn't think a woman would want him the way he was.

His mother couldn't live with an injured man. Maybe no woman could live with him."

Chloe let Mamie's words roll over in her mind as she examined them. She thought of how he initially had resisted her help. She knew he was proud and stubborn; what Mamie had told her gave another layer to his personality.

Then she felt a movement in her abdomen and she felt herself drawn back to another reality. Her own situation. And what she brought to any relationship she and Grady might have.

Another man's child. Could he handle that?

She wasn't sure she wanted to find out. She wasn't sure she could face rejection again.

"You and Grady were meant to be together," Mamie said, squeezing Chloe's hand. "I've prayed so often that Grady would find someone. When you came into his life, I thought those prayers were answered. I don't like to think God was toying with me."

Chloe wasn't sure what to say to that. She knew that relationships were difficult.

"You think about what I said," Mamie urged. "Don't give up on Grady yet. He's a good man, and in spite of what you may think, you're a good woman. Grady is a proud person, but part of me thinks that maybe you have your share of pride, as well."

Chloe felt taken aback by her comment, then, as she thought about it, she understood what Mamie was saying. "I might. It hasn't been easy for me, either, knowing that my father couldn't seem to keep his ranch together. And then me getting a divorce and losing my job." She sighed, trying not to let the despair that hung over her like a cloud darken her perspective. "Maybe I tried to protect myself, as well."

"Of course you have," Mamie said, giving her hands a gentle shake. "But these events are not what define you. These are things that happened to you. These things are not you. You have much to give my grandson. I want you to think about that, as well. And I want you to know that you can trust him with your heart and with that baby you're carrying."

Chloe gave her a half smile. "Thanks for the encouragement." She gave into an impulse and brushed a light kiss over Mamie's cheek. "Thank you for everything."

She got up, picked up Cody and brought him to the porch to get him ready. She needed to get outside and get some fresh air.

Then she needed to figure out what her next step was.

Chapter Fifteen

Grady got out of Ben's truck, then ducked his head against the snow that had started up again just as he'd pulled into the yard. The meeting had dragged on far longer than it had needed to. After what Lucy had hinted at, he'd wanted to leave right away and return to the ranch to talk to Chloe.

But Byron had kept saying how Lucy was dragging her heels and had grilled Grady on the background of the people working at Stillwater Ranch. He had dropped many a broad hint about the lack of thefts from their ranch. Grady had had a hard time not losing his patience. It was only because Lucy had voiced the same concerns that he'd given Byron the information he had. But it bothered him that people were suspecting employees he had known for so many years. People his brother trusted implicitly.

Then the money had brought out another round of protests from Lenora Woods, who'd seemed to think that if anyone needed help it was her, not some single girl who could take care of herself. Byron kept calling for Lucy's resignation. It was tiring and Grady had forgotten what a blowhard Byron could be.

Carson had managed to rein Byron in and they'd finally gotten through the agenda. But throughout the meeting Grady had kept thinking about what Lucy had said.

He made his way into the house, torn between hurrying and making sure he didn't fall again. His leg was getting sore again, but he didn't want to dwell on that. He needed to find Chloe. To figure out what Lucy was talking about.

Don't let her get away from you.

You're not the only one with pride.

Lucy's words had spun around his head all the way home. The smile she'd given him had ignited a tiny spark of hope.

Once inside he shucked his coat, inhaling the scent of cookies, his growling stomach reminding him he hadn't eaten anything since breakfast. He followed his nose to the kitchen, hoping that Chloe would be there. As he wolfed down a couple of cookies, he listened. But the house was silent.

He heard a vehicle pull up and he hurried to the door just as his grandmother came inside.

"Do you know where Chloe and Cody are?" Grady asked.

His grandmother shook her head as she unwound a thick scarf from around her neck, stamping off the snow from her boots. "No. I've been gone for an hour or so. She said she was taking Cody for a walk. She left the same time I did. She isn't back yet?" Mamie's voice took on an edge that added to Grady's concern.

"No. She's not." Grady pulled back, analyzing. Breaking things down. "I'll go check at the barns. She might be there."

He slipped his coat back on, dropped his hat on his head and grabbed his gloves.

"Do you want me to come?" his grandmother asked, worry lacing her voice.

"No. I'm sure it's fine," Grady said, not wanting to add to her concern. *One step at a time*, he told himself. *First plan A. Check the barn.*

He tugged on his gloves, wrapping a scarf around his neck to cut the wind that he heard picking up.

He walked carefully across the yard to the barn, ducking his head against the icy wind. As the snow hit his cheeks he hoped they weren't in for another storm.

But all was quiet in the barn. Just to make sure, he hurried down the alley. Sweetpea whinnied at him as he went past. Babe and Shiloh just watched him go.

Grady's heart turned in his chest. Chloe and Cody weren't here. They weren't in the house. Then, where would they have gone for so long? He tried to call her on her cell phone but didn't receive an answer. He guessed she was in a place with poor reception or her battery was dead. Either way, he had no idea where she could be.

He tried to settle his growing concern. Think. Analyze.

He remembered his grandmother saying the last time Chloe had taken Cody out it was for a ride in his sled toward the south ridge. But how far had they gone? He didn't dare walk on this ice.

No one was around to help and his grandmother couldn't do anything. He had to go find her, but how?

He'd have to saddle up one of the horses.

He found a halter and headed out into the pasture. Thankfully the horses had just been fed and were standing around the hay bale that one of the hands had given them. It took some awkward maneuvering, but he finally caught Apollo, one of the quieter horses, and led him back to the barn where the tack room was located. Once inside, he faced another obstacle trying to saddle up the horse on his own. He hadn't done it since he'd been back and he knew he was wasting valuable time trying to manage. So he swallowed his pride and hurried to the house as quickly as he dared.

His leg was aching by the time he got back to the house.

"Grandma! I need your help," he called out, sticking his head in the door.

"I'm right here." She appeared immediately. "What do you need?"

"Help with the horse. I'm going out to find Chloe and Cody."

Mamie grabbed her coat and shoved her feet into her boots, then headed out.

But she was faster than he was and while he tried to keep up, he was afraid of falling and injuring himself. He would be no good to Chloe if he was flat on his back.

Mamie looked behind her then, came back, tucked her shoulder under his arm and helped him to the barn. Once again he had to fight down his innate sense of independence, thankful that it helped him move just a bit faster.

He and Mamie got Apollo saddled up in record time. He kept telling himself not to panic. Chloe had probably just gone farther than usual and once the wind started up, decided to head back. She wasn't reckless. She was careful.

She was alone.

"You haven't lost your touch," Grady said as he tightened up the cinch, making sure all was snug and secure.

"Like riding a bike." Mamie took the horse's bridle and started leading him away.

"Where are you going?" Grady asked, grabbing his crutch and stumbling along behind her.

"You can't climb up on that horse on your own," Grandma said, leading him to the box they had used when Grady and Ben were youngsters.

Grady almost balked, but he couldn't get all puffed up now. Too much was at stake.

So he took the steps one at a time, then climbed on the horse. Without a word Mamie carefully lifted his injured leg and slipped his foot into the stirrup, then she slipped the reins over Apollo's head and handed them to Grady.

"Ride safe," she said. "Please find them. I'll be praying for you."

"While you're praying, call Clint Daniels and Finn. We could use their expertise. And call Emilio and a couple of the other boys, as well."

She nodded as she walked ahead of him to the entrance of the barn. She opened the door and he rode out into the blowing snow.

Chloe trudged along the packed trail she had walked along down in the draw, pulling Cody on the sled, her mind weighing and measuring what Mamie had told her.

Part of her didn't dare cling to the hope Mamie's words had kindled. Her sense of self-preservation had been honed while living with Jeremy and afterward.

But the part of her that had always yearned for Grady, that had cherished every moment they spent together the past few weeks, greedily latched on to the tiniest crumbs.

"What do you think, Cody?" she asked the little boy, who was sitting like a little mummy on the sled behind her. "Do you think I should tell Grady about my baby? Do you think I should take that chance?"

Cody just sat there grinning at her, his cheeks rosy and his eyes bright.

"You are so adorable," she said, laughing in spite of herself. "You don't even care that your daddy is in a coma and you have no clue who your momma is, do you? As long as you're taken care of it doesn't matter. Maybe I need to be more like you. Just trust that God will take care of me, whatever shape that takes."

Cody waved his mittened hands as if agreeing with her, barely able to move in the restrictive snowsuit, his stocking cap shifting down and covering his eyes. Chloe stopped and gently pushed it back up, squatting down and checking if he was warm enough.

"I just wish I knew what to do," she said, brushing some snow off his snowsuit. "Mamie said I could trust Grady, but part of me wants to let him remember me as this supposedly pure and innocent person."

He would find out the truth soon enough, but by that time she probably would be gone.

She stood and the wind, gusting now, pulled her scarf away from her neck. It seemed the storm was picking up. Down in the draw the sound was muffled, but she knew she would have to go up that hill sooner or later.

Today she had gone farther than she usually did, and now it sounded as if the bad weather they had predicted for tomorrow was coming sooner than expected. She started looking for the path up the hill. Another blast of wind tossed snow at her and she wrapped her scarf closer around her, now feeling irresponsible for taking Cody so far.

She stepped up her pace and looked around to make sure Cody was okay. Then she turned just as she hit an icy patch. Her feet slipped and she tried to catch her balance. Her foot hit a root, rolled onto its side, and she collapsed into the snow in an ungainly heap. Thankfully she kept hold of the rope pulling Cody's sled, but as she tried to get up, searing pain shot through her ankle and up into her leg.

Chloe's heart sank as she dropped into the snow again, riding out the wave of pain.

She sucked in a breath, then another as it subsided into a dull, steady throb.

Wrenched for sure, maybe sprained.

She had a good fifteen-minute walk ahead of her, and she had to get up to the top of the hill yet.

Dread clutched her as another gust of icy wind howled down the gully. On top she and Cody would be out in the open, but she couldn't stay here. If someone went out looking for her, they wouldn't find her.

"Stupid, stupid," she muttered, feeling silly, irresponsible and frightened.

"We're going to be okay," Chloe murmured, as much to herself as to the little boy in the sled. "We'll be okay."

Please, Lord, help me be okay. Help me and Cody to make it out of here. Give me strength to get us home.

She tried not to let desperation pull her down as the wind whistled around her. She pulled her scarf off and wrapped it around the baby's face for extra protection against the wind. All she could see were his bright eyes and, thankfully, he seemed fine. She glanced around, looking for a stick she could use to walk with.

There. To her left. A branch lay half-covered in snow. She clenched her teeth against a wave of pain shooting up from her ankle as she took another hesitant step toward it, then a hop, then a step. Each movement made it feel as if glass was imbedded in her leg. After what seemed like ages, she made it to where the branch was. She pulled it loose from the snow, whimpering as she lost her balance and landed on her sore ankle. She had to think of Grady with each wave of pain, knowing that he dealt with this all the time, surprised it didn't make him grumpy or miserable.

Looping the rope from the sled around one arm, Chloe used the branch to make her clumsy way up the hill. Each time she slipped, the weight of the sled pulled her back. Slowly, slowly she made her way up, dragging the sled behind her. She stopped a couple of times to make sure Cody wasn't toppling off, but he was okay.

After what seemed like hours, she made it to the top of the hill. She sat down, rested a moment, thankful for one small victory. In spite of the chilly wind and biting snow, she was sweating with exertion. Not good, she thought, as she was now exposed and so was Cody.

But he was covered and she knew she couldn't get to the ranch carrying him. She would just have to keep going. She pulled her cell phone out of her pocket and felt another stab of dismay. No service.

Help me, Lord, she prayed, shoving her phone back in her pocket. She got up, grabbed her stick and started hobbling toward the ranch, her head down against the slanting snow. All she could do was take one step. Then another.

And keep praying.

Chapter Sixteen

Grady squinted into the blowing snow, wishing he could see better. The track he had been following was getting snowed in but so far it looked as if Chloe had stayed on this trail. Hopefully she hadn't veered off. The sun was going down. In an hour or so it would be dark.

And then what?

He didn't want to think about that. All he could think about was Chloe and Cody and getting to them and returning them home.

He leaned forward, ignoring the pain in his leg as minor compared to the fear that gripped his heart. It was getting colder. How long would Chloe and Cody last in this weather if he didn't find them?

As he rode, he thought of other missions he'd been on that didn't end well. He pushed those thoughts back. He couldn't think of that. He reminded himself that each time he went out it was with success in mind.

Please, Lord...

His prayer was simple, a cry from his heart.

He didn't know why Chloe had pulled herself back from him. Didn't know why she was avoiding him.

He should have fought for her.

Don't let her get away from you.

Lucy's words spurred him on and he nudged Apollo in the ribs, ignoring the pain in his leg.

Cowboy up, his father had always told Grady and Ben when things got tough and they wanted to quit. Those words were exactly appropriate now.

Please, Lord...

His horse lifted his head, as if sensing something. Grady peered through the now-driving snow, seeing nothing. But if there was one thing he had learned when riding horses in uncertain situations: trust the horse. Pay attention to its body language.

Apollo's ears pricked forward and he slowed. A horse's first reflex was flight so it made sense that, if he saw something, he would slow down. The horse whinnied softly and then he heard a yell.

"Help! Please, help!"

Chloe.

Thank You, Lord.

Grady nudged his horse in the ribs, leaning to one side, favoring his good leg as he tried to look through the driving snow. "Chloe? Where are you?" He still couldn't see her.

"I'm here."

He tried to follow her voice then saw a darker form that eventually took shape. Chloe, leaning against a tree, Cody in the sled behind her.

"Please, help us."

"I'm here," Grady said. "I'm here."

He rode closer and relief spread like warm honey through his veins when he saw Cody waving his arms. Chloe stood, then faltered.

"Are you okay?"

"I sprained my ankle," she said, pain lacing her voice. "Cody's okay, though."

Grady looked from Cody to her, thinking.

"Do you think you can get on the horse?"

"Just get Cody home, I'll get there eventually."

"Not a chance. Hand him to me," Grady said, not daring to get off the horse himself. He knew he couldn't get back on the horse or make his way back without his crutch. "I want you to try to climb on."

Chloe simply nodded, and pulled the sled closer, tugged her mittens off and unbuckling the strap that held the baby in. It took a few moments longer than normal, then she handed Cody up to him.

Grady shifted Cody to one arm and held out his hand to her and kicked his one foot out of the stirrup. "This will hurt, no matter which foot you use, but you can do it. Put your foot in the stirrup, hang on to the horn of the saddle and climb on."

She bit her lip but then nodded, clearly not seeing another way around this predicament. Grady shifted himself as far back in the saddle as he could. She wouldn't be able to swing her leg around, which meant he had to let go of the reins as she clambered on. Hopefully Apollo would behave and not try anything funny.

It took a couple of tries, but finally Chloe was settled in front of him on the saddle, Cody in her arms. She had the presence of mind to lean forward and grab the reins. Grady reached around her and took them in his hands, thankful that the wind was now in their back. As Apollo started walking it felt as if the storm had eased off.

"How's your ankle?" Grady asked, shifting so there was enough room, wincing even as he did so.

"It hurts. How's your leg?"

"It hurts, too."

"Is Cody okay?"

"His hands are toasty warm and so is his head. He's fine."

They rode in silence for a while. The wind that had tossed snow at him and whistled around his ears seemed quieter now that it was behind them. The forest looked peaceful with the snow falling down around them.

Chloe shifted, tossing a look over her shoulder. "Thanks for coming to get me. I shouldn't have gone out. It was risky."

"You didn't know the storm was coming as soon as it did. And you didn't know you would sprain your ankle." He held the reins in one hand as he lifted the collar of his coat, protecting his neck from the snow. "It wasn't your fault."

Chloe said nothing and the questions haunting him circled his brain like ravens.

Ask her why she avoided you. Ask her if your disability is a problem.

But asking the question would make him vulnerable, and he thought of his father and what he went through after his injury. How his mother hadn't been able to handle it. Couldn't deal.

But was Chloe the same?

Somehow, even as he examined the question, he sensed he was giving her short shrift. And having Chloe in his arms felt so good, so right. It was such a stark reminder of what he had been missing. And now that they were alone, he realized how foolish it was to go on acting as if nothing had happened.

Don't let her get away from you.

He had to know.

"Why did you—"

"I need to tell you—"

They both spoke at once, then stopped.

Grady laughed lightly, the awkwardness plaguing both of them apparent in how Chloe hunched her shoulders, how stiffly he held the reins.

He loosened his grip, which meant he was holding Chloe even closer. He could feel her relax against him. He felt a renewed surge of hope.

"What happened, Chloe?" he asked, putting himself out there, making himself vulnerable. "When you turned away from me after we spent that afternoon in the barn. Was it because I fell? Because you were reminded of how less of a man I am?

"What are you talking about?" The question burst out of Chloe. "Is that what you think? That's crazy. Why would you think that?" Her back stiffened as if underlining her reaction to his questions. He wished he could see her face, but he could only keep talking, hoping she understood what he was saying.

"I'm sorry, but it's just that my mother left my father after his accident. She couldn't live with him. Vanessa kept harping how my disability was a problem she was willing to overlook. Guess I'm just a bit sensitive."

"You're not…not less of a man. That's a ridiculous thing to think. I don't know why you would even entertain the idea that I'm that…shallow, unfeeling, and I don't appreciate being compared to Vanessa."

Her chagrin both surprised him and fanned the tiny spark of hope Lucy's comments had created.

"I wasn't comparing, just thinking—"

"That's good, because your mom was wrong to leave, and I'm nothing like Vanessa. I care about you, a lot, and I thought I was…"

"Was what?" he prompted.

But she said nothing. Yet he felt as if she had been on the verge of saying something he wanted to hear.

"I'm sorry," he said, still trying to absorb this angry version of Chloe. "I just thought…after I fell on the ice, that's when you pulled away. If it wasn't what I thought it was, then why?"

She looked down, fussing with Cody's stocking cap, shifting him on her lap, as if putting off her reply. His horse plodded along, picking his way over the icy patches, and Grady hoped and prayed he wouldn't stumble. He was carrying a precarious load.

"Why then?" he urged, sensing that something else was coming. He hoped he was ready.

She pulled in a breath, her shoulders tensing.

"I'm pregnant," she said.

"What?"

"I'm pregnant. Jeremy is the father."

Grady tried to absorb this information, tried to figure out where to put it in his mind.

"So when is the baby due?"

"I'm not quite five months. Our marriage was stumbling along," she said, her voice quiet as if she hardly dared let the information leave her. "But I had made promises and wanted to be faithful. Then I got pregnant. Jeremy never wanted children. He got angry and filed for divorce. He had a judge who was a good friend and managed to get it done extraquick. After that he disappeared. I haven't been able to track him down to discuss child support. I was on my own." Grady had to bend closer to Chloe to hear what she was saying, and each word was like a small blow. Unsettling and surprising at the same time.

"He said he didn't want to have anything to do with the baby. That's why he wanted the divorce. So when you said what you did about Cody... I thought... I thought you would feel the same way, especially because this baby isn't yours the same way Cody isn't."

Her voice broke on the last words and Grady's heart plunged. He felt so bad for her obvious distress and he wrapped one arm more tightly around her, trying to find the right words to say what was spinning through his mind. Yes, he was confused and yes, this was a shock, but for her to think he wouldn't want to have anything to do with her baby?

Chloe took in a shaky breath, which made him feel even worse for her. She was clearly upset, and that bothered him even more than it did to find out she was pregnant.

"Why would you think I would feel the same way that Jeremy did?"

"Because of what you said about Cody. Just before you fell. But it was what you said that made me pull away from you. Not you falling."

Grady skipped back, trying to remember. "I'm sorry. I can't remember."

"You said...you said that you didn't want to think of starting a relationship with the responsibility of a child. You said that was heavy."

"I said that? About Cody?" Grady tried to catch up as he realized what she was referring to.

She nodded, reaching up to swipe at her cheeks with a gloved hand.

Grady's heart melted at the thought of her tears and he cradled her even closer. He wished he could see her face. Wished he could tip her chin up to look into her eyes, wished she could see the sincerity in his own. "What I said was referring to the fact that Cody had a mother we knew nothing about. That he was dumped on my grandmother's doorstep without any notice. It was the mess that came with it. Vanessa, my brother in a coma. I was referring to that. The responsibility of that. The heaviness of all that." He struggled, wishing, hoping he was making himself clear. Because he felt as if he and Chloe were balancing on the edge of something large and life changing, and the right or wrong words could send him in either direction. And he knew he couldn't hold back any longer.

He leaned closer, pressing his cheek to hers. "I don't know if you're ready to hear this or not, but I have to tell you how much I care about you. I've been miserable the past few days, and it isn't just because my leg's been bugging me. My heart's been bugging me more. I missed you and I hope you missed me." He took in a breath, sent up a prayer, then said, "I love you. I want you in my life no matter what happens."

In spite of the movement of the horse, Chloe suddenly became perfectly still. He heard her draw in a shaky breath and he wondered if he had spoken too soon. He shifted a bit to try to see her, but her face, this close in his peripheral vision, was a blur. He couldn't read her expression or guess what she was thinking.

"Oh, Grady," she whispered, bringing one gloved hand up to his face. "I can't believe I'm hearing this. It's so much." She released a light laugh and he could feel her cheek lift in a smile. "I have to say I've been miserable without you, as well. I missed you so much." She pulled in another breath. "And I love you, too."

Grady's heart felt as if it was going to explode out of his chest. At the same time he felt as if a burdensome, uncomfortable pack had slipped off his back leaving him feel weightless. Free.

"You love me?" He could hardly believe it.

"I love you."

He wanted to kiss her. But for now he had to content himself with holding her tight with one arm, his cheek pressed to hers, his heart beating against her back.

I love her.
She loves me.

Chloe wanted to cry, to laugh, to turn and give Grady a hug, but all she could do was press her hand to his cheek, hoping he could feel how her heart sang with a joy she couldn't find words for.

"I shouldn't have assumed" was all she could say. "I should have stayed and talked to you, but I was so afraid."

"So was I," he said. Then he pressed a kiss to her cheek.

She lay her head back against him, still holding Cody who, thankfully, sat quietly in her lap. She was about to say something more when a voice called out from the darkness.

"Grady? Is that you?"

Chloe saw a shadowy figure on horseback coming toward them through the falling snow.

"I just got here. All set to head out and rescue you," Emilio said as he came nearer, sounding disappointed. "Clint is on his way, as well."

"How far is the ranch?" Chloe asked, squinting through the snow and gathering dusk.

"Only a couple hundred yards ahead," Emilio said. "You all okay?"

"We're all fine," Grady said.

"Mamie will be glad to see you. Josh had to hold her back from saddling up and heading out herself," Emilio said as he turned his horse around, waiting for them to catch up. He glanced down at Cody. "You look over-burdened there. You want me to take him?"

"It might be more comfortable for him." Chloe's one arm was growing tired, holding him up and away from the saddle horn. There was only so much room.

Emilio moved his horse closer and, reaching over, took Cody from her. "Hey, little guy," Emilio said, settling the baby in front of him. "You've had an adventure." Emilio looked at Grady. "I'll just bring him to the ranch right away. Let Mamie know you two are okay."

"That'd be good," Grady said, his voice a rumble against her back. "We'll be along shortly. I don't want to rush Apollo."

"Sure thing." Emilio tugged down his hat, hunched his shoulders against the wind and set out back to the ranch.

Chloe couldn't think of what to say as Emilio disappeared into the snow. Part of her wanted to stop right here and now, but her feet were getting cold, her hands were icy and her ankle was throbbing.

What a time to have the man you love express his own love for you.

"We should be there in a couple of minutes," Grady said, wrapping his one arm around her middle, pulling her tightly back against him.

It was less than that by the time they got to the yard. The glow of the house lights was inviting and Emilio's horse was tied up close to the house. Clearly Mamie had already heard the news about their safety and Cody was in good hands.

Grady steered the horse toward the barn. He stopped by the large rolling door and dismounted slowly. Chloe could see he was stiff and sore and struggled with her guilt. She should have been working with him. It was what she had been hired for.

I was going to, she reminded herself as Grady led the horse into the warm, softly lit barn. *Eventually.*

He brought the horse to the nearest stall and tied him up. His crutch was still leaning against a wall. He grabbed it, then he walked to Chloe's side and held his arms up to help her.

She managed to put her weight on her good leg and slowly dismount, Grady supporting her. She got down, but as soon as she put even the smallest amount of weight on her foot, she stumbled.

Grady caught her, wavering, as well.

They stood, leaning against each other.

Grady laughed. "I guess you can identify with me right now."

"I can," she agreed, finding her balance again. She still clung to him, but that was as much for emotional support as physical.

"And I guess right now we need each other. To support each other."

"In more ways than one," she said, looking up at him, tugging off her gloves. Though her fingers were chilled, she cupped his dear face in her hands, the stubble on his chin only making him more rugged and appealing.

Then he did what she had been longing for him to do. He bent his head, pulled her close and kissed her.

She sighed as he pulled away, her heart full.

"Is this real?" she asked, trying to absorb the wonder of it all.

"I hope so," Grady said. He shifted his weight, winced and nodded. "Yup. It's real."

Chloe laughed then grew serious as she looked up at him, asking the question that she both dreaded and yet knew needed to be dealt with. "And my baby?"

Grady put his hand on the tiny swell of her stomach that seemed to have come out in only the past few days, his hand warm, comforting.

"I love you," he said. "I love you so much. And I know I will love this baby, because he or she is a part of you. I won't lie that I'm nervous about it. I think I said what I did about Cody because I'm not sure what kind of father I could be. But this baby, this child, we would be taking care of together. And I know you'll be an amazing mother and will help me learn to be an amazing father. We'll be doing this together. I don't know if I'll be able to be the active father I had always thought I could be—"

Chloe put her finger on his lips. "I love you just the way you are. You are the best man I know. You are everything I want, and you will be everything this baby and any baby we have together needs." She put her weight on one foot, then stretched up to kiss him, underlining her vow.

He smiled back at her then gave her another hug. "I'm so thankful for you. And I pray that God will bless us and our life together." Then he pulled back. "And now we should make our way back to the house to get Emilio to take care of this horse and to tell Mamie. I'm sure she's wondering what's happening."

"I have a feeling she knows exactly what is happening," Chloe said with a grin. "But I'm sure she wants to hear for herself."

"Then, let's go," Grady said. "Let's go back to the house. Let's go back home."

And leaning on each other, supporting one another, they did exactly that.

* * * * *

Belle Calhoune grew up in a small town in Massachusetts. Married to her college sweetheart, she is raising two lovely daughters in Connecticut. A dog lover, she has one mini poodle and a chocolate Lab. Writing for the Love Inspired line is a dream come true. Working at home in her pajamas is one of the best perks of the job. Belle enjoys summers in Cape Cod, traveling and reading.

Visit the Author Profile page at LoveInspired.com.

HEART OF A SOLDIER

Belle Calhoune

Delight yourself in the Lord,
and he will give you the desires of your heart.
—*Psalms* 37:4

For my daughter Sierra. I love your independence, creativity and wisdom. You are beautiful inside and out, with the heart and imagination of a writer. I love watching you soar like an Eagle. Always remember there are no limits to the things you can achieve.

Acknowledgments

For all my family and friends for all their support and love, especially my dad, my sister, Karen, and my friend Lim Riley.

I owe a debt of gratitude to my editor, Emily Rodmell, for catching all the things I tend to overlook and for wholeheartedly embracing my heroine.

I am very grateful to all the readers who wrote to me asking when I was going to write Holly's story. Your enthusiasm inspired me to create a love story worthy of all your expectations.

Chapter One

West Falls, Texas

Holly Lynch quickly made her way to the mailbox, parking her wheelchair next to it so she could scoop the mail out and place it in her lap. Once she'd dumped the mail onto her skirt, she riffled through it, a smile lighting up her face as she saw the familiar handwriting. She ripped the envelope open with her finger, pulling the crisp stationery out and lifting it to her nose to inhale the aroma. She closed her eyes and breathed in the woodsy, spicy scent. She imagined Dylan Hart smelled just like this piece of stationery, as clean and fresh as a pine tree. A photo fell out of the letter, landing on her lap, faceup. She stared down at Dylan—her gorgeous, green-eyed, smiling soldier—her heart doing flip-flops at the sight of him. He was dressed in his uniform and grinning into the camera, showcasing his impressive dimples and unforgettable face.

She opened the letter, noticing it was dated almost three weeks ago. This was how long it took to get a letter to and from Afghanistan. She let out a deep sigh. Three long weeks! A lifetime, as far as she was concerned. Her hands trembled as she began reading the letter.

Dear Holly,
I hope this letter finds you well. On this end, things couldn't be better.

My tour of duty came to an end a few weeks ago. I'm pleased to report that I've received an honorable discharge. Finally, at long last, I'm coming home for good. I arrive stateside on October 1. I'm spending some time with my mom and her new husband, Roy. She's been taking really good care of Leo for me while I've been in Afghanistan. Here's the really good part. I'm planning to come to West Falls on October 15. Sorry for not telling you sooner, but I wanted it to be a surprise.

I hope this is welcome news to you, Holly. We've been talking about our first meeting for so long now. I can hardly believe it's happening. By the time this letter reaches you, I'll almost be there, at your side.

There's so much more I want to say, words that can be said only face-to-face.

Until then, be safe.
Fondly,
Dylan

The letter slipped from Holly's fingers, floating down to the ground like a leaf falling from a tree. Its graceful descent belied the turmoil raging inside her. Dylan Hart, the pen pal she'd been corresponding with for a little over a year while he was stationed in Afghanistan, was coming to West Falls, all the way from Oklahoma to see her. And according to his letter, he'd be arriving sometime today. With mail scattered all over her lap, Holly adroitly maneuvered her wheelchair up the ramp leading to the front porch. She barreled her way inside the house and double locked the front door behind her. Once she was safely inside, she concentrated on breathing normally. She was taking in huge gulps of air, but she still felt as if she couldn't breathe. Her palms were sweaty, and beads of moisture had broken out on her forehead. The sound of her labored breathing thundered in her ears.

Dear Lord, help me. I don't know what to do. Please don't let Dylan come here!

Bingo, her chocolate Lab, padded his way to her side. Sensing her frantic mood, he cocked his head to the side, then began to gently lick her hand. Reaching out, she patted his head, looking deeply into his russet-colored eyes.

"Bingo, what am I going to do?" she asked as panic skittered through her.

She wanted to hide! She wanted to get in her van and drive as fast and far from Horseshoe Bend Ranch as possible. There was no way in the world she could face Dylan. Because as much as she adored him, as much as she ached to see those brilliant green eyes in person, she didn't have the courage to deal with this situation she'd created. She couldn't face the secret she'd kept from him. Somehow, in all the letters they'd exchanged, she'd failed to tell him the single most important fact about herself.

She was a paraplegic. She'd lost the use of her legs

in an accident, and she'd never walk again. Not in this lifetime. Brave, handsome Dylan, who'd proudly served his country in Afghanistan, had no clue that the woman he'd been writing to—the woman he was traveling all this way to see—was not the woman he believed her to be.

Dylan Hart let out a low whistle as he pulled up in front of the Horseshoe Bend Ranch. In all his life he'd never seen anything finer. It made the Bar M back home seem like chopped liver. The massive entrance dwarfed him, making him feel insignificant in the scheme of things. As he drove past the gates, all he could see stretched out before him was lush green grass—acres upon acres of the purest horse land in the entire state.

Although Holly had told him her family owned a ranch and it had been in her family for generations, he hadn't been expecting anything this impressive. For a man who'd been just getting by for most of his life, it left him a little unsettled. Here he was, fresh from a combat zone, with nothing to offer Holly but his sincerity and the special friendship they'd both nurtured. He swallowed past the huge lump in his throat, hoping it was enough to land him the woman of his dreams.

He knew he was getting ahead of himself, but he couldn't help it. He had such a good feeling about Holly—she aroused emotions in him that he hadn't felt in a long time. It wasn't love—he wasn't that deep in— but something in his gut told him she could be the one. While he'd been over in Afghanistan, there had been endless amounts of time to think about his future. When the bottom fell out of his world, everything had become crystal clear. A place to call home, a good woman by his side and a strong sense of community. More than anything else in the world, that was what he wanted.

And here he was in West Falls, Texas, taking a huge leap of faith. It wasn't like him, not even remotely, but here he stood, ready to embrace his future. Even though he didn't have a job lined up and this could all blow up in his face, he was willing to reach for the brass ring. He was prepared to put his painful past firmly in his rearview mirror. He was giving it his best shot.

Holly could be the one to make him forget about roadside bombs and friends who would never make it back home. She could be the one to make him believe that there were true, honest women out there in the world. And today he would be seeing her for the first time, since he didn't own a single picture of her. How he wanted to see those baby-blue eyes she'd described in person! He'd dreamed about meeting Holly for months now. Although excitement was building inside him, there was also a slight feeling of doubt. Was he doing the right thing?

Lord, please let this rash decision to come all the way to West Falls be right! Let Holly be the woman You've picked for me to fall in love with, something lasting and real. I'm so tired of doing this alone. I'm so afraid of ending up by myself.

After driving for about a half mile, he reached a fork in the road. He saw a grand home looming in the distance. As someone who loved architecture, he appreciated its beauty. It was the type of house that made a person sit up and take notice. It was an impressive two-story white structure with a long wraparound porch and shiny black shutters. It looked like the type of house he would have loved to have grown up in. This place,

Dylan thought with amazement, was a far cry from the small trailer where he'd spent the first eighteen years of his life.

He parked his truck and got out, then made his way to the porch steps in a few easy strides. To the left of the stairs was a wheelchair-accessible ramp leading to the front porch. The sight of the bright red door had him grinning. It made the grand house look warm and inviting—the same way Holly had seemed in all her letters. Blue and red rocking chairs sat facing each other, just waiting, he imagined, for someone to plop down and sit for a spell.

He looked down at himself, hoping his favorite blue shirt and well-worn jeans made him look presentable. With a hint of impatience, he rang the doorbell, itching to meet his pen pal after all these days, weeks and months. Seconds later he rang it again, then knocked on the door for good measure. When no one answered after a few tense minutes, he rapped again on the door, this time with a little more force.

He heard something—or someone—inside the house. A rattling noise sounded by the door, and he heard a whirring sound. Every instinct he possessed told him that someone was in there. "Afternoon. I'm looking for Holly Lynch," he called out.

The heavy click of a lock being turned echoed in the stillness of the fall afternoon. With a slow creak, the door opened. A woman was there, sitting in a wheelchair, her blue eyes as wide as saucers. She had dirty-blond hair and a pretty face that gave her a girl-next-door look. A smattering of freckles crisscrossed her nose. Even though the blue eyes held a look of fear, they were beautiful. They reminded him of his mama's favorite flowers—cornflowers. A necklace with a diamond pendant hung around her neck. She was wearing a T-shirt that read I Do My Own Stunts. The shirt made him want to laugh out loud at her spunk and sense of humor.

The young lady was just sitting there, staring at him without saying a single word. Had he scared her that badly with his knocking and ringing the bell? She was looking at him as if he were the Big Bad Wolf ready to pounce on Little Red Riding Hood.

"Sorry to bother you, miss, but I'm looking for Holly." He extended a hand and grinned at her, wanting to take away some of her nervousness. "I'm Dylan Hart. A friend of Holly's."

Tentatively, she reached out and shook his hand, giving him a slight smile. The blue eyes still looked wary, and the half smile never quite made its way to her eyes. She folded her arms across her chest as if she was guarding herself against him. He wasn't sure if he was imagining things, but her posture looked downright uninviting.

"And you are?" he asked, leading her to introduce herself.

"C-Cassidy. I'm Cassidy Blake," she answered in a quiet voice.

Cassidy! Holly had written to him about her best friend, Cassidy, who was engaged to Holly's brother, Tate. Holly had never once mentioned that Cassidy was in a wheelchair. Or had she? No, he wouldn't have forgotten something like that. Maybe Holly was so used to Cassidy's condition that she hadn't thought to mention it. It was a little bit shocking to see such a young woman confined to a wheelchair. He wondered what had happened to put her there.

"I just got into town a little while ago. Is Holly here?" He didn't want to be rude, but cutting to the chase was his style. He'd come all this way for Holly. Just one look in her eyes, and he knew all would feel right in his world.

Cassidy seemed to think for a moment before she answered him. "Um, no, she's not. She went into town to run a few errands. I don't think she was expecting you until later. She just received your letter today."

Dylan glanced at his watch. It was two o'clock. Something told him Cassidy wouldn't want him hanging around the house, waiting for Holly's return. She had a strange look on her face—somewhere between anxiety and horror.

"I guess I'll head back into town and unpack my things to kill some time," he said, wanting to fill the silence with a little conversation. He couldn't shake the sense that she was nervous about his being here. Hopefully she wasn't worried about her safety. As far as he knew, he looked fairly trustworthy, although anyone could be a stalker nowadays.

Her mouth swung open. "You're staying in town?"

"Yeah," he said with a smile. "I rented a small cottage right near Main Street. My landlord is Doc Sampson. He runs a restaurant in town."

"Yes, the Falls Diner. He's a wonderful man." She seemed to gulp. "Are you staying on awhile in West Falls?"

He was feeling somewhat giddy about his impulsive decision. Although he'd wanted Holly to be the first one to hear about his plans, he couldn't resist the impulse to share the news with her closest friend.

"I made plans to stay in West Falls indefinitely. I signed a four-month lease with Doc, and I'm hoping to find some ranch work in the area. I've had a lot of experience breaking in wild horses and doctoring cattle back in Oklahoma."

Her eyes widened. "That can be dangerous."

"I served time in Afghanistan. There's nothing more life threatening than a combat zone."

He couldn't help but smile at her wide-eyed concern. Working with wild horses was something he'd been doing since his teen years, ever since his father had hired him on as a ranch hand at the Bar M Ranch. Every year during summer vacation he'd lived and worked at the Bar M, devoting himself to the business of cattle ranching. The whole reason he'd signed on at first was to repair his fractured relationship with his father. It had hurt his mother terribly to see him working side by side with the man who never publicly claimed him. *Crumbs,* she'd called it. "He's giving you nothing but crumbs," she'd said with tears misting in her eyes. "You deserve so much better." In the end, he'd learned the hard way that some fences could never be mended. It was the best lesson his father had ever taught him.

Yes indeed, working with wild horses could be dicey, but ranching had been in his blood for generations, even though for many years he'd resisted its strong pull. For years he'd asked himself why it appealed to him, and despite his many attempts to figure it all out, all he knew was that it called to him like an irresistible force. It wasn't a choice, he'd come to realize. It was his calling. And someday, he hoped to own his own spread, a little stretch of land he could call his own.

Dragging himself out of his thoughts, Dylan nodded, acknowledging her question. "Yeah, it can be dangerous. When horses are out of control, it can be an unstable situation. That's why training is so important."

She leaned forward in her chair. "And you've had lots of training, right?" She furrowed her brow, concern etched on her face.

He smiled, tickled by her earnestness. "Yeah, lots and lots. But I'm also very careful, and I respect the horses."

It was funny. She seemed to heave a huge sigh of relief. Cassidy was a sweetheart, that was for sure. Her caring so much about a perfect stranger showed she was a loving and giving woman. Again, he found himself wondering what had happened to devastate this young woman's life.

He quickly glanced at his watch. "Well, I should be heading back into town, since it looks like she won't be here for a while. It was nice meeting you, Cassidy."

She mumbled a goodbye. He heard the door close behind him and the turn of the lock as soon as he'd stepped out onto the porch. He stopped in his tracks as a feeling of unease came over him. He didn't know if he was being paranoid, but her actions had been a little strange. Although she seemed to radiate a good vibe, she'd been jumpy and nervous the entire time, even locking the door upon his departure. As he made his way to his car, he looked across the huge expanse of land that stretched out before him for miles and miles. Horseshoe Bend Ranch. He couldn't imagine a more tranquil place to live. It didn't seem the type of place where one had to bolt the door against intruders. What did he know about it anyway? Joy pulsed inside him as the realization hit him full force. He and Holly were now in the same zip code, and it wouldn't be much longer until they could see each other.

Had she really just done that? Rather than come clean with Dylan, she'd introduced herself to him as Cassidy Blake, the name of her best friend. She watched from behind a living room curtain as Dylan made his way off the front porch. He was handsome. That was for sure. Way more good-looking than his pictures captured. Those green eyes of his sparkled and glittered like a flawless gem. He had a beautiful, pearly-white grin. His dark hair was cut into a short military style, which enhanced his masculine features. And he was tall, six feet she would guess, with brawny arms and shoulders. His physicality was hard to ignore. It jumped out at her, reminding her of everything that set them apart from one another. Several times she'd wanted to reach out and grab his hand or ask him about Leo, his bearded dragon. But that would have been a huge tip-off that she wasn't who she was claiming to be. She'd sunk so low in hiding her disability from Dylan. Why hadn't she just told him? Surely it would have been better than these feelings of dread and guilt gnawing at her conscience. Pain sliced through her, causing her to wrap her arms around her middle in an attempt to assuage the hurt she'd inflicted on herself.

Lord, please make this pain go away. I've gotten so used to loss that I never knew it would hurt this much to lose Dylan before I truly had him. I try so hard to walk a righteous path, yet here I am withholding information and pretending to be somebody I'm not.

Was it really so out of the question to admit the truth to him? She squeezed her eyes shut to block out random images flashing into her mind. Dylan's shocked face as she introduced herself as the woman he'd been writing to over the past year. Dylan's disappointed expression. The look of pity that would inevitably pass over his face.

She covered her face with her hands. No, she couldn't do it. She couldn't handle the pain that came with the knowledge that she would never be Dylan's vision of what a partner should be. She was too flawed, too imperfect. He'd traveled all this way to see in person the woman he'd connected with during some of the darkest hours of his life. Never in a million years would Dylan be expecting a woman in a wheelchair. After all he'd been through in Afghanistan, she couldn't deliver him yet another blow. She just couldn't handle it.

As soon as she saw Dylan's truck zoom off into the distance, she picked up her cell phone and dialed the number of Cassidy Blake's art gallery. After a few rings, she heard her best friend's chirpy voice on the other end.

"Hi, Holly. What's up?"

"Cassidy. I need you to come to the ranch as quick as you can get here." She felt out of breath after she finished.

"What is it? Are you okay?" Cassidy asked. Holly could hear the concern in her voice.

"It's not an emergency. I just need my best friend," she explained, trying to convey the urgency without causing Cassidy panic.

"Let me close up the gallery. I'll be there in twenty minutes," Cassidy promised, quickly ending the phone call.

For the next twenty minutes Holly fretted over her situation, wondering how she was going to tell Cassidy she'd impersonated her when Dylan had arrived at the ranch. Hopefully her best friend would understand the impossible position she was in. As soon as Holly heard the crunch of tires in the driveway, she made her way toward the door, opening it and greeting Cassidy as she quickly walked up the front steps.

As usual, her best friend radiated an effortless, breezy look. With her strawberry-blond hair, green eyes and wholesome good looks, she'd always been a showstopper. Even in her simple T-shirt and flouncy skirt, she looked amazing.

Holly couldn't be happier about Cassidy's engagement to her older brother, Tate. They'd all been through a lot together, most notably the terrible accident that had left Holly without the use of her legs. For many years Cassidy had stayed away from West Falls, torn apart by guilt and shame since she had been behind the wheel at the time of the accident. Last summer Cassidy had returned home to help her ailing mother, and in the process, she and Tate had fallen in love all over again.

"You scared me with that phone call. What's going on?" Cassidy asked as she stepped over the threshold. She held out Dylan's letter to Holly. "You must have dropped this. I found it next to the mailbox."

Holly pushed the door closed and wheeled around so she could face Cassidy. She reached for the letter, stuffing it down into her skirt pocket. She took a deep breath.

"Do you remember me telling you about Dylan? The soldier I write to?"

"Of course. He's stationed in Afghanistan, right?"

Holly nodded. "Yes, he was. But he's stateside now. He arrived in West Falls today."

"That's amazing!" Cassidy squealed. "I can't wait to meet him."

Holly stared blankly at her best friend. In her opinion there was absolutely nothing to celebrate, although Cassidy had no way of knowing it.

Cassidy frowned, her eyes filled with concern. "What's the matter? You look as if someone died. I thought you'd be celebrating instead of moping around the house."

Holly looked down, too overcome with shame to look Cassidy in the eye. "Cass, I messed up. I didn't tell him about my being a paraplegic."

Cassidy's eyes bulged, and she shook her head in disbelief. After a few seconds she said, "Tell me everything."

Holly quickly got Cassidy up to speed on Dylan's unexpected visit and her pretense about being Cassidy.

"But how could you pretend to be me? We don't look anything alike. I thought you two sent pictures back and forth," Cassidy asked, her brow furrowed in confusion.

"I kept meaning to send a photo, but I never did. It was difficult to send him a picture without having told him I'm a paraplegic." Holly let out a bitter laugh. "Of course, when he showed up here he wasn't expecting to see his pen pal confined to a wheelchair, since I conveniently left that part out."

Cassidy looked agitated. She bit her lip and ran her fingers through her long hair. "What are you going to do?"

Holly was wringing her hands. She looked up at Cassidy, squashing down the spark of jealousy she felt as she gazed at her beautiful and able-bodied friend. Cassidy's calves were shapely, while hers lacked any muscle tone whatsoever. What she wouldn't give to be able to walk into a room under her own steam instead of always making an entrance by way of her wheelchair. She let out a deep sigh. What was the point of comparing herself to her best friend? She chided herself. Feeling envy wasn't going to change a thing. It wouldn't make her something she wasn't or somebody she could never be.

"I need you to pretend to be me, Cass. Just long enough so you can end things with him and send him on his way. He'll never know that you're not me." The words tumbled out of Holly's mouth at a rapid speed. Intuition told her that it was only a matter of time before Dylan came back to the ranch. He'd had a look of determination and purpose in his eyes. She needed to fix things quickly. Cassidy frowned. "Holly. You can't be serious. Why in the world would you want me to pretend to be you?"

Tears pricked her eyes. "I need you to do this for me, Cass. Seriously. I want Dylan to leave West Falls and go back home to Oklahoma. This is the only way!" She was starting to feel desperate, as if the walls were closing in on her.

Cassidy frowned. "Tricking him isn't the answer. Why can't you just tell him the truth?"

Heat seared her cheeks. "Because I can't face him. I never told him I'm in a wheelchair, that I'm paralyzed from the waist down. How do you think he's going to feel after coming all this way to see me?"

"You're the bravest person I know. Find your words

and tell him the truth. If he's as wonderful as you say he is, he'll understand."

"This is different. Dylan is… He's everything. Smart. Brave. Gorgeous."

Cassidy's brow was furrowed. "And you're all those things, Holly."

Holly shook her head. "No, I'm not, Cass. You don't understand. He's a soldier. The world he lives in is a very physical world. He breaks in wild horses, rides mountain bikes, does marathons. He protects America from harm. He's a hero."

"And you're pretty heroic, too. You've lived through a horrific accident that cost you the use of your legs. You've devoted your life to getting the message out about irresponsible teen driving. You're a woman of faith, Holly. All those things make you an amazing woman."

Although she loved Cassidy like a sister, she didn't want to hear any of this at the moment. It didn't matter how many times people told her she was brave and wonderful. She didn't feel either of those things. Not at the moment. Not when Dylan was most likely on his way back to the ranch to meet up with her. There was no way she could look him in the eye and admit her lies. She needed to get herself straightened out before he showed up.

"Please, Cassidy. I need you to be me when Dylan comes back," she begged in a panicked voice. "You owe me."

The ominous words hung in the air between them. Cassidy's face lost all of its color, and her mouth tightened in a firm line. As soon as the words had tumbled out of her mouth, Holly had deeply regretted them. Cassidy had just come back into her life after an eight-year absence. In the past six months they'd rebuilt a friendship that had been ruined in the aftermath of the accident that had left Holly paralyzed. Cassidy had been at the wheel at the time, and she'd fled West Falls rather than face the town's censure. It had taken a lot of hard work and prayer to get things back to where they once were with their friendship.

Now, due to overwhelming fear, Holly found herself in an awkward position. With three thoughtless words she'd dredged up their painful past and made Cassidy feel as if she were still harboring a grudge. In reality she, along with Cassidy's cousin, Regina Blake, and their childhood friend, Jenna Keegan, all shared in the responsibility. They'd all participated in the reckless-driving game, although Cassidy had taken the fall since she'd been at the wheel when the car had slid off the road. One could make the argument that she, in fact, owed Cassidy everything for having single-handedly shouldered the blame for eight long years.

Before she could apologize, a knock sounded at the door. Holly jerked her head in the direction of the front door, then looked over at Cassidy. Her friend's eyes were wide with alarm, and she was shaking her head back and forth.

"Please, Cassidy. Just pretend to be me. Tell him you started seeing someone, that you're really sorry but it's over," Holly whispered. She felt weak begging Cassidy to do something she knew was wrong, but a part of her didn't care. Right now all she cared about was making sure Dylan didn't figure out his pen pal was confined to a wheelchair.

"Tell the truth, Holly. Before this whole thing spirals out of control," Cassidy said, her eyes full of disappointment.

Feeling defiant, Holly wheeled over to the door and yanked it open. All of the air rushed out of her lungs the moment she saw Dylan. He was wearing a black cowboy hat, but he quickly took it off and placed it by his side. She noticed he'd switched up his clothes and taken a shower. His hair was still slightly damp, and he was wearing a pair of jeans and a white T-shirt. His arms were heavily muscled and toned. Once again, she was hit with the full impact of Dylan's physicality. He looked as if he belonged on the cover of a men's fitness magazine or on television as the star of a healthy-living commercial. All at once it hit her smack on the head. There was no way she belonged in his world. For the past year she'd been living in a world of denial, clinging to a kernel of hope about a possible future with this impossibly perfect man. In his arms was a bouquet of yellow roses and white stargazer lilies, her favorite flowers. Somehow he'd remembered from her letters. She felt a pang run through her at his thoughtfulness. How she wanted to reach out and accept his offering and press her nose against the fragrant blooms.

"Is she back yet?" Dylan asked, his expressive eyes radiating enthusiasm.

With a lump in her throat, all she could do was nod and gesture toward the inside of the house. His handsome face lit up with a wide grin. She smiled at him, feeling light-headed at the sight of his tall, muscular frame. But he wasn't smiling at her. He was looking past her, straight at Cassidy. And he was beaming so widely it almost overtook his whole face. She felt her chest tighten painfully. Loss—sharp and swift—

flooded her. How could it be this painful to lose something she'd never truly had in the first place? Sucking in a ragged breath, she invited him inside, then watched as he walked across the threshold and beat a fast path toward her best friend.

Chapter Two

"Holly! Is it you?" Dylan made his way across the foyer in two quick strides. Cassidy nodded her head in acknowledgment. Holly watched as Dylan wrapped his arms around Cassidy in a warm embrace. She felt her insides lurch as she observed Dylan's intimate gesture. He was so full of life, so enthusiastic and joyful. Watching him was like seeing a force of nature in motion. Her best friend, on the other hand, was acting standoffish. She wasn't hugging Dylan back, and her body language was as stiff as a board. Her expressive face was giving away too much. Maybe it was simply because she knew her so well that she could tell Cassidy looked conflicted and ill at ease. Her pulse started beating at a rapid pace. If Cassidy couldn't pull this off, she'd be forced to explain it all to Dylan. The very thought of it made her palms sweat.

A part of her couldn't help but feel cheated as she watched Dylan's interaction with her best friend. This embrace should have been hers. His gorgeous smile, which lit the room up like sunshine, should have been directed at her. And maybe it would have been, she thought. If only she had been honest with him from the beginning. Perhaps things could have been different.

Cassidy stepped away from the hug, her face paler than usual, her eyes drifting nervously away from Dylan and toward Holly. She seemed as if she was in pain. Guilt speared through her at the agony on her best friend's face. She looked as if she'd rather go swimming with sharks than follow through with this meeting.

"This has been a long time coming." Dylan's voice was infused with sweetness. To Holly it sounded like the sweet sound of rain after a long drought. For a moment she let it wash over her, rejoicing in the rich timbre of it. He held out the bouquet of flowers, saying, "These are for you," as he handed them over.

"Thank you. They're gorgeous," Cassidy said stiffly, reaching out and accepting the stunning flowers.

Dylan grinned, showcasing a pair of dazzling dimples. "I hope you're not upset with me for showing up here in West Falls. I'm not usually a fly-by-the-seat-of-my-pants guy, but I couldn't help myself. The way you described your hometown made me want to see it for myself."

"It's definitely unexpected," Cassidy answered, shooting Holly a meaningful look.

Holly tried to nod discreetly in Cassidy's direction, wanting to encourage her to act normal, but she felt Dylan's gaze land on her. He seemed to have the instincts of a hawk, paying close attention to everything around him. As a soldier, he'd probably honed those skills as a means of survival.

Dylan frowned. "Did I interrupt y'all in the middle of something?"

"No, of course not," Holly said smoothly, her eyes now focused on Dylan's face.

"It's fine. We were just shooting the breeze," Cassidy added. "Would you like something to drink? Some sweet tea or lemonade?"

"I'd love some sweet tea," he answered, looking grateful for the offer.

"Sure thing. It'll give me a chance to put these flowers in a vase." Cassidy scurried off toward the kitchen, as if she couldn't wait to escape, leaving the two of them all by themselves.

"Why don't you make yourself comfortable in the living room." Holly gestured toward the doorway leading to the foyer. Following behind him, she quickly maneuvered her wheelchair into the room. As Dylan folded his tall, rugged body into a leather armchair, her gaze was drawn to the dog tags hanging around his neck.

Filled with curiosity, she blurted, "Are those your tags?"

Dylan reached up and lightly fingered the tags, his face contemplative as he answered. "Just one of 'em is mine. The other one belonged to one of my buddies who died over in Afghanistan."

Died? He must be referring to Benji, the soldier he'd written about in one of his letters. At only eighteen years old, he'd been among the youngest soldiers in the unit. From what she remembered, he'd been killed instantly when their Humvee had been blown up by a roadside bomb. Dylan had been seriously injured as well, but thankfully had rebounded from those injuries. The attack had occurred before they'd started writing each other, and Dylan was very close lipped about it and his subsequent hospitalization and recovery.

Cassidy returned with a tray of drinks and some slices of homemade pumpkin bread. Like a perfect hostess, she served the refreshments, then plopped down onto the sofa directly across from Dylan. Holly discreetly watched him as he thirstily downed the contents of the glass. It was almost impossible to tear her gaze away from him. She felt like a starving person sitting down at an all-you-can-eat buffet. Dylan, in all his cowboy/soldier glory was a sight for sore eyes.

"Horseshoe Bend Ranch is spectacular," he raved, his eyes wide with admiration. "I can't say as I've ever seen a finer spread." His tone was filled with awe.

"It's the largest and most profitable horse-and-cattle-breeding operation in this part of the state." The words rolled off Holly's tongue like quicksilver. She wanted to clap her hands over her mouth to stop herself from inserting herself into the conversation. It wasn't her place to crow about the family ranch. That might raise a red flag in Dylan's eyes.

Dylan grinned at her. "I'm not at all surprised to hear that." He turned his gaze toward Cassidy. "It must make you feel proud knowing what your family has achieved."

"Yes, the Lynches are a hardworking bunch," Cassidy acknowledged. "It's impossible not to feel proud of them."

Holly flashed a smile in her soon-to-be sister-in-law's direction. Her best friend was incredibly sweet and loyal. As far as she was concerned, Cassidy was going to be a perfect addition to the Lynch clan. If Cassidy and Tate would only set a date and put everyone out of their misery!

"So I was thinking you might like to grab a bite to

eat in town," Dylan said, his face full of expectation. "It'll give us a chance to talk for a spell."

White teeth flashed against his sun-burnished skin, causing a little hitch in her heart at the beauty of his smile.

Cassidy pressed her fingertips against her head. "Dylan, I—I'm not feeling too well." She shifted uncomfortably in her seat. "I'm so happy you stopped by, but I think it might be better if we catch up another time."

Dylan's face fell. He recovered quickly, plastering a smile on his face. "Sure thing. Why don't I swing by tomorrow. I think I'll head back to town and grab something to eat. Doc tells me I have a standing invitation at his diner."

Dylan stood up, placing his empty glass down on the tray before reaching for his Stetson and resting it against his chest.

The look on Dylan's face took her breath away. He looked confused. And crushed. Some of the light went out of his eyes. Holly wanted to wrap her arms around him and soothe his disappointment. Although he appeared to be as tough as nails on the outside, with his rugged appearance and soldier's swagger, she knew all too well about his tender side. And even though she felt a twinge of annoyance toward Cassidy for going off script, she knew all the blame for this entire fiasco lay at her feet. She'd done this. Her insecurities about believing a man could fall for her had led her down this path. For more than twelve months she'd neglected to tell him her most basic truth. And now it was all unraveling, bit by bit.

Of course, it had all begun innocently enough. Pastor

Blake had started a pen-pal program so the members of Main Street Church could correspond with soldiers serving in Afghanistan. Wanting to show her support for the brave men and women of the armed forces, she'd quickly signed up. From the very beginning she'd felt a connection with the brave soldier from Madden, Oklahoma. They'd shared their hopes and dreams, as well as favorite movies, stories about their pets and best-loved ice cream flavors. She'd shared tidbits with him about life in West Falls and the joys of Horseshoe Bend Ranch, as well as her loving family.

In turn, he'd described a soldier's day-to-day life in Afghanistan, the triumphs, the tragedies and the struggles. He'd written her about his wonderful mother, who'd raised him as a single parent. One letter led to another until they were receiving letters from each other on a weekly basis. Somehow, without her even realizing it, Dylan Hart had become a huge part of her life. As the door closed behind Dylan, a feeling of emptiness swept through her like a strong gust of wind. A longing to call out to him, to stop him in his tracks so she could make him stay longer, rose up inside her. After so many nights lying awake, thinking about her green-eyed soldier, it was agonizing knowing she would never be able to face him as Holly Lynch. As much as she wished it wasn't true, Dylan Hart would forever be out of her reach.

Dylan didn't know how to explain the feelings roaring through him as he headed out the gates of Horseshoe Bend Ranch. He felt like a deflated balloon. For the life of him, he couldn't figure out why he felt so disappointed. Holly was gorgeous. Stunning. Any normal, red-blooded man would take one look at her and thank the Lord above for placing her in his orbit. But when he'd finally come face-to-face with her, there had been no kismet, no spark. Nothing special. She hadn't even seemed stoked to see him.

Could he have been so wrong about their connection? She'd been much quieter than he'd ever imagined. In her letters, her lively personality had practically jumped off the page. In person, Holly hadn't been at all as he'd imagined. Something felt off between them. There hadn't been a feeling of recognition when he met her. Not at all. Not even for a single minute. Although he knew it would take some time for them to adjust to each other, things still should have flowed more effortlessly between them. There had been no attraction, no pull in her direction. And she wasn't at all like he'd expected her to be. She was skittish and nervous. When he'd moved to pull her into a hug, she'd stood there like a statue, still and unmoving. She hadn't even hugged him back. She didn't seem like the Holly he'd gotten to know over the past twelve months.

And then she'd practically rushed him out the door on the pretext of not feeling well. Not once had she asked about his living arrangements or his four-month rental with Doc Sampson. Truthfully, she hadn't seemed all that happy to see him at Horseshoe Bend Ranch. Disappointment filled him, leaving him frustrated and full of sorrow. He'd been so sure about Holly, more certain of her than anything ever in his life. Yet now it was looking as if he'd made another gigantic mistake.

It wouldn't be the first time, a little voice reminded him. He shook off the memory of his faithless ex-girlfriend, Shawna. It had been a long time since he'd thought about his high school sweetheart, the woman who'd dumped him after his deployment to Afghanistan. After he'd broken his neck and was laid up in a military hospital, he'd been deemed useless in her eyes. He fought against the anger swelling up inside him. There was no time in his life for people who weren't genuine. And he refused to wallow over past hurts. He had enough scars to last a lifetime.

Please don't let me have been so mistaken about Holly. I've been so wrong in the past about so many things—relationships, people, situations. Please let me find in her the strong, faithful woman I've been seeking. Show me I haven't traveled all this way chasing a pipe dream.

Maybe it was just jitters from meeting each other for the first time. It could be that his expectations were way too high. And meeting someone in the flesh was a lot different than writing to one another. She had every right to be nervous, didn't she? Perhaps it just wasn't meant to be, he realized as a sinking sensation settled in his stomach. Being so misguided about a situation would be a hard pill to swallow. Sometimes one just got a sense of a person—who they were down to their very soul. And for the past year, he'd come to know Holly as a warm and loving, God-fearing woman. Her goodness had resonated in every letter she'd written him and wormed its way inside him, serving as a reminder of everything he wanted in a life partner.

Try as he might, he just couldn't shake off the encounter with Holly. There was something bothering him. It was resting right under the surface, but he couldn't put his finger on it. All of a sudden it hit him. Her eyes. They'd been a vivid green, not blue. Holly had said her eyes were blue. Or was he going crazy? And he'd noticed she was wearing a ring when she'd poured him the sweet tea. Not just any ring, he realized. It had been a diamond ring planted on the wedding finger of her left hand.

He pulled his truck over to the side of the road, his breathing shallow as he racked his brain for the facts. Had she been wearing an engagement ring? Could he have been wrong about her eye color? No, absolutely not. He remembered the words she'd written him in her letter. *I'm a blue-eyed girl from West Falls, Texas.*

He slammed his palm against the steering wheel. What in the world was going on? The woman he'd just seen, the one pretending to be Holly, was a fraud. Her eyes were a spectacular green. That fact, coupled with the odd way she'd been acting and the sparkly ring, was all the proof he needed. With a wild groan, he did a U-turn in the road, his tires spewing dust and rocks as he made his way back toward Horseshoe Bend Ranch. He didn't know who was trying to make a fool out of him, but he was surely going to find out.

"That did not go so well." Holly let out a deep sigh. Things had not unfolded the way she'd envisioned. Even though she hated the idea of tricking Dylan, the idea had come to her in a moment of absolute desperation. As an honest woman, it didn't sit well with her that she'd taken the low road instead of coming clean to Dylan. An overwhelming feeling of fear had held her back. She now felt as helpless as a lamb.

"Holly, I'm sorry. I tried, but I—" Cassidy grimaced and shook her head. "I just couldn't pull it off the way you wanted. It didn't feel right giving him the brush-off."

"It's not your fault. I'm responsible." Her tone was clipped. She saw the look of dismay on her best friend's face. She didn't mean to be so abrupt, but she was feeling so wounded. It hurt to lose the possibility of Dylan. Even though they'd shared secrets and dreams ever since they were kids, she wanted to lick her wounds in private. There was no way Cassidy could ever understand what had driven her to keep her disability a secret. Most able-bodied people wouldn't get it in a million years. All Cassidy had to do was walk in a room to have all male eyes drawn to her like moths to a flame. Ever since the accident she'd been single. Alone. For eight long years she hadn't gone out on a date or shared a sweet, tender kiss with a single soul. There had been nobody to hold hands with or catch a movie with at the drive-in. She'd hadn't received flowers on Valentine's Day or kissed anyone under the mistletoe. Although she'd felt the stirrings of something with Deputy Cullen Brand, they'd never managed to get out of the friend zone. And considering the fact that he worked closely with Tate in the sheriff's office, in the long run it might have been a little awkward.

Becoming Dylan's correspondent had allowed her a rare opportunity to connect with someone without her physical condition being front and center. Living in a small town like West Falls where everyone knew her whole life story felt limiting at times. And she'd wanted to experience romance. Pure, wondrous romance.

She'd wanted someone to fall for her without the wheelchair getting in the way. Yes, in retrospect it was selfish of her to withhold the truth, but she hadn't been able to write those words down on the page. She hadn't wanted his opinion of her to change.

Her relationship with Dylan had started out as mere friendship, blossoming into tender, powerful feelings over the course of the past year. Deep in her soul she'd nurtured a fragile hope that he might be the one. She'd never been in love, but she'd hoped to be in a position to fall head over heels in love with Dylan. And to have those tender feelings returned. Now, in light of everything, those dreams had gone up in smoke. She must have been crazy to think this would all work out in the end.

The sound of whirring tires followed by screeching brakes reverberated in the stillness of the October afternoon. A loud rapping on the front door soon followed. Holly locked eyes with Cassidy before moving toward the front door and slowly opening it. Dylan was standing on the front porch, his handsome features marred by a frown. Holly let out a deep breath. He looked so different now. His face was shuttered. He seemed impenetrable, as if he'd built a wall around himself no one or nothing could breach. The way he was standing—his arms were folded in front of him and his chest was rapidly rising and falling—caused a prickle of awareness to race through her. He looked as if he were ready to take on the world.

"May I come in?" The grim set of his features was nothing compared to the iciness in his voice.

Flustered, Holly waved him into the house. All the while her mind was racing. What was he doing back here? And why was his expression so forbidding? Her throat felt constricted, and she didn't think she could utter a single word if she tried. The sound of his boots echoed sharply against the hardwood floor. He moved toward the middle of the foyer so he was facing both of them.

Looking back and forth between them, he ground out, "Make no mistake, we need to get something straight. I don't know what kind of game the two of you are playing with me, but I do know you're not Holly Lynch." He jutted his chin in Cassidy's direction, his eyes blazing with anger. "Are you?"

Resembling a deer caught in headlights, Cassidy froze, her eyes wide with alarm.

Holly maneuvered her wheelchair until she was positioned directly in front of Cassidy. She had no intention of making her best friend take it on the chin. She'd started this whole thing, and even though it wouldn't be easy, facing Dylan was her responsibility. She looked up at him, refusing to lose her courage and look away from his probing gaze.

Before losing her nerve, she dived right in. "You're right. She's not Holly, Dylan. I am."

Chapter Three

"Holly?" His question bristled in the air like a live grenade. The air around them buzzed with electricity.

"Yes. It's me, Dylan." She met his gaze head on, her blue eyes full of intensity.

A hundred different thoughts were swirling through his mind. His first reaction was a strong sense of recognition. Of course this was Holly. It all made sense now, and even though he'd been thrown off by the wheelchair, there was something he'd instantly recognized in her essence.

His second reaction was sorrow. His soul shattered for Holly. *She couldn't walk?* The same woman he'd been corresponding with for more than a solid year was in a wheelchair. Hadn't she written him about being an accomplished rider? About wanting a house full of kids one day? What had happened to her? Had this all been a big scam? Thoughts were whizzing through his brain until he felt himself becoming dizzy.

Confusion covered him like a shroud. His mind went totally blank. Suddenly, he was stumbling around in the darkness without a way out.

"Why?" His voice came out raspy and uneven. He shoved his fingers through his hair as myriad emotions flitted through him. "Why didn't you tell me? What is this all about?" The tone of his voice sounded sharp and raised, but he was well past caring about that. It hurt so badly that Holly had tried to trick him. The chocolate Labrador retriever began growling low in his throat, the hairs on his back raised. The dog sat down in front of Holly, acting as a protector.

"Shush, Bingo. Quiet down," Holly said in a firm voice as she patted the top of his head.

Cassidy cleared her throat and looked over at Holly, her eyes wide with concern. "Holly. What do you want me to do? Should I stay?"

Holly met Cassidy's gaze. She gave her best friend a tentative smile and shook her head. "Go back to the gallery, Cass. I'm sorry I involved you in this."

Cassidy glanced back and forth between them, hesitating for a moment before she headed for the door. She pulled it open and cast a lingering glance over her shoulder at the two of them. The look in her eyes warned him to go easy on Holly. The sound of the door clicking closed behind her rang out in the stillness of the foyer.

The silence that lingered in Cassidy's wake was painful. Considering written communication between them had always felt effortless, it was an odd sensation.

"I'm sorry, Dylan. Please don't blame Cassidy for pretending to be me. It was all my idea. And it's not something I'm proud of by any means."

"Then why'd you do it?" he asked, needing to know what this ruse was all about.

"When I got your letter today, I panicked," she admitted. She gestured toward her legs. "Not telling you about my being paralyzed was cowardly. I should have told you in the very beginning, but as time went by, it became harder and harder." She hung her head. "I should never have kept secrets from you, Dylan. It was wrong of me."

"When? How?" He was fumbling with his words. There was so much he wanted to say, to ask, but he still felt out of sorts. He was still reeling from the news. The shock reverberated down to his very core.

"I was in a car accident when I was eighteen, right after I graduated from high school. My friends and I were playing a reckless-driving game, and I didn't have my seat belt on. The roads were slick that night, and we weren't being responsible. Cassidy lost control and hit a stone wall. I was thrown from the car." Holly's shoulders sagged. "As a result, I lost the use of my legs."

His mouth felt as dry as sandpaper. He had to ask the question, couldn't deal with not knowing. Already it was nagging at him relentlessly.

"Permanently?" His voice sounded like a croak.

"Yes. My spinal cord was partially severed. Even though I still have some sensation, I won't ever walk again. Not in this lifetime."

The words slammed into him with the force of a tidal wave. The news left him feeling unsteady on his feet. It felt like a kick in the gut. He felt so selfish for thinking it, but there it was, settled firmly around his heart. Why hadn't she told him? His hands were trembling like a leaf. He felt such incredible disappointment in her decision to withhold something so important from him. As a person who'd been caught in a web of lies ever since he was born, he was a big believer in the truth. And Holly had seemed so open and forthright in her letters.

Had he been mistaken? Everything he'd dreamed of building with Holly had crashed and burned in a single instant. And he felt nauseous. Sick with loss and grief and dashed hopes. And he also felt devastated for her. Sweet, loyal Holly, who'd written to him over weeks and months without fail. She'd sent him care packages filled with treats and books and stuffed animals. Holly had kept him in her prayers, and in return, he'd asked God to keep her out of harm's way. Wonderful, brave Holly, who'd no doubt been through so much pain and tragedy in her young life. Yet in her letters she'd always projected such positivity, like a strong ray of sunshine beaming down on him in a war-torn, unstable land.

Still, it didn't sit well with him that she hadn't come clean to him. It made him question every single thing he knew about her. He'd traveled all this way to meet her, all in the hopes of starting a life with her. In his mind, he'd begun to think of her in a forever type of way. The ring, the white picket fence, the kids, promises of forever. Once again, he'd been a prize fool. *Counting chickens,* his mother called it, and she'd been warning him against doing so ever since he was knee high to a grasshopper.

And there was something else. Holly being in a wheelchair brought him back to a place and time where he himself had been disabled. A roadside bomb in Afghanistan had blown the Humvee he was driving to smithereens. Two soldiers in his unit had been killed, with another losing his sight. The injuries he'd sustained due to the IED had been life threatening. In the beginning, he'd been told he might never walk again. But, over weeks and months he'd crawled his way out of the dark, black hole and gotten his life back. And to prove a point, he'd volunteered for another tour, just to show he hadn't been beaten. He was still standing.

"I'm sorry you came all the way here only to be disappointed."

Holly's melodic voice dragged him out of the past, so that his feet were solidly planted in the here and now. And even though he wanted to run from this situation, he had no choice but to face it. "No, it's not about that. It's just—" Just what? How could he explain it to Holly without hurting her or making her feel more ashamed of the information she'd withheld? He needed to be sensitive to her feelings, but at the same time, he couldn't sugarcoat things. He had to be honest with himself as well as Holly. So far, things were not playing out as he'd imagined.

"I suppose you had a preconceived notion about me, right? Cute. Blond. Blue-eyed. Standing on two feet." She breathed out a tiny huff of air. "Wheelchairs don't exactly come to mind when you're painting a picture in your head of someone, do they?"

He let out a ragged sigh, then raked his fingers through his military cut. "I don't know what to say, what to think." He rocked back on his boots, then looked away from her intense scrutiny. She seemed to be studying him, and it made him feel slightly uncomfortable. With a groan he turned back toward her. "I'm being honest here. If I'd known from the beginning, I'm sure I wouldn't be feeling this way." He shook his head, trying to rid his mind of all the jumbled thoughts. "Okay, that's not true. Or maybe it is. I don't know how I would feel, Holly. I just feel a little caught off guard. You weren't straight with me. Don't you think I deserved to know? It makes me wonder if you were ever planning to come clean with me." Although it pained him a little to press the point, he felt he deserved an explanation.

Holly nodded, and he saw a soft sheen glimmering in her eyes. Those incredible blue eyes he'd been dreaming about gazing into were awash in tears. For the first time he noticed how pretty she was, and if it hadn't been for the wheelchair, he might have recognized her right off. It had thrown him, since he'd never been given a single hint about her condition. And he hated to admit it, but he'd looked right through her. The wheelchair had served as a barrier to the truth.

He'd been under the belief that there wasn't a single thing about Holly he didn't know. She was his champion. His Texas rose. The woman he'd been so wrapped up in for the past twelve months. But when she'd greeted him at the door, the wheelchair had served as a buffer between them, and it made him feel a little small to realize that he hadn't even really given her more than a cursory glance.

"Of course you had a right to know, especially when we started discussing the future and meeting one another in person. And I did plan to meet you…on my own terms, when I was ready to tell you everything." Tears slid down her face. Her chin trembled and quivered. Despite it all, she held her head up high. Her countenance said a lot about her. She was strong. She'd had to be, he reckoned. Being paralyzed at the tender age of eighteen didn't leave one a lot of choices, did it? He had a hunch Holly had dug in deep and persevered, relying on her faith and family to sustain her.

"Believe it or not, I'm pretty courageous in most other aspects of my life. For some reason, I just didn't have the guts to tell you the truth. I kept promising myself I would with each and every letter, but as time moved on, it became more and more difficult to do so."

Suddenly, the tables had turned. Just like that, his anger fizzled. Instead of feeling upset with her, he was now feeling badly for Holly. It was confusing, since he was the one who'd been deceived. He was the one who had no idea where he went from here. With no job, four months of rent paid up to Doc Sampson and nothing going the way he'd imagined, his future was seriously in question. All he knew was that he wanted to comfort this woman he'd grown to care about.

"Hey, don't cry, Holly. My mama always told me a pretty girl should never cry." He got down on his haunches beside her chair, then leaned over and brushed her tears away with his thumb.

"At least you think I'm pretty," she joked, the corners of her mouth creasing in a slight smile. Her dry comment made him want to grin back at her, even though the circumstances didn't exactly call for it. Wheelchair or no wheelchair, she still had withheld vital information from him. She hadn't been half as transparent as she'd seemed on paper.

Holly was far more than pretty, he realized. Beautiful, even. He started to tell her so, but he stopped, determined not to go down that road. Not today when so many things were up in the air between them. Not when his stomach was tangled up in knots and he couldn't seem to think past this very moment. The intense feeling holding him in its grip was easily recognizable. It was fear. Because even though he was a decorated soldier who had served two tours of duty in Afghanistan, the thought of Holly being in a wheelchair sent anxiety racing through him.

And even though he still cared about her, he wasn't certain he saw a future for the two of them. Call it crazy, but ever since Holly had come into his life, dreams of them together forever filled his head at night as he drifted off to slumber. Although he felt a stab of guilt for even thinking it, he couldn't deny the doubts coursing through him. He'd just made it home from a combat zone after seeing his fellow soldiers and civilians broken and bloodied and lifeless. He wasn't sure he was up to any more challenges. Did knowing he might not be able to handle this make him a bad person?

Dear Lord, please give me some clarity. Holly is such a sweet, warm person, but I don't want to plunge headlong into a situation I can't emotionally handle. And I'm still really confused about where we go from here. A huge curveball was thrown at me when I wasn't expecting it. Life has shown me that everything happens for a reason, yet I can't fathom why I'm here. And I can't wrap my head around Holly being a paraplegic. It reminds me so much of everything I left behind in Afghanistan. Am I strong enough to get past this deception?

"What are you going to do now?" She looked at him sorrowfully, her expression full of regret and a hundred different emotions he didn't want to analyze.

Dylan shrugged as reality set in. He really didn't have anyplace to go. With his mother having recently moved to New Mexico with her new husband, there was no longer anything tying him to his hometown. He'd burned all his bridges with his father a while ago, no longer content with being a dirty little secret. His outside child. The one who didn't matter. It had been almost six years since he'd spoken to him. He wasn't even certain his father knew he'd made it back from

Afghanistan. Nor did he think he even cared. For too long now, he'd been seeking something from the man that he'd never been willing to give. Acceptance. Unconditional love.

At the moment he felt like a ship without a rudder. Here he was in West Falls, Texas, as clueless as the day he was born. For so long he'd been running. From his father. From the painful gibes about his paternity. He'd run away from Madden, Oklahoma, straight into the service. At some point he just had to stand still. And perhaps God had placed him here in West Falls for a reason.

He stroked his chin with his thumb, deep in thought. "My rent is paid up for the next four months, and I really don't have a lot of options. I need to find a job until I can get on my feet. From what I've seen, West Falls is a nice community."

Holly's eyes began to blink, and her mouth was agape. "You're staying?"

He was still filled with so much uncertainty, but this decision to stick around was based more on practicality than anything else. In his current financial situation, losing several months' rent was a big deal. For years he'd been sending the majority of his active-duty paycheck back home to his mother. And even though she'd socked some of it away for him in a bank account, he was still far from being solvent. In order to realize his dreams of owning his own ranch, he needed to keep making positive strides in that direction. Instead of acting impulsively once again, he'd have to stick around West Falls, at least until his lease ran out. And perhaps he could find work to tide him over while he was in town.

Holly's gaze was strong and steady. It made him squirm some. Her eyes were such a deep, piercing blue. They pulled him in, and for a moment, all he could do was stare at her. Holly. His pen pal. His more than a friend but not quite a girlfriend. At the moment she was an enigma. As much as her letters had revealed about her life at Horseshoe Bend Ranch, her family and her abiding faith, she'd kept her disability a secret. Surely there were ripple effects in her daily life because of the accident and her being a paraplegic.

"Yep," he acknowledged begrudgingly. "It looks like I'll be staying for a while."

Holly's eyes widened, and her throat convulsed as she swallowed. "West Falls will welcome you with open arms. And it would be fine with me if you wanted to work here at the ranch. With your background, it would make perfect sense."

Open arms? For some reason he couldn't imagine it. His own hometown hadn't been half as accepting of him and the single mother who'd raised him. No, they'd been considered inferior due to his mother's unmarried status and the lack of a father figure in the picture. It hadn't helped matters that his mother had been stunningly beautiful, making all the married women in town clutch their husbands tightly to their sides whenever she was in their presence. She hadn't deserved their judgment and disapproval. Hurt roared through him as the bitter memories swept over him. There hadn't been an ounce of compassion or goodness in any of them!

Holly shot him a nervous smile. "It's a big place with plenty of work to keep you busy."

He nodded at her, his thoughts a jumbled mess. So far this day had not shaped up as he'd planned. And he had no one to blame but himself for much of it. "I'll think about it. It's mighty nice for you to suggest it," he said. "Especially since I showed up here out of the blue."

"I think it might work out nicely," she said, her expression a bit guarded. "If you're open to it."

He felt himself frowning. There was no way he was getting too optimistic about West Falls, even if the idea of a job at Horseshoe Bend Ranch seemed almost perfect. If he built up his hopes too high, he'd most likely be disappointed. He'd taken this huge leap of faith without thinking things through in a mature manner. And he'd gotten burned by her lie.

All this time he'd been focused on meeting Holly and building on the foundation they'd already established. But perhaps he'd really been doing what he'd always done. Running away. From Madden. From the fear of failure. From a father, who treated him like a castoff. Far away from gossipmongers and painful half-truths. Unknowingly, he'd run straight toward another complicated situation. He'd gotten involved with a woman who didn't think enough of him to be straight with him.

Although he'd been hopeful about finally finding peace in this town, things weren't half as simple as he'd envisioned. Just when he'd thought his life was about to be as calm as a lake in summer, a twist of fate had changed everything. At the moment he felt as uncertain about his future as when he'd been dodging land mines in the fields of Afghanistan.

"Picasso, you're a beauty," Holly cooed as she brushed the onyx-colored colt. With her other hand she reached up and fingered the white star on his forehead. She had a soft spot for the handsome horse who'd been born at Horseshoe Bend Ranch during a terrible storm last summer. Although the storm had greatly damaged Main Street Church, it had served as a catalyst to bring her brother and her best friend back together as a couple. For that she would always be grateful.

Rather than sitting at home fretting about the situation with Dylan, she'd gotten in her van and headed down the road to the stables. Being able to drive gave her a sense of independence. Once she was behind the wheel, the world didn't seem so small anymore. She didn't feel so much like a caged bird. And she was never more centered than when she was spending time with her horses. This was where she felt most comfortable, a place where her dreams resided.

One day, she vowed, she'd get back on a horse and ride across the beautiful landscape of Horseshoe Bend Ranch. Sadly, she'd never be able to ride in the same manner as she had before the car crash—wild, spirited galloping through the countryside. But she would still be able to experience the unforgettable sensation of being at one with her horses. For the first time in a long time, she'd be free.

Malachi, who'd worked at the ranch since she was a teenager, had given her space as soon as she'd gotten out of the van, seeming to know intuitively that she was seeking solitude the moment she'd shown up. With his dark, brooding eyes, prominent cheekbones and solemn expression, he was the strong, introspective type.

A few times he stepped outside the barn and checked on her, his movements stealthy as he watched her. It was almost enough to make her smile, watching Malachi observing her when he thought she wasn't paying attention.

Holly heard the crunch of tires on the dirt and the slam of a car door. Shuffling noises let her know someone was walking toward her. As the steps got closer and closer, she called out, "Uh-oh. I must be in trouble if the sheriff of West Falls is paying me a visit in the middle of the afternoon."

"What in the world is going on out here?" a male voice barked.

The sound of her brother's voice confirmed her hunch. She swiveled her head around and made eye contact with Tate, taking in his furrowed brow and the deep scowl on his face.

"Something tells me you already know." She knew Cassidy like the back of her hand. There was a time when she'd kept secrets from Tate—things that had almost doomed their relationship. Now that they were happily engaged, Cassidy wasn't going to hold back anything from the man she loved. She wouldn't do it, not even for her best friend. The stern look on her brother's face confirmed what she already suspected—Tate knew all about the circumstances surrounding Dylan's visit.

"Cassidy was quite upset. She told me the whole story. I had to practically pry it out of her to find out what you'd said to hurt her feelings so badly." Tate's mouth was pinched tightly, his brown eyes narrowed into slits. "Did you seriously throw the past in her face like that?"

Holly looked away and tucked her chin against her chest. She couldn't bear to see such disappointment in Tate's eyes. "I messed up. Big time. What I said to her about owing me—" Heat burned her cheeks as her own words came back to her.

"—should never have been said," Tate finished. His features were etched in grim lines.

Holly wiped her hand across her face, getting rid of the beads of sweat gathered on her forehead. "You have no idea how much I regret saying those words. I wouldn't hurt Cassidy for the world. You know that. I'm just not myself today. And I fully plan to meet up with her tomorrow and apologize."

Tate raised an eyebrow. His features softened. "Seems to me if it wasn't for this soldier friend of yours, you would never have gone to that hurtful place with Cassidy."

She fought against a rising sense of irritation with her brother. At twenty-six years old, she was responsible for her own actions. It was high time Tate stopped giving her a free pass.

"Please don't blame Dylan. None of this is his fault."

"So what exactly is he to you? A friend? Pen pal? Or something more?" Tate's voice was tinged with curiosity.

Holly sighed. Tate's question hit a sore spot. Although it was clear feelings had blossomed between the two of them over the course of more than a year, neither of them had ever laid their feelings on the line. And having a letter-writing relationship couldn't begin to compare to a real face-to-face interaction. Other than gut instinct, she didn't have any proof of Dylan's feelings. She had the feeling that coming to West Falls had been his way of exploring their relationship and showing her how much he wanted them to meet one-on-one. After all, hadn't Dylan written about wanting to say certain things to her in person? But now everything had changed. She'd been a fool to ever think she was on Dylan's level.

"We were building toward something. I'm pretty sure that's why he came all this way to see me." She let out a ragged breath, releasing the weight of the world from her shoulders. "For the first time since the accident, I felt as if I was developing a romantic rapport with someone. And I got carried away with those feelings. I can admit that. It felt so good to be treated like a whole person. I just didn't want that to end. That's why I hid the truth from him in all of my letters."

"Being a paraplegic doesn't make you any less of a person." Tate made a clucking sound. "The sight of you in a wheelchair shouldn't send him running."

"He has every right to be mad. And upset. And disappointed." She lowered her head, unable to look her brother in the eye.

Tate reached down and lifted up her chin. "Don't even go down that road. You could never be a disappointment. You're beautiful and funny and smart, with a heart as big as the outdoors."

"He doesn't see a future with me." The words clogged in her throat, and she fought the sudden urge to cry. Where had all her strength gone? Why did her insides feel like mush?

Tate scowled, looking every inch the tough Texas lawman. He clenched his jaw. "Did he say that to you?"

She swallowed. It was painful admitting the truth. "He didn't have to, Tate. I could see it in his eyes. In the way he looked at me. All the life went out of them."

He made a clucking sound with his tongue. "Then he's not worth a single second more of your time."

She could see the raw emotion on her brother's face.

It mirrored how she felt inside. Her throat clogged up. "That's not fair. I was the one who wasn't honest. No matter how I justified it at the time, it was wrong of me."

Tate rocked back on his heels, his silver-tipped cowboy boots glinting in the sun. He jammed his fists into his front pockets.

"Any man would be blessed to have you." He gazed off into the distance, his expression steely. "I worry about you, little sis. And it has nothing to do with you being in a wheelchair. You've worn your emotions on your sleeve ever since you were a kid. It kills me to think of someone hurting you."

"It's part of being alive. It happens when you live life." She shrugged. "Let's face it. It comes with the territory. Even tough lawmen like you aren't immune to it."

Tate swung his gaze back in her direction. His eyes were moist. "You've always been a wise soul, do you know that? Even when we were kids and I was trying to protect you from the world, you always had a strong head on your shoulders. You never really needed me to fight your battles, did you?"

Holly chuckled as memories of her overprotective brother ran through her mind. "Nope, I didn't. But I always loved the fact that you cared enough to be my protector. It made me feel special."

"I'll never give up that role, you know," Tate said with a smirk. "It's a lifelong assignment."

Holly playfully rolled her eyes. "I can't wait till you and Cassidy get married and have a house full of kids. You'll be so busy chasing after them you won't have time to watch over me."

The thought of it made her a little wistful. Would she ever have a husband and a house full of kids? Or would she be relegated to the role of spinster auntie? Even before the accident, she'd always dreamed of rocking a baby to sleep in her arms. Now that might never happen. Was it realistic to dream of things that might not come to pass?

"It's hard to believe we're finally getting married." His larger-than-life grin was threatening to take over his entire face. It was nice to see Tate so overjoyed and on the verge of having all his dreams come to fruition. For a few minutes the two of them simply savored the moment, basking in the promise of tomorrow. Each and every day, Holly found great inspiration in Tate and Cassidy's love story. It kept her hoping and dreaming and praying. Perhaps she, too, would find her happily ever after.

"By the way, Dylan's not running." She tried to keep her tone conversational, despite the rapid quickening of her pulse. "For the next few months, anyway, he's sticking around in West Falls."

Her brother raised an eyebrow. "So what does that mean for the two of you?"

"We're just friends," she said. "I even told him to apply for a job here at the ranch. He's plenty qualified."

Tate furrowed his brow. "You're okay with him working here?"

She nodded her head vigorously. "I think it would be great. Hopefully I'll get the chance to win back his trust, if he'll allow me to."

Even though her statement was technically true about being in the friend zone with Dylan, she couldn't deny the rush of adrenaline she felt at the mere thought of him. Dylan Hart, her gorgeous, green-eyed pen pal. Her brave soldier. The man who'd traveled all the way from Oklahoma to see her, based on the connection they'd established.

For a woman who'd fought tooth and nail to rebuild her life after losing the ability to walk, it didn't feel good to feel so conflicted. She wished she could turn back time and rewrite all the letters she'd sent to Dylan. This time around she wouldn't hesitate to tell him the truth. Pressing her eyes closed, she prayed that she might have the opportunity to show Dylan she was the kind of woman he'd believed her to be before he'd arrived in West Falls.

Chapter Four

⌒⬩

Dylan revved the engine of his truck, hoping the loud noise would rid his mind of all the chaotic thoughts swirling around him. The urge to leave Horseshoe Bend Ranch felt overwhelming. He slammed his hand against the steering wheel, letting out a low groan as he did so. Frustration speared him. Why would God allow a young girl to lose the use of her legs? Why did things like this happen?

The feelings of helplessness roared through him like thunder. It was the same question he'd pondered when Benji and Simon Akol had been killed in such a senseless, violent way. Where was He that day? In the days following Benji's and Simon's deaths, he'd been flat on his back, recovering from a broken neck, a hairline skull fracture and facial lacerations. For endless hours he'd replayed the explosion in his mind—the wreckage, the blood, the cries of pain, which still rang out in his ears. All the while he'd had no clue that two members of his squad had been killed, wiped out in a single deadly blast. His focus had been on staying alive.

Dark memories swept over him, threatening to take

him to a place he didn't want to revisit. He'd tried so hard to forget the feelings of despair that had consumed him in the days and weeks after the bomb blast. And the fear of the unknown. He didn't want to lash out at God, not when he'd come so far on his spiritual journey. Although he still had a ways to go, he knew he'd turned a corner two and a half years ago. There was no way he was going back to that place in time when he'd been a nonbeliever.

Pressing his eyes closed, he tried to stop the flood of images from rushing through his mind. He didn't like to go back to those moments when dread had been ever present. It made him feel vulnerable and weak and not in control of his own destiny.

Son, you may never walk again. The military chaplain had clasped his hand and broken the news to him in the most compassionate way possible. He'd completely broken down, unable to comprehend a life without the use of his legs. During the bleakest days of his life, his mother had been at his side. They'd prayed together, asking God to grant him mercy and healing. In the end, once all the swelling subsided, he'd experienced sensation in his toes. From there he'd endured months of physical therapy, resulting in his regaining 100 percent function.

As the beautiful West Falls landscape passed by his window, a feeling of uncertainty grabbed hold of him. *What am I doing here? I thought by coming to West Falls I was following a path that would lead me toward the next chapter of my life.* Had this entire journey been nothing more than a pipe dream? A rash, foolish mistake?

The downtown area of West Falls was a vibrant section filled with quaint businesses. It looked like something one might see on a festive postcard. Colorful awnings, old-fashioned lampposts, kids skipping along the sidewalk. The Bowlarama caught his eye. Bowling had been one of his favorite pastimes as a kid growing up in Madden. For some reason Holly's image flashed before his eyes, and he wondered if she bowled. Was it even possible?

The cream-and-purple sign advertising the Falls Diner beckoned him like a beacon. West Falls was a far cry from the town he'd grown up in. Everyone greeted him with a warm hello or a smile in his direction. Many eyed him with curiosity. It didn't offend him one bit since the townsfolk seemed hospitable, not standoffish. No one made him feel like an outsider, something he'd been feeling for most of his life. It was a unique experience to have the welcome mat rolled out for him.

For Dylan, walking through the doors of the diner felt like stepping into another world. Delightful aromas wafted in the air as a pink-haired waitress poured coffee into nice-size mugs and chatted amiably with customers. Salmon-colored seats and aqua menus jumped out at him. The rhythmic beat of a blues band emanated from the jukebox. He looked down at a black-and-white parquet floor so clean he could almost see his reflection.

"Couldn't resist the smell, could you?" The gravelly voice drew his attention toward the counter area where Doc Sampson stood watching him. He wore a snowy apron with the word *Doc* emblazoned in red across the front. With a head full of white hair, warm brown eyes and a kindly expression, he was the quintessential small-town proprietor.

"I have to admit, you had me as soon as I spotted

your sign." He patted his stomach. "I'm starving. What do you recommend?"

"Take a seat, son," Doc said as he gestured toward the counter. "How about the blue plate special with all the trimmings? It's the best buffalo chicken and sweet-potato fries you'll ever eat."

He slid onto the stool, feeling like a little kid again as he eyed one of the waitresses making a milk shake in the blender. "Sure. Sounds great, Mr. Sampson." In fact, it sounded so amazing his stomach began to grumble noisily. He hadn't eaten a bite since this morning. His eagerness to meet Holly had trumped his legendary appetite.

"What's with the Mr. Sampson business? Everyone around these parts calls me Doc."

He nodded his head in agreement. "Doc it is, then. And the blue plate special will do just fine."

"Coming right up, son." He studied Dylan for a moment, his silver brows furrowed. "I don't mean to pry, but I heard you were out at Horseshoe Bend Ranch. Were you looking for a job? I know they're looking for a few ranch hands. I'd be happy to put in a good word for you with the foreman, Malachi Finley."

Dylan tried to stuff down a feeling of discomfort. Doc Sampson seemed like a great guy, but after living in a gossipy town like Madden, he wasn't interested in revisiting the experience. It was only his first day in town, yet rumors about his comings and goings were already swirling around like dust on a windy day.

"No, I wasn't looking for a job, although I do need one," he acknowledged in a tone much lighter than his current mood. Doc was his landlord after all, and he needed to keep things cordial between them. "I went

out there to meet my friend, Holly. She corresponded
with me while I was in Afghanistan. It's because of her
that I'm here in West Falls."

Doc's face lit up, and he let out a loud whoop of excitement. "Holly Lynch! She's one of my favorite people." He grinned at Dylan. "I imagine it was nice to
finally meet her."

He hesitated, not sure how to answer the question.
It hadn't been a good feeling to be played for a fool
by Holly and Cassidy. On the other hand, he couldn't
ignore all she'd meant to him over the past year. He
couldn't forget what it felt like to hold one of her letters
in his hand and to know someone cared, other than his
mom, whether he lived or died. Warm sentiments didn't
just evaporate in an instant, especially not the type of
tight bond he and Holly had forged.

"I didn't know she was in a wheelchair." The words
tumbled out of his lips before he could rein them back
in. He was still grappling with Holly's lie, still unsure
what to make of it all.

Doc's shoulders sagged, and he let out a deep sigh.
"The poor thing lost the use of her legs before she even
got a chance to spread her wings and fly." He shook his
head as if trying to rid himself of the memories. "After
the accident it felt like an earthquake hit this town. It
was hard on the roses—that's what everyone calls her
and her three friends—but Holly had it the worst. She
had to learn to live life in a totally different way. No
riding horses, no driving, no independence." His slight
frame was racked by a huge shudder. "She struggled at
first, but with her family and an abundance of faith, she
pulled herself up by her bootstraps. That young lady is

an inspiration." Doc winked at him and headed through the swinging doors into the kitchen.

Doc's heartfelt words about Holly nudged themselves straight into the center of his heart. He'd always known she was special. In a million years he could never convey all she'd done to keep his mind focused on living and making it back home rather than on the death and devastation he'd encountered on his last tour of duty. Her lively, warm letters had served as a lifeline, reminding him of everything he'd be coming back to in the States. And now he was discovering she'd had to climb mountains in her own life in order to overcome tragedy.

If he was being honest with himself, the urge to stick around West Falls had everything to do with Holly and the bond they'd forged. The idea of Holly bravely rebuilding her life in the aftermath of the accident made him want to get to know her in a way he hadn't been able to through their letters. Suddenly, staying in town had nothing to with practicality. He wanted to discover firsthand everything he possibly could about Holly Lynch.

The early-morning sun cast its stunning rays over the pastoral landscape. A calm feeling settled over him as he drove down the country lane. All he could see on the horizon was a cloudless sky the color of a robin's egg. It was shaping up to being a beautiful October day in West Falls. If he lived to be a hundred, he would never tire of this perfect, sacred land. Thankfully, he was miles and miles away from IEDs, missiles and military strikes. For the first time in a long time he didn't have to think about whether or not this day would be his last. He wouldn't have to struggle to breathe the dank, fetid air. Ever since he'd left Afghanistan, his prayers had been full of mercy and protection for the soldiers he'd left behind. Husbands, mothers, brothers, friends— each and every one of them yearning to make it home to their loved ones.

Without warning, Horseshoe Bend Ranch came into spectacular view. Once again he allowed himself to take it all in. The raw beauty of the land rendered him speechless. It went on for acres and acres, as far as the eye could see. Green, verdant, unspoiled land. Even though Oklahoma had some breathtaking vistas, he'd never laid eyes on anything so pristine and majestic. He couldn't help but think that the Lord had left his finger-prints all over this spread. His chest swelled at the idea of one day owning his own cattle ranch, a dream he'd nurtured since he was a small boy. What would it feel like, he wondered, to experience the sense of pride as-sociated with building up the land into a thing of raw beauty and distinction?

After talking to Doc yesterday, he'd decided to speak to the foreman about being hired on as a ranch hand. It was hard to ignore that he was sorely in need of a job. And Horseshoe Bend Ranch was hiring.

The Lord will provide. His mother's velvety voice rang in his ears, instantly bringing him back to his up-bringing in Oklahoma. If he had a dollar for every time Mama had uttered that sentiment, he'd be a millionaire. More times than not, money and food had been scarce, and they'd lived on the edge of poverty. Finally, in an act of humility, his mother had reached out to his father for financial help, which he'd immediately given. Al-though things had quickly improved after that, Dylan was left with a bitter taste in his mouth about accepting money from the father who didn't acknowledge him. It amounted to little more than charity. For so long he'd struggled with the notion of not being good enough. He'd been fighting to prove otherwise ever since.

After entering the gates, he traveled down a gravel-filled road. When he reached the fork in the road, he turned to the left as Doc had instructed. He glanced over to his right, catching sight of the sprawling main house. Had it just been yesterday he'd been sipping sweet tea inside those walls? He wondered where Holly was at the moment and what she was doing. Even though Holly had given him the go-ahead to seek employment on her family's ranch, he wondered if she might change her mind. Perhaps it would be awkward under the circumstances. Suddenly, he felt himself second-guessing his decision. Should he just turn the truck around and head back to town?

"Too late to turn back now." He glanced down at his bearded dragon, who was sitting in his carrier looking happy to be along for the ride. Leo enjoyed hanging out with him and he didn't mind the swaying movement. Dylan could always tell when he was happy, as well as the times when he wasn't. Being alone for long periods didn't seem to suit him. Rather than leave Leo by himself, he'd decided to bring him on his trip out to the ranch. Lizards thrived in hot desertlike weather, so being stuck in a carrier on a warm October morning wasn't a problem. He looked down at the piece of paper in his hand. Doc had scribbled down the name for him. Malachi Finley.

According to Doc, he was the one who did all the hiring at the ranch. He pulled up to the stables and parked his truck alongside a few cars. Knowing he'd come too far to turn back, he unfolded his long legs and exited. The stable door was wide-open, giving him a clear view of two ranch hands who were trying to rein in a bucking miniature horse.

"Are either of you Malachi Finley?"

Neither man bothered to look up. One of them gestured outside. "Nope. He's out in the corral."

"Thanks," Dylan said as he turned on his heel and made his way back outside. If he wasn't here on such pressing business, he might have been tempted to stay in the stables and watch the struggle between the miniature horse and the ranchers. Something told him that the spirited animal might win the battle. As he stepped out into the sunlight, he had to raise his arm across his face to protect himself from the glare. Because of the rays shining directly in his face, he could make out only two indistinct figures—one astride a horse, the other standing close by. The first thing he noticed was the glint of blond hair shimmering in the sun. Goose bumps broke out on his arms as the realization hit him hard. It was Holly.

She was seated on an alabaster, medium-size horse. A Native American man, who he assumed to be Malachi, stood by her side, holding the lead rope and directing the horse. Holly's focus was 100 percent on the task at hand. Her hands were clutching the bridle. She was so focused that she didn't seem to notice he was thirty feet away, observing her.

Only a moment ago, he'd deliberated as to whether he should even be at Horseshoe Bend Ranch. But now he was transfixed by the sight of Holly on her horse. She looked scared. Even from where he was standing, way across the yard, he could see the signs of it. Her blue eyes were open wide, and she was blinking, giving her the look of a frightened owl. Seeing her discomfort made him want to do something—anything—to help her. It made him want to jump the fence and ride to her rescue. Malachi was being gentle with her. Maybe he was going too easy on her, he realized. No doubt he was well-meaning, but Holly wasn't making any progress. She resembled a statue perched on a horse. Her head was moving back and forth, as if she was arguing with Malachi. Not a single thing about her indicated she was happy or feeling joyful. Hadn't Holly written to him about her love of horses? Shouldn't she at least be smiling?

"Holly, you can't show him you're scared. If he senses it, it'll spook him," he called out. None of this was his business, but he couldn't just sit back and watch her fall apart.

She glanced in his direction, her eyes opening even wider as soon as she spotted him. Wobbling a little in her seat, she let out cry of alarm. Malachi steadied her, and for the first time, he could see the special saddle she was using. There was a belt attached to the saddle that was looped around her waist, as well as a padded back to the saddle. Between Malachi and the saddle, there really hadn't been any real danger of her falling. But, as he well knew, fear lived in one's mind.

"Spook him? I'm the one whose hands are trembling. He's got the easy part," she yelled back.

"Malachi, do you mind if I come inside?" he called out. He didn't want to step on his toes, but helping Holly feel at ease was his primary concern. He watched as Malachi looked up at Holly, his dark eyes questioning her. Holly gave him a quick nod. Malachi gestured him in.

Dylan entered the arena, his movements calm and easy. The last thing he wanted to do was startle Holly's horse. At the moment, both rider and horse seemed unsettled. When he edged closer, he was able to see the elastic bands attached to the stirrup. He imagined they were being used to stabilize her feet. As soon as he reached her side, he was able to read the saying on her shirt—I'm Paralyzed. There's Nothing Wrong With My Hearing. The corners of his mouth twitched, but he didn't want Holly to see his amusement. She needed to dig down deep and take control of the situation. There was no time for distractions.

Without saying a word, Malachi moved a few steps away and folded his arms across his chest. It was clear to Dylan that he wanted to be close enough where he could still keep an eye on the situation. He didn't blame him. As far as Malachi was concerned, he was a stranger. There hadn't even been time to introduce himself. What would he have said anyway? "Hi, I'm Dylan, Holly's pen pal from Afghanistan"? Something told him Malachi wasn't big on chitchat.

Dylan looked up at Holly, immediately noticing the tension lines creasing her pretty features. Resisting the impulse to smooth away those crinkles, he tried to assess the situation. He didn't know whether this was her fourth time back in the saddle or her fortieth. At the Bar M, he'd worked with plenty of disabled riders, most of whom were missing limbs or suffering from war injuries. They called it therapeutic riding.

Because of his experience in Afghanistan, he knew

what fear looked like, up close and personal. At the moment, anxiety held Holly firmly in its grip.

"Sometimes life's not easy." He threw the words out like a challenge, wanting to remind Holly of everything she was too scared to see right now. She'd written those words to him when he'd been full of despair and dejected, having been inundated with bad news about failed missions, roadside bombs and fallen soldiers. Holly and her sweet, spirited letters always served as a shining beacon of hope in the darkness. Now, in some small way, he wanted to give back to her a little bit of inspiration.

"Hey, it's not fair to use my own words against me!" she protested. The beginnings of a small smile hovered on her lips.

Pleasure filled him at the sight of it. She was starting to relax. Her posture didn't look so rigid anymore, and her features weren't so strained.

"What's your horse's name? He's a beauty, that's for sure." He reached out and stroked the stallion's glorious mane. He'd missed being on a ranch—all the sights, smells, sounds and the glorious animals. Being with horses filled a piece of his soul as nothing else could.

"His name is Sundance. He's a Camarillo."

He let out a low whistle. Camarillo horses, categorized by their pure-white appearance, were a rare breed of horse. Although he knew of their existence, he'd never seen one until now. It shouldn't surprise him since, according to Doc, Horseshoe Bend Ranch was among the most successful horse-breeding operations in the country. No doubt the Lynches could afford the best horses money could buy.

She thoughtfully studied him. "What brought you out here today?"

Dylan met her gaze, startled by the jolt he felt as he looked into her eyes. "Doc convinced me to swing by and see Malachi about a job, since I'm sticking around for a while." He shrugged, feeling a bit sheepish.

"Why'd you decide to ride today?" he asked, quickly veering off the topic.

She shot him a look of frustration. "It's one of my goals. I've been trying to get back into riding for years. Before the accident I rode all the time. Every time I get up here for my lesson, I freeze up." She pointed her chin in Malachi's direction. "Every single time. Just ask Malachi."

"You're afraid." His words were simple and to the point. Even a blind man could sense her fear. It was palpable.

She vehemently shook her head, blond hair tumbling over her eyes. "I love horses, Dylan. I'm not afraid. I just—"

Their gazes locked, and he could see stark terror looking back at him. He didn't want to push her too hard, since she already seemed to be on edge. She looked as if all the steam had left her. He deliberately softened his voice.

"It's understandable, you know. You don't need to feel ashamed about it. Being involved in the accident, not riding for so long... It's bound to mess with your confidence." Compassion flared within him. "I know what it feels like. When I became injured, I was laid up in a military hospital for months. By the time they discharged me and I'd redeployed, I was a mess. Physically, I healed." He tapped two fingers against his temple. "But mentally, I was scared to death of every loud noise and shadow."

Holly bit her lip and looked away. "I guess I am a little scared. Not of the horses," she quickly added. "It's been such a long time since I've done this. Almost a lifetime ago. I just don't want to fail at it again."

"You can do this, Holly," he said in a firm voice. "I know you can."

She studied him for a moment, her eyes roaming over his face. He watched her take a deep breath, then sit up straight in her saddle, shoulders back, her mouth pressed in a thin line. With a simple nod of her head, she let Malachi know she was ready to try again. Soundlessly, Malachi appeared at Sundance's side, his eyes carefully trained on Holly. Sensing Malachi possessed some special training he didn't have, Dylan retreated a few steps but still kept his gaze trained on horse and rider.

In a soothing voice, Holly began talking to Sundance, uttering words he couldn't hear. She gently grazed her knuckles against his temple. The stallion nickered softly in response. Holly picked up the reins and instructed Sundance to move. The horse obeyed, gracefully moving into a simple trot. Holly patted his side forcefully, urging him to trot a little faster. Dylan held his breath as she cantered around the corral. Although her pace wasn't fast by any means, it was a clear victory for Holly as she settled into the natural rhythms of riding. Malachi hovered nearby, his eyes trained on both horse and rider, ready to jump in at any moment.

After twenty minutes or so, Holly began showing signs of fatigue. She slowed Sundance to a halt, then gestured to Malachi, who was at her side in seconds.

He watched as they headed toward a ramp and a wheelchair, both set off to the side of the corral. Strangely, in the past half hour, he'd allowed himself to forget about Holly's disability. All he'd wanted to do was rush in and make things better. But now the reality of her situation hit him squarely in the stomach. Feelings of helplessness washed over him. Fear grabbed him by the throat. As Malachi helped Holly off Sundance, he squared his shoulders and turned away, swallowing hard as memories of his own stint in a wheelchair bombarded him. He fisted his palms, determined not to go into a dark place.

"Atta girl. I knew you'd get back in the saddle one of these days," a deep masculine voice rang out as long legs began walking toward them.

Dylan held his hand up to block out the glare from the sun, catching a glimpse of dark hair and a strong jaw. Holly lit up the moment the tall, broad-shouldered man came into view. He felt a twinge of discomfort, knowing there was someone who could make Holly shine like the sun.

The dark-haired man stopped midstride, giving him the once-over as he planted himself next to him. Holly adroitly wheeled over to them, making introductions as she reached their side.

"Tate, this is Dylan Hart. Dylan, this is my brother, Sheriff Tate Lynch."

Dylan stuck out his hand, and for a moment, the sheriff seemed to hesitate before putting his hand out and vigorously shaking it. His gold badge glinted in the sun, serving as a reminder that Tate Lynch ran things in West Falls.

"He's come to talk to Malachi about a job on the

ranch." She looked toward Malachi, who'd just walked over and joined them. "Malachi, officially meet Dylan."

Malachi nodded his head almost imperceptibly in his direction.

Tate jutted his chin toward him. His blue eyes sized him up, not giving a thing away. "Holly mentioned you have some ranch experience."

"Yeah, I spent summers working as a ranch hand at the Bar M Ranch in Madden, Oklahoma. You name it, I did it. Breaking in horses. Wrangling. Roping. Doctoring livestock. Calving. Fence repair."

Tate nodded, his eyes alight with interest. "I've heard of the Bar M. Nice little operation. I remember meeting the owner a few years back at a cattle auction. McDermott, isn't it?"

Dylan tensed up the moment at the mention of his father's name. He allowed himself to relax. It wasn't as if anyone would ever guess the connection. "Yes, that's right. R. J. McDermott. I cut my teeth there and learned a lot."

"He's got a nice way with horses," Malachi added. "I'd say he knows his way around a ranch." Dylan blinked in surprise. Malachi hadn't said two words to him, yet he'd clearly been taking stock of him the whole time.

With a lot of eyebrow raising and head nods, Tate and Malachi seemed to be communicating to one another without uttering a single word.

Tate folded his arms across his chest. "We just had two of our ranch hands up and quit on us, so we need to bring someone on right away to fill the slack. Most folks say it's a nice place to work."

"I think Tate's offering you a job," Holly said in a dry tone. "If he ever gets around to it."

"Is that right?" Dylan asked, shooting a grin in Holly's direction. Joy swept through him at the prospect of being offered a job on his own merits. Other than his service in the military, the only employment he'd ever secured was at the Bar M, and that had been due to his father. In the end, that hadn't worked out too well.

Tate glanced over at Malachi, who nodded his head and added, "The job is yours if you want it."

Gratitude swelled inside him. Who wouldn't want to work at this magnificent ranch, this little slice of paradise? He reached out and shook Malachi's hand. "Thanks for the offer. I'd be happy to come on board."

He couldn't resist looking over at Holly. Her expression bore no hint of any discomfort. If she was surprised by the turn of events, she didn't show it. She looked serene, as if all was right in her world. It seemed that having successfully ridden Sundance had left Holly with a permanent glow on her face.

Thank You, Lord. Thanks for giving Holly back a small piece of something she lost. And for giving me this amazing opportunity at Horseshoe Bend Ranch. I still don't know why You called me to West Falls, but at the moment I'm feeling mighty grateful to be here.

Having Dylan show up unexpectedly at the ranch left Holly with mixed emotions. At first she'd been embarrassed by having him witness her pitiful attempts at riding Sundance. Her lack of finesse was painful, particularly since she'd once been a top-notch rider. Her childhood bedroom had been littered with blue ribbons and trophies. She'd loved galloping across her family's massive acreage with the wind flying through her hair. Sometimes she missed riding so much it caused a physical pain in her body. It was a relentless ache in her soul that wouldn't quit. At times she missed having the use of her legs so much she started to believe she felt normal sensation in her lower extremities.

When Dylan came striding into the corral looking every inch a cowboy on a mission, she'd been surprised and full of jitters. He'd quickly made her feel at ease, soothing not only her but the horse, as well. With his strong, gentle hands and soft voice, he'd made everything better. In his presence she'd felt safe. Not many people made her feel that way. His actions also showed her that he wasn't harboring any ill will toward her, even though he'd distanced himself once Malachi helped her dismount.

Tate's eyes were full of questions as his gaze shifted between her and Dylan. Not that she didn't have her own. There were so many times over the past year she'd felt there might be something more than friendship brewing between them. And having Dylan show up in West Falls seemed to confirm he was leaning toward more than a platonic relationship. Until he'd discovered she was in a wheelchair. Until she'd pretended to be somebody she wasn't.

A little while ago Dylan had disappeared into the stables with Tate and Malachi, no doubt to talk shop and get the particulars about his new job. A part of her ached to tag along so she could show Dylan around the stables herself and introduce him to Fiddlesticks, Picasso and all the other horses. If her parents had been at the ranch, she would have introduced them to Dylan as well, but they were out of town at a horse auction and would be on the road indefinitely.

Wanting to give Dylan his space, she'd stayed outside to give Sundance some apple treats and water before grooming him. As she worked her way with a comb through Sundance's tail, she heaped praise on the magnificent stallion.

"Hey, I thought you might like to meet someone." When she looked up, Dylan was standing there holding a lizard in his arms. A dark cowboy hat was now perched on his head. The bearded dragon was a light green color with dark brown spots scattered across his back. He was beautiful.

"It's Leo! Oh, he's amazing," she gushed. She maneuvered herself away from where Sundance was tethered to his post, not wanting him to be frightened by the lizard. "And he's so much bigger than I imagined."

Dylan laughed. "Yeah, he is, isn't he? He's about a foot now and still growing. I have to make a stop at the market so I can stock up on the veggies and fruits he likes to eat, not to mention I have to find some silkworms and grubs."

Hearing Dylan talk about Leo was like listening to a parent crow over a child. He was acting like a proud papa. And she didn't blame him one bit. Leo was fantastic. She leaned forward in her chair, anxious to get a better look at the lizard.

"Can I hold him? I promise I'll be careful."

His eyes widened at her request. A slow, wide smile began to break out on his face. "Sure thing. Just hold out both of your palms to support him."

She held out her hands and Dylan adroitly handed

Leo over to her. The first thing she noticed was his solid weight. "Whoa. He's a big boy!"

"You got that right. Make sure you support his front arms with your fingers. You can put him in your lap if you want. Might make it easier."

Holly placed Leo in her lap and ran her finger down his back, surprised at the rough texture of his skin. Leo just sat there bobbing his head.

"Most people are a little nervous about holding Leo."

"Not me," she said with a grin. "He's adorable. And he's such a sweetheart to let a stranger hold him."

"Leo's an attention hound. The more he gets, the better he likes it." Dylan's face held a pleased expression. "Bearded dragons get a bad rap. They're actually very gentle creatures despite their name."

"Aw, you're just misunderstood, aren't you? Don't worry, Leo. I don't judge by appearances," she cooed. Leo lay snuggled in her lap as if he planned to stay for a while. She wouldn't mind a bit if he did. "I think he likes me."

"Wouldn't surprise me a bit." Dylan crossed his arms across his chest and studied the two of them. The satisfied expression on his face only served to enhance his good looks. "Leo has good taste."

Dylan's compliment washed over her like a gentle breeze. The wind kicked up a bit, blowing her hair all around her face. As it was, it already had a habit of being on the unruly side. She didn't need the elements to make things worse. *Especially in front of Dylan,* a little voice whispered. Without warning, he reached out and brushed a few strands out of her eyes, his fingers gently grazing her cheek in the process. His touch was warm and tender, making her want to burrow her face against his palm. She looked up at him, and as their eyes met, she felt something electric hovering in the air. There was a slight tension that hadn't been there a moment ago. It crackled and buzzed around them.

Dylan took a step backward, his eyes flickering with an emotion she couldn't decipher. "I should really be getting back to town. I've barely gotten settled in, and I'm supposed to be reporting to work tomorrow."

"I'm thrilled you'll be working at Horseshoe Bend Ranch." She smiled up at him, hoping he felt as good about his decision as she did. "And in case I didn't make it clear yesterday, I'm happy you decided to stay in West Falls."

"Thanks for saying so, Holly. I'm glad to be here." Dylan nodded his head and sent her a lazy smile before tipping his cowboy hat in her direction and turning to leave.

As he walked away, she wavered between joy and discomfort. There was no denying she felt a tremendous pull in his direction. Her insides did flip-flops whenever he was nearby. She felt breathless around him, as if she'd ridden Sundance through the countryside for a whole hour without stopping. Just one glance from him caused her to feel slightly off-kilter. It had been years and years since she'd felt anything like it, and even then, it had been nothing more than a high school romance.

On the other hand, having him nearby didn't help get him out of her mind. And she knew the more she thought about him, the harder it would be for her when he left town. He'd made it pretty clear he wasn't sticking around past the duration of his lease with Doc.

Even though things were now way more complicated between them, he was still there, firmly rooted in her heart. Over the past year, she'd read and reread his letters, almost to the point of memorizing every word and detail. In her mind, there had been an unspoken closeness between them, one that hinted of a future together. Somehow, their physical separation had allowed her to forget the wide chasm between them and all the reasons why they were so very ill suited for one another.

Every time she glanced in his direction, it became even more crystal clear. Dylan was the embodiment of the perfect male specimen. Tall. Rugged. Muscular. The personification of health and good living. Although she'd gotten used to being different a long time ago, those differences were magnified when she was side by side with Dylan.

She couldn't remember ever feeling such an intense longing for someone, one that reached all the way down to her toes. It was an exhilarating, breathless feeling. And as much as it excited her, it also frightened her. She'd been without male companionship for so long that she'd convinced herself she was fine without love in her life. With his piercing green eyes and laid-back demeanor, Dylan was quickly showing her how wrong she'd been in her thinking. *Just fine* wasn't enough. She wanted more than that. Dylan's presence in West Falls was igniting a whole new world of possibilities. For the first time since she was a little girl, she was dreaming of happily ever afters.

And she had the feeling, if she wasn't really careful, that in a few months' time, Dylan was going to leave West Falls with her heart firmly nestled in the palm of his hand.

Chapter Five

Twenty-four hours had passed since her riding lesson, and Holly found herself gritting her teeth as she battled waves of pain. She maneuvered herself over the threshold of her house, then quickly wheeled herself down the ramp and made her way over to her van. She paused for a moment, gritting her teeth against the ripples of pain threatening to overwhelm her. The sensations pulsating through her body were agonizing. Her legs were tingling as if they were on fire. Her arms were burning. Sucking in a deep breath, she reminded herself to breathe.

She didn't have time for this, not when she was supposed to be at Main Street Church in fifteen minutes, speaking to the youth group about distracted driving. Her motivational-speaking gigs were very important to her. As well as providing her with independence and an income, it gave her an opportunity to give back to the community she loved so much. At the moment, the chances of her making it to the church on time were getting smaller by the second.

She inhaled, slowly breathing in through her nose.

There were so many ups and downs with her pain levels. Yesterday she'd felt fine. She'd even made her way over to Cassidy's house to apologize for her careless words. Over chamomile tea and shortbread cookies they'd shed a few tears and hugged it out. Now, less than twenty-four hours later, her body was racked with pain.

"Hold it together. *This too shall pass*," she whispered, willing the agony to disappear. As it was, she could hardly focus, and there was absolutely no way she could lift herself into the van. She just didn't have the strength to push past the pain. Tears pricked her eyes as she imagined having to call Pastor Blake and cancel her speaking engagement. She'd fought so hard to not be limited by her disability, and yet here she was, sidelined by it. She shared a very special relationship with Pastor Blake. Not only was he Cassidy's father but he was also the one who'd led her back to her faith after the accident. The thought of disappointing him left her feeling dispirited.

"'Fear not, for I am with you.'" She repeated the words over and over again, firmly shutting her eyes to try to assuage the pain.

"Is everything okay over here?" Dylan's voice washed over her, making her forget for a moment about the agony coursing through her body. She heard the crunch of his cowboy boots on the pebbled driveway right before he popped into view. Dressed in a pair of dark jeans and an olive-colored T-shirt, he was a welcome sight.

Holly grimaced as waves of pain enveloped her. As much as she didn't want Dylan to pity her, she couldn't hide that she was hurting.

"Yep, everything's fine." Somehow she managed to choke the words out.

Green eyes skimmed over her like lasers. "No, it's not. Something's wrong. You're all tensed up. You're suffering, aren't you, Holly?"

Dylan was frowning at her as if he knew she was trying to pull the wool over his eyes. Despite everything, he still connected with her so well. He was so in tune with her that he sensed something was amiss. Although it felt good to see that their connection hadn't been severed, it was a little unnerving at the moment to meet his probing gaze head-on. His eyes emitted such intensity. It felt as if he could see much more than she wanted to reveal. She broke eye contact, not wanting him to see the distress radiating from her eyes. If she could just have a moment to herself, she could dig in her purse for her medication, then call Pastor Blake and cancel her speaking engagement. The last thing she wanted was for Dylan to see her as a helpless invalid.

"Just having some nerve pain. I'll be all right."

The only thing she could do at the moment to alleviate the pain was to massage her legs and take another pill. Despite her inability to walk, she still had sensation and partial movement in her legs. Earlier this morning she'd taken her medication, but it seemed to be having no effect on her symptoms. She began kneading her legs with her fingers, willing the pain to go away. This harrowing side effect of the accident was unpredictable and jarring.

Dylan frowned. "It looks pretty bad. I can tell by the way you're clenching your teeth."

He got low to the ground so he was sitting on his haunches. Dylan reached for her hand, clasping it firmly in his. His touch felt comforting, like an infusion of warmth invading her body.

"Tell me what I can do. There must be something, Holly. Anything," he said, his tone urgent.

She blinked away tears of frustration. Time was slipping through her fingers, and she was still no closer to being able to get in the van. And even if she did somehow manage to get in the driver's seat, she wasn't confident she'd be able to block out the pain so she could safely drive into town. Her options were rapidly evaporating.

"I'm supposed to be at Main Street Church in ten minutes for a speaking engagement, but I don't think I can drive. I need to call Pastor Blake and cancel. He's been so wonderful about finding me outlets as a motivational speaker."

"There's no need to cancel, Holly, unless you're feeling too poorly to go. I can drive you over there. It'll take about fifteen minutes, but I'll get you there."

"Can you?" she asked, relief flooding through her at the offer. With her parents in Kentucky looking at horses and Tate on the clock at the sheriff's office, she didn't have many options. Malachi was notorious for not owning a cell phone, so even though he was just down the road at the stables, reaching him was impossible.

"I don't want to put you out." If Dylan was heading into work, she didn't want to take up his time. Under the circumstances, Malachi would be understanding, but she didn't want to make it appear as if Dylan were shirking his duties, especially as a new hire.

Dylan's brow furrowed. "Don't worry. It's fine. I was just heading back into town after working a shift when I spotted you over here. Don't ask me how I knew, but something didn't seem right. You were sitting there for quite a spell without getting into your van, and you were a little hunched over." He looked down at his dirt-stained shirt and chuckled. "I'm in need of a hot shower, so bear with me."

From where she was sitting, he looked pretty easy on the eyes, if a little rough around the edges. Having grown up on a ranch, she was used to cowboys in all their rugged glory. It would take a whole lot more than a grimy shirt and some smudges on his face to make Dylan look unappealing.

Realizing she was staring, she felt her cheeks redden. "You're going to have to lift me into the passenger seat, then put my chair in the back."

With a curt nod, Dylan said, "Let's do this." He stood up and brushed some dirt off his jeans. He went behind her chair and began pushing her toward his truck.

After pulling the door open on the passenger side, he turned back toward Holly. He reached down and placed his hands under one of her legs, then slid them underneath the other so he could scoop her up. Ever so gently, he raised her out of the wheelchair, pressing her firmly against his rock-solid chest. Slight fear kicked in. Although she trusted Dylan, being held in someone's arms was an extremely vulnerable position to be in. There were so few people in her life whom she trusted to carry her.

"Just don't drop me," she blurted, giving voice to her fears.

He drew her in closer. His grip tightened. The scent of hay and sandalwood rose to her nostrils.

"Everything's okay," he answered, his voice soft and

soothing. "I'm not going to let anything happen to you. Wrap your arms around my neck."

With wide eyes Holly obeyed, her tight grip betraying her nervousness. "I've got you," he whispered in her ear, his lips grazing against her skin. "And there's no way I'm letting go."

As Dylan walked toward his truck, his mind was racing a few paces ahead of his footsteps. He wanted to be as gentle as possible when he placed her in the passenger seat of the car. A few seconds ago she'd seemed anxious, and he wanted her to feel at ease with him. He wanted to show her that her faith in him wasn't misguided. Even though his nerves were rattled by this huge responsibility and his breathing was a bit ragged, he wasn't going to let Holly down. After all, trust was a precious gift.

When he lowered her onto the seat, strands of golden hair brushed against his cheek. Her scent hovered in the air—a sweet perfumed smell reminiscent of sunshine and roses. She was shivering, no doubt in response to the pain, which sent his protective instincts into high gear. Unlike the other times he'd seen Holly, she looked more professional today. She'd ditched her humorously worded T-shirts for a bright blue button-down top and a dark pair of trousers. Silver-tipped cowboy boots peeked out from under the hem of her pants. She looked beautiful.

He made sure she was safely buckled in before he put her chair in the back, moved around to the driver's side and settled himself in. As they exited the gates of Horseshoe Bend Ranch, he shot a quick glance in her direction. "You look really nice today," he said, trying to make his voice sound casual.

She turned toward him, her cornflower-blue eyes widening at the compliment. It made him wonder if she wasn't used to receiving them or if she was just surprised he'd commented on her appearance. The corners of her perfectly shaped mouth turned up, instantly transforming into a glorious smile. Since he was so close to her, he got a good look at the light freckles scattered across her nose and cheeks. "Thanks," she said, smoothing down the front of her shirt. "Most of the kids come to this program after school, so I try to make an effort, even though I'm more comfortable in a T-shirt and jeans."

"Nothing wrong with that. It's my unofficial uniform," he said with a chuckle. "So how did you get started as a motivational speaker?"

"Well, I've kind of grown in to it. Right after the accident, I was pretty messed up." She darted a quick glance in his direction. "Emotionally, I mean, not just physically. I was angry at God for not sparing me the loss of my legs, so I floundered for a while, both spiritually and socially. Cassidy had been my best friend for most of my life, so when she left town without warning after the accident, I didn't have anyone to lean on. My family was wonderful, but sometimes you just need your girlfriends."

The roses. The tight circle Doc had mentioned the other day at the diner.

Holly continued, "Jenna and Regina are two of my friends who were in the car wreck that night. Afterward they both retreated into their own shells, no doubt because of the circumstances of the accident. It was traumatic for all of us. There was so much fear and secrecy. It was the end of our innocence." She let out a deep sigh. "Our immaturity cost us all so much."

"You most of all." There was no question in his mind that Holly had paid the highest price of anyone. Everyone else had been able to carry on with their lives without permanent scars. Except Holly. Her injuries would last a lifetime.

"Most would say that, but I wasn't wearing a seat belt the night of the accident, Dylan. I'm embarrassed to admit that I was hanging out the window at the time of the crash."

Dylan tried to shutter his expression so Holly wouldn't see the shock roaring through him. *Hanging out the window of a moving vehicle?* He cleared his throat. "That doesn't sound like you, Holly. If you don't mind me asking, what made you do such a thing?"

She bowed her head. "No, I don't mind you asking. And you're right. It's not something I would do at this point in my life, but at eighteen years old, I was a bit of a risk taker, a free spirit of sorts. I was the one in the group who was always pushing the envelope." She shrugged. "You never think anything bad can happen to you when you're that age. You think you're invincible."

"You're right," he agreed, as images of his own youthful foolishness raced through his mind. "Been there, done that."

She let out a deep sigh. "My girlfriends and I were enjoying a fun night out on the town when we ran out of things to do. I guess we were bored. We'd played this game before called chicken, where whoever was driving would mess around with the car and veer into the other lane. I'm ashamed to say we thought it was entertaining. Cassidy was driving, and I was in the front passenger seat. I remember taking my seat belt off so I could hang out the window and feel the rain pour down on my face as I let out a few screams of frustration." He darted a glance at her, aching a little as he saw the bleak expression on her face. "My parents were really strict about my curfew, so I was chafing against their house rules. I thought they were treating me like a child. The car hit a slick patch in the rain and we crashed. Since Cassidy was driving, she bore the brunt of the blame and responsibility. We vowed among the four of us we'd never tell about our reckless behavior. It's only recently that we began telling the truth about that night."

Although Holly's tone was matter-of-fact, the actual details of the accident and its chilling aftermath were anything but routine. He couldn't seem to wrap his head around how quickly things had changed for Holly, how irrevocably her life had been transformed in a matter of minutes.

"And as a result, life as you'd known it ceased to exist," he said as a gnawing sensation tugged at his stomach. "You were forever changed."

Holly turned toward him, the corners of her mouth hinting at the beginnings of a smile. "That's true. Nothing has been the same since that night. But believe it or not, I'm one of the fortunate ones. I could so easily have lost my life when I was ejected from the car. God was watching out for me even though I failed to watch out for myself."

"Wow. It's amazing you can be so…so at peace with it."

"Well, it didn't happen overnight. It took me a long time to come to that realization."

Chills raced along his spine at the thought of a battered and broken Holly, after being thrown from the car, lying on the road hovering between life and death. Hearing Holly's story was shocking and moving at the same time. One moment she'd been a typical teenager having a girls' night out. The next thing she knew she'd woken up in the hospital with catastrophic injuries. It was mind-blowing just thinking about all she'd endured. And everything she had to live with on a daily basis. His own experience with being paralyzed had been of such short duration that he couldn't compare his situation to Holly's. There were so many things that able-bodied people like himself were clueless about. He knew he wouldn't have handled things quite so well if the injuries he'd sustained in the bomb blast had been permanent. As it was, he'd been severely depressed and filled with uncertainty about his future. He'd lived in fear for months. Holly seemed to have navigated her way through her own terrible storm with grace and courage.

"Don't get me wrong. In the beginning I was bitter and apathetic. I kept asking myself why God had chosen me to be so horribly affected by the accident. I'm ashamed to admit it, but I kept wondering why the other girls had remained unscathed. That type of thinking did nothing to move me forward. One day I attended services at Main Street Church, and it was as if a lightbulb went off in my head when I heard Pastor Blake's sermon. I realized it was time to stop feeling sorry for myself and blaming God for my troubles. It was time to start living. After that, I committed myself not only to leading a more faith-driven life but to giving back to my community. This town has stood behind me every step of my journey, so it's only fitting that I talk to the teens about my own experience with reckless driving."

He nodded. "There's certainly a need for it. You hear about teen-driving fatalities all the time."

"Teenagers don't have fully formed brains, so decisions made on the spur of the moment can be life altering. I don't want to lecture them. I just want them to see with their own eyes what can happen when poor decision-making spirals out of control."

Holly was spot-on. Teens didn't want some know-it-all telling them the dos and don'ts of adolescence. That was a surefire way of losing an audience and having them block out anything anyone tried to tell them. He knew this all too well from his own experiences with eighteen-year-old recruits, who chafed at being told what to do. Over time they'd learned the value of listening to more experienced soldiers. Sometimes their very lives depended on it.

Something told him Holly made a powerful impression all on her own.

Fifteen minutes later, they arrived at Main Street Church. After Dylan parked the truck, he retrieved the wheelchair from the back, then scooped Holly up and settled her back in the chair. Having done it once before gave him the confidence to know he could handle it without complications. Once he was finished, Dylan stood on the curb, craning his neck up toward the towering structure. He remembered Holly writing him about the storm that had damaged the church's roof and toppled its historic steeple. Although the roof had been fully restored, the church was still missing its crowning glory. According to Holly, the church was having ongoing fund-raising events to pay for the costly repair.

Little by little, she said, they were moving toward their goal. Even without the steeple, the house of worship was still magnificent.

A good-looking man with salt-and-pepper hair and a kind expression stood at the top of the stairs by the entrance. His slate-gray eyes were welcoming. A smile lit up his face. Dylan had a good hunch this was Pastor Blake, the inspiring man he'd heard so much about over the past year.

"Holly! So glad you could make it after all," he called out as Holly wheeled herself up the ramp and toward the entrance. "I was getting a little worried. You're usually the first one to arrive."

"Sorry, Pastor Blake. I'm running a few minutes late. I needed some help getting here today." She cast a glance in Dylan's direction, her eyes filled with gratitude. "Thankfully, my friend Dylan was able to help me out."

Pastor Blake heartily clapped him on the back. "We're mighty grateful to you, son. She's a bright ray of sunshine around here. The teens are already in the rec room waiting for her arrival."

"Let's get to it, then," Holly said with a grin as she sailed through the open door.

Pastor Blake chuckled and shook his head, then ushered Dylan inside the church. The interior was cool and dimly lit. After following Holly down the aisle, he stopped in his tracks, awed by the way the sunlight streamed like gold ribbons through the stained-glass windows, bathing the altar in natural light.

Pastor Blake paused beside him. "Beautiful, isn't it? Sometimes in the middle of the day I just sit down in one of the pews and enjoy a moment of reflection."

Dylan nodded. He didn't know what to say, even though the idea of enjoying a peaceful moment here appealed to him. It had been a long time since he'd been in God's house. He'd spent some time in the chapel at the hospital while he was recuperating from his injuries, but that had been the extent of it. It shamed him to acknowledge he hadn't lived up to his vow. At the time, he'd made a lot of promises about living a more spiritual life. He'd been so grateful to God for giving him back the use of his legs, so relieved that he didn't have to spend the rest of his life in a wheelchair, promises had flowed out of his mouth like quicksilver. As he walked behind Holly's wheelchair as she led the way to the recreation room, the irony struck him square in the chest. He'd been spared while Holly had been dealt a crushing blow.

Once they reached the hallway, the sounds of animated voices drifted toward them. The recreation room was a large-size area with a brightly colored mural on the wall. There were about twenty teenagers seated around the room. As soon as they spotted Holly, a roar went up in the place. Looking pleased with the warm reception, Holly introduced him to the group. Some of the girls sent him flirty looks and smiles so sweet they almost gave him a toothache. The boys seemed to be sizing him up, staring at him with curious gazes. He held up his hand in greeting before stepping aside and settling into a seat at the back of the room, right before Holly began speaking.

"Hi guys. It's nice to see so many people could make it. I know we've talked a lot about reckless driving, but today I want to talk about personal responsibility." She positioned herself right in the center of the room, where everyone had a good view of her sitting in her wheel-chair. "The way I see it, if you're a passenger in a car, you also have an obligation to make sure the driver is being safe. No texting. No drinking. No game play-ing. Bottom line…if the driver isn't being responsible, you're putting your own life in danger. Take it from me. It isn't worth it."

For the next half hour Holly went over different sce-narios and had the teens role-play. Although a few of the teens were making jokes and goofing around, most of them were taking their assignments very seriously. Throughout, Holly handled herself in a professional manner, gently reining in the kids when they veered off track. She never sounded preachy or holier-than-thou. Authenticity rang out in every syllable. She'd clearly walked the walk, and the kids all knew it. The teens peppered her with questions about her own accident, and she painstakingly answered every one of them, even the ones that made his jaw drop. Her bravery and trans-parency were awe inspiring.

At the end of the session, a pretty dark-skinned girl raised her hand. "Sarah, do you have a question?" Holly asked, her attention focused solely on her.

"Miss Holly, we were talking before you got here about how we can give back to the community. So we—"

A tall boy with ginger hair and freckles chimed in. "We want to have a bake sale at school to help with the steeple fund."

"We know it probably won't make a dent in the over-all cost," Sarah added, "but we think it's important to make a contribution."

"Oh, I think that's wonderful," Holly said, a huge

smile lighting up her face. She clasped her hands together and placed them in her lap. "Every bit helps. And
just think, when the steeple is finally finished, this entire community can take pride that we all chipped in
toward the restoration."

Pastor Blake clapped enthusiastically, grinning from
ear to ear, a huge smile that rivaled the one plastered
on Holly's face. Dylan felt a sudden yearning. The fellowship and community he was witnessing within the
walls of Main Street Church left him awestruck. Never
in his life had he experienced something so profound.
As he gazed upon Holly, her face radiant with joy, he
felt the stirrings of something so powerful inside him it
caused a painful tightening in his chest. Rooted to the
spot, he didn't think he could take his eyes off Holly if
his life depended on it. A longing swept through him,
pure and deep, and although he didn't fully understand
the scope of it, he knew that he wanted to be a part of
this community, this wonderful landscape. This little
oasis from the storms of life.

Every day he was finding new things to appreciate about life in West Falls. The warm, down-to-earth
townsfolk. Doc, his wise landlord. Pastor Blake and
Main Street Church. Horseshoe Bend Ranch and all
its many opportunities. And above all else, Holly. In
many ways she was everything he'd always wanted in
a woman—kind, beautiful, spiritual, funny.

But as much as he was beginning to enjoy life in
West Falls and his budding relationship with Holly, he
couldn't run the risk of getting involved with her and
then finding himself in a situation that was over his
head. Not when he was filled with so much uncertainty.
Not when the chances of hurting her were so great if

things didn't work out. The life she led wasn't easy by any means. Every day presented new challenges and ongoing struggles. And if he was being completely honest with himself, the ramifications of his new life scared him to death.

Chapter Six

Dylan gently held the colt's hoof in his hand, his attention focused on the small stone stuck in the heel. With all the precision he possessed, he extracted the stone, soothing the horse afterward by patting him on his side. He sure was a looker, Dylan noted. The spirited colt had been limping for a few days, a fact that was causing great worry to Holly, according to Malachi. Thankfully, he was none the worse for wear.

"Good boy, Picasso," he crooned. "You're a real champ. I know it must have hurt to have me poking around, but you handled it like a trooper." The colt let out a nicker in response, giving Dylan a reason to chuckle.

"Keep that up and you're going to make yourself indispensable around here." The low timbre of Malachi's voice slid into the silence of the stables. "You saved me a call to Shep, our local vet."

Dylan wasn't surprised by his presence. He'd known the minute Malachi entered the stables, despite his attempts to be unobtrusive. It was a skill he'd learned in

Afghanistan. Being aware of your surroundings had been a matter of life and death in a combat zone.

From what he was discovering about the ranch foreman, he was a keen observer of all things and a lot more talkative than he'd appeared the first day they'd met.

Dylan swiped his arm across his forehead. "The good news is it was only a stone. The way he was limping around the corral, I thought he might have a puncture wound that developed into an abscess. Or possibly a case of thrush."

"That's something to be thankful for. This colt means an awful lot to Holly and Tate. Cassidy, too."

"I figured as much. From what Holly told me about the night of his birth, Picasso is a little superstar around here."

"He came into the world with a real bang, that's for sure." Malachi seemed to be studying him as if he was trying to read his mind. "Dylan, there's something I'd like to talk to you about."

Dylan stood up and faced him, giving the other man his full attention.

"I have to leave the ranch for a bit. A week at the very least. My grandfather on the reservation isn't doing too well."

"I'm sorry to hear that," he said. "I'll remember to keep him in my prayers." Ever since the explosion he'd gotten real good at praying. For some reason, praying for others was more satisfying than asking for his own to be answered. Perhaps because ever since he was a kid he'd been praying for a lot of things that had never come to pass. And somehow, it made him feel more connected to the people around him to offer up prayers on their behalf. It made him feel like part of a community.

Pray for one another, that you shall be healed. The words of his hometown pastor rang in his ears, reminding him that there were certain things from childhood he'd held onto. Not everything had been bad. There were some things he proudly carried with him. Within him there were remnants of a childhood scattered with random acts of kindness and generosity. A pastor who'd taken him under his wing. A schoolteacher who'd encouraged him to reach for the stars. A mother who'd loved him unconditionally.

Malachi stood before him and scratched his chin, deep in thought. "Problem is, Holly depends on me for her riding lessons. I'd hate to slow down her momentum, since she's turned a corner."

"She's certainly making progress," Dylan said with a nod of his head. Over the past two weeks, he'd caught glimpses of Holly riding Sundance in the corral, aided by Malachi. She looked stronger and more in control. Her face no longer reflected fear. "Her confidence seems to be growing, and she's building up her endurance a bit."

"She's definitely stronger, although she tries to push herself past exhaustion at times. You said you worked with disabled riders back in Oklahoma, so it wouldn't be too much of a stretch for you to spot Holly while she's riding. Can you handle filling in for me?" The question hovered in the air between them. It was also the most words Malachi had uttered to him since he'd come on board several weeks ago.

Could he handle it? His initial reaction was to bristle at the suggestion that he might not be able to. He'd handled two tours of duty in Afghanistan, hadn't he? It didn't get any tougher than that. Then, as Malachi's question settled in, he began to wonder. Could he? On one hand, he loved spending time with Holly. The emotional attachment he felt toward her was strong, cemented by months and months of writing to one another and reading her wonderful, lively letters. Even before he'd shown up in West Falls, he had a keen sense of who she was as a person. Kind. Warm. Spirited. A woman of faith. Being in close contact with her would serve only to tighten their bond, and he wasn't sure he wanted that to happen. It would only make it harder to walk away from her in a few months' time. And he did intend to leave West Falls. Being in Holly's presence reminded him way too much of the fragility of life. It made him feel defenseless and vulnerable. He hated feeling that way. Stepping in with a few words of advice while she was riding Sundance was one thing. Driving her into town so she could meet with the teen group had been the right thing to do under the circumstances. Being solely responsible for Holly's care and safety during the lesson was something completely different. It made him responsible for her.

There was no way he was going to admit it to Malachi, but the very thought of it terrified him. *What if something happens? What if I don't know how to care for her needs?* Just the idea of it made him feel uneasy. It put him way too close to that dark space he'd been trapped in, that netherworld of fear and doubt. It served as a constant reminder of what he might have lost if he hadn't regained the use of his legs. It forced him to face his worst fear head-on. What was he thinking to even consider it?

He swallowed past the huge lump in his throat. "Isn't there anybody else?"

Malachi shook his head. "Holly's parents would step in if they were here, but they won't be back from their horse auction trip for a few more days." Malachi was staring at him, barely blinking as he waited for an answer. "How about it?"

"I'd rather not," he said in a no-nonsense, clipped tone. He reached up and fidgeted with the collar of his T-shirt as heat suffused his face.

Malachi frowned, his onyx-colored eyes widening in surprise. "Why?" he said, seeming to lose his composure a little bit. He'd never heard such consternation in Malachi's voice. "What's the problem?" Malachi pressed.

Why? There were dozens of answers to that question, none of which he wanted to share with Malachi. The idea of getting so near Holly was nerve-racking. The thought of getting pulled in any deeper than he already was sent waves of uncertainty crashing over him. Without knowing it, Malachi was putting him in a corner by asking him to fill in during his absence. He was pushing his buttons.

"Why?" he snapped. "I'm just not comfortable doing it, that's all."

He heard the slight whirring sound just before Holly's voice sliced into the silence. "Don't worry about it, Malachi. At the moment I don't want a single thing from Dylan, least of all his help." With eyes blazing and a mutinous look stamped on her face, Holly wheeled herself around and barreled out the door, her blond hair flying around her like a whirlwind. There was no doubt in his mind that she was attempting to get as far away as possible from the very sight of him.

* * *

Heat crept up the back of her neck as she flew out of the stables and quickly made her way toward her van. The path in front of her was clouded by a red haze swirling around her. Hot, pulsing anger was flowing through her veins. She moved to get as far away from Dylan as her chair would take her.

"Arrogant, selfish jerk," she muttered. "As if the world revolves around him!"

The crunching noise of cowboy boots rang out in the stillness of the afternoon.

"Holly, wait up! Please." The sound of Dylan's voice grated in her ears like nails on a chalkboard. She didn't even bother turning around. There was nothing he could say at the moment that she wanted to hear. She couldn't recall a moment in recent memory when she'd been so disappointed in a person.

All of sudden Dylan planted himself in front of her, causing her to almost crash into him. She gritted her teeth, scowling up at him. "Get out of my way before I run you over!" she growled. "I mean it."

He leaned over till they were eye level, firmly placing his hands on the chair arms to stop her from moving away from him.

"Please give me a chance to explain," Dylan said. His features were strained, his mouth creased with tension. Steely determination shone from his eyes. He pushed up his cowboy hat so she was able to see his eyes.

She shook her head, feeling mutinous. "I heard what you said. You made it sound as if Malachi asked you to babysit me! And you made it crystal clear that you don't intend to help me with my lessons. As far as I can see, there's really nothing to explain."

His mouth quirked. Green eyes bore into hers so intently she wrapped her arms around her middle in a protective gesture. There was no way she was going to let him hurt her any further. As it was, she found herself with a racing pulse and abnormal breathing. She couldn't remember the last time she'd been so fired up about something. Or someone.

"I'm sorry if I sounded callous back there. It wasn't my intention." His tone softened to the point of gentleness. "When Malachi asked me about the riding lessons, I felt put on the spot. I'll admit it. I felt a little boxed in."

Her chest was rising and falling sharply. She felt her nostrils flaring as her temper spiked. "Boxed in? Did you seriously just say that?" She rolled her eyes. "Wherever did you get that silver tongue of yours?"

Dylan let out a wild groan. His expression was sheepish. "I just keep putting my foot in my mouth, don't I?" He stood up, pacing back and forth in front of her, his fingers idly toying with the brim of his cowboy hat. "Truth is, the idea of being responsible for your welfare during the lesson rattles me." He threw his hands up and let out a huff of air. "There! I said it out loud. I'm afraid that I won't know what I'm doing—that I'll hurt you. And the thought of hurting you tears me up inside." The vulnerability in his voice touched a tender part of her. Against her will, she found her anger dissipating. He was afraid? This strong, fierce soldier was nervous about hurting her? In a way, it made sense. Hadn't it taken her a while to get comfortable in her own skin after the accident? Hadn't she been a bit overwhelmed by the enormity of her challenges? How could she expect him to feel any differently? This was all new to him.

"Everything could have been avoided if you'd just been straight with Malachi." She frowned at him, annoyed at his ability to worm his way back into her good graces so rapidly. Why did he have so much power over her emotions?

"I'm only here for a short stint, Holly. The more time we spend together—" He seemed to be searching wildly for the right words. "I don't want to complicate your life."

She snorted. "My life? Or yours?"

He wrinkled his forehead, his handsome face looking perplexed. "What do you mean by that?"

"Ever since you arrived in West Falls, you've been tiptoeing around me, pretending that you didn't come here to start a relationship with me. Avoiding the elephant in the room." She slapped her palms against her legs. "Well! It's right here. My legs. My disability. The reason you can't possibly think of me in the same way as you did before you met me in person."

Tension crackled in the air between them. Their gazes were locked on each other, neither one blinking. She spotted a muscle twitching over his eyelid, saw the stress in his clenched jaw. He seemed to be breathing out of his nose.

"Holly, I'd be lying if I said nothing's changed between us. I know you had your reasons, but you hid a very essential truth about yourself from me. That in itself changed our relationship, because you didn't trust me enough to be straight with me. You didn't give me a chance to make up my own mind about whether or not it was something I could handle. For someone who's been lied to ever since he was a child, that's a lot to swallow." He brushed his hand across his face, appearing worn

out. "But there's plenty of things that have stayed the
same. When I'm around you, I still feel as if I've known
you my whole life. I get that easy, laid-back feeling that
doesn't come around very often. At least not for me. I
still care about you. Very much."

She swallowed, overwhelmed by Dylan's heartfelt
words. She felt the same way. From the very beginning
she'd known their friendship was special, a once-in-a-
lifetime connection. And she'd been hoping for more.
Much, much more. But she couldn't put those feelings
into words because she didn't want to put Dylan in any
more of an awkward position than he was already in.
Truth be told, she didn't want to deal with rejection.
And he'd referenced being deceived ever since childhood, something she couldn't even fathom. His words
spoke of deep layers of pain.

"And by the way, you're wrong about something,"
he continued. "Thinking about you is all I've done for
the past year. Thinking. Dreaming. Wanting. Hoping.
And it hasn't changed all that much, even though I've
tried my best to get you out of my mind."

She wet her lips, eager to know why he was trying
to rid her from his thoughts. "Why are you trying so
hard?" she asked in a raspy voice.

He reached down and touched her cheek with his
fingers, slowly trailing them down to the side of her
neck. His tenderness caused her to tremble. "You want
to know why? Since you're tired of me tiptoeing around,
here goes. I've been running away from things for most
of my life. When things get tough or too hot to handle,
I shut down. I leave." He closed his eyes for a second.
"I'm not proud of it, but it's true. What kind of man

would I be if I started something with you that I wasn't sure I could finish?"

Confusion flooded her. Was he trying to say he was sparing her from being hurt down the road? Or that he was scared? She didn't know what to make of either scenario.

"I don't know, Dylan. Maybe you should ask yourself what's worse—not being able to finish something or not even having the gumption to try."

Before Dylan could respond, she made her way to her van, not even bothering to glance back at him before she lifted herself up and into the center console, then reached down to pull her manual wheelchair in behind her. In a matter of minutes she roared off, leaving Dylan in her wake.

Chapter Seven

Ever since leaving Dylan the previous day at the stables, Holly hadn't been able to stop herself from replaying their encounter in her mind. It didn't sit well with her that things were so up in the air between them. Rather than sit around at home and fret over the situation, she was headed to lunch with the roses. If that didn't get her mind off Dylan, she didn't know what would.

As Holly wheeled herself up the ramp entrance to the Falls Diner, a thrill of anticipation fluttered in her chest. As she swung the door open, the smell of downhome cooking assailed her senses, causing her belly to rumble with appreciation. A strong sense of nostalgia swept over her. Robin, a waitress at the diner and Doc Sampson's granddaughter, greeted her with a friendly smile before ushering her to her regular table. As she made her way down the aisle, she spotted the girls at the table chatting animatedly amongst themselves. They were sitting at the booth next to the neon-colored jukebox. It had always been their favorite, the one they'd sat in when they were in high school.

The four roses—Holly, Cassidy, Jenna and Regina. The nickname had been attached to them since their teen years. Best friends since childhood, they'd been inseparable throughout their youth. When they were in high school, Doc had laughingly declared this particular table as the roses' table, due to their frequent visits. And they'd seized every opportunity to sit there, like princesses on a throne. The diner had been the local hangout for the teenagers in West Falls, and the four of them had been regular customers. Doc's best customers, if she remembered correctly. This place held a lot of great memories. As a matter of fact, she'd had her first date here. At the time she'd been crazy about Bobby Simons. For a while there, they'd been the "it" couple of the senior class, until he'd broken things off after the accident. Although she'd been crushed by his abrupt decision, she'd soon realized the wisdom in ending things. At eighteen years old, he hadn't wanted to be saddled with a young woman recovering from traumatic injuries. After being dumped by Bobby, she'd guarded her heart against any man she thought might break it. Until now. Until Dylan had entered her life with his inspiring, wonderful letters.

After putting the brake on her wheelchair, she placed her purse on the table. Using her arms, she raised herself up and swung her legs over so she was seated in the booth next to Cassidy. Since she was a regular customer, Robin knew the drill. The waitress pushed the wheelchair to the back of the restaurant, where she would fold it up and park it in the coatroom.

Holly looked around the table at the three roses, the best friends any girl would be blessed to have in their lives. They all greeted her warmly, their faces lit up with smiles. There was such comfort in knowing their weekly routine of having lunch together was still going strong after four months. In many ways it was the highlight of her week, especially since their ties had been severed for so many years. It was fun catching up and falling into their old, familiar rhythms. The laughter they shared was good for the soul.

"Four volcano cheeseburgers with curly fries. Am I right?" Robin asked upon returning to the table.

They all nodded their heads. It was their standard order, just as it had been back in high school. A warmth settled in her chest at the knowledge that some things never changed. It was a comforting thought in an ever-changing world.

Robin twirled a finger through her pink, shoulder-length hair. "And four chocolate shakes?"

"Yep. Might as well go all out," Jenna declared, patting her nonexistent belly.

"Make mine strawberry," Regina corrected. "I'm living on the edge today."

The girls all burst into laughter at the notion of Regina taking a walk on the wild side with a strawberry shake. Jenna laughed harder than anyone, a fact Holly found hard to ignore. With her long dark hair, caramel-hued eyes and exotic coloring, Jenna was stunning. And for more years than she'd like to count, her friend had been standoffish, staying as far away from the West Falls community as possible. Getting Jenna back into the fold had been a gradual process over the past few months. Even though she still remained a bit reserved, she seemed genuinely happy to be spending time with them. Because of her deep love for animals, she'd even started working as an assistant with Shep, the local veterinarian.

All four of the roses had been forced to realize that the car accident had torpedoed their friendships, turning best friends into distant strangers. When Cassidy had returned to West Falls last spring, old secrets had been revealed, creating a healing balm for all of them. They'd vowed never to let their connections be severed again and to accept responsibility for the accident as a foursome. The townsfolk were still grappling with the revelation that the accident had been the result of horseplay. At first, Jenna had been opposed to revealing their secret, insisting that they'd all promised to uphold their vow to one another. In the end, truth won out, and the four roses were now dealing with the fallout as best they could. They were still in the process of rebuilding their once-unbreakable bond and moving forward with their lives.

Cassidy picked up a spoon and rattled it against her glass. "Ladies, I have an announcement to make." Once she had their full attention, Cassidy continued, "I wanted to let you know that Tate and I have set a date for the wedding. It's December 10." Jenna, Regina and Holly began to hoot and holler, causing Cassidy to raise her hands to cover her ears because of the commotion. A few customers at neighboring tables swiveled around and regarded them with curiosity.

"So," Cassidy continued, "I would like to formally ask the three of you to be my bridesmaids." A momentary hush fell over the table.

"Oh, Cassidy, I'd be honored," Holly said, breaking the silence. She was over the moon for the couple. Words couldn't express the joy she felt in having her best friend become her sister-in-law. After all these years, it was finally coming to fruition.

"I wouldn't miss the chance to be part of this town's wedding of the year," Regina added. She was beaming at her cousin. It was nice to see, Holly thought, considering there had always been a slight rivalry between the two. Regina had always felt second best to Cassidy, and for many years, she'd felt as if she'd stood in her cousin's shadow. Being the daughter of two self-absorbed, neglectful parents had left Regina with a lot of baggage. Most times she hid it behind a veneer, but Holly knew the pain was still there, resting under the surface.

Jenna sat across the table, biting her lip and twiddling her fingers. "Are you sure you'd like me to be in the wedding?" she asked in a tentative voice.

Cassidy reached out and clasped Jenna's hand in her own. "Of course I am, Jenna. I wouldn't have it any other way. Now that we're all back in each other's lives, I'm hoping we can get back to that place in time where we could finish each other's sentences."

Jenna let out a relieved breath and smoothed back her long dark hair. "Thanks for asking me to be part of your and Tate's special day. It means a lot."

"It will be fun to wear a formal gown and get a little fancy," Holly said with a grin. "A nice change of pace for me."

Regina shook her head as she pointed in Holly's direction. "Yes, it will. I can't believe you're still wearing those T-shirts."

Holly frowned as she looked down at her You Rock, I Roll T-shirt. "What's wrong with it?"

"The shirts are cute—" Regina seemed to be struggling for the right words.

Holly crinkled her nose. "But?"

Regina, Cassidy and Jenna exchanged looks.

Cassidy spoke in a gentle, supportive tone. "You could mix it up a bit. Blues and pinks are great with your coloring."

"Hey!" Holly protested. "I got all dolled up for the benefit for Main Street Church, didn't I?"

"You sure did. And you looked amazing," Regina gushed.

She racked her brain for more evidence that she wasn't a walking fashion disaster. "And I wear a nice outfit every time I do my speaking engagements."

"Ease up, girls. If she's happy with herself, she shouldn't have to change who she is," Jenna insisted.

Cassidy pressed on. "Are those T-shirts who you are, Holly? Or simply your way of telling the world you've accepted your situation and you can be irreverent about it?"

Cassidy's question caused her to stop and think for a moment. At first the T-shirts had been a statement to the world, her way of saying, "Yes, I'm paralyzed. I'm in a wheelchair. I've accepted it. Let's move on." She'd gotten used to wearing them, almost like a protective covering. Now that the roses mentioned it, she couldn't remember the last time she'd opted for anything other than a T-shirt. She hadn't even realized how far she'd taken it.

She bit her lip. "I guess I have been hiding behind them." She let out a ragged sigh. "Why go to all the effort when my dating prospects have been slim to none?"

Regina leaned forward across the table. "So what's going on between you and your soldier? Cassidy said he was hired on at the ranch."

"We're just friends, Regina. It's not romantic," she quickly answered. "And yes, he'll be working at the ranch for a few months." She bit her lip as she contemplated laying it all on the table. The four roses had made a deal to be honest with one another about the goings-on in their lives. There was no time like the present.

"He didn't know until he showed up here that I was in a wheelchair."

Regina's eyes bulged. Jenna let out a little squeak. Cassidy reached out and put her arm around her.

"You never told him about the accident in any of the letters you exchanged?" a wide-eyed Jenna asked.

Regina eyed her with curiosity. "Not even a hint?"

Holly shook her head. There was no point in being embarrassed about it now. She couldn't go back in time and change things, despite how fervently she wished it were possible. All she could do was learn from her mistake. And try to understand why she'd lacked the courage to be completely transparent to Dylan. Why hadn't she felt as if she were enough?

"No, I didn't tell him. For some reason even I don't fully understand, I couldn't. I'm more ashamed of that than anything I've ever done since the accident." She wet her lips, determined to confide in the roses. "I got so caught up in Dylan. I guess I just didn't want him to view me any differently."

Jenna squeezed her hand. "You're allowed to make mistakes. Don't beat yourself up about it."

Regina's gaze was focused somewhere in the distance. Clearly, she hadn't even been listening to her moment of introspection.

"Sorry to go off topic, but who's that tall drink of

water standing at the counter? There should be a law against someone being that good-looking."

A frisson of awareness rippled through her. In a small town like West Falls, there weren't too many strangers who would fit that description. Holly glanced over her shoulder only to clap eyes on Dylan as he stood at the counter, chatting up Doc. He wore a light brown cowboy hat on his head, a white cotton T-shirt and a pair of well-worn jeans. His muscles were on full display. She quickly turned back toward the table, not wanting him to feel obligated to come over, especially after their dust-up the previous day. This was the first time she'd seen him since then, and it was bound to be awkward for both of them. As she'd made it clear to Dylan, obligation was the last thing she wanted from him.

"That's him… Dylan," she explained to the girls, her voice sounding way calmer than she felt on the inside. In response, Regina let out a low whistle. Her friend's enthusiasm made Holly smile.

There was no denying Dylan's masculine appeal. The short dark hair paired with the startling green eyes. His chiseled features. His rugged, manly build. She imagined his good looks garnered a lot of female attention wherever he went. She stuffed down the twinge of jealousy she felt at the idea of Dylan being sought after by the female population in West Falls. After all, it wasn't as if she had any claim on him. He was as free as a bird.

"He is handsome, isn't he?" she asked the roses. All three women nodded their heads at Holly, echoing her sentiment. She felt her pulse quicken at the thought of Dylan being in such close proximity. Although she was trying to play it cool, she felt a huge grin overtaking her face.

"He's coming this way," Regina announced, her voice laced with excitement.

Holly felt a stab of uncertainty in her midsection. This might not be the most pleasant encounter in light of the fiery words they'd exchanged yesterday at the stables. There hadn't been an opportunity to clear the air, and it wouldn't have surprised her a single bit if he tried to avoid her. Seconds later she heard the clicking sound of cowboy boots on the parquet floor, right before she felt a tall, solid presence looming beside her. Holly tilted up her head, her pulse pounding as she met his gaze head-on. His brilliant green eyes glittered with an emotion she couldn't quite decipher. Dylan took off his cowboy hat and held it against his chest. He ran a hand through his rumpled hair.

"Afternoon, Holly," he said with a nod. His husky voice sent goose bumps racing up her arms. He scanned the faces around the table and nodded his head in greeting as he murmured, "Ladies. Nice to see you."

"Dylan, these are my friends, Jenna and Regina. You've already met Cassidy." Dylan's expression as he locked gazes with Cassidy could only be described as guarded. Turning toward Holly, he held up a to-go bag. With a sheepish grin that showcased his dimples he said, "These curly fries are addictive. This is my third order this week."

The knot in her stomach slowly began to ease up. Their spat seemed to be forgotten. "You're preaching to the choir. We've been eating them for most of our lives."

"Would you care to join us? We can pull up a seat," Regina offered.

"No, I've got to head back to the ranch. But thanks for asking." He shifted from one foot to the other.

"Holly, I've got some free time this afternoon if you'd like a riding lesson."

She fidgeted uncomfortably in the booth. "A-are you sure? I wouldn't want to put you out."

"The only thing that would put me out is if you didn't accept my offer," he said smoothly, an expectant expression on his face. "It would be my pleasure."

"Well, then, I accept," she said, trying not to give in to the wild impulse to wrap her arms around his neck and place a grateful kiss on his cheek. He was instantly forgiven for being ornery yesterday. Words couldn't express how desperate she was to get back in the saddle. This unexpected offer from Dylan filled her with joy.

A smile tugged at the corners of his mouth. His handsome face held a relieved expression. "Well, then, I'll see you at two o'clock or so." He placed his cowboy hat back on his head and drawled, "Nice to meet you, roses."

After saying their goodbyes, silence reigned at the table until it was clear Dylan was out of earshot.

"Be still my heart," Regina murmured as she fanned herself with her hand.

Cassidy turned to Holly and raised her eyebrow. "I thought you said the two of you were just friends?"

"We are," Holly insisted, resisting the impulse to turn around and catch a last glimpse of Dylan as he exited the diner. She knew if she did the roses would never let her live it down.

Jenna playfully rolled her eyes. "Friends, huh? Is that why your face is lit up like a Christmas tree?"

Regina sent Holly an all-knowing look. "He's crazy about you. I can tell."

Holly felt her cheeks reddening. "No, he's not."

"She's right. He couldn't take his eyes off you," Jenna added. "Just be sure he's someone you can trust." She blurted out the words almost against her will. A shadow crossed her face and she broke eye contact, suddenly immersing herself in the contents of her plate.

Although Holly appreciated the subtle warning from Jenna, she sensed her friend was coming from a place of hurt. She couldn't put her finger on it, and Jenna had never revealed a single thing to confirm her suspicions, but she firmly believed something had happened to wound her soul. Something life changing.

Not for the first time, she prayed Jenna would find healing.

With regards to Dylan, she knew she could trust him. He was a good man, a strong and courageous soldier who'd devoted himself to keeping America out of harm's way. And he was a forgiving person. If not, he would have left West Falls as soon as he discovered her closely guarded secret. He'd never given her even the slightest reason not to have faith in him.

This was all foreign territory for her, Holly realized. It had been ages since she'd sat with the roses and talked about boys and tender feelings. There hadn't been any romantic prospects in her life for eight long years. And although Dylan was a far cry from a boy, she still had nervous flutters in her stomach when it came to him, the same ones she'd dealt with as a teenager with her first crush. In the aftermath of the accident she'd been so focused on getting her bearings that she'd put romance on the back burner. Although it was a heady feeling to be the center of attention because a handsome cowboy paid attention to you, she was determined not to get carried away. Doing so had already caused a big mess and created friction between herself and Dylan. Besides, he wasn't interested in anything more complicated than friendship. He'd told her as much the other day.

"We had a pretty intense connection over the past year, but I could tell when we met in person he was uncomfortable with my being in a wheelchair. It was written all over his face," she confessed.

"Holly! That's not fair," Cassidy protested, her emerald eyes flashing with indignation. "He was taken by surprise, that's all. Anyone would have felt uncomfortable under the circumstances."

"I suppose you're right, Cass. I have to own that," she admitted, shrugging her shoulders.

"None of it matters anyway. He's only here for a short time, until his lease with Doc runs out."

"That's what I said when I came back to West Falls," Cassidy said drily. The roses laughed as she wiggled her engagement ring at them.

Yes, indeed. Cassidy had gotten her happily ever after with Tate. And she was now a permanent fixture in West Falls, even though she'd only planned on staying for the summer to care for her ill mother. *But you're not Cassidy,* a little voice whispered. *All you shared with Dylan were poignant letters exchanged during a period in his life when he was in a war zone and seeking normalcy. It wasn't real life!*

Perhaps their connection wasn't as strong as she'd hoped. In her fantasies she'd imagined a glorious future for the two of them, filled with a courtship, a wedding and a white picket fence. No, she wasn't going to wrap her head around those pipe dreams. She just couldn't. Allowing herself to hope for something to blossom between her and Dylan was asking for trouble. And a world of hurt. Because, regardless of what the roses seemed to think, she couldn't shake the feeling that when Dylan looked at her he couldn't see past her lie of omission about being in a wheelchair and the complications it presented.

Two hours later Dylan had saddled up Sundance and assisted Holly in the process of mounting her horse. It surprised him how smoothly things were going. With the ramp, Holly was able to mount Sundance at the top of the platform where her wheelchair was level with the horse. His assistance was primarily making sure the horse was steady, lifting her up by the waist and helping her get situated on Sundance. Her upper-body strength showcased amazing power. Despite the fear gnawing at him, everything was working out just fine. Way better than he'd imagined.

As he'd discussed with Malachi, Holly's skills were rapidly improving, fueled by an increase in her endurance and a boost in confidence. After an hour's worth of riding, he could see the fatigue etched on Holly's face. Even though she didn't want to stop the lesson, he knew she'd reached her limit. Pushing her past it wasn't a good idea. Malachi had warned him about such a scenario. Against her wishes, he put an end to the session, earning himself a gigantic smile by promising to give her another one tomorrow. Once he'd helped Holly dismount and get back in her chair, she wheeled herself toward the stables, coming back out in a matter of minutes with a picnic basket and a blanket in her lap. She smiled at him mischievously.

"I think we've earned a little break," she said, holding out the blanket to him. He looked around him for the perfect place to set up, noticing a small tree a few feet away from the stables. When he reached the spot, he began spreading out the black-and-red checkered blanket, appreciative of the shade the tree provided. Holly was right behind him, the picnic basket in her hands. After taking it from her, Dylan watched as Holly put the brake on her chair, then lowered herself down onto the blanket. He settled himself beside her, marveling at her quiet strength and independence.

Barely able to contain his curiosity, Dylan asked, "So what's in the basket?"

"It's a peace offering of sorts." Holly looked him straight in the eye, her face full of contrition. "I had no business blowing up at you the other day."

"Are you kidding me? You had every right to blow off some steam. It makes me cringe just thinking how I must have sounded." He made a clucking sound with his teeth. "I know you must have been calling me all kinds of a fool."

"Were your ears burning?" she asked, sending him a mischievous look.

Holly flipped the lid of the picnic basket and pulled out two napkins and two bottles of water, then reached in again and pulled out two mouthwatering cupcakes. She placed one in front of him on the napkin.

"Are these carrot cakes?" The sight of the sweet treat had him practically salivating. A low rumble began emanating from his stomach, causing Holly to laugh.

"Yes, they are. I remember you writing in one of your letters how you couldn't wait to get one of your mother's carrot cakes." She held up her hands. "Doc deserves the credit, though. I bought them at the diner."

"She made me a batch for my homecoming ceremony." He reached out and picked up one from his napkin, letting out a sound of satisfaction as the rich taste hit his tongue. "Mmm. They've always been my favorite." He put a finger to his lips. "Just don't tell my mama, but these are almost as good."

Amusement flickered in Holly's eyes. "I'm glad you're enjoying them."

Gratitude swelled inside him for Holly's thoughtful gesture. More and more he was seeing the complete picture of Holly and who she was as a person based on her unselfish actions and sweet nature. Caring. Giving. Grateful. Ever faithful.

"You didn't have to do this, Holly."

"Are you kidding me? You've gone above and beyond with the riding lessons. The least I could do is feed you."

"I'm grateful for it, but you don't have to be beholden to me. I'm an employee here."

Holly visibly stiffened and stopped nibbling her cupcake, midbite. Her eyes held a wounded expression. Within seconds she'd masked her countenance, no longer appearing stricken.

"I didn't mean—" He fumbled with his words. "That's not the only reason I helped out today. You're my friend, Holly. I enjoy spending time with you."

Friends? Who was he trying to kid? They were clearly more than friends, although he didn't know how to categorize her. On some level, both of them knew he hadn't come all the way to Texas for friendship. Even though things were more complicated than he'd imagined before coming to town, he still felt much more than friendship for her. Denying it wouldn't change a thing. It was still there, resting against his heart. And it was growing stronger each and every day.

"I've never felt as close to someone as I do to you," he blurted. "And I've never properly thanked you for writing me. Your letters meant the world to me. In fact, hearing all about your life in West Falls opened up a whole new world for me. Hearing about this ranch kept me sane. It helped me stay strong in moments when I thought I couldn't last another day over there. So thank you, Holly Lynch."

She sent a pearly grin in his direction. "You don't have to thank me. I got as much from your letters as I gave to you. Your stories about military life made me want to be brave, even when I didn't particularly feel like it."

Dylan frowned. "Something tells me you didn't need me to give you courage. You're pretty humble about your recovery, but Doc told me all about the accident and how you endured. You persevered, Holly. And now you're thriving. That makes you a very strong woman."

"I've always had my family by my side, as well as the doctors. They make the world of difference."

The world of difference. He'd felt the same way when his mother had flown to his side at the military hospital and willed him back to good health with equal doses of prayer, love and devotion.

"I know what you mean," he admitted. "Mama did the same for me. She'd never even been on a plane before, but she flew all the way overseas to be with me. She pretty much used all her life savings to fly to the hospital and stay with me during my recovery." His throat clogged, and tears pricked at his eyes. The memory of her dedication never failed to move him. "She was my lifeline."

Holly reached out and clasped his hand, giving it a

comforting squeeze. "From everything you wrote to me about her, she sounds like a good woman and an even greater mom."

He nodded, not even trusting himself to speak at the moment. His emotions were too close to the surface, too raw. For so long, it had been the two of them against the world, fighting all the battles together as a united front. She'd never let him down. Not one single time. She'd never missed any of his baseball games, and she'd sat in the bleachers and cheered for him at his high school graduation. He was overjoyed that she'd finally found a man worthy of her love and affection, even though her new life had led her to New Mexico.

"My mother and I are going through a rough patch at the moment," Holly said, her eyes swirling with emotion. "She kept some information from me that I had every right to know. Things have been strained between us for the past few months."

Dylan frowned. "I don't mean to pry, but is it something that can be mended?" He knew all too well about fractured family dynamics.

Holly shook her head, her expression muted. "I'm praying on it. Dad called me the other night. My parents will be back in a few days from their horse-scouting trip, so it might be a good time to try to mend some fences."

"I'm sure she'll meet you halfway," Dylan said, a smile tugging at the corners of his mouth. "From what you've told me about your family, there's a lot of love and devotion there."

"Dylan, if you don't mind my asking, what about your father? In all your letters, you never once mentioned him."

For a moment he hesitated. He felt his back tensing up. His hands tightened into fists. The topic of his father was a prickly one. There were still so many unresolved issues between them, so much animosity and bitterness. It was embarrassing to admit to this amazing woman that his father had never wanted him. He'd been cast off.

Clearing his throat, he said, "Basically, I didn't have a father. Not one to speak of anyway. He bailed on me and Mama before I was even born."

"I'm so sorry," Holly said in a mournful voice. "That must have been difficult."

He shrugged, not wanting Holly to pity him. "He and my mother loved each other at one point. Or so she says. They grew up together in Madden, even though she came from a rougher side of town. My mom says they were high school sweethearts. So when she found herself pregnant, he proposed." He let out a ragged sigh. "They never made it down the aisle, though."

Holly's blue eyes shone with surprise. "No? What happened?"

"When the daughter of the richest man in town took a fancy to him, my so-called father took off in a flash." He fiddled with his collar as heat suffused his neck. It was tough to admit his father was a man of such dubious morals. "I guess he saw a better deal with her."

She nibbled at her nail, then shoved her fingers under her legs so she wouldn't be tempted to bite them. "Did he end up marrying the other woman?"

Yes." He spit the word out as if it were poison. "And he had two perfect kids with her, all the while refusing to do right by me and my mama. He never acknowledged me as his kid, although everyone figured it out and we became the target of the town gossipmongers. Every now and then he would throw me a bone and take me to a baseball game or the circus. It was usually in the next town over where no one would see us."

He fought past the lump in his throat. It was painful to dredge up a lifetime of hurt and disappointment. He wondered if he'd be choking on it for the rest of his life.

She nodded, her eyes radiating compassion and understanding, even though he imagined Holly's childhood had been picture-perfect. How in the world could she relate to such a messed-up situation? She chewed on her lip. "How awful, Dylan!"

Awful. That didn't even begin to describe it. It had been pure torment. But living in Madden had taught him a lot about survival, lessons he'd taken right along with him to Afghanistan. He liked to think those early lessons had kept him alive in a war zone. They had made him sharper and stronger, with an ability to land on his feet no matter what was thrown at him.

His gaze locked with Holly's. There was so much emotion in their azure depths. Despite all she'd been through, things that might have hardened a person, she still had empathy for him. Her eyes said it all. She ached for all he'd endured.

But he still hadn't told her the extent of the injuries he'd sustained. He hadn't yet revealed his own devastating experience with losing the use of his legs. As difficult as his ordeal had been, it was nothing compared to all Holly suffered. And she still had day-to-day challenges. Guilt began to creep in on him.

"I hate to complain about it after all you've been through. It must have been terrifying to wake up in a hospital bed and have a doctor tell you about your paralysis."

Her mouth tightened. "It was actually my parents and Tate who delivered the news. They made sure to be the ones to tell me." The look on her face spoke of hardship and loss. "Even though it was devastating, learning about the gravity of the situation from my loved ones was a blessing. When I lost it, at least I had the three of them there to hold me as I fell apart."

"And your recovery. What was that like?" he prodded, overwhelmed by curiosity about her journey.

She winced. "It took months to learn how to roll over, get dressed by myself, feed myself. I had to learn all the things most able-bodied people take for granted. That's one of the reasons these lessons mean the world to me. Riding Sundance makes me feel like my old self. It helps me feel independent. I still have a lot of mountains to climb on this journey, but I'm determined to get there."

He felt something tighten in his chest and he knew that he couldn't hold out on her a minute longer. It wasn't fair to just sit here and listen while she bared her soul. He owed her so much more than that. Clumsily, he searched for the right words to say. "Do you remember what I wrote to you about the injuries I sustained two and a half years ago?"

Her eyes went wide. "Of course. The Humvee you were traveling in… It was attacked, wasn't it? That's when your friend Benji was killed."

Benji. He tried not to think of him too often. Benji, with his Southern twang and gentle demeanor. He'd told more knock-knock jokes than Dylan had even knew existed. Even when they'd been stinkers, he'd found himself laughing. There was something so genuine and good-hearted about him. Dylan had never met a soldier more proud of his origins. Benji didn't hesitate to boast about hailing from the finest town in Virginia. Manassas, Virginia. Benji told anyone who would listen about his hometown being the site of the First Battle of Bull Run in 1861. His friend's patriotism has come at a devastating price. He'd lost his life protecting the freedoms most people took for granted.

"Holly, what I want to tell you—" He put his cupcake down on his napkin and fiddled clumsily with his fingers. "What I need to let you know is that I can relate to your situation more than most. My injuries were quite serious. For a while there I was in really rough shape. I was out of commission for months."

Holly made a tutting sound. "That's tough. I know what it's like to be confined to a hospital bed and staring at four walls. It makes you value the normal, everyday life you lived before everything tilted on its axis and changed."

He sucked in a deep breath. "Holly, there's more. We have more in common than you know. The reason I was in the hospital for so long was because I lost the use of my legs, just like you did."

Chapter Eight

❧

I lost the use of my legs, just like you did.

The words slammed into her with the force of an explosion. She grappled with Dylan's words, immediately assuming she'd misheard him.

"Wh-what do you mean?"

"My neck was broken as a result of the explosion. The force of the blast threw me from the Humvee. The doctors didn't think I would ever walk again. They told me as much when I woke up from a medically induced coma."

Broken neck. Legs. Coma. The details were whizzing around her like hummingbirds. But she couldn't seem to get past the shock induced by Dylan's announcement. Dylan had been paralyzed?

"How long? How long were you—?" She stumbled over the words, still reeling from his admission. So much of Dylan was reflected in his physicality. Being a soldier. His work around the ranch. Riding horses. For the life of her she couldn't imagine strong, powerful Dylan paralyzed.

"I couldn't walk for two months. Once the swelling

on my spinal cord went down, I began doing physical therapy." Just reliving his experience seemed to have a drastic effect on Dylan. His complexion was ashen. Tight lines were drawn around his mouth and eyes. A look of stark terror flashed in his eyes.

"To be honest, the pain was excruciating. Fear was my biggest motivator. The thought of never walking again—" He stopped midsentence, appearing worried that he might have put his foot in his mouth again.

"It's okay to say it. You're being honest. For a while after the accident, I had this recurring dream where I regained the use of my legs." She let out a shaky laugh. "I grew to hate that dream, because as good as it felt while it was happening, there was a world of disappointment when I woke up and realized it wasn't true."

Silence stretched out between them. She was still grappling with this new information about Dylan. Her mind was working overtime trying to sort it all out when something clicked into place. Finding out the specifics of his injuries explained so much about Dylan and the way he viewed her.

She tilted her head toward him, eager to see his reaction to her question. "When you look at me, there's something else you see, isn't there?"

His brows shot up. "Something else? I'm not sure what you're talking about."

"I couldn't put my finger on it until this very moment, but I get it now. Every time you look at me it's as if you're reminded of your darkest hour, your worst fear. My being in a wheelchair really brings it all back for you, doesn't it? I'm the living, breathing embodiment of your nightmare, aren't I?"

Tears pricked at the back of her eyes, but she blinked

them away. She could handle this, no matter what he had to say, no matter how badly it crushed her. It hurt so deeply to know that the very sight of her caused pain to Dylan. Because she cared for him. Deeply. And the sight of him did the very opposite to her. Her feelings were growing stronger and stronger every day. He was so much more now than the pen pal she'd reached out to as part of Main Street Church's ministry.

Dylan met her gaze without backing down. "Holly, you're right. When I first got to the ranch and realized you were paralyzed, the memories from the bomb blast came rushing back to me. They were like a tidal surge I couldn't hold back even if I tried."

His body shuddered. "I'm not sure I ever fully faced up to the events of that day. Losing Benji, having to deal with a devastating injury, feeling guilty about being alive when others weren't so fortunate. Being around you has helped me heal from all that. It's helped me face my fears. Seeing you working with the teens at Main Street Church and watching you tackle this rid-ing thing head-on—" He shook his head. "It inspires me. I've been forced to take a good long look at myself and the things I haven't faced up to. More important, it's made me even more certain of what kind of man I want to be. I don't want to be the type of man who runs away when things get tough, even though I've done that a time or two in the past. I want to be more grounded in my faith so I don't feel so alone during the rough times."

"You never walk alone, Dylan. He's right beside you. Always."

"Thanks to you, I'm beginning to realize that, for the first time in my life. I'm so proud to know you, Holly Lynch."

She ducked her head down, overwhelmed by raw emotion and the beautiful sentiment he'd expressed. "I'm proud to know you, too, Dylan. In case I never told you in any of my letters, thank you for bravely serving this country. I know it wasn't easy."

Shivers went through her as she remembered some of the harrowing details from his letters. IEDs. Insurgents. Friends killed in the line of duty.

"It was my pleasure to serve and protect this country," he said with an easy grin, his adorable dimples on full display. "There are few things more important to me than family, good friends and this amazing country we call home."

Dylan reached out to her, clasping her smaller hand in the grip of his larger, roughened one. He leaned toward her, his shoulder brushing against hers as he swept a kiss across her forehead. As his lips moved over her skin, she pressed her eyes closed, cherishing this tender interlude, which she feared would pass all too soon.

This sweet moment of perfection, she thought, *will forever linger in my dreams.*

Sometime in the future—months and months after Dylan was gone for good—she could relive it over and over again. She wanted to take this moment and brand it on her soul so the feelings it evoked would never leave her. It would give her a sense of peace just knowing they'd shared something so special. As she opened her eyes she found Dylan gazing into them with a tenderness that left her breathless. They sat in companionable silence until Dylan made mention of getting back to work. They began packing up the empty water bottles and trash.

She said her goodbyes to Dylan, casting one lingering look over her shoulder as he ambled off toward the stables, his gait full of cowboy swagger. And even though she knew there were mountains standing between them, a small kernel of hope began to take flight within her soul. Could this really be happening? Was there a possibility of winning Dylan's heart before he left West Falls?

For the next week, Malachi stayed put at the reservation, during which time Dylan gave Holly almost daily lessons. He wasn't as nervous anymore about helping her out. So far, things had worked out well, although the past few times, she'd balked when he'd tried to end the lessons. At the moment, she was sitting on Sundance, her arms wrapped around her middle in a mutinous gesture.

"Dylan, I'm fine," she protested. "I could go another fifteen, twenty minutes."

"You don't want to wear yourself out," he said, trying to sound diplomatic. Although she was building up her endurance, he didn't want to push her too hard. As it was, she looked wiped out. He couldn't miss the signs—sweat gathered lightly on her forehead, winded breath, slumped posture. Her plucky personality made it impossible for her to say she'd had enough, even though she was dragging. Holly wanted so desperately to be back in the saddle and to make forward strides. She wouldn't hesitate to push past her limits in order to get there. As far as he was concerned, it wasn't happening. Not on his watch.

"Are you saying I look worn-out?" she huffed, placing a runaway curl back in place and wiping the sweat from her brow. At times he'd noticed her hair had a mind of its own, with the locks breaking free from the pony-tail she'd placed it in. He liked seeing her hair falling all around her face. It softened some of her rough, tomboy edges. It made her look prettier than usual, if that were possible. As it was, she was stunning.

"Right now you're acting as stubborn as Rooster Cogburn."

Holly sputtered at the mention of her family's feisty rooster, a legendary character at the ranch. "Seriously? You're comparing me to a rooster?" Although her voice sounded indignant, Dylan could detect the amusement on her face and the twinkle in her eyes. She was seconds away from bursting into laughter.

"If the shoe fits," he drawled, intent on riling her up a little. "Come to think of it, your hair does get a little spiky from time to time."

She sputtered, her face resembling a storm cloud as she frowned at him. "One thing you better learn real fast about us Texas girls—never, ever insult our hair!"

Dylan threw back his head and laughed out loud. He couldn't remember the last time he'd had so much fun with someone. He liked the spirited side of Holly, even if it meant she was digging in her heels and acting ornery. Their easy banter made him feel almost weightless, and a happy feeling settled over him every time they went head-to-head. He'd never met anyone quite like her. He had the feeling if he searched the whole world over he'd never find another woman like Holly.

The sound of an approaching vehicle drew their attention away from their squabble and toward the dirt road situated just past the stables. The biggest horse trailer he'd ever seen came into view, then slowly made its way around the bends and stopped.

Holly let out a high-pitched squeal and began to fidget in the saddle. "Dylan, please help me down. My parents are here. They're back!"

As Dylan helped her down from Sundance, his mind began to whirl with the news. After several weeks on the road, the Lynches had finally returned from picking up their newly acquired horses. Holly had talked a blue streak about her parents during several of her riding lessons. From what he'd learned about them, they were exceptional people. Maggie Benson Lynch had grown up as the princess of Horseshoe Bend Ranch, with all the rights and privileges of being the daughter of a wealthy horse breeder. She'd been born with the proverbial silver spoon in her mouth. According to Holly it had been love at first sight when Frank Lynch had clapped eyes on Maggie.

"My dad was working at the ranch as a cowhand. My grandfather forbade the ranch hands from dating my mother, but once they laid eyes on each other… there wasn't a force on earth that could stop it." Clearly, Holly loved relaying the story. Her eyes had twinkled. Her skin had held a rosy glow.

"Your parents have built a beautiful life for themselves," he'd said, trying to keep a grip on his amazement. It was hard not to be impressed with all they'd achieved. Horseshoe Bend Ranch was a stunning monument to hard work and dedication.

"My grandfather, Lucas Benson, had a lot to do with it. He came to West Falls from Kentucky with barely a nickel to his name." Holly had shaken her head and chuckled.

"So how did your father win your grandpa's approval?" A cowhand winning the hand of the ranch owner's daughter? It sounded like a fairy tale to him.

"The old-fashioned way," Holly had answered, her voice tinged with pride. "He earned it by dedicating himself to this ranch and by making it his mission in life to generate more revenue and higher standards. And by chasing all the other boys away." She'd winked at him. "Gramps couldn't resist that."

Dylan shook himself out of his thoughts as two figures emerged from the cabin of the rig. He followed in Holly's wake as she quickly wheeled herself in their direction. A man he assumed to be her father strode toward her, meeting her halfway. As soon as he got within touching distance Holly wrapped her arms around his middle and hung on for dear life. He bent over and placed a kiss on the top of her head. Her mother walked over and ran her hands through Holly's hair, her gesture full of affection.

"If that hug was any indication, I dare say you missed us," Frank said as Holly released him from her grip.

"Maybe just a little bit," Holly teased, her voice breathless. "Mama. Daddy. I'd like you to meet Dylan Hart, a friend of mine. He's been hired on as a ranch hand and he's been giving me riding lessons, as well."

Dylan stuck his hand out to Mrs. Lynch. "I've heard an awful lot about the two of you. It's great to finally meet you."

"Nice to meet you, too, Dylan. Please call me Maggie. No one calls me Mrs. Lynch around here. It makes me feel ancient. And I don't do handshakes. Only hugs." Before he could comment, Maggie wrapped her arms around his shoulders and embraced him enthusiastically. Afterward, she stood back and grinned at him, her full cheeks resembling small plums.

Maggie Lynch was an attractive woman who exuded a vibe of ease and charm. With her expressive eyes and delicate features, she reminded him a bit of her daughter. The dark hair tinged with streaks of gray and the glasses perched on the bridge of her nose were uniquely her own. Frank Lynch was a bear of a man, well over six feet and broad shouldered. Frank reached out and clapped him on the shoulder, his twinkling blue eyes and warm smile immediately dispelling any doubts about his kindly nature.

"Welcome aboard, son. Any friend of my number one girl is always welcome at Horseshoe Bend Ranch," Frank said, his voice laced with enthusiasm.

Holly grinned at her father. "How was your trip home? You look a little tuckered out." Frank reached down and tugged lightly on a strand of Holly's hair. It was obvious that father and daughter shared a special bond. He didn't know if he was imagining it or not, but there seemed to be a slight tension between Holly and Maggie. Their interaction seemed a little strained.

"We made good time," Frank answered. "Every three to four hours we stopped to give the horses a water break. We spent last night in Houston, so the trip wasn't too bad. Wanted to make it home in time for the rodeo."

"The rodeo is not to be missed," Holly explained. "At least if you're a Lynch."

Maggie looked over at him. "One of the reasons we do our scouting in October is because of the temperature," Maggie explained. "The summer months are too brutally hot to safely transport horses any kind of distance. And we want to make sure all our horses are comfortable and healthy."

Frank chuckled. "In case you haven't guessed, this is more than a job for us. It's our life's passion. That and our two wonderful children."

Pride and an abundance of love rang out in Frank's voice as he spoke about Holly and Tate. Dylan felt a small stab of jealousy. What he wouldn't give to have a father who felt that way about him. To just once hear his father brag on him or hail his latest achievement would mean the world to him. Other than a few "atta boys" when he'd worked at the Bar M, there had been nothing to speak of. And he'd yearned for it. Like a starving person in search of a meal, he'd gone after any scrap of affection from him. Just when he'd felt as if they'd begun to establish a father-son bond, the rug had been pulled out from under him.

The memory of it still seared his insides. Because of it, he continued to harbor bitter feelings toward his father. It was like a festering sore that just wouldn't heal. And even though he was a fully grown adult, thinking about his father made him feel like that six-year-old boy who'd waited up half the night on Christmas Eve for his father to show up with his presents. Presents that hadn't made an appearance until a week later.

What kind of father will I be? Or husband? How can I give someone something that I never received? That I was never taught?

The questions roared through his mind like a freight train. He'd asked himself these things a hundred times or more. And even though he'd prayed on it, answers still eluded him. Finally, when he couldn't take it anymore, he glanced away from Holly and Frank, his throat clogged with a resentment that threatened to choke him.

"They're getting on like a house on fire, aren't they?" Her mother crept up on her while she was watching Dylan and her father standing side by side outside the trailer, talking and laughing as they sized up the horses.

"They seem to be," Holly answered, casting her mother a sideways glance. A little while ago her mother had gone up to the house and changed into a pair of dark-washed jeans and a long-sleeved shirt. Her father had been showing off the horses like a proud papa. She'd been content just watching Dylan's excitement over the animals.

Her mother reached down and tweaked her nose. "Penny for your thoughts. You seem to be miles and miles away from here."

"No, Mama. I'm right here." She let out a contented sigh. "I was just wishing this perfect moment could stretch out a little longer."

"Why? So you and your young man could canoodle as the sun goes down?" Maggie teased.

"He's not my young man," she said, a wistful tone echoing in her voice.

"Well, he could be if the two of you would only open your eyes and realize how right you are for one another."

"Mama! You've only just met Dylan. How on earth could you know that?" she scolded.

"You're so comfortable together. And you make such a handsome couple. With his dark head of hair and you being so fair, it's—"

"It's not that simple!" She cut her mother off. "Please, let's not pretend it's not a complicated issue. My life isn't easy. Doctor's appointments, daily medicine, doctor's bills, physical therapy."

"And everything you bring to the table counterbalances that—joy, laughter, support, faith."

She fought against a rising sense of annoyance. Why did her mother always try so hard to be her cheerleader? She didn't want anyone in her life to sugarcoat the situation with Dylan. That would only lead to disappointment and heartbreak. After everything she'd done to protect her daughter from hurt and rejection, surely her mother wouldn't want that.

Rebellion rose up inside her. Looking at things through rose-colored glasses wasn't going to do her any favors. "Dylan could be with anyone he wants! Look at him," Holly said, jutting her chin in his direction. No doubt at her father's insistence, Dylan had mounted one of the horses and was galloping around the arena, his every movement full of power and agility.

Her mother knitted her brows together. "And what if he wants to be with you? Is that so hard to fathom?"

Yes! she wanted to scream. *In a world full of able-bodied women, why would he ever choose me? Why would he choose a difficult road when he could easily take the path of least resistance?* She didn't know why it was difficult to believe Dylan might have actual feelings for her. Why was it easier to believe she wasn't good enough to earn Dylan's love?

"Holly Lynch! Don't you dare look at me like that. You're good enough." Tears pooled in her mother's eyes and she choked out the words. "You're plenty good enough, baby girl." Without her even uttering a single word, her mother was able to read her like a book and tap into her innermost fears.

She glared at her mother, all her anger rising to the surface. "I'm not your baby girl, Mama. I haven't been for a very long time." Her voice bristled with things left unspoken. Tension crackled in the air between them. Her mother's face crumpled, and she let out a ragged sigh.

"Is there something you want to air out with me?" A heavy silence descended upon them. She tilted up her head, meeting her mother's gaze as she battled her bottled up emotions.

"Why did you do it? Why did you keep Cassidy's letters from me?" Her voice broke and she stifled a sob. After leaving West Falls eight years ago in the aftermath of the accident, Cassidy had written her dozens of letters, all of which her mother had intercepted in the mail and kept from her. It was only when Cassidy returned to town that her mother's actions had been uncovered. For months now, she'd avoided this confrontation, too frightened by the depth of her fury to deal with it head-on. She'd tamped down her feelings of betrayal, which had only made them fester.

"I can't believe I didn't come to you and admit what I'd done. Cassidy told me you knew someone kept her letters from you. By process of elimination, you must have guessed it was me."

Holly couldn't bring herself to speak. She simply nodded, acknowledging that she had indeed figured it all out. It was a painful discovery, but the facts had all pointed toward her mother.

"It's no excuse, but I suppose my shame was too great. Your whole life I've tried to teach you right from wrong and to walk a righteous path, yet I failed to do the same thing when I was presented with a choice. What I did—I could say it was done of out of love, but that wouldn't fully explain it. I was nervous and afraid—I was so angry at Cassidy for leaving after the accident. I blamed her for your injuries and for inflicting so much devastation. Not just on you but Tate, as well. He was heartbroken and humiliated when she broke off the engagement. And you were broken, in every possible way. When the letters started coming I told myself I would just tuck them away somewhere until you came home from the hospital. Until you were stronger. One day turned into another and another, until years had gone by…and the letters finally stopped coming."

"Were you ever going to tell me?" Her voice was raised, and it must have carried over to the driveway. Dylan glanced at them, his face creased with worry. She nodded in his direction, letting him know everything was fine. Or at least as fine as it could be under the circumstances.

"I like to think that I would have come clean eventually," her mother answered in a quiet voice. "I've learned from this, Holly. Forgiving Cassidy is the hardest thing I've ever done in my life. Gaining forgiveness from her for withholding those letters and keeping the two of you apart… It deeply humbles me. I can only pray you forgive me, as well."

She folded her hands in her lap. As much as she loved her mother, there was no way she could ignore all the resentment bubbling under the surface. And it wasn't just going to disappear because they'd aired things out. For eight long years she'd believed her best friend had turned her back on her. If her mother hadn't intercepted the letters, she could have been spared a world of pain. There was no way she could put into words what the loss of her best friend had done to her. Losing Cassidy had caused a physical ache in her soul that had never truly subsided until she came back to town.

She cast her eyes downward and cleared her throat. "I need time, Mama. Forgiveness isn't something I can just snap my fingers and give you. I wish it were that simple."

Her soul felt heavy as she forced the words out of her mouth. She wanted to be merciful, but she still ached for all those lost years between her and Cassidy.

When she looked up, the tears glistening in her mother's eyes made her heart sink. She'd been honest, but at what cost? Hurting a woman she loved beyond measure created an ache in her soul.

"Take it from me, Holly. Holding on to anger is debilitating. It wears you down. I lived it for a very long time. It changes who you are as a person. I don't ever want you to be in such limbo. No matter how long it takes, I'll be here waiting for you."

Holly felt her mother's fingers lightly run through the ends of her hair as she walked away from her and into the stables.

Dylan made his way over to her in a few easy strides. "Is everything okay?" he asked, his brows knitted together.

"It's fine," she answered. Her voice sounded a tad wobbly to her own ears. She was doing all she could not to scream with frustration.

He cocked his head to one side. "You sure about that? Things sounded pretty intense."

Raw emotion clogged her throat. "We're just going through something at the moment."

Keeping her family issues private was a habit she'd perfected during the years when her parents had been mad at the entire town. Furious that town officials hadn't filed charges against Cassidy for the accident, they'd closed ranks and withdrawn from the West Falls community, including Pastor Blake and Main Street Church. As a result, she was accustomed to holding everything in and not confiding in anyone about her family. She'd learned at an early age to close ranks. Old habits die hard, she realized.

Dylan narrowed his eyes as he gazed at her. "I don't know what the problem is, and it's certainly none of my business, but I can tell she loves you very much. They both do. Take it from me. You're real fortunate to have them in your life."

"I know, Dylan," she said with sigh. "But that doesn't mean we don't have our problems."

Dylan shot her a look resembling disbelief. From the outside looking in, her family appeared to be picture-perfect. Dylan had no idea that her family had been embroiled in such a firestorm. Thankfully, things had changed for the better when fences were mended in the aftermath of the big storm. It had taken years for the emotional scars left over from the accident to fade away. And still, the residual affects lingered.

How could she put it all into words and make Dylan understand? She threw her hands up in the air.

"Okay. If you don't believe me, here it is. For eight years my mother kept Cassidy's letters from me and made me think she'd totally turned her back on me when she moved to Phoenix after the accident. Instead, she was reaching out to me and writing heartfelt letters I never got to read."

She fisted her hands in her lap. "Those letters would have meant the world to me at a time when I hit rock bottom. I thought my best friend had abandoned me!"

Dylan let out a low whistle. "That's pretty rough. I can see how that would make your head spin."

She released a deep breath. "Our relationship has always been based on trust. I can't believe my mom would withhold something so important from me."

"Did she tell you why she did it?" Dylan prodded. "She must have thought she had good reason."

"After the accident, she was overwhelmed by pain and fear. Her feelings toward Cassidy were ones of anger and rage. But that's no excuse!" She shuddered as the dark memories swept over her. "It was a horrible time, that's for sure. But it's just so hard for me to accept the lengths she went to out of some misguided desire to protect me."

A tremor rippled along his jawline. He opened his mouth, then shut it. His eyes were focused on her like lasers. Although looking into Dylan's eyes wasn't a hardship, there was something unnerving about his perusal. He was staring at her so intently. She couldn't shake the feeling that he was itching to weigh in on the situation.

She frowned. "What? Why are you looking at me like that?"

He stalled for a moment, chewing on his lip. He narrowed his eyes as he looked at her. "Holly, forgiveness doesn't just work one way," he finally said, his voice low and measured. "If I hadn't forgiven you when I first arrived in West Falls, we probably wouldn't be sitting here right now. And when you made your pact with the roses, you chose to keep information about the accident just among the four of you. Sometimes we all fall short of who we want to be. Perhaps you should remember that when you're dealing with your mother."

Chapter Nine

Holly's reaction to his pointed comment about forgiveness was weighing heavily on Dylan's mind. She hadn't said much in response, making him feel as if he'd overstepped a boundary. Her reddened cheeks and the firm set of her mouth had done all the talking for her. As soon as Frank and Maggie emerged from the stables, she'd quickly excused herself to take care of Picasso. Although his gut instinct was to follow her and make amends, he'd decided to give her some space.

His intention hadn't been to rile her up or get her all twisted up inside. Speaking from the heart, especially to Holly, was second nature to him. More than anything he'd wanted her to realize that her mother's actions were rooted in fear, as much as her own had been when she'd failed to tell him about her being in a wheelchair and in the aftermath of her accident. Fear was not an excuse, but it did sometimes explain lapses in judgment.

Why are you getting so invested in this anyway? Why does it bother you so much that Holly and Maggie are at odds?

In the long run it wasn't something life altering for

him. He wouldn't be around long enough to see the fall-out. But why did it feel so very important to him? Why was his first instinct to step in and make things better? To help them both heal from their estrangement? Why was he allowing himself to get sucked into their lives?

An hour after his conversation with Holly, Dylan found himself enjoying some downtime in his cottage. After making some popcorn in the microwave, spending some quality time with Leo and taking a long, hot shower, he'd gotten his second wind. Even though it was just a temporary place to rest his head until he left town, he was enjoying the peaceful vibe of his abode. Located near the center of town, it was a cheerful little place with large windows that allowed sunlight to stream effortlessly into the kitchen and living room. He'd made a few fixes to the place—nothing major, just a little paint and spackle. But somehow it was beginning to feel like home. And for a man like him, it felt like a big deal.

Earlier that afternoon, Frank and Maggie had invited him to an event at the ranch this evening, a coming-out of sorts for the horses. He was honored to be included in the festivities. According to the Lynches, it was customary at Horseshoe Bend Ranch to usher in the new horses by putting them on display and inviting friends to stop by and admire them.

"It also gives us a chance to visit with everyone after being on the road for so long," Frank had said with a wink in his wife's direction.

By the time Dylan made his way back to Horseshoe Bend Ranch, a dozen or so people were gathered around the stables. He almost did a double take when he got out of his truck and laid eyes on the nicely decorated table set up in the grassy area next to the stables. A red-and-white checkered tablecloth, small vases filled with lavender and softly flickering lanterns created a festive vibe. The tangy smell of barbecue drifted in his direction, causing a low grumble in his stomach. The aroma made him realize how hungry he was for some down-home cooking.

Several of the ranch hands welcomed him with raucous greetings. They were a great group to work with—easygoing, hardworking and friendly. They'd gone out of their way to make him feel as if he was one of them, as if he was a part of Horseshoe Bend Ranch. Strangely enough, he did feel a sense of belonging, and it left a warm, settled feeling in his bones.

He cast his gaze over the area, hoping for a glimpse of Holly. Within seconds his eyes focused in on her. She was sitting a few feet away by the stable doors, her face lit up with joy as she chatted with a tall dark-haired man. Dylan gave him the once-over, honing in on the shiny gold badge attached to his khaki-colored jacket. Something about the way they were talking caused a kernel of discomfort to pass over him. Holly seemed so at ease, so lighthearted. Was there something about this particular man triggering these feelings in her? He shook off his irritation, not enjoying the stab of jealousy slicing through him, leaving his stomach in ribbons.

He felt a little hitch in his heart at the sight of Holly. Instead of her normal T-shirt and jeans, she was wearing a burgundy-colored long-sleeved shirt, a denim skirt and a pair of black cowboy boots. Her hair hung in loose waves around her face. A pair of dazzling earrings glittered by her ears. Her gaze locked with his. She sent him a hesitant smile.

In three easy strides he was at her side, drawn in by the welcoming look stamped on her face. He hadn't planned on intruding on her conversation with the lawman, but there was something pulling him in Holly's direction. It was a strong force he couldn't ignore, like a magnet tugging him toward her. There was no point in fighting it, he reckoned.

"Glad you could make it," Holly said as soon as he reached her side.

"Mighty glad to be here this evening," he said, tipping his hat in her direction. "I'm grateful for the invite."

"Cullen Brand." A hand shot out in his direction, and he reached out to shake it, nodding at Cullen as he introduced himself. He had the distinct impression the other man was sizing him up just as much as he was taking stock of the lawman.

"Cullen works with Tate at the sheriff's office. He's a deputy," Holly explained.

"I hear you're just back from Afghanistan, Dylan." Cullen's eyes were alight with interest.

"That's right. I've been back stateside for over a month now. I'm still getting my bearings, though."

"Well, welcome to town. West Falls has a lot to offer."

His gaze shifted back toward Holly, giving Dylan the distinct impression he was making reference to her. "Especially here at Horseshoe Bend Ranch." He looked Dylan straight in the eye, his expression hardening. "We're a real tight community, too. Always looking out for one another."

"As it should be," Dylan drawled, meeting Cullen's unwavering stare head-on.

"Cullen!" Tate's voice carried across the yard. He was motioning for him to come over. Cullen acknowledged him with a wave before excusing himself to go join him. Dylan shook his head in disbelief as Cullen walked away from them. When he turned back toward Holly, he noticed the corners of her mouth were twitching with laughter. "Don't mind Cullen. He's a little protective of me." She covered her mouth with her hand in an attempt to hide her amusement.

"Did the two of you date or something?" he asked gruffly. Again, his gut tightened at the thought of Cullen and Holly's seemingly close relationship. It was a distinctly uncomfortable feeling.

"No, we never dated. He's just a good friend. And an all-around great guy."

The pressure in his chest loosened up so that it no longer felt uncomfortable. The thought of Cullen and Holly being more than friends didn't sit well with him. With Holly's reassuring words, he began to relax again.

"I hope what I said earlier about your mother didn't upset you." He studied her face, looking for any signs of distress.

Holly shook her head. "I wasn't upset. Not with you anyway." She twisted her lips. "I was pretty mad at myself, though. And embarrassed. You held a mirror up to me, and I was forced to take a long look at myself. For months now I've been angry at Mama for keeping information from me, but I did the very same thing to you. Not to mention that the roses and I kept a huge secret for eight years about the cause of the accident. How could I not have seen that I was holding her to a different standard than myself?"

"Sometimes we're too close to a situation to see it

clearly. Don't beat yourself up about it. It happens to the best of us."

She looked away from him. "You must think I'm a hypocrite. 'Judge not, that you be not judged.' I've read that scripture dozens of times, yet I've failed to practice it in my own life."

His heart cracked a little at her somber tone, coupled with the lost expression on her face. A strong urge to console her swept over him.

"Listen, Holly, I'm the last one to point any fingers at anyone. My relationship with my father is a train wreck. For most of my life I've been angry at him because all I ever wanted was for him to be present in my life. And he wasn't." He paused for a moment, determined to stave off a rising tide of emotions. "You've got something special. Two parents who are involved in your day-to-day world and who love you. All I was trying to say is, don't let anything get in the way of that. It's a beautiful thing."

Her shoulders sagged. She looked frustrated and defeated.

"I know what you're saying is true, but I'm just not there yet. In my own way and in my own time, I'll patch things up with Mama."

Dylan reached out and captured her chin in his palm. He stroked her jaw with his fingers, enjoying the feel of her silky-smooth skin. "Just don't wait too long, okay? My mama used to tell me not to let the sun go down on my anger."

Holly cocked her head to the side, her brow furrowed. "Did you always listen to her?"

"Nope," he said with a chuckle. "I was an ornery

little fella. A few times she had to wash my mouth out with soap due to my sassing her."

"Thanks. Now I've got that image in my head," Holly said with a smirk. She began laughing, which caused Dylan to chortle even louder at the memory of his pint-size self. She threw her head back and clutched her belly, her face contorted with merriment.

A feeling of joy slid through him until he was filled to overflowing with it. It was moments like this, when it was just the two of them, that it seemed as if all was right with the world. And it felt as if this was all he would ever need to be perfectly, deliriously happy.

By the time the sun began to slide beneath the horizon, two dozen or so people were gathered at the ranch. Tate, Cassidy, Doc Sampson, Jenna, Pastor Blake and his wife were some of the faces he recognized, as well as Frank and Maggie. Holly introduced him to the local vet, Vicky Shepard, and her husband, Tom. Everyone gathered around the table and feasted on barbecued ribs and chicken, corn on the cob, baked beans, biscuits and peach cobbler. Even though he didn't know everyone, he felt at ease in their company, as if they were old friends with whom he was getting reacquainted.

After dinner Maggie invited everyone to head toward the arena. It was lit up with lanterns and twinkling lights. There were six horses in all being led inside. Three Arabians, one chestnut, two onyx. The other three were bay-colored American quarter horses. It was a sight more breathtaking than any he'd ever seen. Each was more beautiful and graceful than the next.

Holly was radiant. As much as he found himself captivated by the horses, he found his gaze straying toward her. His sweet, beautiful Holly.

"This is incredible," he said. "I've never seen so many fine horses all at once!"

"Believe it or not, it moves me every single time," Holly gushed. "I can't even count how many runnings of the horses I've witnessed, but each and every one is special."

Frank walked by, leading an Arabian. He stopped right next to them, a glint in his eyes as he addressed Dylan. "We have a tradition around here. Since you're our newest hire, we'd like you to showcase one of the horses. His name's Warrior. I think it's pretty fitting."

Frank held out the reins to him. His smile was full of encouragement. For a moment Dylan was frozen, unable to reach out and take Frank's offering. He swiveled his head toward Holly, filled with disbelief at the gesture.

"Go on, Dylan," Holly urged. "What are you waiting for?"

She gave him a nudge. Dylan took the leather straps, running his fingers over them for a moment before guiding Warrior into the arena and mounting him. Once he sat astride the Arabian, Dylan cast a quick glance in Holly's direction, his pulse quickening as their gazes locked. She was clapping for him and the other riders, her face lit up with happiness. His heart seized up at the sight of her.

Against every instinct warning him not to get too invested in his temporary life in West Falls, he was becoming tethered to Horseshoe Bend Ranch and all its inhabitants. As each day rolled into the next, it was becoming harder and harder to imagine himself leaving this wonderful place. And most of all, saying goodbye to Holly.

* * *

Watching Dylan mount Warrior and then lead him in a trot around the arena caused a fierce swell of emotion to course through her. Together they were pure poetry in motion. Her cowboy soldier. He was constantly surprising her, just when she thought she knew him like the back of her hand. The restrained emotion he'd shown just before taking Warrior's reins had almost done her in. His expression had been full of gratitude. Why had he been so surprised by her father's gesture? Why had he acted as if he didn't deserve it?

More than anything in the world, she'd wanted to share this special moment with Dylan, to see it reflected through his eyes. And she'd seen it all—the wonder, the admiration, his deep love of horses—shining back at her. He'd gotten choked up when her father asked him to ride one of the Arabians because of the respect he had for Horseshoe Bend Ranch.

Dylan got it. He understood her family's passion. He had reverence for the horses and livestock. Some people were simply impressed with Horseshoe Bend Ranch and the grandeur and majesty of it. Dylan saw past the surface. He was all about the horses and the day-to-day running of the ranch. The lifestyle. Those values went way down deep to his very core.

The sound of boots rustling in the dirt had her swiveling around. Malachi was standing there, his gaze transfixed by the horses trotting around the arena. She grabbed him by the arm. "Malachi! You're back. How's your grandfather?"

He winced, letting out a slow hiss of air before he responded. "He passed on to a better world. We had his burial earlier today."

Holly knew enough about Native American traditions to know the ceremony had been sacred and simple. She reached out and placed her hand in his, squeezing it gently.

"Oh, Malachi. I'm so sorry. I know how much he meant to you. He practically raised you."

A slight tremor danced along his jawline. "I was glad to be there with him in the end as he drew his last breath. He lived a good life. That's all that really matters in the end. And the things we take away from our loved ones. The lessons they leave behind."

"I'm sure Jacob left you with enough of his wisdom to sustain you for the rest of your life."

"What he taught me most is that life is too short to be afraid." He turned toward her, staring at her pointedly. "I think that's something we have in common, Holly. Fear."

"You? Afraid?" Holly scoffed. "I can't ever remember you being intimidated by a single thing."

Malachi grimaced. "It seems that way, doesn't it? Sure, I can tackle a rattlesnake head-on and break in a wild horse, but when it comes to opening myself up… to a woman…that's where I let the fear take over."

"What do you have to be afraid of?" she asked, swallowing past the huge lump in her throat. It suddenly dawned on her that Malachi avoided relationships like the plague. Why hadn't she ever asked him about it? For the life of her, she couldn't remember the last time he'd had a woman in his life.

"Rejection. Opening myself up to someone who can hurt me again."

Again? When had Malachi's heart been broken? And by whom? She crossed her hands in front of her, fiddling with her thumbs as her mind raced. "And you think I'm like you?"

Malachi leaned down and brushed a kiss across her cheek. "I think you might believe you're not good enough, just like me. But from where I'm standing, there's nobody better than you."

Tears filled Holly's eyes as the beautiful compliment washed over her. Malachi smiled at her and ambled away, heading straight toward Tate and Cassidy. She watched through misty eyes as Malachi delivered his news, and Cassidy and Tate hugged him. She loved this man like a brother, yet until this very moment, she'd been clueless about his doubts and fears. And his heartache. It was so true that you never knew the burdens people carried around with them.

"One ice-cold lemonade for the pretty lady." Suddenly Dylan was standing in front of her, offering her a glass. While she was busy talking to Malachi, he must have finished up in the arena. She'd been so consumed by their conversation that she hadn't even noticed.

Dylan took one look at her and frowned. "Hey, what's wrong? Why are you crying?"

"Malachi's back. He was just telling me his grandfather passed away." She wiped a tear away from her cheek.

Dylan got down on his haunches, setting the drink on the ground beside him. "I'm awful sorry to hear that. Losing someone is never easy."

"I'll be praying for Malachi and his family. Now, more than ever, it makes me realize I really need to set things straight with Mama. I don't want to live in regret. If something ever happened to her, and I hadn't fixed things—"

He clutched her hand. "Nothing's going to happen to her. Talk to her tonight and tell her how you feel. Don't let another day go by without forgiving her, especially if it's weighing this heavily on your mind."

She nodded. "I will. For sure. As soon as the evening winds down, I'll talk to her."

He reached up and grazed her cheek with his palm. "Hey, what can I do to bring back that gorgeous smile of yours? I don't like seeing you so sad."

"I'll be fine. I just got a reality check, that's all," she reassured him, reaching out and brushing her knuckles against his hand. The desire to touch him, to connect with him, was overwhelming. Yet it took all of her courage to initiate contact with him. Malachi was right. The fear of rejection still lived close to the surface. Thanks to Dylan and his rock-solid presence, those fears were slowly fading.

"Hey, c'mere, Holly. I want to show you something."

Dylan gestured for her to follow him as he walked past the stables and headed toward the pasture. The area was peaceful, with not a single person in sight. He walked right up to the fence and threw his head back, causing his cowboy hat to come tumbling down to the ground. He stretched out his arms and looked up toward the heavens. Glancing back over his shoulder, he grinned at her, then pointed up at the full moon dazzling an otherwise onyx sky.

Watching Dylan revel in the beautiful fall evening was a humbling experience. She'd lived on this ranch her entire life, and although she loved it, she knew there were times she took it for granted. He'd told her enough about his time in Afghanistan for her to truly appreciate what the great outdoors meant to him. Clean air. Wide-open spaces. Freedom. Safety.

She was in awe of the way he appreciated the simple things that couldn't be bought or sold. Of the way he could rejoice in God's most wondrous creations and show such sincere gratitude for all his blessings. As she gazed at him, her mind and her heart felt full, almost to the point of overflowing. And she knew in this moment no other man would ever do, because Dylan was wedged firmly in her soul. For now and always.

Holly followed behind him, maneuvering herself over to the fence until she was parked beside where he stood. She was smiling now, which was a good thing. It had been painful to see her with tears in her eyes. It made him realize he'd do anything to make her feel better. And who wouldn't feel their spirits lift by looking up at this incredible full moon? Who wouldn't feel buoyed by this beautiful backdrop? It was a reminder of how insignificant they all were in the scheme of things. Their problems were nothing compared to the celestial splendor of the sky.

He couldn't remember a time in his life when he'd felt so content. For so long he'd had this feeling of unhappiness lodged inside his chest. He hadn't even realized until recently how much it was weighing him down. Ever since he'd arrived in West Falls, those feelings had begun to dissipate, like fog lifting after the rain. He felt almost weightless. Content.

"The look on your face when you're here in your element… It's pure joy," Holly said. "I've spent my life around cowboys. Not all of them light up from the inside when they're working the ranch. Not all of them feel what you feel when they're surrounded by nothing more than land and sky and horses."

"I come from a long line of ranchers on my dad's side. I think it runs through my veins," he said, acknowledging for the first time his ranching ties.

"Whether you realize it or not, Dylan, you've found your sweet spot." She grinned at him, appearing delighted at the prospect of him finding his way.

He was just happy he'd gotten her to smile. "I think you're right," he acknowledged. "For so long I resisted it, this gravitational pull toward ranching. That was one of the reasons I enlisted. I was so afraid of being like my dad, so scared I'd turn out to be his carbon copy. I wanted to go down a road he'd never traveled."

He shuddered, suddenly overcome by a feeling of vulnerability. "But here I am again. Right back where I started."

"Just because you love ranching doesn't mean you're like him. It just means you're a cowboy, down to the bone. He doesn't own that."

"I know that here." He tapped the side of his temple. "But here." He placed his palm over his heart. "That's where the doubts live. And sometimes they rattle around my brain until I can't even think straight."

Holly nodded her head, her expression full of understanding. "I get it. That happens to me sometimes, too. The voice of doubt in your head becomes louder than your own instincts. When those thoughts creep in, I just have to focus on something to center me."

She reached out and placed her hand on the fence enclosure. "Most times it's Horseshoe Bench Ranch that settles me. Being here reminds me of what's truly important."

There was a wistful feeling rising up inside him as he listened to Holly's words. His gaze focused on a place far in the distance. "Lately I've been thinking more and more about my dreams of owning my own ranch."

He cast a quick glance in her direction, needing to see her reaction to his statement. More times than he could count, his dreams had been scoffed at and deemed out of his reach, so much so that he no longer shared them. Confiding his aspirations to Holly wasn't easy. It left him wide-open.

"Nothing as grand as your family's spread," he qualified, "but something all of my own. A legacy for my children. Something they can feel proud to be a part of."

Children. He'd gone and said it out loud. That desire was something he'd wrestled with for some time. As much as he wanted to experience being a parent, there was still so much doubt about whether or not he would be a good one. For him, fatherhood seemed like this elusive thing he couldn't quite put his finger on. It was a mystery he wasn't sure he could unravel.

"Oh, Dylan, that's wonderful," Holly said, enthusiasm laced in her voice. "I may be biased, but owning a ranch, working the land and seeing it grow into something more beautiful than you ever imagined… That's as good as it gets."

It was as if she was reading his thoughts. Truthfully, he couldn't imagine a better life. Unless, of course, that life included a woman with whom he could share those aspirations. Someone he could cleave to for the rest of his days, the way the good Lord intended. That would be a fulfilling life.

Holly bit her lip, her expression thoughtful. "Having children is something I think about all the time. I'm not sure if I'll ever be able to have a child of my own, but if I could, it would be a dream come true."

Although he'd wondered if Holly was able to bear children, he never would have asked such a delicate question. But now that she'd brought it up herself, he could tell her how he felt about the subject. "I can't imagine you not being a mother someday. Your outlook on life is incredible. You'd bring so much to a child's life. Hope. Kindness. Faith. And most of all, an abundance of love. You deserve to live out that dream."

"Thank you," Holly whispered, emotion shimmering in her eyes. "Coming from you, that means a lot."

Dylan reached out and clasped Holly's hand in his, enjoying the way their hands felt wrapped together.

He looked up at the endless stretch of sky. Set against a velvet backdrop, the luminescent moon sat surrounded by twinkling, dancing stars. He sucked in a deep breath, inhaling the clean country air.

"It doesn't make any sense at all, but somehow the moon seems bigger here, and I don't ever think I've seen a sky so picture-perfect. Being here at the ranch settles me. It makes me feel as if anything is possible. I feel centered," he said.

He turned toward her, admiring the way the moon gleamed off her dewy skin. "That's in large part due to you."

Her eyes widened and her mouth curved in a sweet smile.

"Me? I haven't done anything."

"Haven't you?" he asked, his voice a low whisper. "I beg to differ. You've changed my whole world."

Holly's expression was one of pure joy. He leaned over and brushed the side of her face with his knuckles.

Their eyes met, and for an instant, he saw something so beautiful and pure in their depths. It took his breath away. He dipped his head down and captured her lips in a tender, romantic kiss.

As his lips moved over hers, he felt a powerful stirring inside his chest. He wanted this kiss to go on and on until the sun crept up over the horizon. She was kissing him back with a gentleness he'd never experienced before in his life. She was cracking his heart wide-open in the process.

As the kiss ended, he found it hard to pull away from her. For long seconds he just laid his forehead against hers. From the moment he'd found out Holly was in a wheelchair, he'd resisted the magnetic pull in her direction, even though he'd felt it from the moment he'd read her first letter. Since he'd arrived in West Falls, he'd been fighting their attraction with everything he had in him. But it seemed as if every time he dug in his heels, something happened to show him how wrong he was to deny the way she made him feel.

Was it wise of him to get so close to her when he knew his time in West Falls was limited? He wasn't sure. Sometimes feelings trumped wisdom, he realized, particularly when you were with someone who made you feel things you hadn't felt in a very long time. If ever.

Holly was biting down on her lip, cheeks flushed, her eyes shining brightly. "Was that a friends-only kiss?"

"Friends don't usually kiss by the light of the moon," he teased.

He was feeling cocky, buoyed by their amazing kiss. It gave him a rush sharing something so sweet and wonderful with Holly. He'd dreamed of moments like this while he was in Afghanistan, in the quiet hours between darkness and dawn. The reality was far better than his dreams.

"I always want us to be friends, Dylan. No matter what." Her voice rang out with a sincerity he couldn't ignore. She held out her hand. "Shake on it?"

Suppressing the urge to grin, he got down on his haunches and clasped it in a firm handshake. "I promise we'll always be friends."

Holly let out a relieved sigh, her mouth creasing into the beginnings of a smile.

"But something tells me we're headed toward something way more special," he said.

As the fireflies danced in the cool night air, Dylan took off his denim jacket and draped it around Holly's shoulders. He leaned in so their shoulders were touching, then placed his arm around her. He wanted to be close to her, because being with her was the one thing that made everything else fade away. It was the thing that made the most sense. All the doubts and second-guessing seemed to vanish in a puff of smoke whenever he just focused on her and stopped worrying about the future.

With a lifetime of imperfect moments in his past, this night with Holly was shaping up to be a memorable one. As impossible as he knew it was, he wished he could capture the moment in a bottle for all time. That way he could go back and uncork the bottle whenever he had the urge, allowing the memories of this evening to wash over him like a warm summer shower.

As euphoric as he felt, as deeply satisfied as he'd ever been in his life, he had a niggling feeling in the pit of his stomach. Try as he might, he couldn't seem to make it go away. Something told him that this rare feeling of contentment wasn't going to last.

As the celebration drew to a close, Dylan asked her if he could drive her back to the main house. Without skipping a beat, she accepted his offer. Being courted by her cowboy soldier was a heady experience. He'd barely left her side all night. She got goose pimples when his arm brushed against hers as they sat side by side in his truck. Joy speared through her as they sang along in unison to the chart-topping hit on the radio.

When they reached the house, they sat on the porch for a spell, listening to the quiet sounds of a Texas evening. The howl of a coyote rang out in the stillness, cutting through the silence. Dylan reached out and laced his fingers through her own. It had been ages since she'd held hands this way with someone who made her heart skip a beat. It had been so long since she'd felt this in tune with another human being. Many days she'd doubted whether it would ever happen for her.

When Dylan finally saw her to the door, he bent down and brushed a kiss across her cheek, then rubbed his thumb alongside her jawline. "I'd like to take you to the rodeo on Friday night. As my date."

All night she'd been hoping he would ask her. At one point she'd almost swallowed her pride and asked him to go with her. The annual rodeo, held out at the fairgrounds, was a two-day event that drew in crowds from all across the state. The only rodeo she'd ever missed was the one held a few months after her accident.

Being asked on a date by Dylan was a dream come true. Most twenty-six-year-old women took things like this for granted. But not her. The last time she'd been asked out on a date had been in high school. Her outings with Cullen didn't really count, since they'd never made it past friendship. As attractive as he was and as much as she enjoyed his company, she'd never felt for him one iota of what Dylan sparked inside her. There had been no pull in his direction, no tugging at her heartstrings.

"That would be great, Dylan." She could feel a huge sappy grin overtaking her face, but at the moment, she didn't even care. How could she not smile at the prospect of spending an evening in Dylan's company? Better yet, as his date.

Dylan smiled back at her, a self-assured grin that made her think he'd been counting on a yes.

"See you tomorrow?" He said it like a question. She simply smiled and nodded her head, secure in the knowledge that they would make time to see each other at some point during the day.

Finally they said their goodbyes, even though she felt a strong impulse to stretch the evening out until the stars were stamped out from the velvet sky. Dylan seemed reluctant, also. He kept turning around to look back at her as he made his way off the front porch and into his truck. Once she was inside the house, she listened for the sound of its engine roaring to life as he vanished into the night.

She couldn't remember a time when she'd felt so hopeful. So wonderfully alive. This evening had been full of fellowship and romance. Lots and lots of romance. And there had been such tenderness in the moments she'd shared with Dylan. His denim coat was still wrapped around her shoulders, serving as a reminder of his chivalry. The best thing about being with Dylan was that he never made her feel helpless. Most important of all, he acknowledged all the things she was capable of doing. He didn't treat her as if she were broken.

A pang coursed through her as she remembered one of the things they'd discussed. *Children.* Listening to him talk about his future was an eye-opener. Carrying a child to full term was difficult for paraplegics. In order to conceive, she might have to go off most of her medications. She'd done the research and talked to her doctor at length about the possibility of someday having a child. Although she had a referral to a top specialist in the field, she'd been putting it off, nervous about the prospect of flying to Boston by herself for the consultation.

A huge sigh bubbled up inside her. Ever since the accident she'd refused to fly alone. The very thought of it triggered an anxious response, a panicky feeling that raced straight through her, leaving her breathless and perspiring. On the few occasions she'd flown, her father had accompanied her. Although she'd been grateful at the time, she couldn't help but wonder if his protectiveness had held her back. How could she even think about raising a child if she couldn't stand on her own two feet and face her fears?

And how could she even hope for a future with Dylan when she wasn't certain she could ever give him the children he dreamed of making part of his legacy?

Chapter Ten

The following day passed by in a flurry of activity at Horseshoe Bend Ranch. There was an undercurrent of excitement as the buzz surrounding the rodeo reached a fever pitch. Holly didn't come across anyone—not a ranch hand nor a wrangler—who wasn't itching to attend. She didn't know a soul in town who wouldn't be putting in an appearance at the two-day event, including her three best friends. Although she'd promised to meet up with the roses, something told her there was bound to be a big reaction from them when they saw her with Dylan. They were going to tease her for sure, especially since she'd told them they were simply friends. Just the thought of it brought a smile to her face.

After her riding lesson with Malachi, she was able to spend some time with Dylan as he groomed Picasso in the stables. It was nice to be around someone without having to work in order to fill up the silence. Everything flowed so easily between them, even the quiet moments. Before Dylan headed off to the northern pasture to repair fences, they finalized their plans for the evening. He told her he'd pick her up at the main house a little before six o'clock.

The remainder of the day passed quickly, leaving her with little or no time to fret about her outfit or to get nervous about her first date in eight years.

But before she could allow herself to fully enjoy the evening ahead, she needed to make amends with her mother. She'd tossed and turned all night just thinking about their estrangement and her own unwillingness to grant forgiveness. She didn't want to be the type of person who harbored grudges, particularly against someone she loved with all her heart.

At this time of day, she knew where her mother could easily be found. As Holly maneuvered her chair across the side lawn, she spotted her mother in the distance, up to her elbows in mulch and compost in her garden. When she came closer, her mother whirled around, a surprised expression etched on her face. "Holly! I'm surprised to see you out here."

Holly's heart sank. There was a time when her mother wouldn't have been startled at all to see her in the garden. It showed just how wide the gap was between them. Gone were the days when she'd just show up unexpectedly with a glass of sweet tea and lemon bars.

"I've always loved this place and being able to see your green thumb in action. What are you planting?"

Her mother wiped her brow with her gloved hand. "Just trying to plant these wildflower seeds next. Blue bonnets will add a nice touch to the garden. They need a sunny spot in order to thrive. I finished with the pansies and violas. And of course my favorites, snapdragons." She looked up at Holly, squinting against the sun's glare.

"Is something troubling you, sweetheart?"

Holly swallowed past the lump in her throat. There was so much she wanted to say, yet she didn't know where to start. She folded her hands in her lap and fumbled with her fingers.

"I'm tired of being angry at you. I've been blaming you for all the lost years with Cassidy. But the truth is, you weren't solely responsible for that. There were so many ripples after the accident. It was like a domino effect that toppled down everything in its path."

Tears freely ran down Holly's face, and she didn't even bother to wipe them away.

Her mother's face crumpled. "I did an awful thing. I should never have kept those letters from you. You had every right to read them and decide for yourself if you wanted Cassidy in your life."

Holly nodded. "Yes, it was wrong, Mama. But I forgive you. And I know why you did it. You were protecting me the only way you knew how. Someday I hope to be a mother myself. From what I've heard, protecting one's child is a strong instinct."

"Yes, it is," she acknowledged with a nod. "It's the most powerful force on earth. But in the past few years I've come to realize you don't need me or Tate or anyone else to fight your battles. You've grown into a strong, independent and wise young woman, Holly Lynch. And I'm so very proud to call you my daughter."

Her mother swiftly bridged the gap between them. Holly threw herself into her mother's open arms like a force of nature. It felt so nice to be embracing her mother without a single issue standing between them. Now there was nothing but love and mutual admiration pulsing in the air around them.

As they broke away from one another, Holly watched as her mother swiped at her eyes with the back of her hand. They were happy tears, born of reconciliation and hope. It was a joyful moment, especially in the aftermath of so much heartache and loss.

"So I heard Dylan talking about taking you to the rodeo tonight." A sweet smile hovered on her mother's lips. She nodded her head approvingly.

Holly couldn't hold back her grin. Suddenly it felt as if all was right in her world. Now that she'd bridged the gap with her mother, her thoughts were full to overflowing about her date with Dylan.

"Our first real date," she said. "I have to admit I'm a little nervous, but more than anything, I'm excited to take this journey with him, wherever it leads."

Her mother reached out and tightly clasped Holly's hand. "It's what your father and I want for you, Holly. To continue to make strides and move forward on your journey. If you decide to follow that path with Dylan at your side, we'll support you."

Holly felt her cheeks flush with excitement. There were no guarantees about her future with Dylan, but she had every reason to believe they were headed toward something wonderful. Knowing she had her parents' blessing made it even more special. Anticipation about this evening was building inside of her, as fragile and precious as a burgeoning flower in springtime.

When Dylan arrived at the house at five minutes before six, Holly was there to greet him. He was standing on her front porch with a bouquet of wildflowers in his hands, dressed in a dark pair of jeans, a long-sleeved shirt and a black cowboy hat.

"I've been wanting to give you flowers for a long

time," he drawled. His grin made him even more handsome than anyone had a right to be. She had to tear her gaze away from him or run the risk of staring as if she were a kid looking through the candy store window.

She reached for the flowers, raising them so she could inhale their sweet scent.

"Thank you. This is way better than the first time," she said, making reference to the flowers he'd inadvertently given to Cassidy on the day they'd met.

Dylan laughed and shook his head. She felt happy he could look back on that moment and chuckle about it. At the time it hadn't been a laughing matter. Things had changed so much between them in the past few weeks. It was humbling to acknowledge she'd made such a major mistake with Dylan, yet he was still in her life.

As her parents looked on with barely contained excitement, she sailed out the door with Dylan, eager to get to the rodeo and start enjoying the festivities. It was more practical for her to drive since her van was tailored to her specifications and she had a placard designating her as a disabled driver. With the placard, they'd be able to park close to the venue so she wouldn't have to travel all the way across the dusty, uneven lot. Being in a wheelchair meant having to plan every aspect of an outing, from the parking situation to making sure the seats were wheelchair accessible.

From the moment they entered the gates, they could see the atmosphere at the rodeo was lively and bustling with spectators. It was a little tricky at times navigating her way through the sea of people, but Dylan was a huge asset. With his commanding height, broad shoulders and no-nonsense demeanor, he easily cut a path for them through the crowd, never leaving her side for a moment.

By the time they made it to their seats, the first event—barrel racing—was about to start. Holly was rooting for West Fall's own, Lacy Kidd, one of the strongest competitors. She cheered loudly along with Dylan as Lacy outperformed all the other riders and was awarded first prize. Bronc riding, bull riding and steer wrestling quickly followed, making for a thrilling event. When Dylan put his arm around her and asked her if she wanted to go get some refreshments, she almost had to pinch herself. Spending time with him at the rodeo was the most fun she'd had in a very long while. Their rapport was effortless, and she couldn't help but feel as if she'd known him her whole life. There was no nervousness, no awkwardness during her first date in eight years. Being with him made her feel as comfortable in her own skin as she'd ever been since the accident.

When her stomach started grumbling loudly as they made their way toward the concession stand, they both broke out in laughter. It was funny how she didn't even feel embarrassed. She felt so comfortable with him, so natural. It was the way her brother had always described the ease he felt whenever he was with Cassidy.

Dylan suddenly stopped in his tracks. When she looked up at him, his entire face had been transformed. His jaw was tight. Stress lines had formed around his eyes. Her eyes quickly skimmed over him. A few moments ago he'd been having a wonderful time. What had caused such a drastic change in him?

"What is it? Is something wrong?"

"It's nothing. I just want to get out of here," he said.

His tone was abrupt. His face had an ashen look. It seemed as if he might snap in two.

"Something happened. Tell me. It's written all over your face." She wasn't letting this go, not when she sensed something was terribly wrong.

"Dylan." At the sound of the deep masculine voice, Holly swiveled her head just in time to see a man reach out and grab Dylan by the arm. She watched as Dylan violently jerked away from the man's grip, his face contorted in anger. The older man was tall, broad shouldered, with a full head of sandy-brown hair. Tension crackled in the air as they faced each other, both holding fierce expressions.

Holly reached out and gripped Dylan by the wrist, pulling him toward her in the process. When he turned toward her, his eyebrows were furrowed, his cheeks reddened.

"What's going on? Who is this?" She darted a look at the man, who was still standing a few feet away, his expression as tension filled as Dylan's. Matter of fact, he bore a strong resemblance to Dylan—same eye color, a similar build, the exact same dimple in the chin. Suddenly, bells were clanging in her head.

"Nothing. Nobody." Dylan's tone was clipped and riddled with barely suppressed rage. An angry vein thrummed above his eyebrow. He looked as if he was coming undone.

"Dylan. Please. Tell me the truth. What's got you so twisted up inside?" She was begging him now, filled with fear and uncertainty about his state of mind. Something had to have happened to create such a change in him. What in the world was going on?

Dear Lord, please hear my prayer. Whatever war is

*raging inside Dylan, please give me the tools and the
wisdom to help him through it. I care so deeply for him,
and it hurts me to see him so torn up inside. With Your
guidance, we can get through this.*

His face hardened into a mask of granite. His eyes
were bristling with anger, his teeth gritted. He jerked
his chin in the man's direction as he spit out, "That's R.
J. McDermott, owner of the Bar M Ranch." He shoved
his fists into his pockets and looked away from her. "He
also happens to be my father."

Tension crackled in the air in the wake of his announcement. He swung his gaze back toward Holly,
needing to see her reaction to his admission. The look of
shock and pity on Holly's face made him want to turn on
his cowboy-booted heel and leave the fairgrounds. Even
though he wanted to get as far away from R. J. McDermott as humanly possible, he couldn't very well leave
Holly behind. And he was sick and tired of running
away from things. So far, it hadn't done him any good.

"Son, please just give me a few minutes." He couldn't
remember ever hearing such a pleading tone in his father's voice. He almost sounded human. For a moment
he almost thought R.J.'s expression was one of humility. Surely he must be seeing things, since there wasn't
anything humble about his father.

He left out a harsh laugh. "Why should I? That's a
lot more than you ever gave me." He pointed his chin
in his father's direction. "What do you want?"

"I've been trying to find you for years, ever since you
left Madden. I heard you were in the service, but your
mama wouldn't give me any information about where
you were stationed."

"Don't talk about my mother." His voice rang out sharply. "You don't have the right."

R.J. held up his hands as if warding off an enraged bull. "I know you're angry at me. And you have every right to be. For a very long time I didn't do the right thing. I'm hoping to change all that."

Seeing his father after such a long time was a shock to the system. It rocked him to his core. He hadn't expected it in a million years. Not here of all places. Not in West Falls, miles and miles away from Oklahoma. He'd believed his father had written him off years ago.

What was he doing here? How had he tracked him down?

"Dylan. Son. Hear me out." Hearing the word *son* roll off his father's tongue made him grit his teeth even harder.

Looking at R. J. McDermott was like staring into a mirror. They shared the same sea-green eyes, a similar rugged build, the exact dimple in their chins and identical noses. Because of the striking resemblance, his paternity had become a hotly debated topic in his hometown. Although his mama's advice had been to hold his head up high and ignore the petty gossip and whispers, it hadn't been easy.

Seeing his father again forced him to relive those soul-crushing moments. It reminded him of every slight, every snub, every father-son event he'd missed out on as a kid. It brought back the pain of having to witness his father sitting with his wife and other kids in the front pew at church while he'd hidden himself in the back. And he'd never forget all the fights he'd waged in his mother's honor when some kid had called her a foul name. It had all been because of R. J. McDermott and his shaky moral compass.

A muscle twitched in his jaw. His stood up tall, steeling himself against the onslaught of painful memories. He wanted to appear as impenetrable as granite. "There's nothing you could ever say to me to make up for everything you put me through."

R.J.'s mouth twisted. "But I'd like to try. That's why I hired a private detective to find you. Because I want to be in your life. I want to build a relationship with you."

"Since when?" he demanded.

His father winced. "Son, I've always loved you. I may not have shown it in the ways that mattered, but I've loved you since the day you were born."

He let out a snort. "You've been in and out of my life since the day I was born. We don't even share the same last name. Any number of times you could have claimed me. You didn't!"

Dylan took a few steps until he was nose to nose with his father.

"So what's changed? Why are you so all fired up about us reconciling? Why now?"

His father's chin trembled. "Because I realized how wrong I've been. I've done a lot of soul-searching. I heard through the grapevine you'd enlisted. For years I've been filled with worry about whether you were going to make it back home alive. It killed me knowing that the only information I had about you came from a few of your high school buddies. And even then, the information was sketchy. Life doesn't often give us second chances. I mean to make the most of mine. If you'll let me."

For a moment he stood and stared into his father's

eyes, noticing for the first time how the past six years had aged him. There were tiny wrinkles surrounding his mouth, and his sandy hair was peppered with a few strands of gray.

For his entire life R. J. McDermott had seemed larger than life. Now he seemed vulnerable. Even though he'd always seemed like a giant to Dylan, he was merely a man. The very notion had him questioning everything he thought he knew. It made his thoughts and emotions feel jumbled. Wanting to get as far away as possible from the situation, he took a step backward, coming up against Holly's wheelchair in the process. Turning toward her, he could see the confused expression on her face. "Holly, let's go. There's nothing more I need to hear from him."

Holly looked up at him, her blue eyes wide. "Are you sure? He came all this way to see you."

"Son, please don't go," his father pleaded.

"I'm not your son. You made that mighty clear six years ago."

"You'll always be my son."

"Go back to Oklahoma," he answered.

"I'm not going anywhere, Dylan! Not until the two of us can hash things out." The sound of his father's deep voice was thunderous.

Making sure Holly was right beside him, Dylan charged away from his father and headed toward the exits. It wasn't until he was a good distance away that he finally allowed himself to release the choppy breath he'd been holding.

Dylan's powerful tread made it hard for her to keep up with him as he strode toward the parking lot. His steps were full of anger—an unbridled rage that might have frightened her if it wasn't Dylan she was observing. She knew he wouldn't take it out on her. His emotion went inward. He was a quiet storm brewing. It had nothing to do with her and everything to do with his unexpected run-in with his father.

It was all so confusing. Dylan's father was R. J. Mc-Dermott, the same man who'd hired him at the Bar M Ranch and mentored him in the ways of ranching. But he was also the man who'd refused to give his son the family name or any acknowledgment of his paternity. Yet he was here in West Falls after hiring a private detective, begging his estranged son to give him another chance. Even though she resented him for every scar he'd inflicted on Dylan, she couldn't help but nurture a fragile hope about reconciliation between father and son. Judging from the mutinous expression on Dylan's face, the likelihood of it happening was slim to none.

The facts were still whirling all around her. She was trying to make sense of it, to put the pieces of the puzzle together. Dylan and R.J. Father and son. Six long years of estrangement.

"Dylan, are you all right?" They'd reached her van, and instead of moving toward the passenger side, he was just standing there staring off into space. He was breathing heavily through his nose, his jaw tightly clenched. His face looked as ominous as a storm-filled sky.

"I'm fine," he said with a small nod of his head. "I just couldn't stay in there a minute longer, listening to him."

"I have to admit I'm a little confused. You said a while back that you worked at the Bar M. That's where you learned all about ranching and breaking in wild horses, wasn't it?"

Dylan nodded, which gave her the go-ahead to keep talking. "If your relationship with him was so fractured, how did all that happen?"

Shoving his hands in his pockets, he began pacing back and forth, his cowboy boots stirring up a cloud of dust. "When I was a teenager, he gave me a job, taught me about ranching. I guess you could say he took me under his wing. But he never acknowledged me as his son. He never gave me that sense of belonging, even though I wanted it more than anything. Even though the whole town knew and gossiped about the situation, he never publicly claimed me, never once offered me the McDermott family name."

Seeing the pain etched on Dylan's face was agonizing. Hearing the ragged, broken tone of his voice brought tears to her eyes. She couldn't imagine someone not claiming this wonderful, brave man. How could R. J. McDermott have denied his own son his place in the world? She didn't have to ask what it had done to Dylan. The emotions rippling across his face and laced in the ragged tone of his voice spoke volumes.

"Yet, you ask, why should not the son suffer for the iniquity of the father?" The scripture from Ezekiel roared through her mind. It was so unfair the price Dylan had paid for his father's pride and selfishness. Because of R. J. McDermott's unwillingness to acknowledge his son, Dylan had been forced to pay for his father's sins. And he was still paying, judging from the torment he was going through. He was still suffering. She knew from her own painful experience that some wounds might never fully heal. But she was a firm believer that with faith and love all things were possible.

Her mouth felt as dry as sawdust. "What happened six years ago?"

He shoved his hands in his back pockets and rocked back on his heels. She could see the tension in his jaw. "I was working at the Bar M right alongside R.J. Being together like that, day in, day out… We got real close. For the first time in my life, I thought maybe just maybe, we were building toward something real. Something lasting. A local television crew was coming to do a feature on the Bar M. He promised me I'd be part of it, that he'd introduce me as his son. He said I'd be standing right there next to Jane and Roger Jr. I felt so blessed to finally be acknowledged. It was like this huge cloud lifted and the sun was bursting through."

He shuddered, his whole body heaving with the effort. "Mama tried to warn me. Told me he wouldn't follow through."

He hung his head, focusing on the ground as he drew circles in the dust with the toe of his boot. A wild chuckle burst from his lips. "On the day of the shoot, he pulled me aside and told me he couldn't go through with it, that his wife wouldn't let him publicly acknowledge me. He said it would hurt his other children. I left that day and never went back. I haven't seen him since… Not till this evening."

"Not once in six years?" She couldn't hide the shock in her voice.

Although Dylan had told her about being estranged from his father, she'd had no clue about the reasons. The circumstances behind it were devastating. Again and again, his father had wounded him, and even when he'd given him another opportunity to get it right, he'd broken his promise and shattered the last vestiges of Dylan's belief in him. She felt a strong urge to turn back around and give R. J. McDermott a piece of her mind.

"Not once. Not a call or a letter or an email. He tried to reach out to me, said he wanted to make things right, but I wasn't interested. Not after what he did." His voice sounded raspy, and she sensed he was fighting against a tide of emotion.

"Do you think there's any way the two of you could—" she began.

"No," he said sharply. "Too much water has passed under that bridge. I'm not some little kid looking for his father's love and approval."

She wanted to remind Dylan about what he'd said to her about forgiving her mother, but she stopped herself. The situation wasn't the same, not by a long shot. Dylan had suffered a lifetime of not feeling good enough due to his father's actions. Over and over again, he'd been hurt. That wasn't a simple fix. There were so many layers to the situation, so many undercurrents swirling around.

As she drove back to the ranch, she couldn't help but notice the strained vibe between them. Dylan's body language had closed him off. He sat in the passenger seat and stared out the window. A few times she tried to make light conversation, but he wasn't giving her anything more than monosyllabic answers. When they arrived back at Horseshoe Bend Ranch, Dylan saw her to the door, then brushed a quick kiss across her forehead. She stuffed down her feelings of disappointment that the kiss wasn't as romantic as she'd hoped for. In a perfect world they would have sat down together on the porch and held hands or kissed underneath the stars.

When Dylan headed off into the night he didn't once look back at her. She willed him to turn around, to give her one last, lingering look to let her know that nothing had changed between them. There was no look, nor a goodbye wave as he heaved himself into the truck and started its engine. A chill ran down her arms as his truck roared off into the onyx night, leaving her staring after him with a strong sense of foreboding settling over her.

Chapter Eleven

I'm not going anywhere, Dylan. Not until we can hash things out.

His father's parting words had thundered in his ears all through the night, resulting in a fitful sleep. He'd given up trying to get some shut-eye, knowing his turbulent thoughts would keep him awake. The simple truth was he didn't want to hash anything out with his father. He didn't want to listen to what he had to say.

Why not? a little voice inside him nudged. *What are you afraid of? That you still care? That you still have love for him even though you don't want to? That he still has the power to make you feel like that wide-eyed child who cried his eyes out when Daddy didn't show up on Christmas morning?*

He shrugged off the torturous thoughts as he headed toward the ranch for a full day's work. West Falls had been his safe haven, his brand-new shiny start. Now it had been tainted by his father's unexpected arrival. More and more as of late, he'd begun to like the man he was becoming. A man who wasn't bogged down by past disappointments and family dysfunction. A man who knew that his worth wasn't determined by his last name.

Right now he felt as confused as he'd been six years ago. In the span of a few minutes in R. J. McDermott's presence, all his confidence had been shattered. All his doubts had returned. About himself. And his father. And Holly. A half dozen times last night, he'd had to stop himself from throwing his things into a suitcase and taking off for parts unknown. The only thing stopping him was Holly. He owed her more than that. More, probably, than he'd ever be able to deliver.

She didn't deserve to pin her hopes and dreams on someone like him. Cullen's image popped into his head. Solid, dependable Cullen. He was a deputy. He was part of the fabric of this town. Her brother's right-hand man. A man like Cullen wouldn't disappoint Holly. He'd be as sturdy as a brick wall.

It wouldn't be fair to lead Holly on without knowing for certain if he could go the distance with her. Memories of his mother came into sharp focus. Her face puffy from lack of sleep. Her eyes red rimmed from crying. All because she'd never gotten over loving his father. Pain seared through him at the notion that he could inflict such damage on Holly. *Like father, like son.* Hadn't that always been his worst fear?

Spunky, amazing Holly. She was too good for him and the uncertainty that plagued him. She didn't deserve to be with someone who was filled with so much indecision. After all she'd been through, he couldn't be the person who hurt her. He wouldn't! It was far better to slightly wound her now than to devastate her further down the road. As loving as she was, he knew it was only a matter of time before she surrendered her heart to him. If she hadn't already.

All morning he kept himself busy at the ranch. He spent hours working with the Angus cattle in the southern pasture. And when he was done, he went straight to work on a project in the stables. Around midday he caught sight of Holly in the corral, having her lesson with Malachi, but he didn't venture outside to watch. After last night, he didn't have the slightest idea how to get things back to normal. He still felt so off-kilter, with his mind racing in a hundred different directions. He was afraid she would see the uncertainty in his eyes and call him on it. How could he tell her everything that was bottled up inside him?

After her lesson, Holly sought him out as he was trimming Warrior's hooves. She kept a respectable distance until he was finished. Having grown up around horses, Holly knew all too well the dangers of startling a horse.

"He's really taken to you," she said once he'd finished the job.

"I think he likes having my undivided attention," he answered as he rewarded Warrior with a sugar cube. "Haven't met a horse yet who didn't like to be pampered a little bit."

Within seconds, the conversation between them stalled out. The silence between them was weighty. Holly kept casting him curious glances, as if she was trying to figure something out. And he couldn't seem to find his way back to that comfortable, easy rapport they'd established. He kept wanting to look over his shoulder to make sure his father wasn't going to show up and shatter the sweet peace he'd found.

Holly frowned at him. "You seem a million miles away from here."

He tried to smile at her in an attempt to lighten the mood, but his mouth didn't seem to want to cooperate.

"What are you talking about? A man can't be in two places at the same time," he said, trying to make his tone sound light.

"Something's changed in you since last night," she said in a quiet voice. "You haven't been the same ever since you ran into your father."

He shot her a questioning look. Was his mood that heavy? Was there a dark storm cloud hovering over his head?

She continued, "You seem somber. Distracted. And right now you just seem to be going through the motions."

He bowed his head. It was already happening. He could tell by the wounded tone in Holly's voice that she was hurt by his behavior. Confused about his moody temperament. Disillusioned. Pretty soon everything would fall apart. Everything was slipping away from him.

"I'm sorry if I'm disappointing you." And he was sorry. More than he could put into words.

Holly met his gaze, her eyes flashing with surprise. "You haven't disappointed me. I just wish you'd let me in. I know you're hurting. I know your father showing up knocked you off balance. But you're holding it all in. I thought we could talk about anything." She let out a sigh. "In our letters we always managed to cut through everything and get straight to the important stuff. Has that changed?"

He didn't know how to answer that question. Truthfully, with his father being in West Falls, it felt as if everything had changed. How could he put it all into words and make her understand?

"Holly, I'm not sure you could ever see where I'm coming from. How I feel. Your whole life you've had this solid, intact family unit. Me, I don't know what a real family is. What it looks like. Seeing my dad just reminds me of what I am, where I come from."

Holly shook her head fiercely. "Your mother was your family, Dylan. And she did a wonderful job raising you, despite all the financial hardships, the gossipmongers and being a single mother."

"Yeah, she did," he said with a nod. "But my father—he bailed on us. Me, especially. I have no idea what it's like to have a father, one who puts you first and loves you unconditionally. He didn't even give me his last name. You have no idea what that does to a person."

She looked stricken, and her cheeks were flushed crimson. "No, I don't know. I can't imagine how much pain you've gone through. To tell you the truth, it hurts me to even think about it. But what I do know is that you can't let your past determine your future."

"But what if I'm like him, Holly? What if I bail on you when things get tough?" He turned toward her, seeking an outlet from all the turbulent emotions he was waging war against. "I don't want to ever hurt you like that. I don't ever want to be the one to cause you pain. I can't let that happen!"

* * *

Fear trickled along her spine. The intensity in Dylan's voice was causing warning signs to flash before her very eyes. He sounded so unsure, as if he were precariously straddling a fence, with no certainty as to which side he might land on.

Suddenly, she felt as if everything was slipping away from her. Every dream she'd nurtured for herself and Dylan hung in the balance. And there was nothing she could do to change things. He was wavering. He was backing away from what they'd built. She could hear it in his voice. It shimmered in his eyes and in the way he looked at her. Her heart sank into her belly.

In some ways she'd always expected this. Ever since Dylan had arrived in West Falls, she'd been dreading this moment. He'd always been just out of reach, like a high-flying kite she'd never been able to hold on to. So far she'd been savoring all the precious moments they'd shared, just in case things didn't work out the way she hoped. Instead of prolonging the agony, she wanted to cut to the chase. It was always better to rip off the bandage rather than to tug at it, bit by bit. Either way, she knew it was going to be unbearably painful.

"What are you saying?" Her mouth felt as dry as sandpaper, yet she somehow pushed the words out. "It's best if you just spit it out."

Dylan raked his fingers through his hair. "I stayed up last night, thinking this through." Dylan's eyes were bleak. Empty. "I'm going to be moving on from West Falls."

"Moving on?" she asked dully. Had she heard him right? "But I thought—"

She swallowed painfully. Her tongue felt heavy.

What had she thought? That Dylan would stay in West Falls forever? That they would ride off into the sunset together? That he would love her?

"I thought we were—" Her throat constricted as she tried to utter the words. Pride wouldn't let her finish her sentence.

"I know. So did I." He let out an agonized groan, and his tortured gaze swept over her. "I'm not the man you need. Don't you see, Holly? I'm broken. Seeing my father brought a lot of issues to the surface. It made me realize how unfair I was being to you. How can I promise you a future when I'm not even sure of anything myself? Coming face-to-face with him after all this time brings back all the doubts and insecurities. I thought I'd closed a door on that, but I haven't."

"I haven't asked for promises," she said in a quiet voice. She hadn't asked for anything from him other than his forgiveness. It still surprised her that he'd given it to her so freely. But the truth was, she wanted so much more.

Dylan was rattling off a string of excuses, each and every one sounding like a platitude. The bottom line was he didn't want her. And he wasn't sticking around to fight for the life they could have together. He was giving up. He was running.

Waves of pain washed over her. She pressed her hands against her belly as her insides roiled and twisted. Was this Dylan's version of "it's not you, it's me"?

"I know you haven't asked for anything, Holly. And you probably never would. You believe in people, and you give everyone the benefit of the doubt." A poignant smile swept across his face. "But you deserve promises…and commitment and devotion. I have no doubt you'll find those things."

"Just not with you." She choked the words out, almost against her will. Dylan locked gazes with her, and she watched as a tremor ran along his jaw. He seemed to be fighting some invisible battle. He opened his mouth, then shut it. He clenched his teeth.

A look of pain was etched on his face. He sucked in a deep breath. "I've got to go pack up my things and talk to Doc."

She now knew what it felt like to lose the love of her life. It was so much more incredibly painful than she'd ever imagined. Why hadn't she known it would be this awful, this devastating? Why hadn't she prepared herself for this possibility? How could she have allowed herself to get so wrapped up in loving him that she'd forgotten to wear her suit of armor? For so long she'd been shielding her heart, yet in one fell swoop, Dylan had torn down all her defenses and wedged his way into her very soul. And now she was going to lose him. She was going to have to live a life without him.

Dear Lord, give me enough strength to let go of Dylan with grace and humility. I love him more than words can ever say, but I know that doesn't give me the right to hold on to him. I have to love him enough to let him go and make a life for himself on his own terms.

She wanted him to stay. If begging would do the trick, she'd have done it, throwing her pride to the wind in the process. But what would she gain by having Dylan stick around out of pity? No, that was the furthest thing from what she wanted. He'd marked her, branded her very soul with his gentleness and goodness. Because of him she would never be the same. Despite

her fear of rejection, she'd opened up her heart to him.
She'd cast away all her fears and insecurities, all in the
hopes of making a future with him.

And since she loved him—with every fiber of her
being—she had to let him go.

"Dylan, I'm not going to beg you to stay. If something inside of you is telling you that a life in West Falls
isn't the life you want for yourself, I have to respect
that. From the moment I read your first letter, I wanted
nothing but good things to come your way. And that
hasn't changed one bit."

He reached out and swept his palm across her cheek,
his fingers trembling as they grazed her skin.

"Will you—?" His voice broke off, swallowed up
by emotion.

She knew instinctively what he was asking. "Don't
worry about me. I'm going to live my life," she said in
a strangled voice. "I'm going to stretch myself, to go
after all the things I want to accomplish. Whether it's
rock climbing or going on a plane by myself or carrying a child, I'm reaching for the brass ring."

He brushed his hand over his face and heaved a tremendous sigh. "Holly, you deserve all that and so much
more. I wish I was the man who could make all your
dreams come true."

He bent down and brushed a fleeting kiss across her
lips. His lips tasted salty, and she realized it was her
own tears, which had slid down her face onto her mouth.
Bravely, she wiped them away. Before she knew it, he
was walking away from her and out of the stables, dis-
appearing from view within seconds. She steeled herself
against the ripples of pain coursing through her body.

Loving Dylan was out of her control. Losing him

wasn't something she'd ever wanted to face, although from the moment he'd arrived in West Falls, a part of her had always feared it would happen. But her life wasn't over. She still had miles and miles to go on her journey. In a few weeks, she'd be heading to Boston in order to meet one of the top specialists in the world. An unexpected phone call from the doctor's office had forced her to make a swift decision. She'd said yes to the consultation, knowing it would allow her to get the answers she needed. She was going to swallow her fear so she could create positive changes in her life. Although a part of her soul would always belong to Dylan, she loved herself enough to know she deserved happiness.

She was no different from Cassidy or Regina or Jenna. They all yearned for the same things. A family. Faith. Someone special to adore and be adored by. A soft place to rest their heads at night when the day was done. Cherished friends. She wanted it all. A life she would proudly live out for as long as she graced this earth.

Before Dylan had come into her life, she'd really not been sure what she could give back as a partner. Now she knew. She'd never really considered herself worthy of the happily ever after. In the back of her mind, there had always been a niggling idea that she wasn't wife material. But that was yesterday. In God's eyes, she was perfect. Now there were no more doubts about whether she was whole enough or whether her disability would be a burden. Real, lasting love saw past all that. Someone who loved her, truly loved her, wouldn't allow obstacles to get in his way. And she knew Dylan's doubts had nothing to do with her disability. It was about his feelings of self-doubt and his fear of following in his father's footsteps. He was tangled up in the past. He was stuck. She wasn't. Not any longer.

Dylan drew in a sharp breath as he made his way to his truck. An agonizing sensation seized his chest. He wasn't breathing normally. Everything was a blur. He didn't feel steady on his feet.

He'd just hurt the most wonderful woman he'd ever known, and even though he knew he was sparing her pain in the long run, it still gutted him to do it. The urge to turn around and run back toward Holly was overwhelming. Every step he took in the opposite direction caused him to physically ache.

He vaulted into his truck, revved his engine and drove away from Horseshoe Bend Ranch as fast as he possibly could. Maybe, just maybe, he could outrun the pain. That was what he was good at, wasn't it? Running. Instead of easing up, the hurt was intensifying.

Walking away from Holly might just kill me, he realized. Never in his life had he felt this overwhelming sense of loss. There was a twisting sensation in his stomach, threatening to double him over. He was battling a tidal wave of emotions. The urge to run away was strong. It was what he always did, wasn't it?

He didn't belong here! Holly was a vital part of this town. She was the all-American girl who everyone adored. He, on the other hand, was just a visitor passing through West Falls. So why did it feel as if his right arm was being chopped off? Somewhere along the way he'd become a part of the fabric of this town. Aside from Holly, he'd forged relationships with Doc Sampson, Malachi, as well as Frank and Maggie. And the ranch hands were quickly becoming some of his closest buddies. It killed him to think how deeply he'd wounded Holly. He'd seen the devastation and confusion in her eyes. It mirrored all the emotions he'd been at war with ever since his father had waltzed back into his life.

As he reached the cottage, he parked his truck and got out. For a few minutes he stood in front of the door, not fully understanding why he couldn't force himself over the threshold. He stalked back toward his truck, then retreated a few paces. He continued to walk back and forth between the cottage and his truck, his mind whirling with a hundred different thoughts.

Despite all he'd accomplished in his twenty-seven years, he still didn't feel good enough. That was what this was all about. The wounds were still there, just under the surface, always ready to creep back into existence. The childhood he'd experienced could never be undone. And the scars would carry over into his relationships—his ability to fully commit, to believe in the durability of love.

All this time he'd thought his doubts were about Holly. But in actuality, they had always been about him. His past. His fears. His running away. His doubts about being able to fully love a woman for the long haul. The legacy he'd inherited from his father.

He sat down on the front stoop. Wasn't it time he dealt with it? He was tired of running, and he was emotionally exhausted. It was one thing when his past caused him pain, but now it was hurting Holly, as well. And he didn't have to run away from West Falls to know that he couldn't breathe properly without her. He couldn't think straight, couldn't smile, laugh or do much of anything. Without her, he wasn't complete. There was a big, gaping hole in his life without Holly in it.

He was in love with Holly Lynch. The knowledge came sweeping over him like a strong gust of wind. Over-the-moon, can't-stop-thinking-about-her, soul-shattering love. He could try to push away those feelings for all eternity and they would still be there, nestled around his heart like a vise.

He loved Holly. He would always love her. She was a beautiful, healing balm. The letters she'd written to him had turned his whole life around. She'd strengthened his faith and given him the strongest motivation possible to survive Afghanistan. She soothed his soul in a way no one else ever had. There was no one else who would ever be able to, he imagined. Holly made him laugh out loud. She'd brought him closer to the Lord and made him believe that all things were possible. Her humble spirit and giving nature made him want to be a better man.

And each time he looked into her soulful eyes, he saw every dream he'd ever wished for reflected back at him. He couldn't imagine finding all those things in another woman, not if he searched the whole world over. And running away from West Falls, away from Holly, wouldn't change the way he felt. A home. Kids. A woman who would stand by his side, come what may. The possibilities were endless.

He heard someone calling his name. Doc was standing there, staring at him with a furrowed brow and a bewildered expression.

"Son, are you okay? I got your message that you needed to see me immediately. Is something wrong?" Doc's gravelly voice was laced with worry.

He'd completely forgotten that he'd left a message at the diner for Doc. A few hours ago he'd had every intention of giving the keys to the cottage back to him and saying his goodbyes before heading out of West Falls. Now nothing could be further from the truth. He wasn't going anywhere. It just wasn't possible. For the first time in his life, he knew he was planted right where he belonged. And he intended to let Holly know in no uncertain terms how he felt about her. As a feeling of euphoria washed over him, he reached out and clapped his hand on Doc's shoulder. His hand landed more forcefully than he'd intended, causing Doc to jump a little.

"I'm good." He threw back his head and let out a cackle of laughter. "No, I'm better than good. I'm great. Fantastic, actually."

Try as he might to contain it, he was acting like a giddy fool. And even though he was slightly embarrassed, the other emotions he was feeling were way more important.

Doc cocked his head to one side and studied him. "Dylan, was there a reason you wanted to see me? If not, I'm going to head back to the diner. I'm not sure Robin can handle the dinner rush all by her lonesome."

"Go on. Head back to the diner. I've got to drive back to the ranch and see Holly."

Pure adrenaline was racing through his veins. He suspected that a silly grin had popped up on his face.

Doc nodded. "Okay, then. If you're sure you don't need me. I'll see you later."

Doc walked away and headed down the street toward the Falls Diner. He cast a few curious glances back in Dylan's direction.

Dylan waved at him and jumped into his truck, full of fire to get back to Holly. All of a sudden his palms began to moisten as he gripped the steering wheel. What if Holly didn't want to see him? What if he'd blown it? No, he wasn't going to get his head tangled up in negative thinking. He had to take action! He had to make things right with her before the sun went down on this day. As he made his way back toward Horseshoe Bend Ranch, he prayed that he hadn't burned any bridges he couldn't rebuild.

Chapter Twelve

Holly sat in the stables, watching as the sunset dipped down beneath the horizon. A riot of colors lit up the sky. Oranges, pinks and purples. For the past few hours she'd been putting off heading back to the house. It would soon be nighttime, and once this day was done, Dylan would be out of her life. She'd wake up tomorrow morning to the stark reality of his absence. And even though she was willing herself to be strong, her body trembled at the daunting task stretched out before her. How would she manage to carry on without falling apart at the seams?

Count your blessings. She'd grown up hearing those words roll off her mother's tongue. She and Tate used to joke about how frequently that sentiment was ingrained in their minds. Although she knew it was true, she was having trouble practicing it at the moment. Try as she might to stay positive, her head was pounding with tension while her thoughts were jumbled and chaotic.

Over time she'd really grown to believe that she had a future with Dylan. *Fool,* a little voice whispered. Fool for believing in happily ever afters and fairy-tale endings. It worked out that way for some people, but not for her.

She heard a rustling sound behind her. It sounded like cowboy boots crunching against the wood floor. *Malachi.* She couldn't face him. He'd see it all on her face in an instant, the same way he always did. It was too soon to share her sorrow. She wasn't ready to tell anyone yet. She ducked her head down, determined to avoid eye contact with him. There would be time later to tell him Dylan was gone.

And Tate, also. Although he wasn't an I-told-you-so type of person, she still cringed at the prospect of having to broach the subject with her overprotective brother. She raised her hands to her mouth as a tight, familiar sensation gripped her. She had to stop herself from crying out. Loss. It made her whole body ache. Having been down this road before, she knew the loneliness and pain that awaited her. The endless nights between darkness and dawn where nothing could fill the void. The very thought of it made her clench her fists at her side. Once again, she'd have to be as strong as granite, even when it felt as if her world was spinning out of control.

"Holly." The deep pitch of the voice surprised her. She whirled her chair around, her eyes drinking in the sight of Dylan. He was standing a few feet away from her, his short dark hair tousled, a sheepish expression on his face as he gazed at her. For a moment her mind went blank. Why was he here? Wasn't he supposed to be on the road, hightailing it out of West Falls? Wasn't he supposed to be gone?

She said the first thing that came to mind. "Did you forget something?"

He nodded his head. "Yes, I did. I forgot you, Holly."

"Wh-what are you talking about?" Had she heard him right? He'd forgotten her?

He moved toward her, reaching her side in seconds. His eyes skimmed over her face with a look of such tenderness it robbed her of the ability to speak. She had so many questions sitting on the tip of her tongue, but she couldn't give voice to any of them. All she could do was stare at Dylan. She'd truly believed that she would never see him again. He was smiling at her now, a full-on, gorgeous, pearly-toothed smile, which reached right into her chest cavity and tugged at her heart.

"For a little while there, I forgot about us. About what you mean to me, what you've always meant to me. I forgot that running away from my problems has never worked out in the long run. And I forgot how very much I love you."

I love you. Three little words, spoken with such tenderness. And conviction. The raw intensity in his voice brought tears to her eyes. But a little while ago, he hadn't been so certain. He'd been on the verge of walking away from her, hadn't he? How could she believe in this when she'd come so close to losing him?

"I see the confusion on your face, and I don't blame you one bit. A few hours ago I walked away from you, and now I'm back telling you that I'm in love with you." He reached out and clasped her hand. "But it's true. I love you, Holly."

She pulled her hand away from him, needing to focus on her feelings rather than get swallowed up by the emotion of the moment. More than anything in the world, she'd wanted this declaration of love from Dylan. As their relationship had developed, she'd dreamed of a moment like this. She'd hoped and prayed for it. Having him here in West Falls had served only to intensify her feelings toward him. He was everything she'd ever hoped for wrapped up in a rugged, handsome package. Brave. Kind. True. They shared the same values, and there weren't many men who cherished the land the way Dylan did.

But he was also still tormented by his past, so much so that it might affect their future. She needed to be certain Dylan's feelings were strong enough to pin all her hopes and dreams on. If not, how could they ever make it through the hard times that were sure to come their way? She swallowed past the lump in her throat. There were things she needed to say to Dylan if they were ever to move forward.

"I thought I'd lost you. You have no idea of what that felt like, what the past few hours have been like for me. It was the death of everything I've been holding close to my heart for the past year."

Dylan winced. "Holly, I'm so sorry for hurting you. As a man, I'm far from perfect. For a moment I faltered, and I let fear take over. But the truth is, I could never have left town, because the love I feel for you wouldn't let me." He let out a harsh laugh. "I didn't even realize it until I tried to leave. The weight of it hit me full force when I couldn't even bring myself to gather up my belongings."

His rugged frame shuddered. "No matter how I tried, I couldn't leave. Because it didn't make sense to be separated from the woman I love. And I do love you, so very much. It's been building up these past few weeks and months, but it wasn't until I got to know you up close and personal that I fell right over the edge. I got to see how truly amazing you are. My precious, courageous Holly. I'm completely, absolutely crazy about you."

His words were so humble and powerful. He was admitting his imperfections and his mistakes. He was laying it all out for her, warts and all. And he was telling her from the depths of his soul how deeply he loved her. She couldn't ask for more. Moisture stung her eyes as the full impact of his declaration washed over her. Finally, after all her years of wishing him into being, she'd found her other half.

"Dylan, I love you, too." She bowed her head as tears slid down her cheeks. "And I feel so overwhelmed to be loved by you. I'm so grateful that you turned your truck around and came back to me."

"I'm the one who's grateful. The day I received your first letter was the beginning of a whole new life for me." He squatted down so that they were near eye level. He brushed a lock of hair out of her eyes, then reached for her hand again. This time she didn't pull away. She squeezed his hand tightly. At this rate she might never let it go.

She bit her lip, feeling conflicted about shattering this perfect moment. "Dylan, you have to promise me something."

He lightly caressed her palm, his huge smile highlighting the dimple in his chin. "Anything, beautiful. You know that."

"You have to try to broker peace between you and your father." Dylan immediately tensed up and pulled away from her. He let out a low groan. Abruptly, he turned his face away from her. She reached out and grasped his chin, slowly turning his face back toward her. "I'm not saying you have to forgive him. That's between you and God. But in order to move forward, you need to get your house in order. You need to tie up all the loose ends, otherwise our future together could be clouded by everything you're holding on to."

Dylan frowned at her. A slow hiss escaped his lips. "You're right. I know you are. It's hard to move forward when there are still things from the past I'm conflicted about."

"So you'll do it?" she asked. She was almost holding her breath in anticipation of his response. There were mountains standing between Dylan and his father, but she truly believed reconciliation was possible. In her own life she'd reconciled with Cassidy after not speaking to her or seeing her for eight years. And she'd managed to forgive her mother for keeping Cassidy's letters from her. Deep down, Dylan loved his father, and she suspected R. J. McDermott loved his son, otherwise he wouldn't have made the effort to find Dylan. Everything in her life had taught her that with love, all things were possible.

"I'll try my best to meet him halfway, to hear him out. I'm not making any promises, but I'll give it a shot," Dylan said. His expression softened. "It won't be easy, but I've been trying to be a better man. I reckon forgiveness is a big part of that. It's a very humbling thought."

"All I ask is that you try. When and if you close the door on your relationship with your father, you need to be at peace with it. I just want you to be at peace, Dylan."

The corners of his eyes creased as a slow smile began forming on his face. "When did you become such a wise woman, Holly Lynch?"

"I don't know. Maybe it was the day I decided to become your pen pal," she teased. "It forever changed both our lives."

Dylan raised his head and delivered a quick kiss to her forehead. "I'm so very thankful that God placed the two of us in each other's paths. I promise never to take our love it for granted again."

She shook her head and smiled. "Nor will I. We're truly blessed, aren't we?" She leaned forward and placed a sweet, triumphant kiss on Dylan's lips. He reached out so that his palms could cradle both sides of her face as the kiss deepened into one of pure celebration. As the kiss ended, Holly murmured his name, rejoicing over the love she'd found with her cowboy soldier.

Epilogue

Three weeks later

The stack of letters was sitting on her bedside table when she woke up in the morning. Her mother had promised weeks ago to find the letters from Cassidy she'd hidden up in the attic all those years ago. There were twenty-one letters in all. One by one, she read the entire stack. Some made her laugh out loud, while others made her shed a few tears. Over the years the letters dwindled down to almost nothing. No doubt Cassidy had gotten the message loud and clear after not hearing back from her. She was so thankful her mother had saved them. In all those years Cassidy had never really left her. She'd been there in spirit, if not in body. That knowledge filled her with such hope. Even when things seemed darkest, the dawn still came.

God had given her that message when Dylan had showed up at Horseshoe Bend Ranch with his heart in his hands. In the end, love was stronger than fear and self-doubt. It trumped every other emotion known to man. She felt so very blessed to be this cherished. Life had never been so good. The very last envelope was a pretty blue, the color of a robin's egg. The handwriting that spelled out her name belonged to Dylan. She would recognize the graceful slope of his script anywhere. Careful not to tear the envelope, she lifted the flap, then gently pulled out the stationery.

She took the letter and pressed it up to her nose, relishing the woodsy, rugged scent. She hadn't realized how much she'd missed receiving Dylan's sweet, endearing letters. Her heart began to beat a little faster as her eyes scanned the page.

Dear Holly,
The simple act of writing your name down on this piece of paper makes me realize how much I've missed writing to you. All those weeks and months when I was in Afghanistan, and at this very moment as I'm putting these words to paper, I feel such a deep connection to you. Mere letters written on a piece of paper cannot express the depth of what you mean to me. I'd like to tell you with words while gazing into your eyes what you've brought into my world. I'm not sure if there are enough words in the English language to do it justice, but I'd like to try.

Please meet me at noon at this location—31 Trinity Pass Road. Just past the covered bridge. With all my love,
Dylan

Holly pressed the letter against her chest, heaving a sigh at the beauty of Dylan's sentiments. Her heart was thumping wildly in her chest. After everything they'd been through, the letter deeply resonated with her. Dylan had changed her world in so many amazing ways. He'd made her realize that she was capable and resilient and worthy of her own happy ending. And by loving her, he'd restored her faith in a bright future.

As her GPS navigated her toward the destination, she began to wonder where this journey was taking her. There was nothing out here but wide-open spaces. She came upon a stone entrance with a hunter-green placard announcing it as 31 Trinity Pass Road. Turning into the driveway, she rode for about half a mile until she spotted Dylan standing next to a stone house, with Leo cradled in the crook of his arm. She drew in a deep breath at the sight of him.

Dylan waved to her, and she beeped her horn at him in response. She parked in the makeshift driveway, maneuvering her wheelchair and then herself out of the driver's seat with more speed than usual. Her curiosity was spurring her on. Why in the world had Dylan invited her all the way out here?

"Thanks for coming," Dylan said with a welcoming smile as she wheeled herself over to his side.

"Of course," she said. "Your note piqued my curiosity. I was counting the minutes down till noontime."

Dylan placed Leo down on the ground and moved a step closer toward her. "Holly, I've never really had a place to call my own. In Madden I always felt not good enough. Even though it was my hometown, I never felt a sense of belonging. Being the object of gossip and innuendo doesn't really lend itself to feeling accepted by the community."

Just thinking about Dylan's sense of isolation and lack of self-worth made her want to weep. It wasn't fair that he'd been made to feel unworthy and an object of scorn.

"I'm so sorry you went through so much," she said. It still amazed her how cruel people could be, particularly to a child.

"Being here in West Falls… It's allowed me to put all that behind me. I finally feel as if I'm home. And I wouldn't change the past, even if I could, because every step led me straight to you."

"Oh, Dylan," Holly whispered, her voice tight with emotion. "That makes me so happy."

"You've brought tremendous joy into my life. Before I met you, I was lost. Running away was how I dealt with feelings I didn't want to confront. I was so afraid of the past, so stuck on the painful things I endured that it was hard to believe I could find happiness. And I was terrified of not being strong enough to stay around. Growing up, I never saw any examples of true, enduring love. For me, it seemed like this elusive thing I could never grab hold of. You changed all that, Holly."

He lowered his head and brushed a sweet kiss across her lips. He stood back and looked at her, his eyes brimming with wonder. "What you've taught me—grace, humility, forgiveness. And most of all, resilience."

He reached into his pocket and pulled out a piece of rolled-up paper. He just stood there grinning at her, not saying another word.

She wrinkled her nose. "What is that?"

Dylan unfurled it and held it up for her to see. "It's the deed to this property. I own it."

She felt her eyes widening. "Dylan. Are you joking?" She choked out the words. He handed her the document and she ran her eyes over it, quickly scanning the deed proclaiming Dylan Hart as the owner of one thousand acres of prime Texas land. She swung her eyes up from the parchment so she could look at him.

"How?" There was no way in the world she could utter anything other than a single word.

Shock and awe had her in its grip. *Was this really happening?*

"R.J.... My father...wanted me to have something to call my own. He wanted to give me part ownership of the Bar M along with Jane and Roger Jr., but I told him I'd be sticking around these parts. He understood that I want to settle down in West Falls. Next thing you know, we're out scouting properties, and he's giving me a big fat check and calling it my inheritance."

Holly felt tears pooling in her eyes. "This is incredible. Not just the land, which is amazing in itself, but your reconciliation with your father. I knew the two of you were making progress, but I didn't dare hope for something like this. After everything that happened in the past, you've allowed yourself to try to forgive him. You're moving forward."

Dylan blinked several times. He seemed to steady himself against a swell of emotion.

"He offered me a huge olive branch. And he stuck around West Falls so he could try to bridge the gap between us. I couldn't ignore that or what it meant. In his own way, he loves me. At first, pride prevented me from seeing it, but I had to let go of the past and try to forge a new path with him. He was young and he made a lot of mistakes as a parent. I'll never forget how it feels not to have a father in my life and to not be acknowledged, but I do want to try to build a relationship with him. He says he wants to make amends. I want to be the type of man who can grant forgiveness. So we're going to work on our relationship, one step at a time. I want to move forward. I want to have faith." He gestured around him at the land stretched out before them. "I'd say this is a major step in the right direction."

As far as she was concerned, it was an excellent step toward healing and reconciliation. It was a grand gesture from his father, which would cement their future. Loving Dylan as fiercely as she did, she needed to make sure he wouldn't harbor any regrets.

"Are you sure you want to relinquish your ties with the Bar M? Your whole life you wanted to be acknowledged, to be part of the McDermott clan. Doesn't it feel strange to give up the opportunity to go back to Madden and take your rightful place at the family ranch?"

He leaned down and planted a light kiss on her forehead. His large palm caressed the back of her head, his fingers swirling through her hair. She closed her eyes, wishing she could make this moment last for more than a fleeting moment. So many things were changing for Dylan. His world was suddenly becoming a whole lot bigger and more centered. Was there still room for her in his life? Or would he soar away from her like a comet blazing through the sky?

"Holly, I'm not giving up a single thing. How could I be? All of my life I've been chasing a feeling. I wanted to belong somewhere, to have the sense of community you've had your whole life. I've been running in so many different directions, trying to fill up that hole, only to realize that you've already done that. From the moment I received your first letter, I knew in my soul you were meant for me. And when I first met you and I was filled with fear and second-guessing my feelings, my heart always recognized you. I'm so sorry I fought it for so long. But I promise you, the only place that will ever feel like home is where you are."

He reached into his jacket pocket and pulled out a sparkling diamond ring. She gasped as Dylan bent down on one knee and clasped her hand firmly with his own. He looked into her eyes, and what she saw reflected there caused tears to brim over her lids and trickle down her face. Deep in the darkest regions of her soul, she'd feared no man would ever look at her with such love and wonder in his eyes. She'd always worried that the accident had cost her a future with a loving man at her side. With one single gesture, Dylan had put all those fears to rest.

He reached out and brushed her tears away with his fingertips in a light caress that skimmed over her skin. "Holly, I want to be your husband. If you'll have me, that is. I've made a lot of mistakes with you. And I'm sure I'll make a bunch more over the years."

His eyes filled with tears, and his voice turned husky. "But if you'll agree to be my wife, I promise to be by your side for the rest of our days, loving and honoring you. I want to be that person you lean on when you get weary and the road becomes a little bumpy. And I want to lean on you, too, Holly. Through everything that life has in store for us, I want you to take the journey with me."

So many emotions were coursing through her. Joy. Hope. Disbelief. But she needed to make sure he understood the realities of her everyday life before he made any pledges. She had to be certain that he wasn't looking at their future with rose-colored glasses.

"Dylan. You need to know a life with me isn't going

to be easy. There will be so many challenges, so many ups and downs. And my daily regimen of medication, all the physical therapy and doctor appointments. And I still may never be able to conceive a child, let alone carry one to term. It's possible, but not a given. I know how much you want children in your future."

Dylan reached up and pressed his lips against hers, silencing her in an instant. His lips moved over hers with conviction and certainty. When he pulled away from her, she saw everything shining forth in his eyes. Truth. Love. Forever. Everything she'd always dreamed of having.

He brushed his hand across her temple. "A life with you is all I've ever wanted. If you're willing to take this journey with me, you'll make me the happiest man alive. I think I've known you were my future from the moment I read your very first letter. And I know it won't be easy at times. I know we'll face challenges other couples don't have to worry about. But I believe in us, Holly. And there's no other woman I'd want by my side other than you. I want to prove myself to you, every day of our lives, from this moment forward."

She reached out and placed a finger over his lips. "Shh. You've already proved yourself. By coming back to me. By being here, right by my side. By loving me."

He cradled her face in his hands. "Holly Lynch. My pen pal. My best friend. My other half. Will you do me the honor of becoming my wife?"

"There's nothing in this world I want more," she answered as she wiped away tears from her cheeks. "And there's nobody I'd rather go through life with than you. My cowboy soldier."

Dylan placed the diamond ring on her finger, letting out a "Hallelujah" when it fit perfectly.

Holly tugged at his collar and pulled him close enough that she could show him her gratitude for all the joy he'd brought into her life. Her lips brushed against his in a wonderful celebration of the love they'd found and everything their future held in store for them. They both knew with a deep certainty that their love was enough to weather all the storms, come what may.

* * * * *

LOVE INSPIRED

Stories to uplift and inspire

Fall in love with Love Inspired—
inspirational and uplifting stories of faith
and hope. Find strength and comfort in
the bonds of friendship and community.
Revel in the warmth of possibility and the
promise of new beginnings.

Sign up for the Love Inspired newsletter
at **LoveInspired.com** to be the first
to find out about upcoming titles,
special promotions and exclusive content.

CONNECT WITH US AT:

f Facebook.com/LoveInspiredBooks

🐦 Twitter.com/LoveInspiredBks

Get 4 FREE REWARDS!

We'll send you 2 FREE Books plus 2 FREE Mystery Gifts.

FREE
Value Over
$20

Both the **Love Inspired®** and **Love Inspired® Suspense** series feature compelling novels filled with inspirational romance, faith, forgiveness, and hope.

YES! Please send me 2 FREE novels from the Love Inspired or Love Inspired Suspense series and my 2 FREE gifts (gifts are worth about $10 retail). After receiving them, if I don't wish to receive any more books, I can return the shipping statement marked "cancel." If I don't cancel, I will receive 6 brand-new Love Inspired Larger-Print books or Love Inspired Suspense Larger-Print books every month and be billed just $5.99 each in the U.S. or $6.24 each in Canada. That is a savings of at least 17% off the cover price. It's quite a bargain! Shipping and handling is just 50¢ per book in the U.S. and $1.25 per book in Canada.* I understand that accepting the 2 free books and gifts places me under no obligation to buy anything. I can always return a shipment and cancel at any time. The free books and gifts are mine to keep no matter what I decide.

Choose one: ☐ **Love Inspired**   ☐ **Love Inspired Suspense**
                 Larger-Print   **Larger-Print**
                 (122/322 IDN GNWC)   (107/307 IDN GNWN)

Name (please print)

Address   Apt. #

City   State/Province   Zip/Postal Code

Email: Please check this box ☐ if you would like to receive newsletters and promotional emails from Harlequin Enterprises ULC and its affiliates. You can unsubscribe anytime.

Mail to the **Harlequin Reader Service**:
IN U.S.A.: P.O. Box 1341, Buffalo, NY 14240-8531
IN CANADA: P.O. Box 603, Fort Erie, Ontario L2A 5X3

Want to try 2 free books from another series? Call 1-800-873-8635 or visit www.ReaderService.com.

---

*Terms and prices subject to change without notice. Prices do not include sales taxes, which will be charged (if applicable) based on your state or country of residence. Canadian residents will be charged applicable taxes. Offer not valid in Quebec. This offer is limited to one order per household. Books received may not be as shown. Not valid for current subscribers to the Love Inspired or Love Inspired Suspense series. All orders subject to approval. Credit or debit balances in a customer's account(s) may be offset by any other outstanding balance owed by or to the customer. Please allow 4 to 6 weeks for delivery. Offer available while quantities last.

Your Privacy—Your information is being collected by Harlequin Enterprises ULC, operating as Harlequin Reader Service. For a complete summary of the information we collect, how we use this information and to whom it is disclosed, please visit our privacy notice located at corporate.harlequin.com/privacy-notice. From time to time we may also exchange your personal information with reputable third parties. If you wish to opt out of this sharing of your personal information, please visit readerservice.com/consumerschoice or call 1-800-873-8635. **Notice to California Residents**—Under California law, you have specific rights to control and access your data. For more information on these rights and how to exercise them, visit corporate.harlequin.com/california-privacy.

LIRLIS22

Someone was shooting at them!

Liam hit the gas and Shauna braced herself for the worst. Her body began to shake uncontrollably as the SUV sped up and jerked from side to side as Liam attempted to escape.

They were shooting at her this time. Not just attempting to run her off the road.

These people, whoever they were, wanted her *dead*.

Just like her mother.

Why? She couldn't seem to grasp why she'd suddenly become a target. It just didn't make any sense. Tears pricked her eyes, but she held them back.

After what seemed like eons but was likely only fifteen minutes, the vehicle slowed to a normal rate of speed.

"Are you okay?" Liam asked tersely.

She hesitantly lifted her head, scanning the area. "I—Yes. You?"

"Fine. Thankfully the shooter missed us. I wish I knew exactly where the gunfire came from." He sounded frustrated. "This is my fault. I knew you were in danger, but I didn't expect anyone to fire at us in broad daylight."

"At me." Her voice was soft but firm. "Not you, Liam. This is all about me."

He glanced sharply at her. "They could have easily shot me, too, Shauna. Thankfully, they missed, but that was too close. And you still don't know why these people have come after you?" He hesitated, then added, "Or why they killed your mother?"

"No." She shrugged helplessly. "I'm not lying. There is no reason I can come up with that would cause this sort of action. No one hated either of us this much."

"Revenge?" He divided his attention between her and the road. She didn't recognize the highway they were on, but then again, she didn't know much of anything about Green Lake.

Other than she'd brought danger to the quaint tourist town.

Don't miss
Hiding in Plain Sight *by Laura Scott,*
available September 2022 wherever
Love Inspired Suspense books and ebooks are sold.

LoveInspired.com

IF YOU ENJOYED THIS BOOK, DON'T MISS NEW EXTENDED-LENGTH NOVELS FROM LOVE INSPIRED!

In addition to the Love Inspired books you know and love, we're excited to introduce even more uplifting stories in a longer format, with more inspiring fresh starts and page-turning thrills!

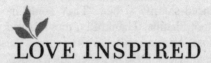

LOVE INSPIRED

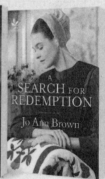

Stories to uplift and inspire.

Fall in love with Love Inspired—inspirational and uplifting stories of faith and hope. Find strength and comfort in the bonds of friendship and community. Revel in the warmth of possibility, and the promise of new beginnings.

LOOK FOR THESE LOVE INSPIRED TITLES ONLINE AND IN THE BOOK DEPARTMENT OF YOUR FAVORITE RETAILER!

LITRADE0622